HALINA FILIPINA
A New Yorker in Manila

A graphic novel by
ARNOLD ARRE

TUTTLE Publishing
Tokyo | Rutland, Vermont | Singapore

Published by Tuttle Publishing, an imprint of Periplus Editions (HK) Ltd.

www.tuttlepublishing.com

Copyright (c) 2022 Arnold Arre

All rights reserved. No part of this publication may be reproduced, stored in a retrieval system, or transmitted, in any form or by any means, electronic, mechanical, photocopying, recording or otherwise, without the prior written permission of the publisher.

Library of Congress Control Number: 2022931223

ISBN 978-0-8048-5544-0

25 24 23 22
8 7 6 5 4 3 2 1

Printed in Singapore
2203TP

Distributed by:
North America, Latin America & Europe
Tuttle Publishing
364 Innovation Drive, North Clarendon,
VT 05759-9436 U.S.A.
Tel: 1 (802) 773-8930
Fax: 1 (802) 773-6993
info@tuttlepublishing.com
www.tuttlepublishing.com

Asia Pacific
Berkeley Books Pte Ltd
3 Kallang Sector #04-01
Singapore 349278
Tel: (65) 6741 2178
Fax: (65) 6741 2179
inquiries@periplus.com.sg
www.tuttlepublishing.com

TUTTLE PUBLISHING® is a registered trademark of Tuttle Publishing,
a division of Periplus Editions (HK) Ltd.

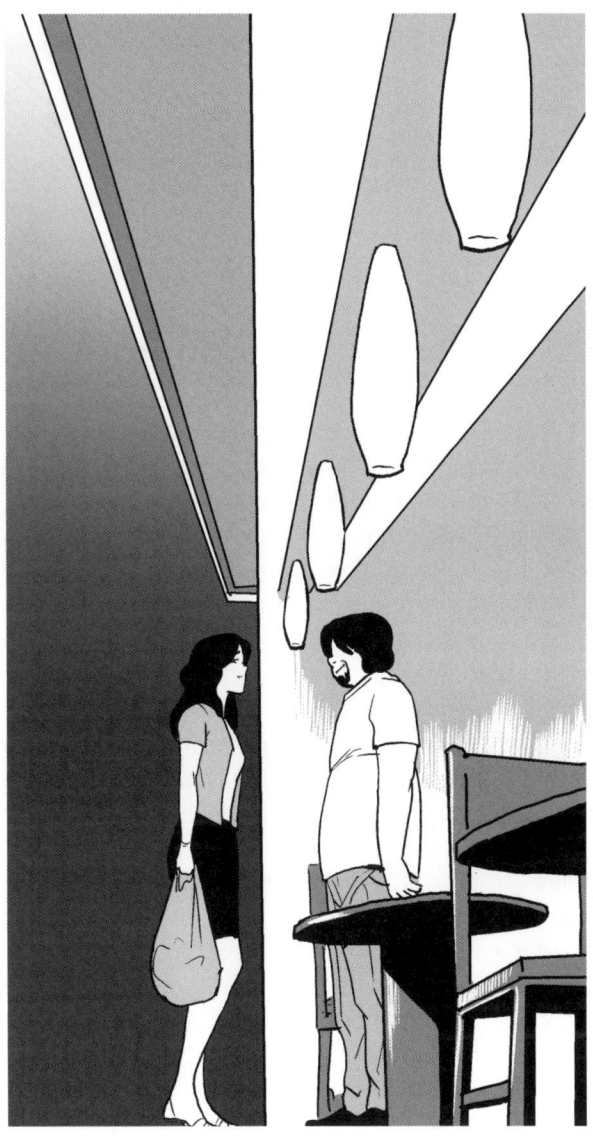

"The identity of the Filipino today is of a person asking what is his identity."

– Nick Joaquin, *Culture and History*

Introduction

One of the best pieces of advice I've ever heard was from Tom Kelley of IDEO during his talk for Stanford's *Entrepreneurial Thought Leaders* series. He said that one of the ways to stay innovative was to "think like a traveler." He noted that when you visit another country as a tourist, you are immediately aware of the unique little things about that place that the locals have probably taken for granted: the way people greet each other on the street, the proper etiquette when entering a house, table manners, the design tropes of their advertising. Kelley says that if one keeps that mindset no matter where you are, you become sensitive to all the little things that make society work and are in a better position to find solutions to make it better.

This idea of "thinking like a traveller", I believe, is what makes Arnold Arre one of the most innovative Filipino comic creators of our time. Many Filipino comics try to highlight their Filipino identity by relying mainly on visual and verbal cues that come dangerously close to caricature, like having superheroes with design elements of the Philippine flag in it, or wearing a salakot or a barong. Others use Philippine mythology or history as their mark of being Filipino, no doubt following in the footsteps of Arnold himself who pioneered this particular genre with his award-winning graphic novel *The Mythology Class* back at the start of the millennium. Yet many of them still fail to capture that feeling of authenticity and sincerity with their stories, creating Westernized superheroes or manga story clones draped in Philippine clichés or spouting Taglish dialogue. But when you read any of Arnold's works set in the Philippines, the characters and the settings genuinely feel Filipino. They feel like they are set in very specific parts of the Philippines from very specific parts of society. The way the characters talk, their body language, the distinct background details that pepper the setting of every scene, they all contribute to making the stories feel genuine. Filipinos who read it will feel right at home, and those from other countries will swear they've just taken a virtual Philippine vacation. And yet Arnold's stories don't just mimic and recreate Philippine culture and society. His stories comment on them and subtly

try to reshape them into something better. I believe he is able to achieve this because he "thinks like a traveller" and notices all these little quirks and nuances about our lives as Filipinos that most of us have become numb to. He takes them and crafts them into a narrative experience that enthralls us with seemingly little effort, like an artist transforming street junk into multi-million dollar sculptures.

Halina Filipina is probably one of my favorite Arnold Arre stories so far. One reason is that I'm a sucker for romantic slice-of-life stories, so this just hits me in all the right places. But it's also a story about two people meeting in the Philippines: Halina, a traveller and who is discovering just what the Philippines has to offer, and Cris, a local who is all-too familiar with the country and perhaps even a little bit sick of it. With any other author, it would be a nice set-up for a simple comedic romance. But Arnold uses his traveller's thinking in telling this story, making us reflect on the concepts of identity, of both pride and shame towards our country and ourselves, and how all that ties into the way we feel about those closest to us. It's a graphic novel that feels simultaneously comfortable yet also challenging. Only an author as observant and as skillful as Arnold could tackle such themes in such a subtle, entertaining, and heart-filling manner.

So as you turn the page, be prepared to see the Philippines through the eyes of Halina and Cris. Be prepared to see a little bit of yourself as well in them. And in both cases, I guarantee you'll find something familiar, yet also something unexpected and new. That's what happens when you travel with Arnold Arre.

Jamie Bautista
Alabang 2015

> *"Arnold's stories don't just mimic and recreate Philippine culture and society. His stories comment on them and subtly try to reshape them into something better. "*

PRESENT DAY

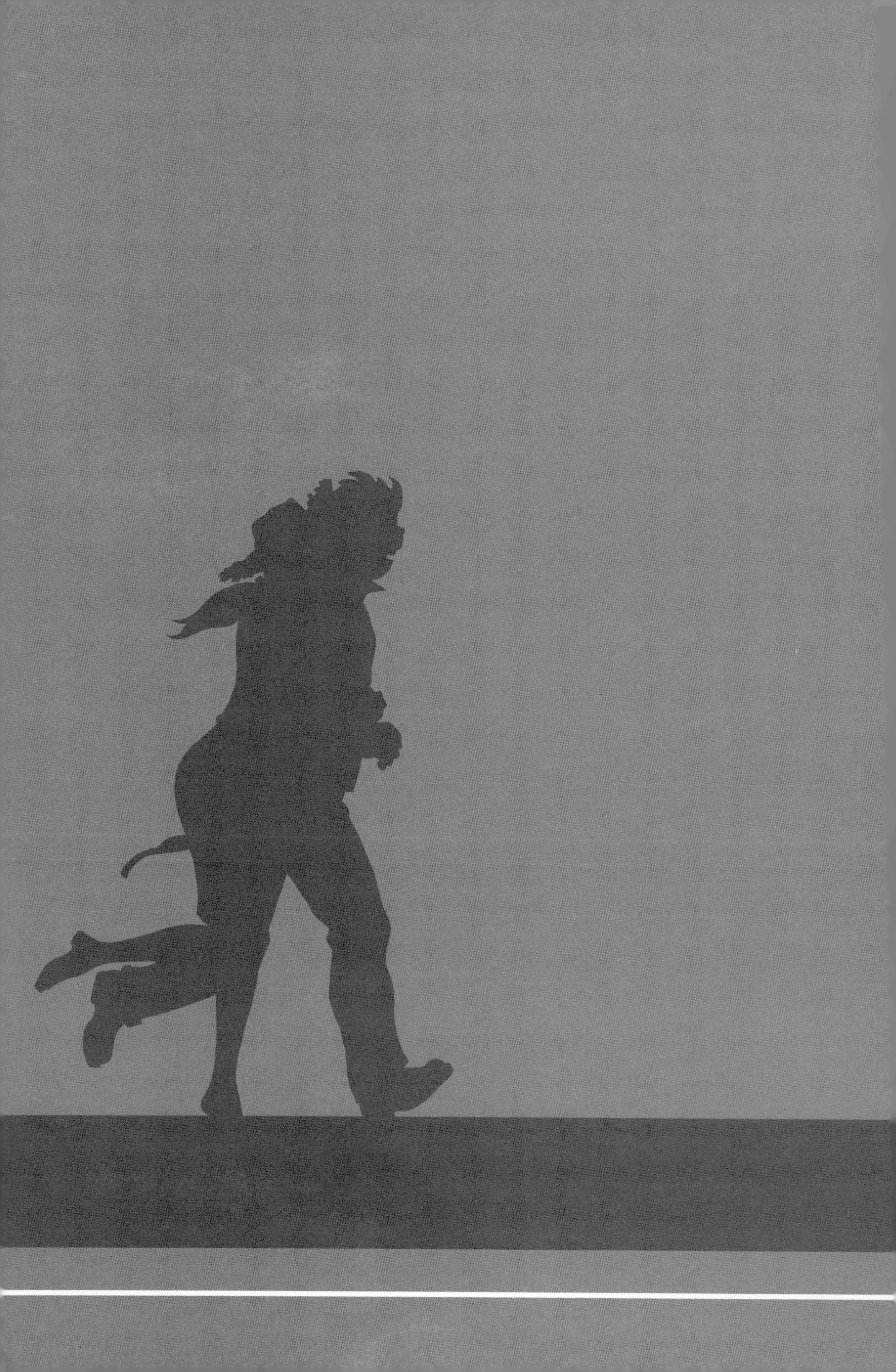

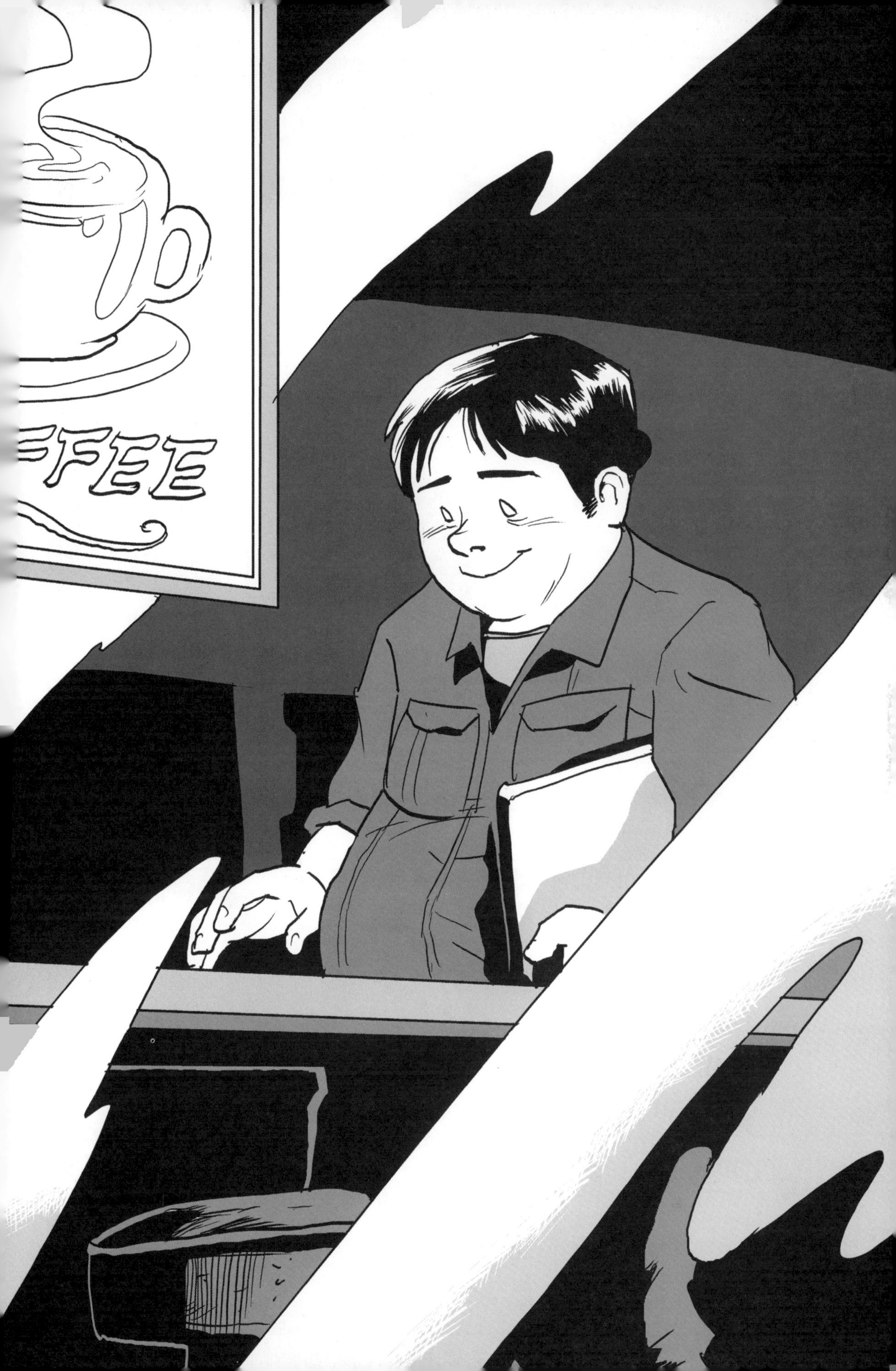
FFEE

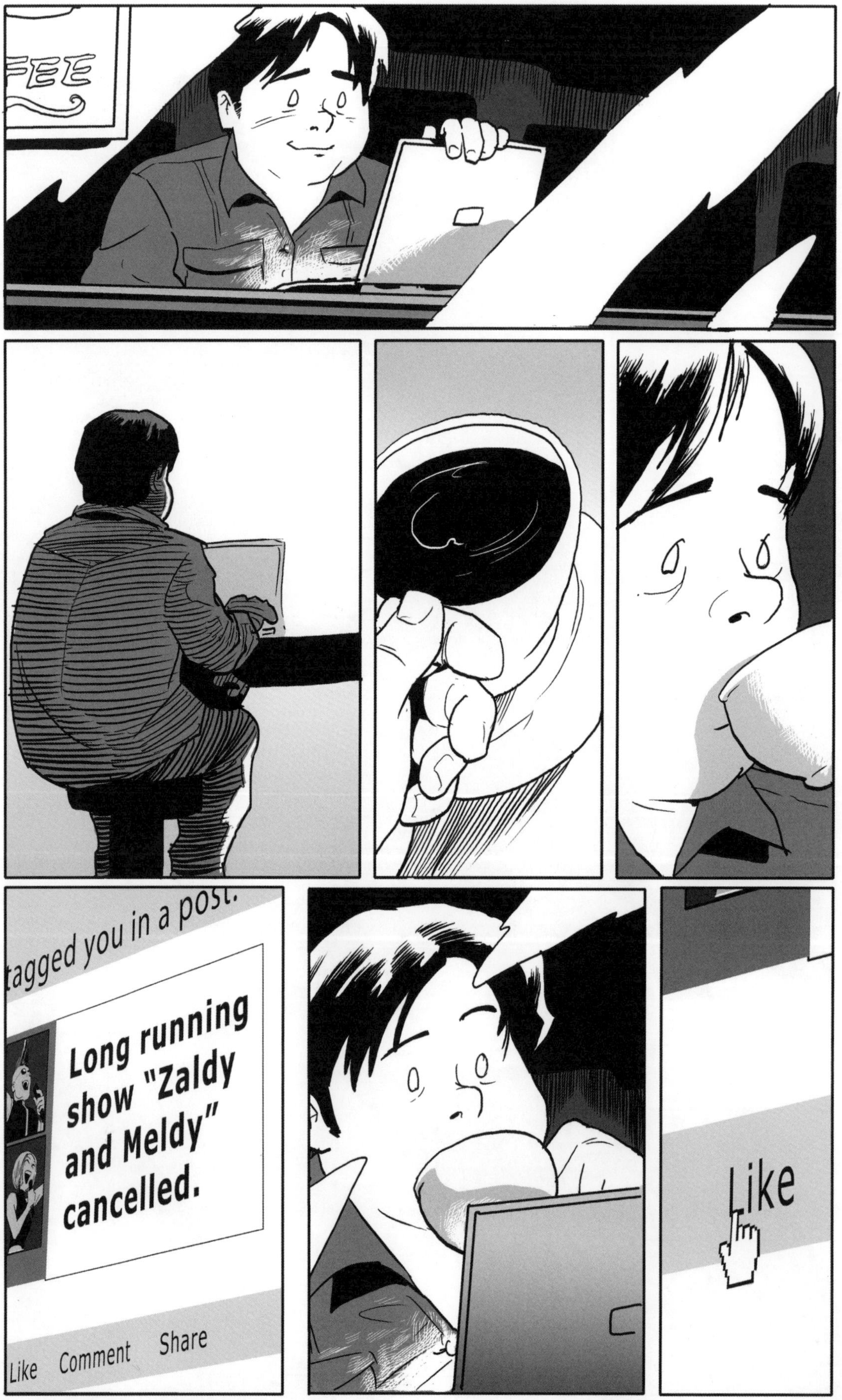
FEE
tagged you in a post.
Long running show "Zaldy and Meldy" cancelled.
Like
Comment
Share
Like

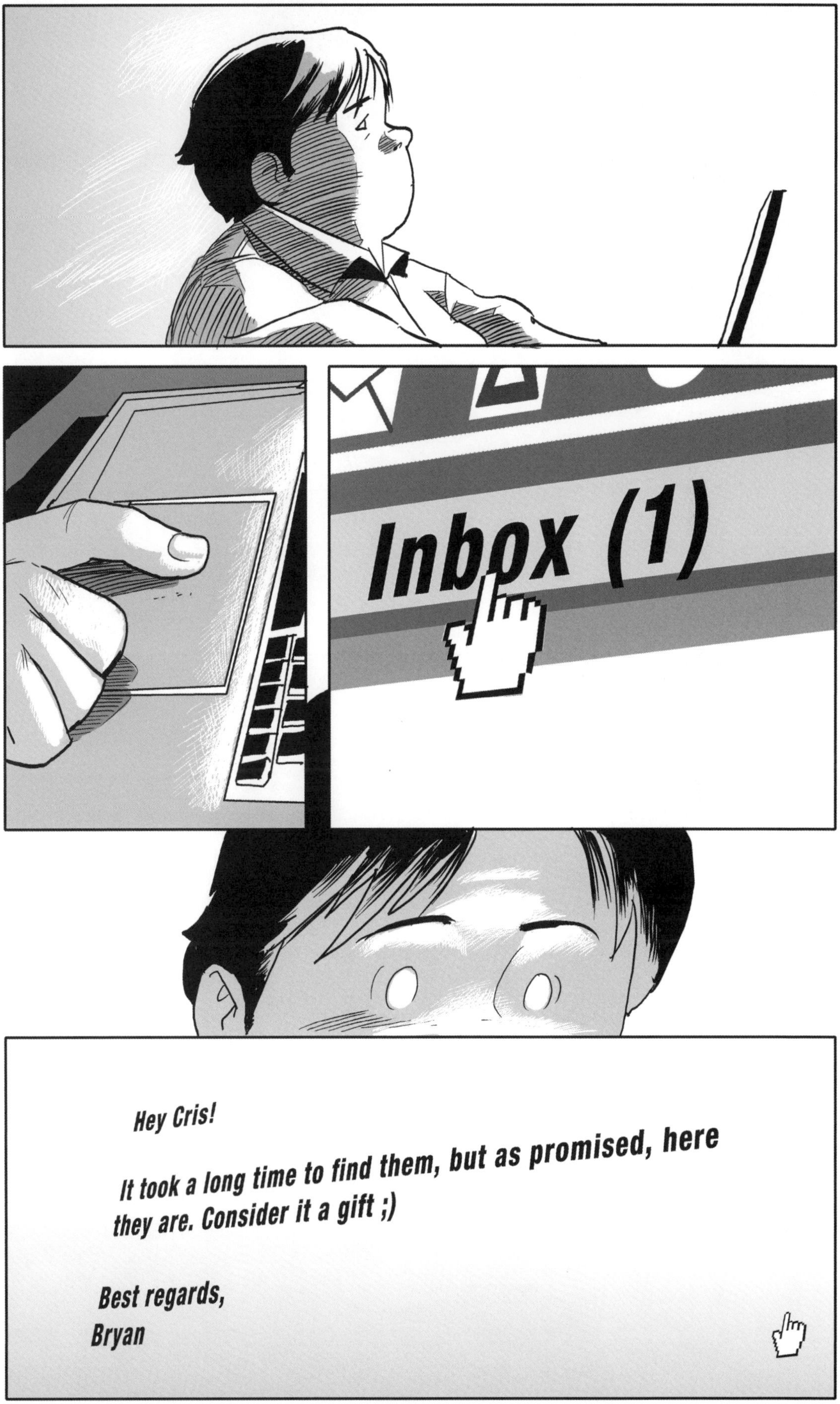
Inbox (1)
Hey Cris!
It took a long time to find them, but as promised, here they are. Consider it a gift ;)
Best regards,
Bryan

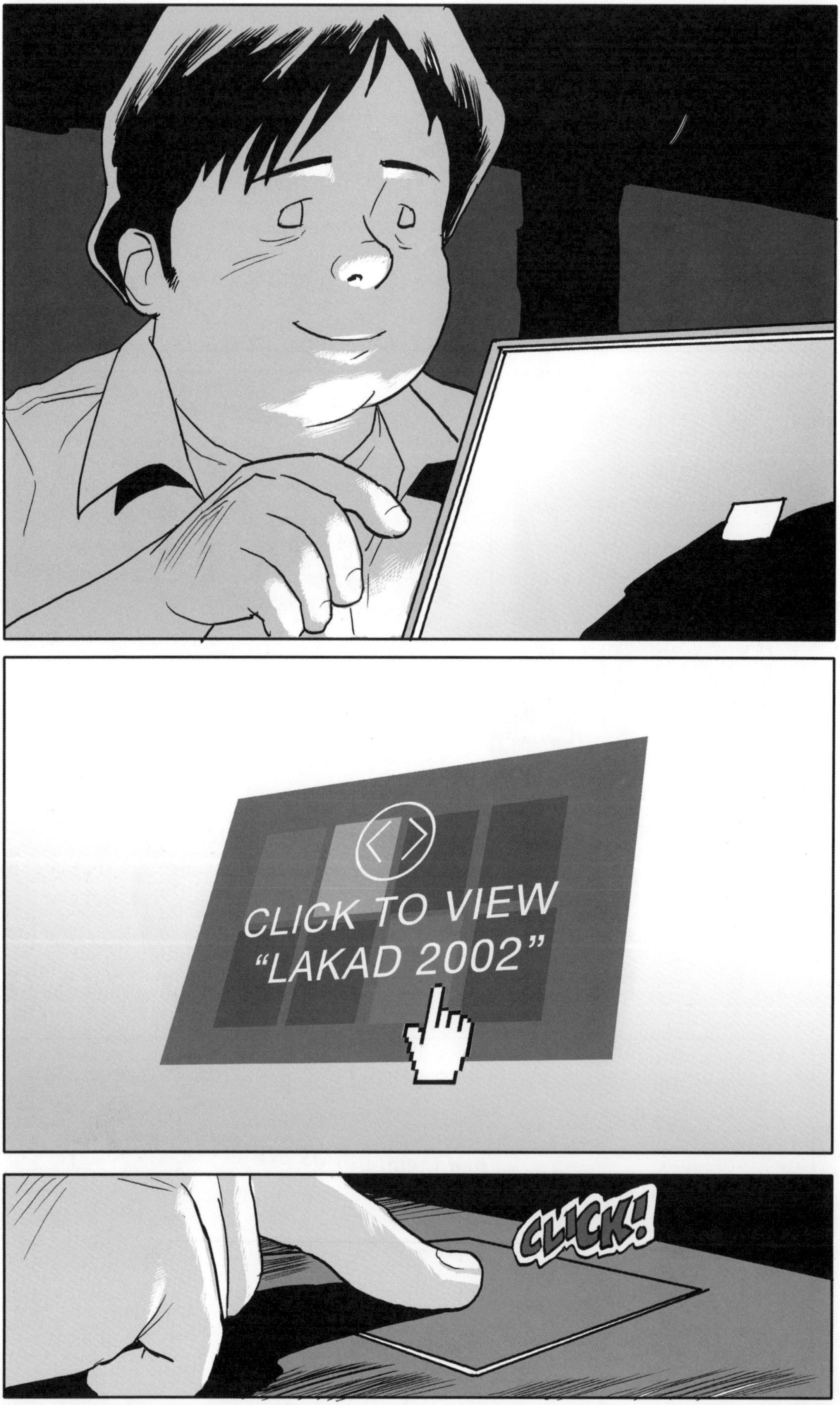
CLICK TO VIEW
"LAKAD 2002"
CLICK!

FEBRUARY 2002

Chapter 1
The Meeting

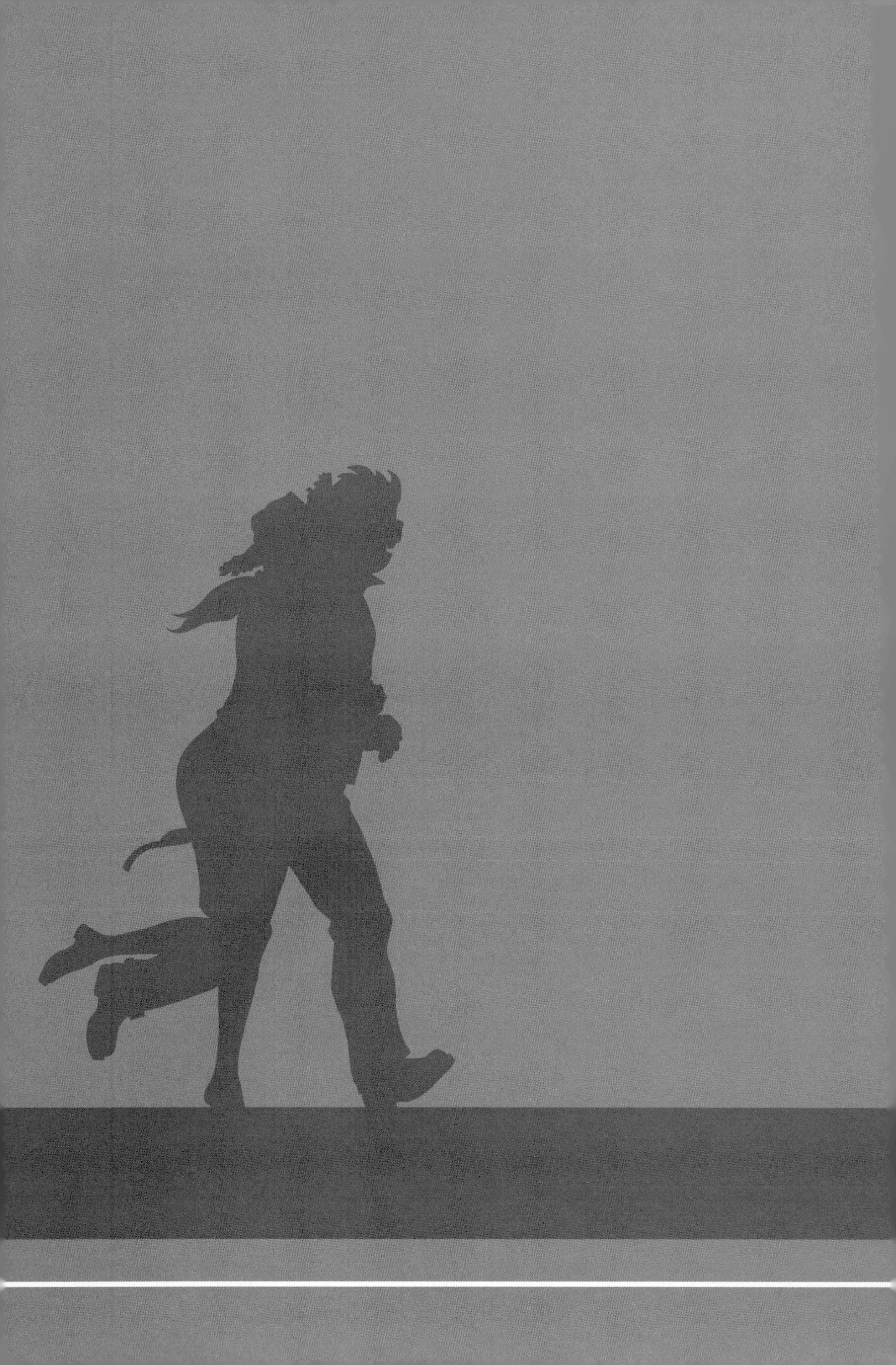

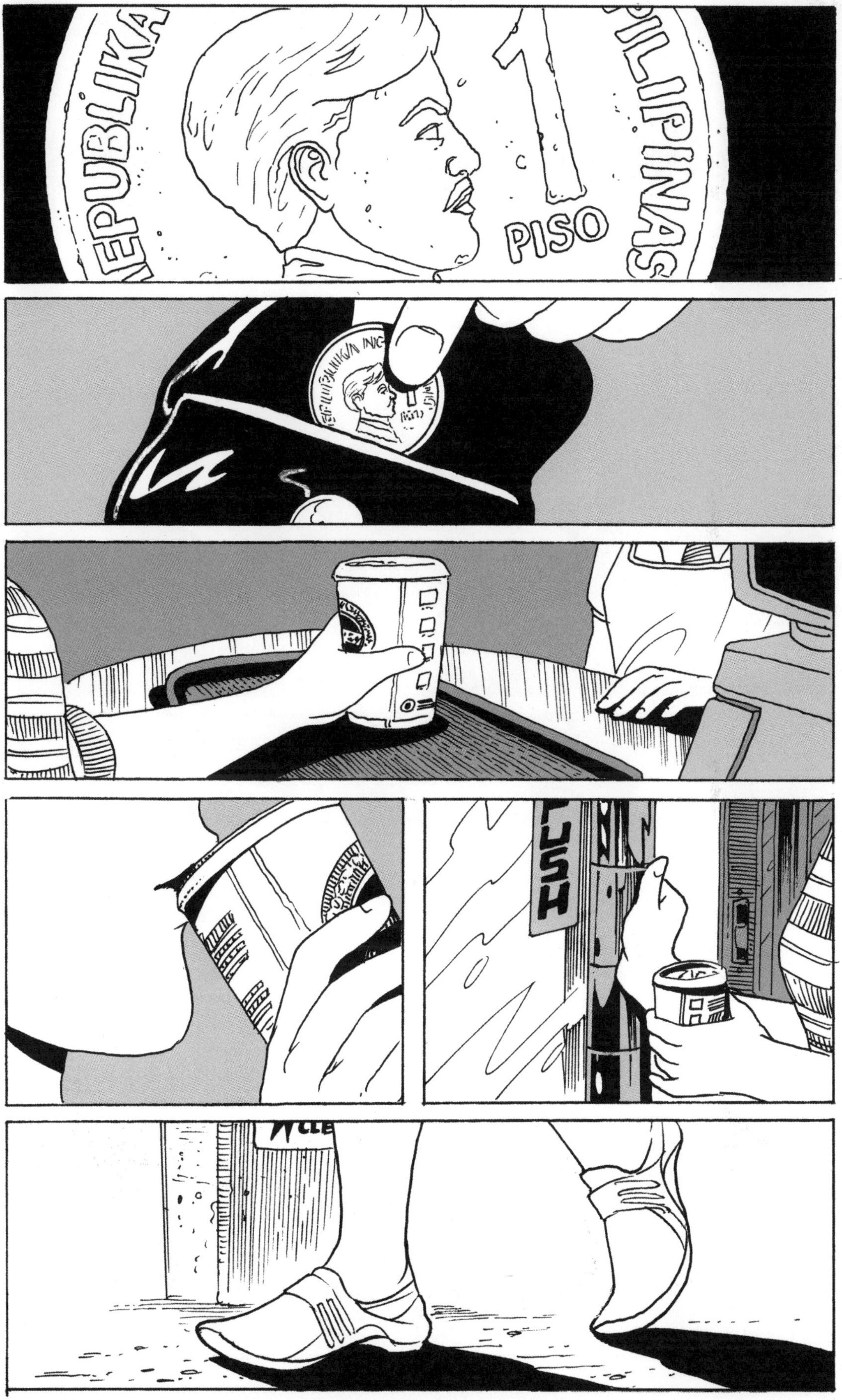
PILIPINAS
1
PISO
PUSH

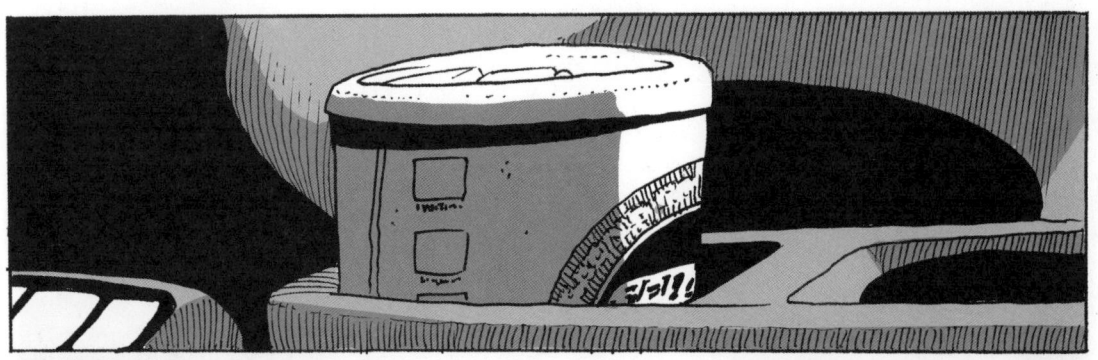

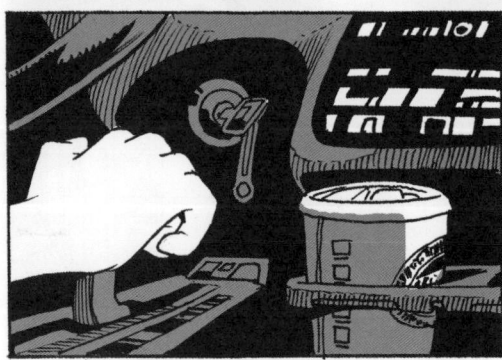

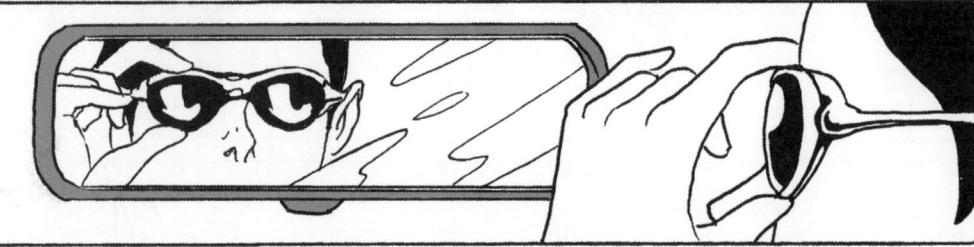
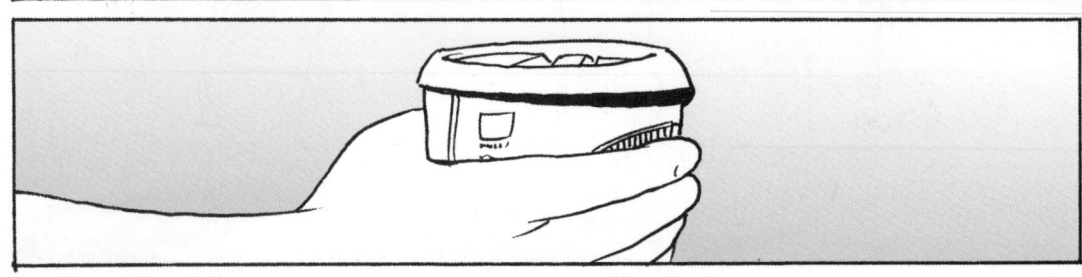

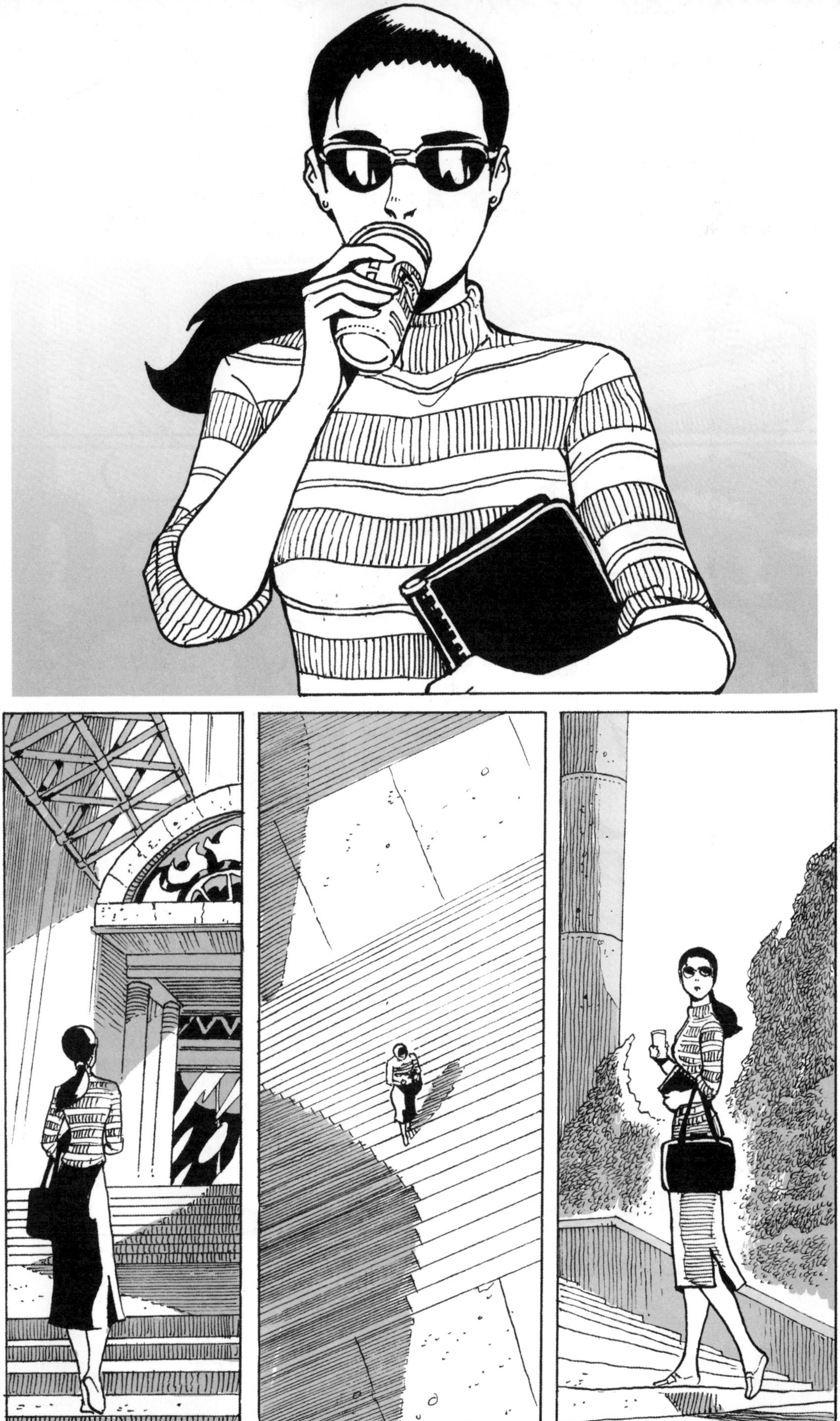

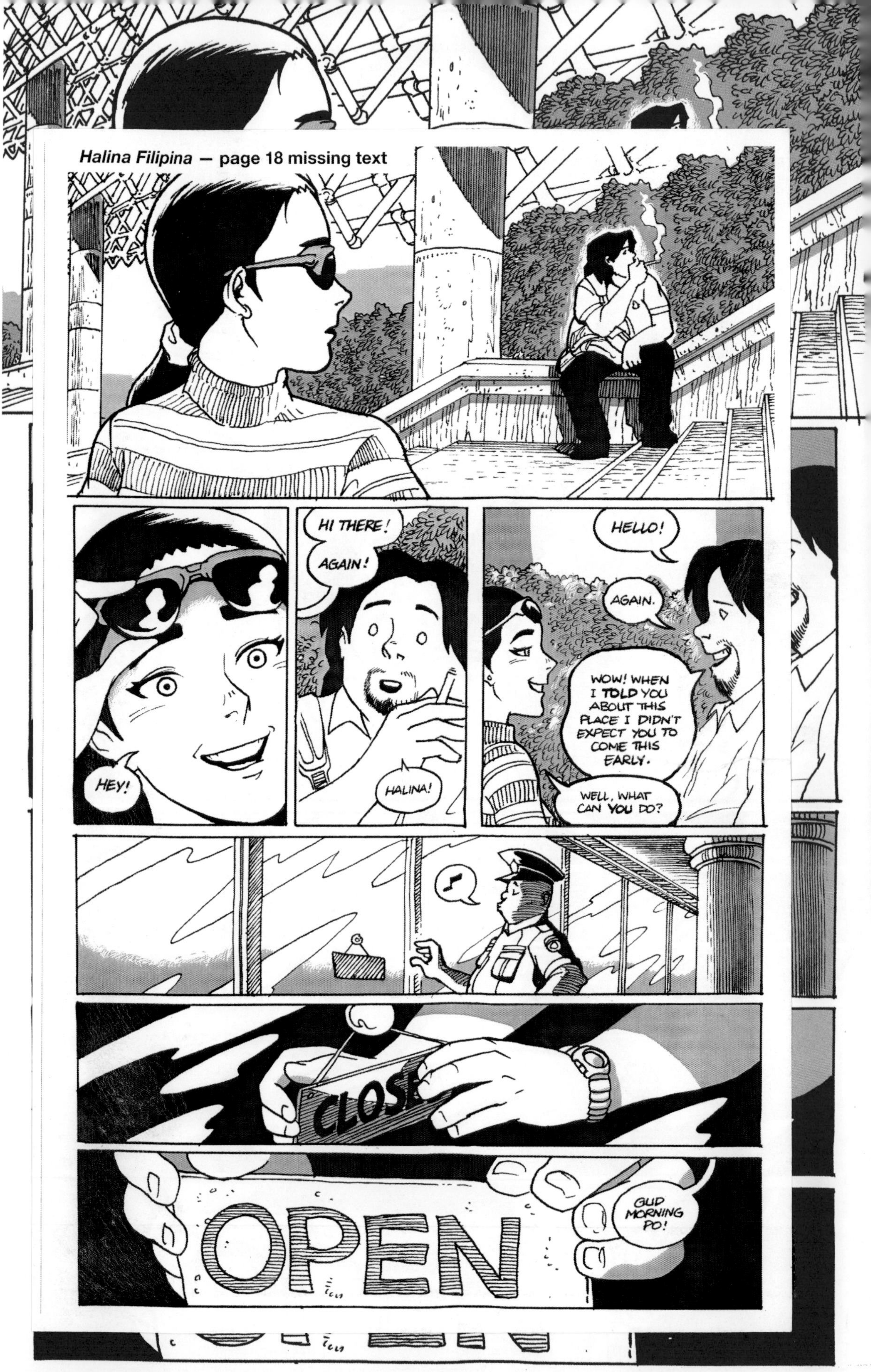
Halina Filipina — page 18 missing text
HEY!
HI THERE!
AGAIN!
HALINA!
HELLO!
AGAIN.
WOW! WHEN I TOLD YOU ABOUT THIS PLACE I DIDN'T EXPECT YOU TO COME THIS EARLY.
WELL, WHAT CAN YOU DO?
CLOSE
OPEN
GUD MORNING PO!

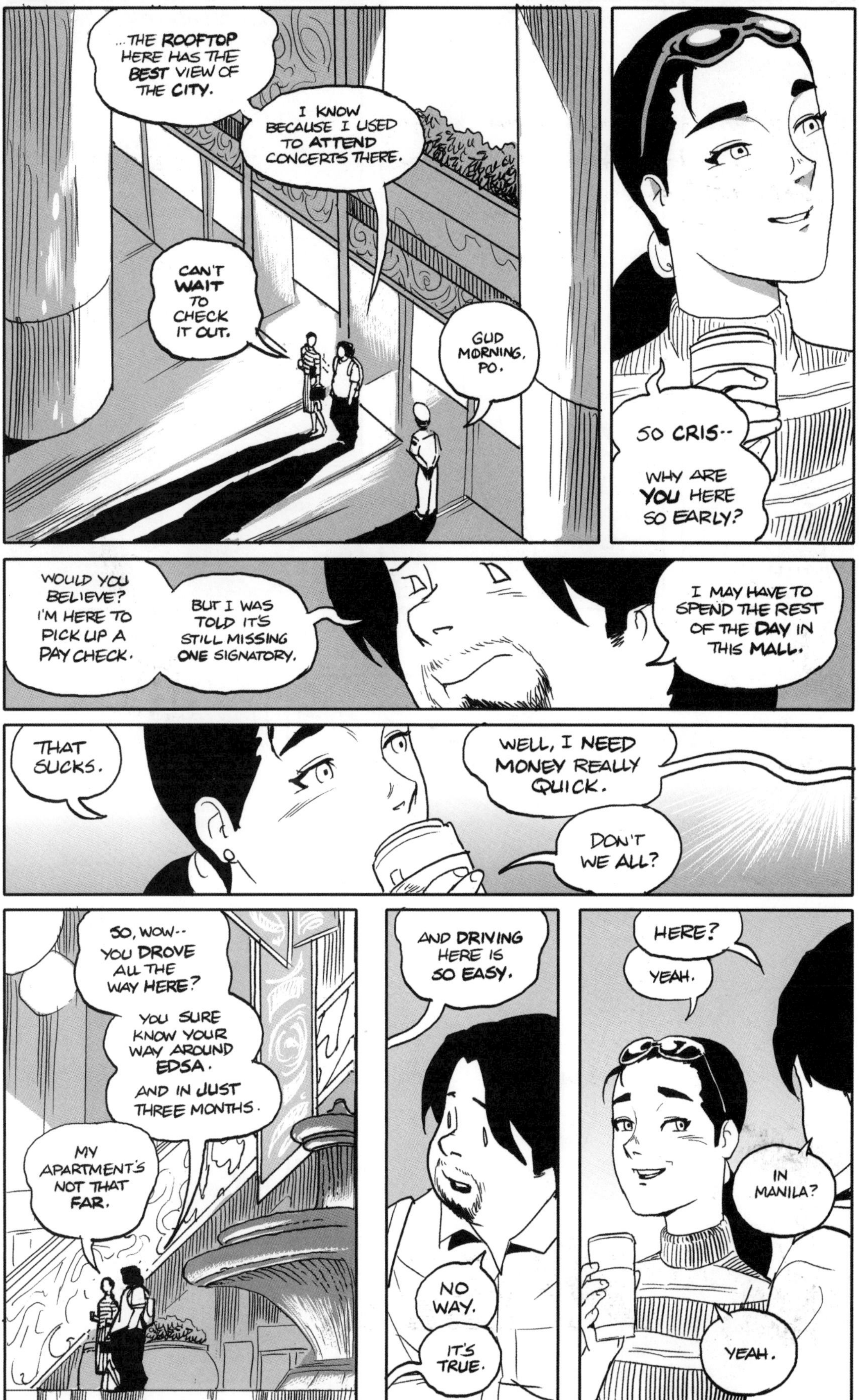
...THE ROOFTOP HERE HAS THE BEST VIEW OF THE CITY.
I KNOW BECAUSE I USED TO ATTEND CONCERTS THERE.
CAN'T WAIT TO CHECK IT OUT.
GUD MORNING, PO.
SO CRIS--
WHY ARE YOU HERE SO EARLY?
WOULD YOU BELIEVE? I'M HERE TO PICK UP A PAY CHECK.
BUT I WAS TOLD IT'S STILL MISSING ONE SIGNATORY.
I MAY HAVE TO SPEND THE REST OF THE DAY IN THIS MALL.
THAT SUCKS.
WELL, I NEED MONEY REALLY QUICK.
DON'T WE ALL?
SO, WOW-- YOU DROVE ALL THE WAY HERE?
YOU SURE KNOW YOUR WAY AROUND EDSA.
AND IN JUST THREE MONTHS.
MY APARTMENT'S NOT THAT FAR.
AND DRIVING HERE IS SO EASY.
NO WAY.
IT'S TRUE.
HERE?
YEAH.
IN MANILA?
YEAH.

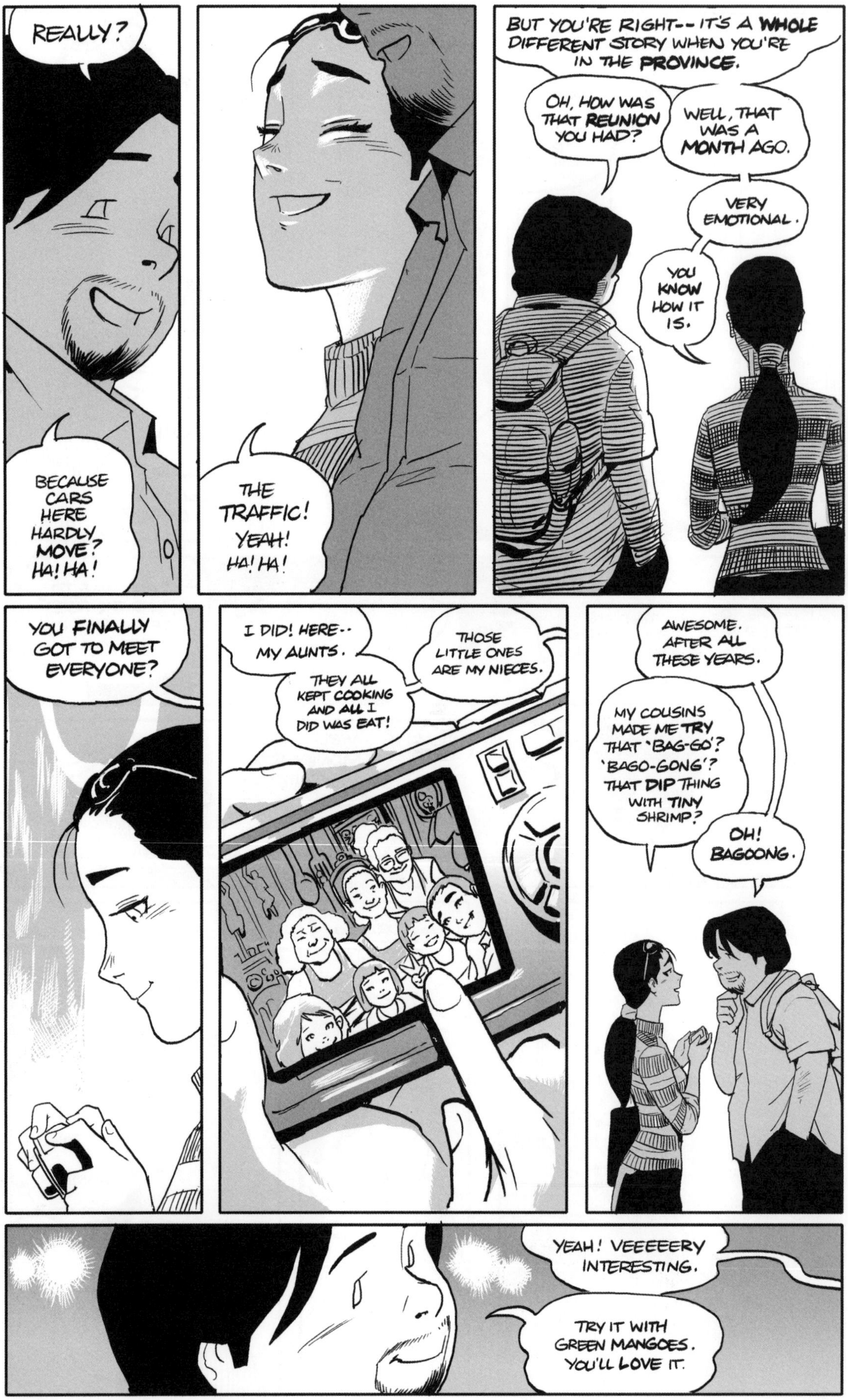
REALLY?
BECAUSE CARS HERE HARDLY MOVE? HA! HA!
THE TRAFFIC! YEAH! HA! HA!
BUT YOU'RE RIGHT-- IT'S A WHOLE DIFFERENT STORY WHEN YOU'RE IN THE PROVINCE.
OH, HOW WAS THAT REUNION YOU HAD?
WELL, THAT WAS A MONTH AGO.
VERY EMOTIONAL.
YOU KNOW HOW IT IS.
YOU FINALLY GOT TO MEET EVERYONE?
I DID! HERE-- MY AUNTS.
THEY ALL KEPT COOKING AND ALL I DID WAS EAT!
THOSE LITTLE ONES ARE MY NIECES.
AWESOME. AFTER ALL THESE YEARS.
MY COUSINS MADE ME TRY THAT 'BAG-GO'? 'BAGO-GONG'? THAT DIP THING WITH TINY SHRIMP?
OH! BAGOONG.
YEAH! VEEEEERY INTERESTING.
TRY IT WITH GREEN MANGOES. YOU'LL LOVE IT.

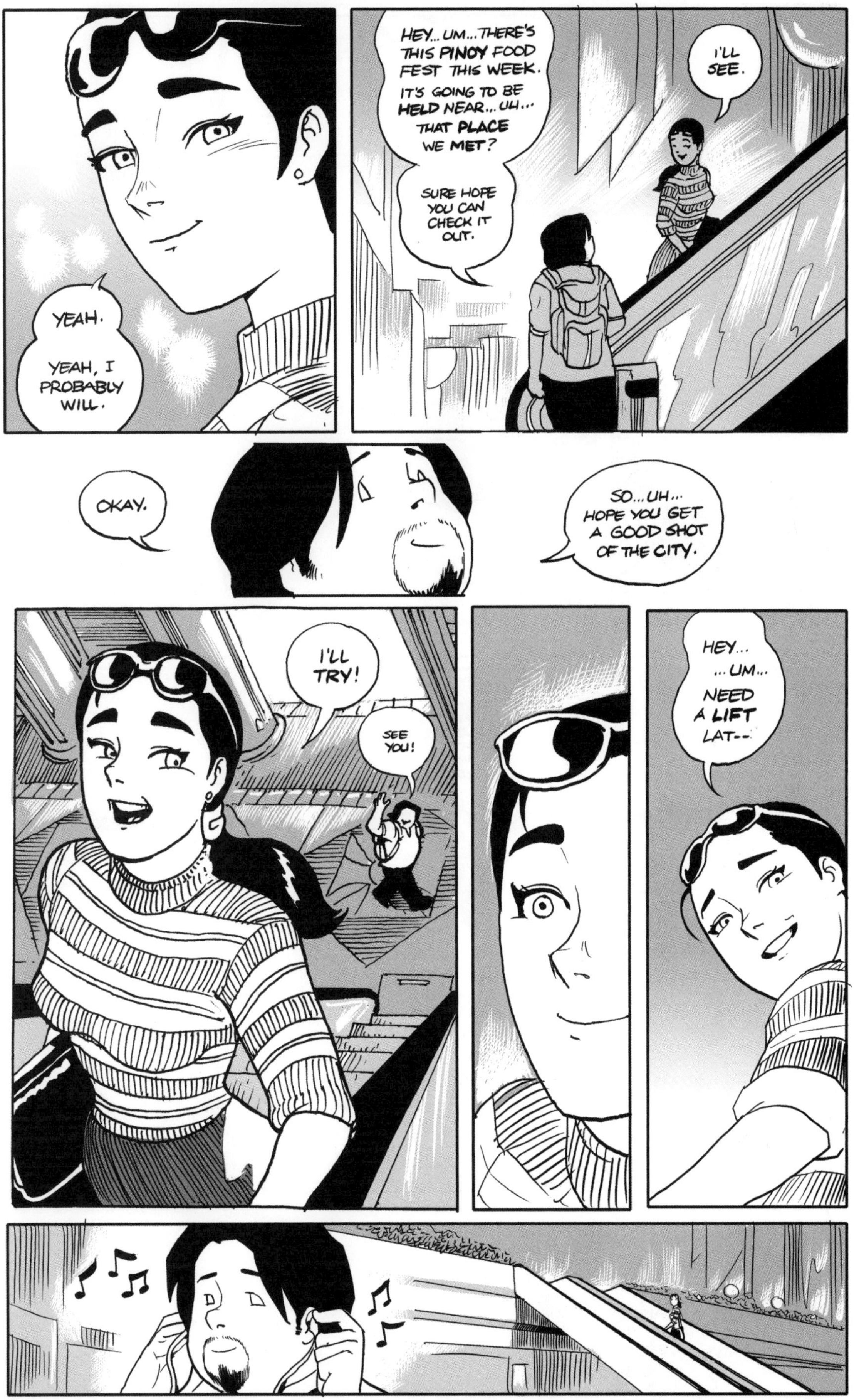
YEAH.
YEAH, I PROBABLY WILL.
HEY... UM... THERE'S THIS PINOY FOOD FEST THIS WEEK.
IT'S GOING TO BE HELD NEAR... UH... THAT PLACE WE MET?
SURE HOPE YOU CAN CHECK IT OUT.
I'LL SEE.
OKAY.
SO... UH... HOPE YOU GET A GOOD SHOT OF THE CITY.
I'LL TRY!
SEE YOU!
HEY... ...UM... NEED A LIFT LAT--

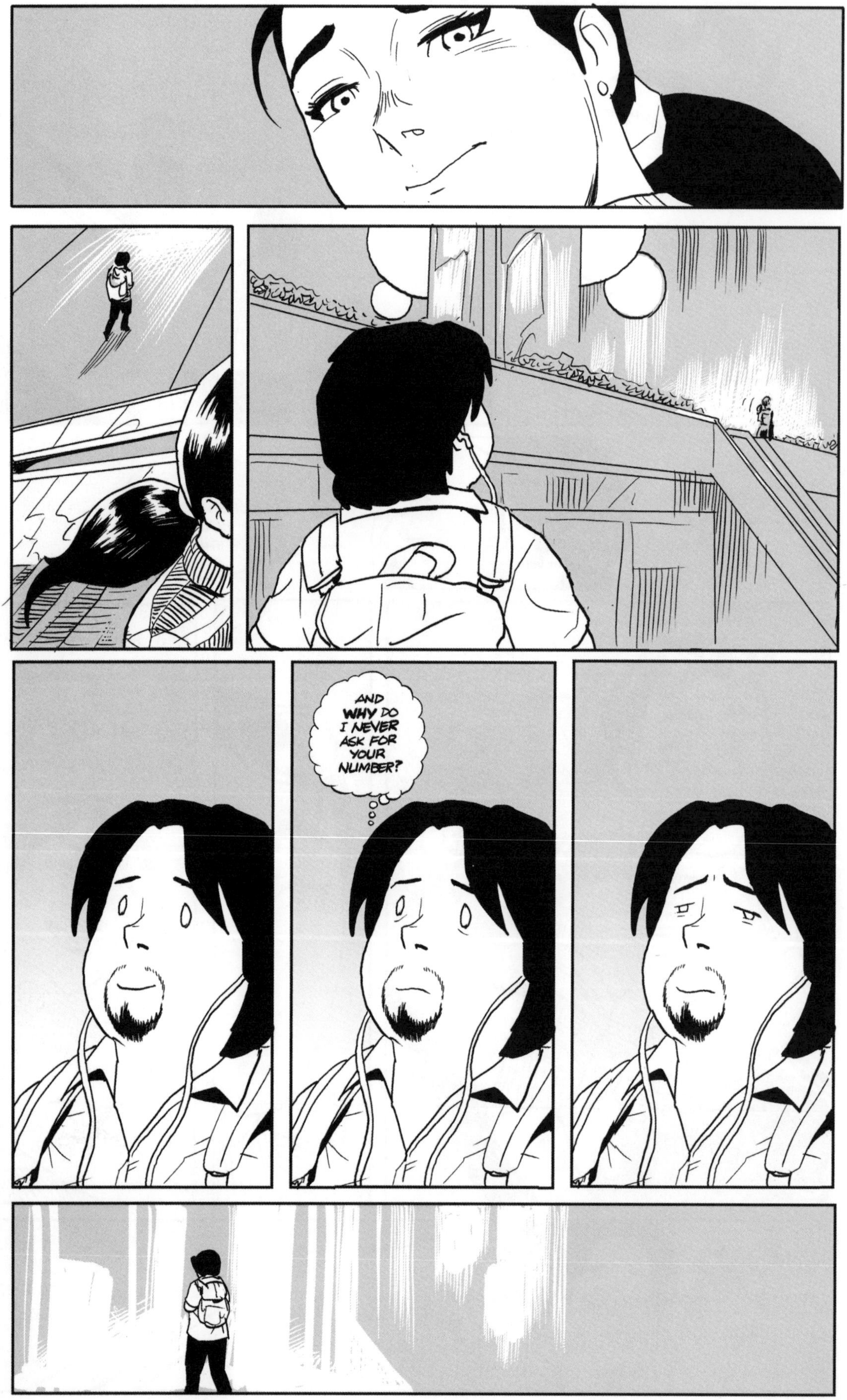
AND WHY DO I NEVER ASK FOR YOUR NUMBER?

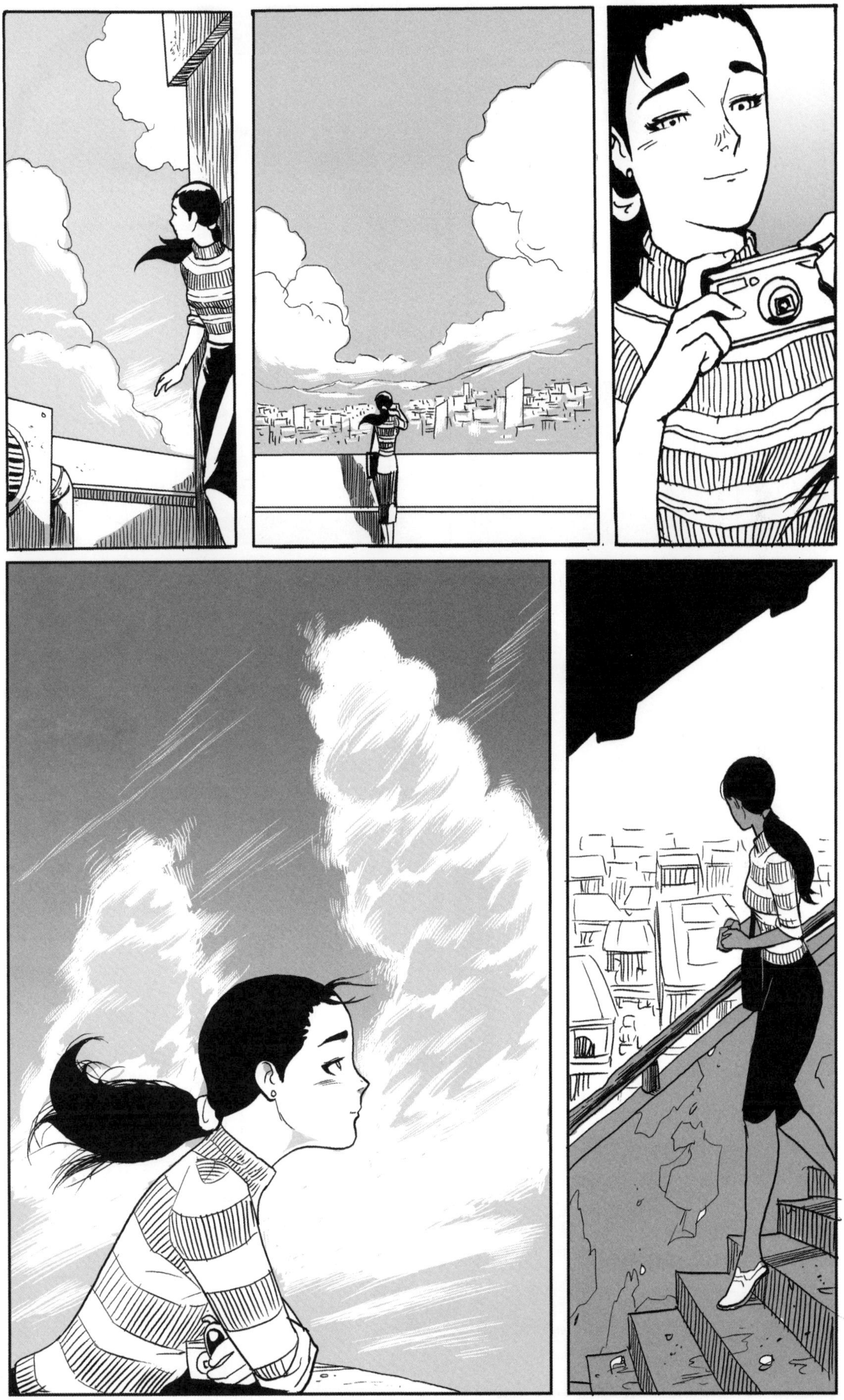

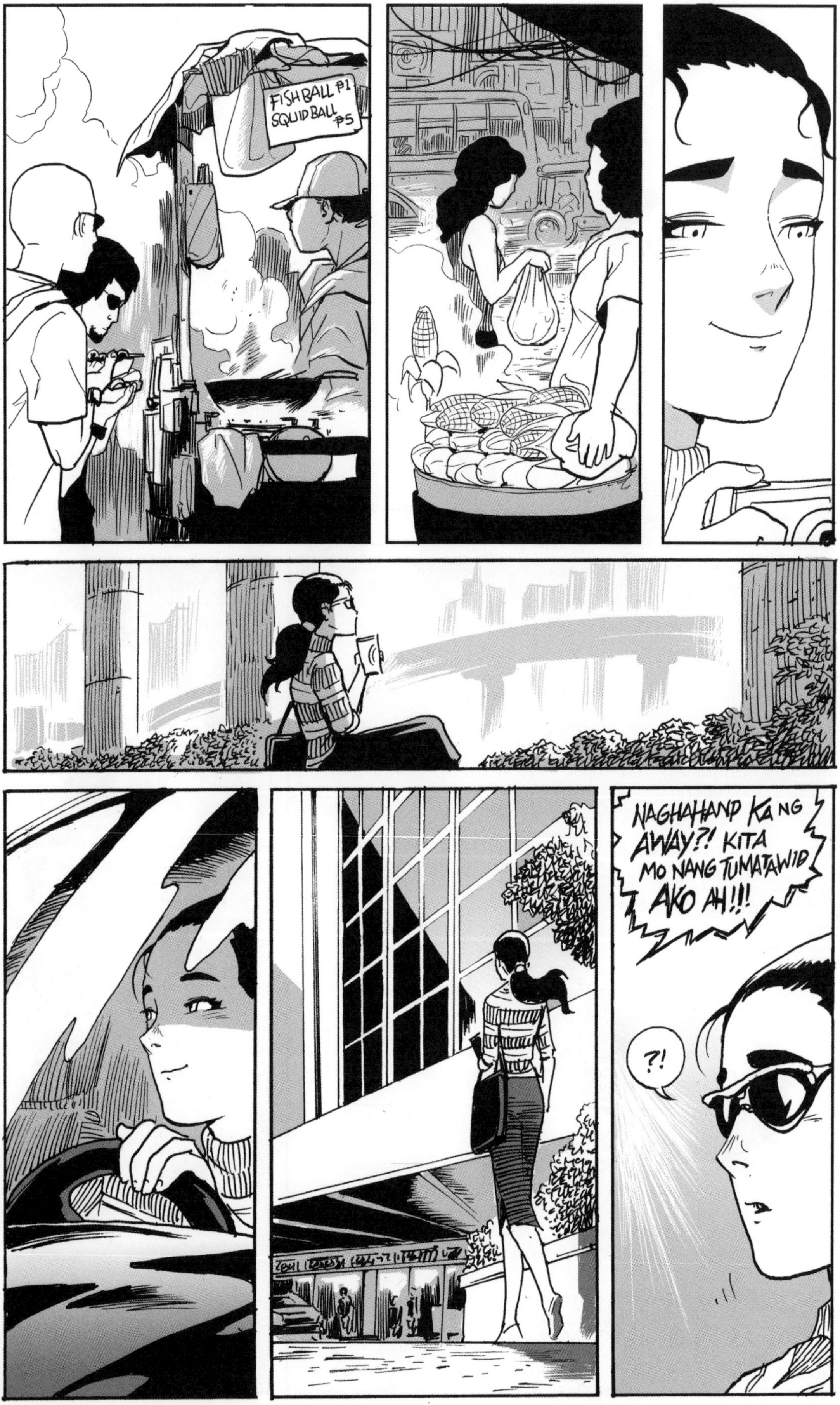
FISH BALL ₱1
SQUID BALL ₱5
NAGHAHANP KA NG AWAY?! KITA MO NANG TUMATAWID AKO AH!!!
?!

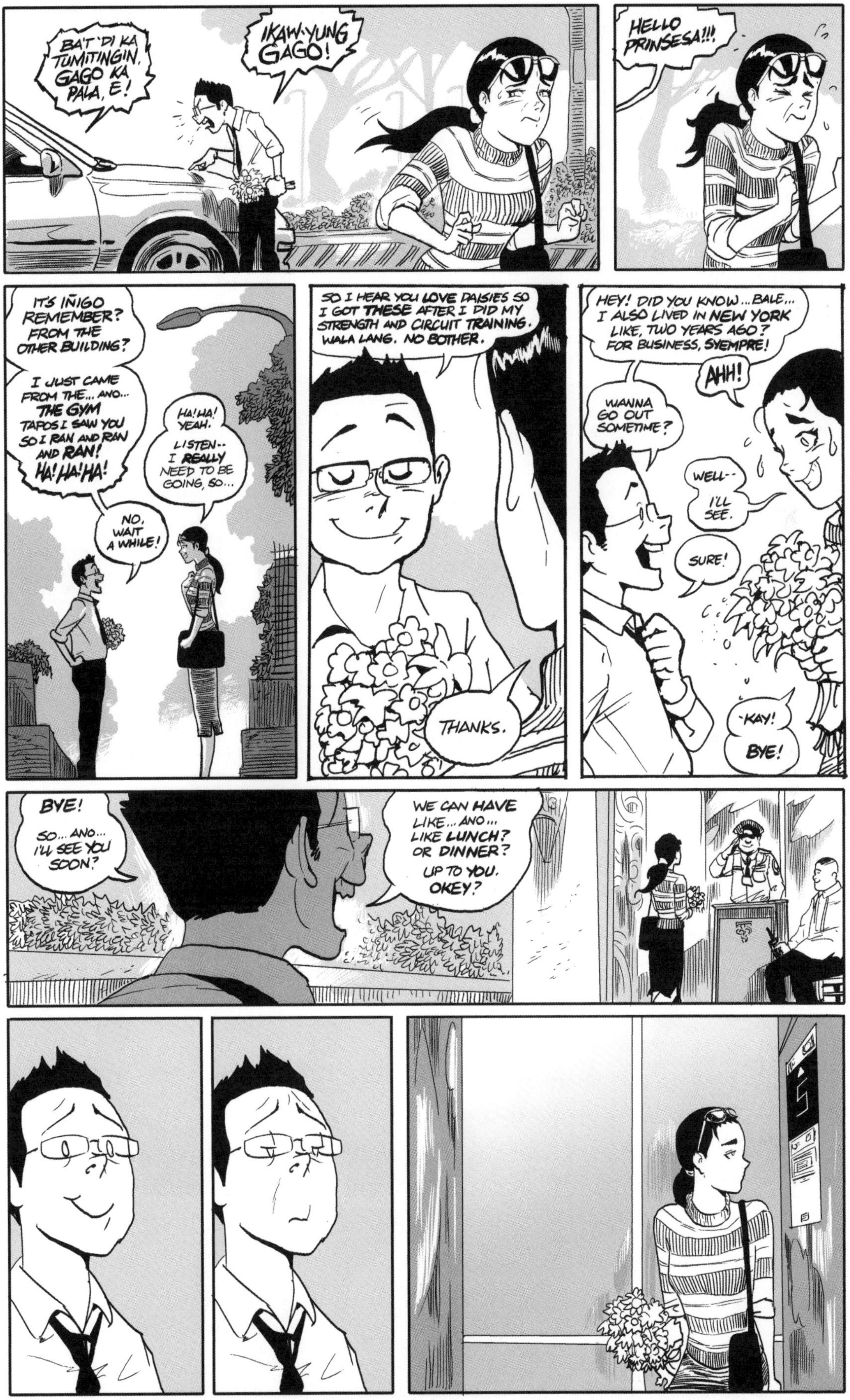
BAT 'DI KA TUMITINGIN, GAGO KA PALA, E!
IKAW-YUNG GAGO!
HELLO PRINSESA!!!
IT'S IÑIGO REMEMBER? FROM THE OTHER BUILDING?
I JUST CAME FROM THE... ANO... THE GYM TAPOS I SAW YOU SO I RAN AND RAN AND RAN! HA! HA! HA!
HA! HA! YEAH.
LISTEN-- I REALLY NEED TO BE GOING, SO...
NO, WAIT A WHILE!
SO I HEAR YOU LOVE DAISIES SO I GOT THESE AFTER I DID MY STRENGTH AND CIRCUIT TRAINING. WALA LANG. NO BOTHER.
THANKS.
HEY! DID YOU KNOW... BALE... I ALSO LIVED IN NEW YORK LIKE, TWO YEARS AGO? FOR BUSINESS, SYEMPRE!
AHH!
WANNA GO OUT SOMETIME?
WELL-- I'LL SEE.
SURE!
'KAY! BYE!
BYE!
SO... ANO... I'LL SEE YOU SOON?
WE CAN HAVE LIKE... ANO... LIKE LUNCH? OR DINNER? UP TO YOU. OKEY?

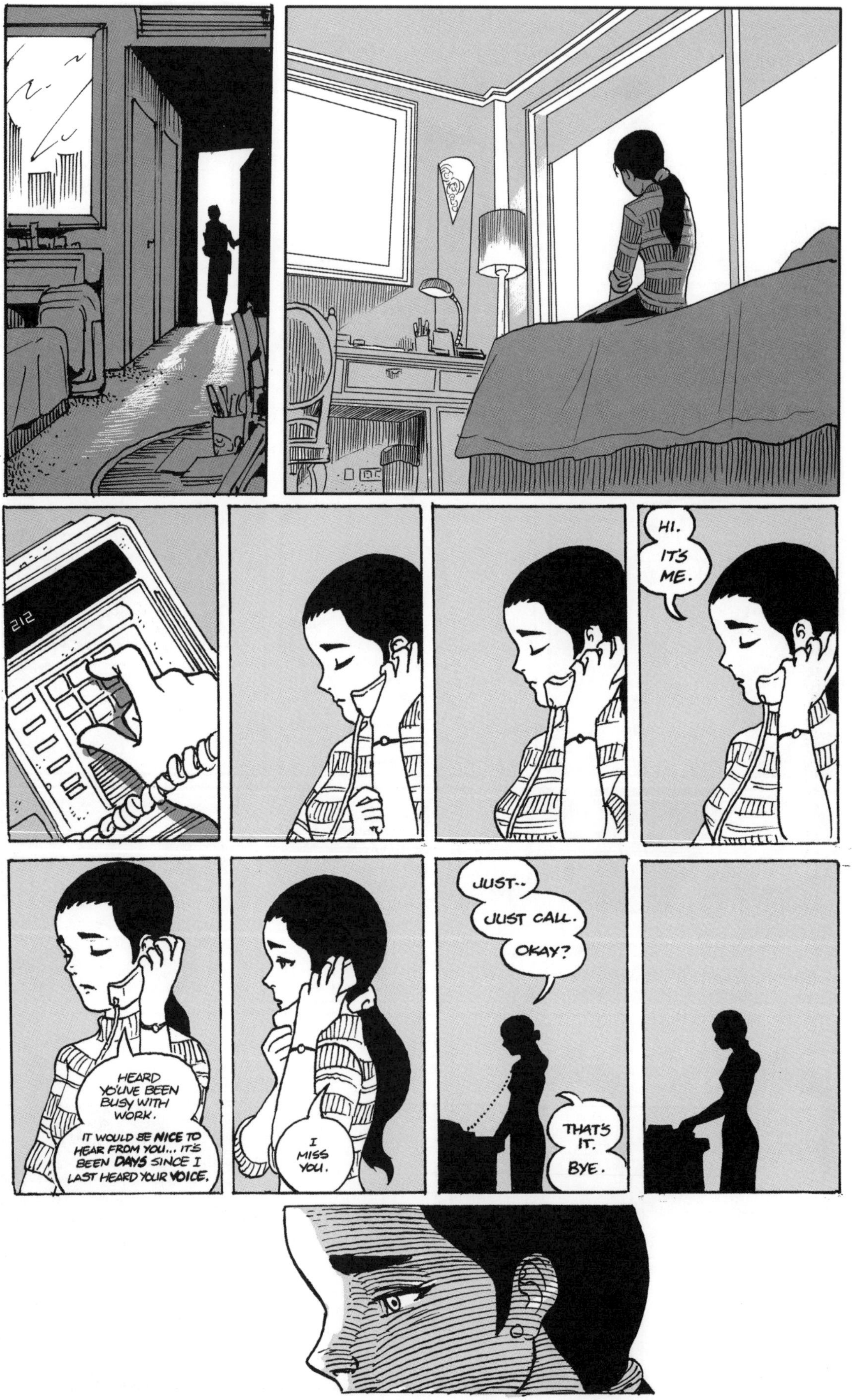
212
HI.
IT'S ME.
HEARD YOU'VE BEEN BUSY WITH WORK.
IT WOULD BE NICE TO HEAR FROM YOU... IT'S BEEN DAYS SINCE I LAST HEARD YOUR VOICE.
I MISS YOU.
JUST--
JUST CALL.
OKAY?
THAT'S IT.
BYE.

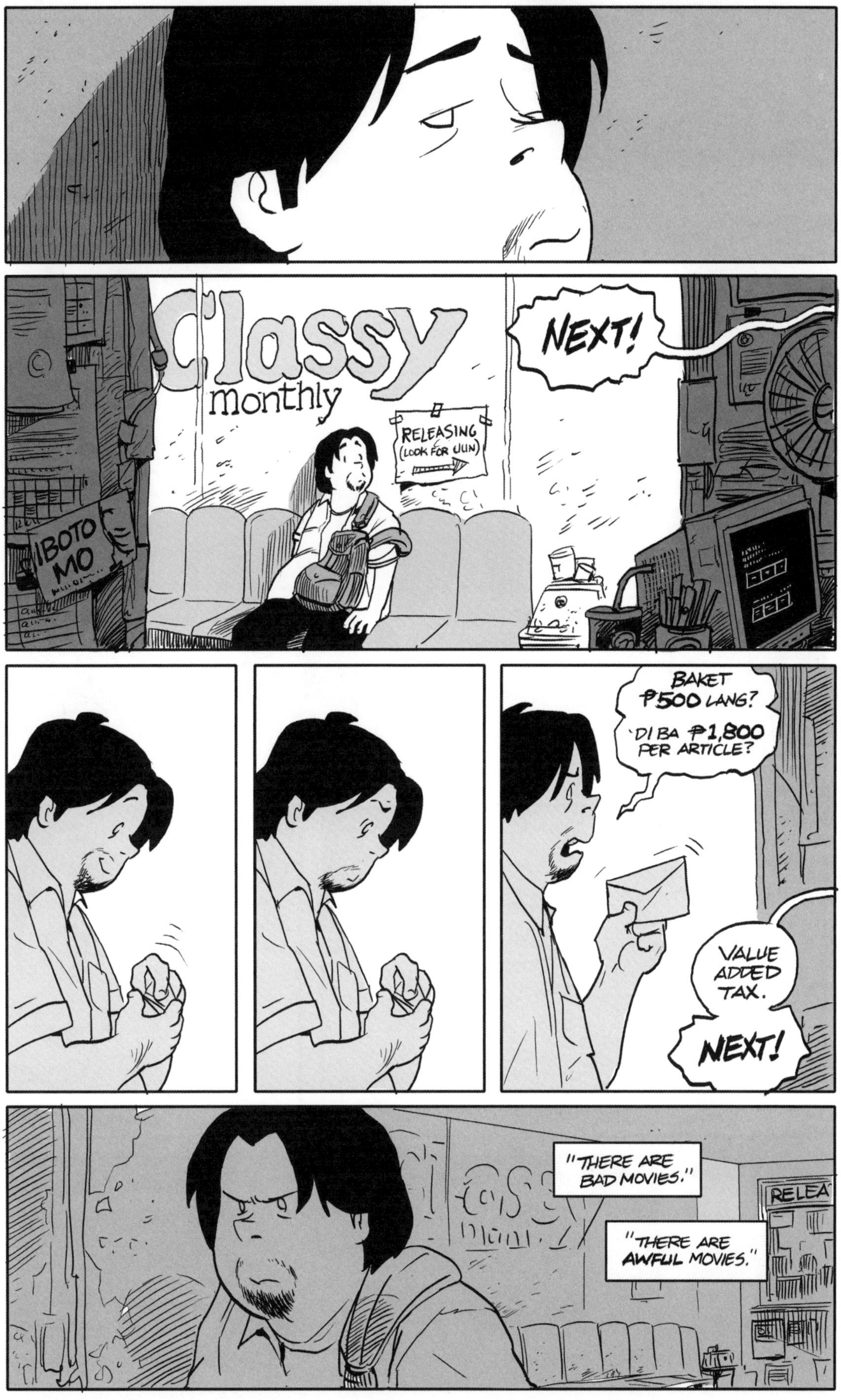
Classy
monthly
RELEASING
(LOOK FOR JUN)
IBOTO MO
NEXT!
BAKET ₱500 LANG?
'DI BA ₱1,800 PER ARTICLE?
VALUE ADDED TAX.
NEXT!
"THERE ARE BAD MOVIES."
"THERE ARE AWFUL MOVIES."
RELEA

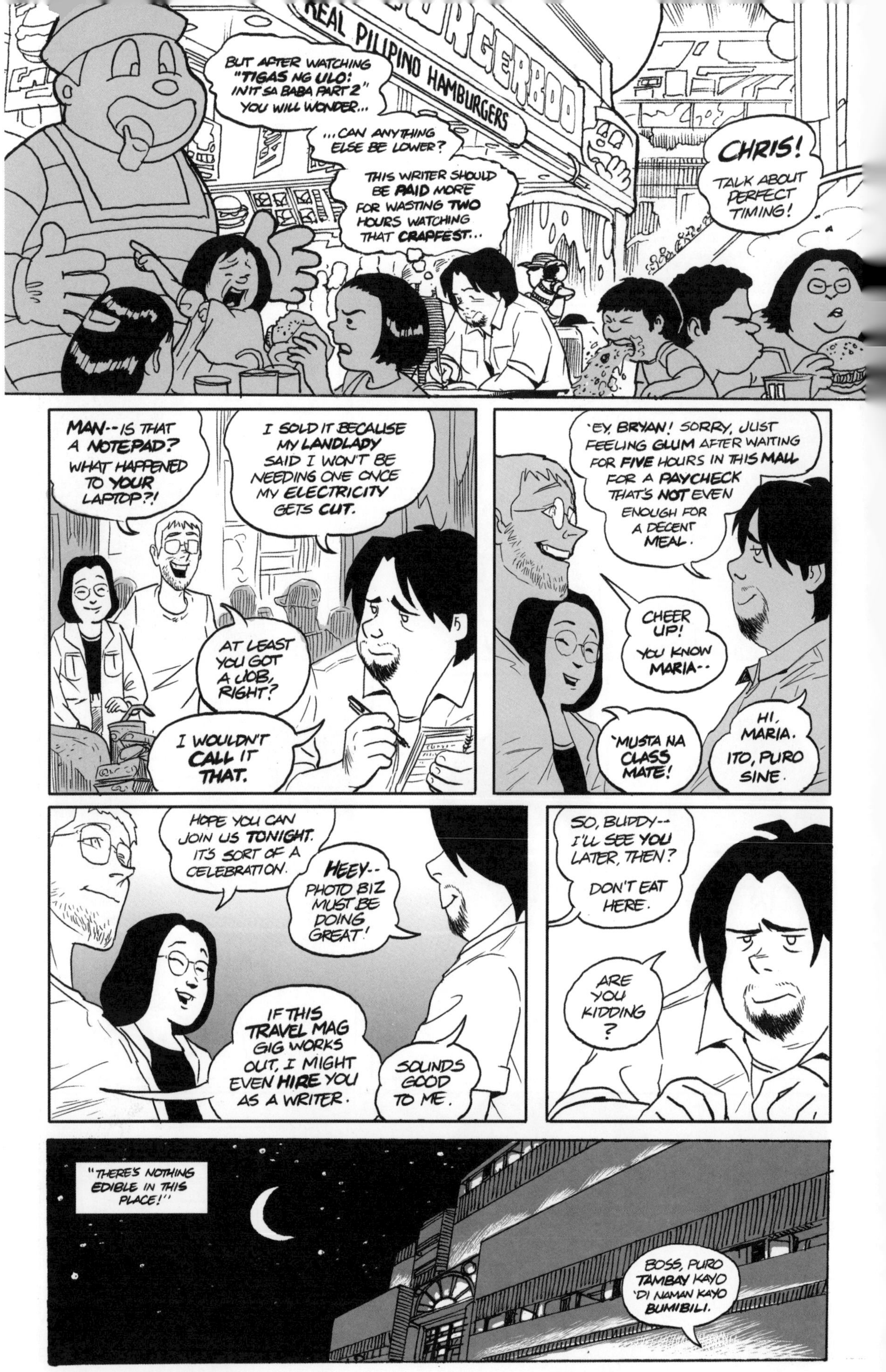
REAL PILIPINO HAMBURGERS
BUT AFTER WATCHING "TIGAS NG ULO: INIT SA BABA PART 2" YOU WILL WONDER...
...CAN ANYTHING ELSE BE LOWER?
THIS WRITER SHOULD BE PAID MORE FOR WASTING TWO HOURS WATCHING THAT CRAPFEST...
CHRIS! TALK ABOUT PERFECT TIMING!
MAN-- IS THAT A NOTEPAD? WHAT HAPPENED TO YOUR LAPTOP?!
I SOLD IT BECAUSE MY LANDLADY SAID I WON'T BE NEEDING ONE ONCE MY ELECTRICITY GETS CUT.
AT LEAST YOU GOT A JOB, RIGHT?
I WOULDN'T CALL IT THAT.
`EY, BRYAN! SORRY, JUST FEELING GLUM AFTER WAITING FOR FIVE HOURS IN THIS MALL FOR A PAYCHECK THAT'S NOT EVEN ENOUGH FOR A DECENT MEAL.
CHEER UP! YOU KNOW MARIA--
`MUSTA NA CLASSMATE!
HI, MARIA. ITO, PURO SINE.
HOPE YOU CAN JOIN US TONIGHT. IT'S SORT OF A CELEBRATION.
HEEY-- PHOTO BIZ MUST BE DOING GREAT!
IF THIS TRAVEL MAG GIG WORKS OUT, I MIGHT EVEN HIRE YOU AS A WRITER.
SOUNDS GOOD TO ME.
SO, BUDDY-- I'LL SEE YOU LATER, THEN?
DON'T EAT HERE.
ARE YOU KIDDING?
"THERE'S NOTHING EDIBLE IN THIS PLACE!"
BOSS, PURO TAMBAY KAYO 'DI NAMAN KAYO BUMIBILI.

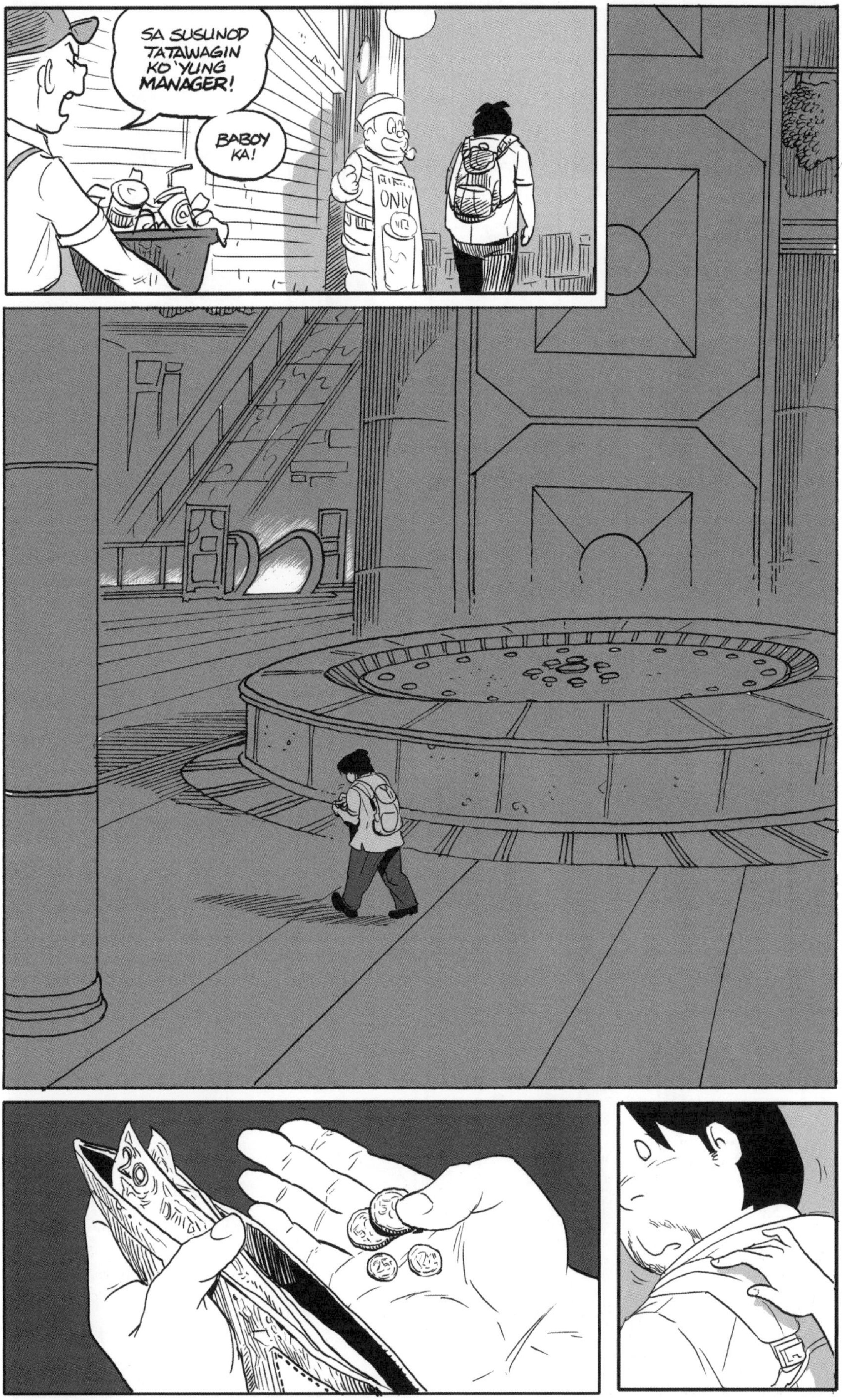
SA SUSUNOD TATAWAGIN KO'YUNG MANAGER!
BABOY KA!
ONLY

HEY THERE BIG GUY! NEED A LIFT?
WH!!
HA!HA! YOU! AND HOW WAS YOUR DAY?
NOT AS BAD AS YOURS'!
HA!HA! HA!HA!HA! HA!
AWWW MAN! I NEEDED THAT.
HEY! UM... ...CAN WE...
CAN WE EXCHANGE NUMBERS THIS TIME?
SO I WON'T HAVE TO GIVE YOU A SHOCK EACH TIME?
SURE!
COME ON!
LET'S START OVER.
LIKE LAST WEEK.
CRISOSTOMO.
CRIS.
HALINA.

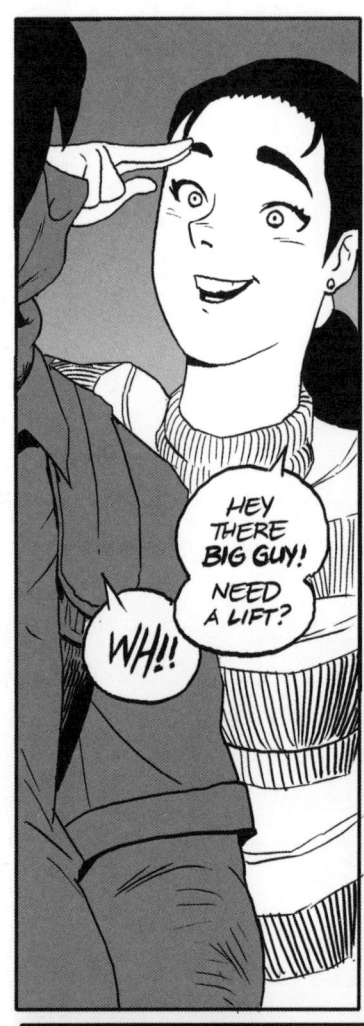

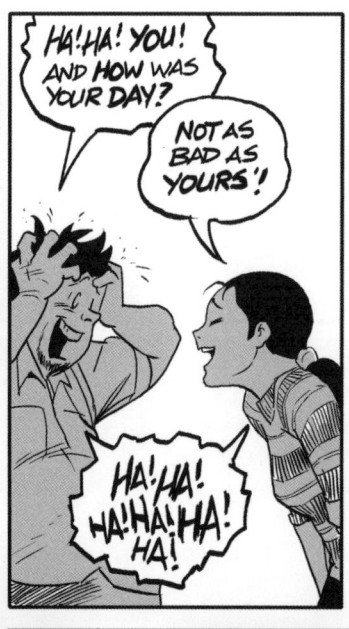

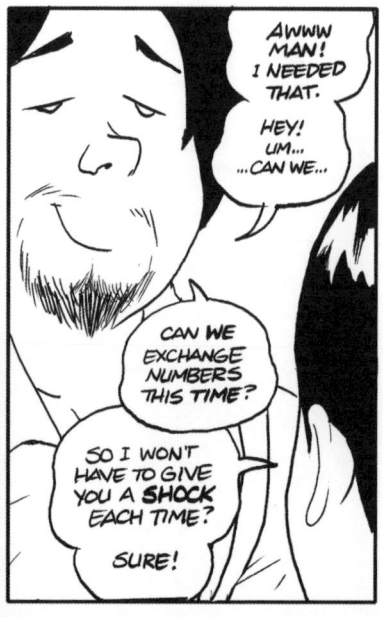

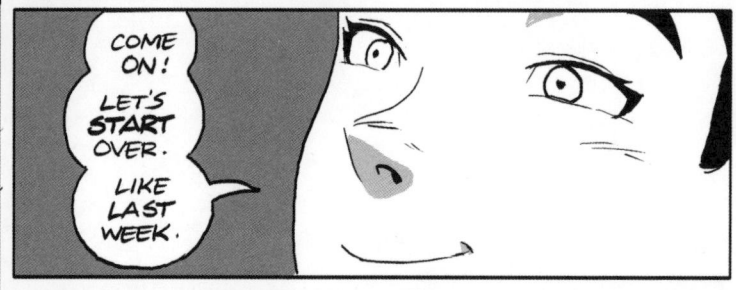

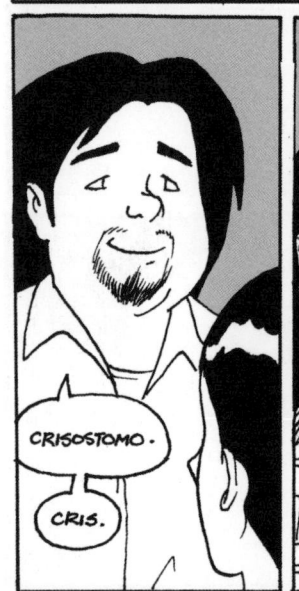

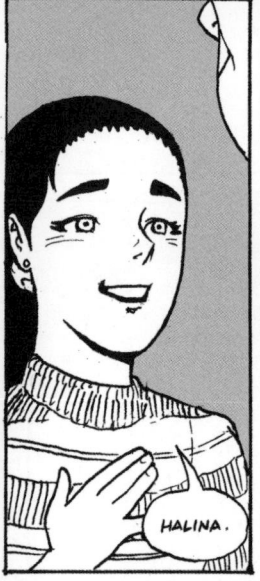

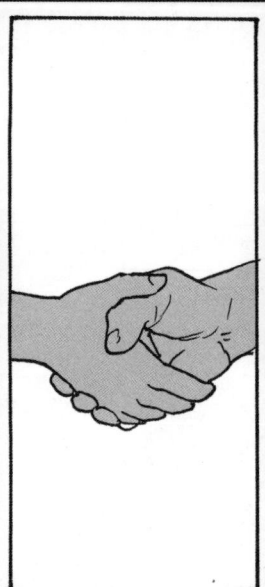

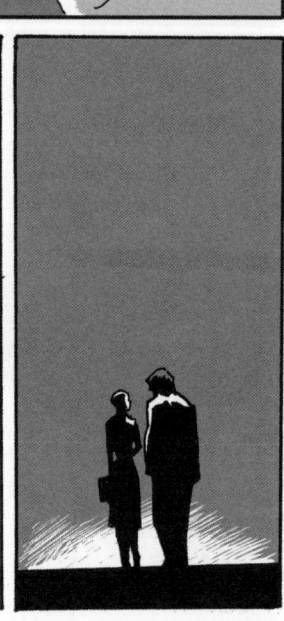

Chapter 2
Manila Nights

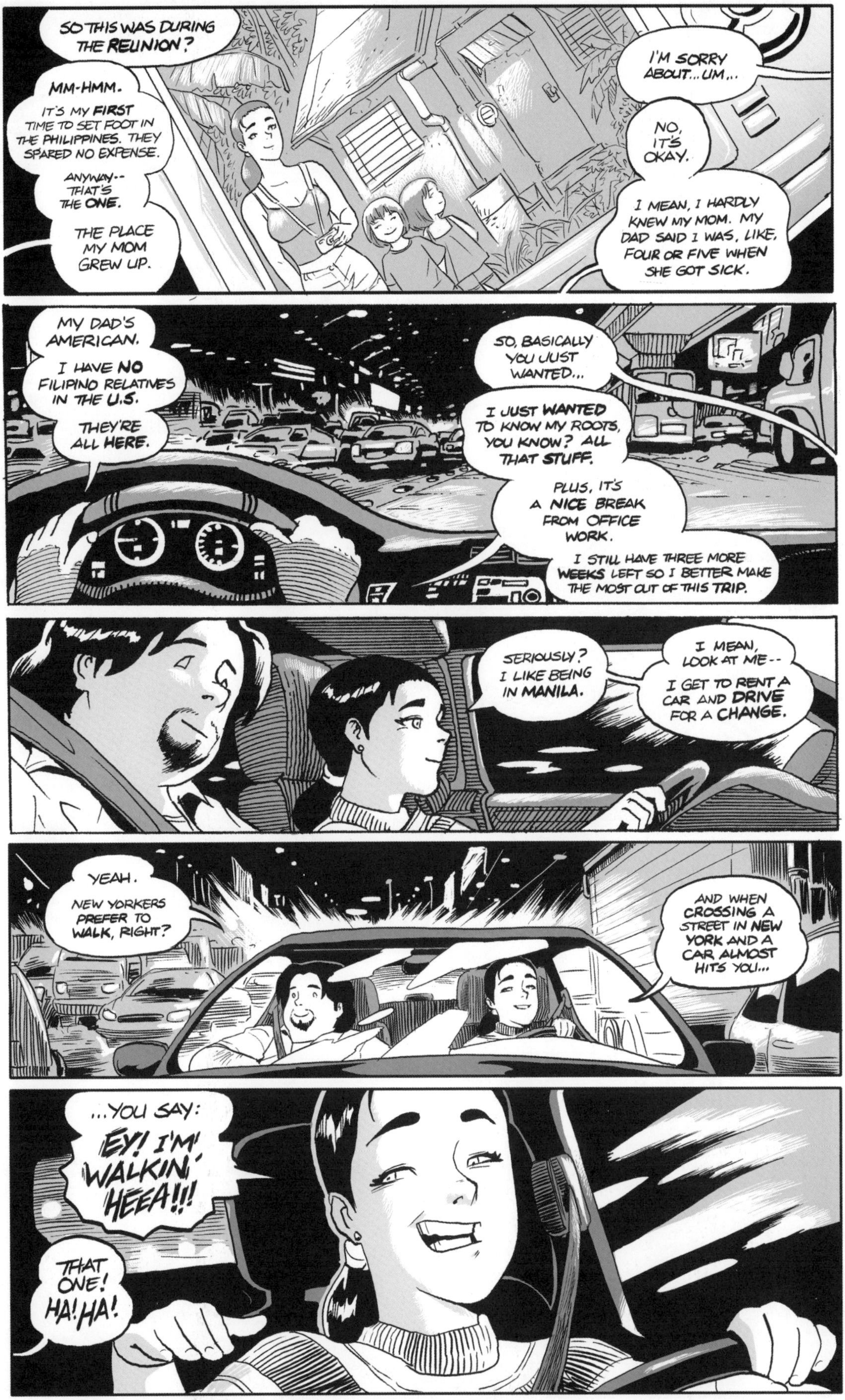
SO THIS WAS DURING THE REUNION?
MM-HMM.
IT'S MY FIRST TIME TO SET FOOT IN THE PHILIPPINES. THEY SPARED NO EXPENSE.
ANYWAY-- THAT'S THE ONE.
THE PLACE MY MOM GREW UP.
I'M SORRY ABOUT... UM...
NO, IT'S OKAY.
I MEAN, I HARDLY KNEW MY MOM. MY DAD SAID I WAS, LIKE, FOUR OR FIVE WHEN SHE GOT SICK.
MY DAD'S AMERICAN.
I HAVE NO FILIPINO RELATIVES IN THE U.S.
THEY'RE ALL HERE.
SO, BASICALLY YOU JUST WANTED...
I JUST WANTED TO KNOW MY ROOTS, YOU KNOW? ALL THAT STUFF.
PLUS, IT'S A NICE BREAK FROM OFFICE WORK.
I STILL HAVE THREE MORE WEEKS LEFT SO I BETTER MAKE THE MOST OUT OF THIS TRIP.
SERIOUSLY? I LIKE BEING IN MANILA.
I MEAN, LOOK AT ME--
I GET TO RENT A CAR AND DRIVE FOR A CHANGE.
YEAH.
NEW YORKERS PREFER TO WALK, RIGHT?
AND WHEN CROSSING A STREET IN NEW YORK AND A CAR ALMOST HITS YOU...
...YOU SAY:
EY! I'M WALKIN' HEEA!!!
THAT ONE! HA! HA!

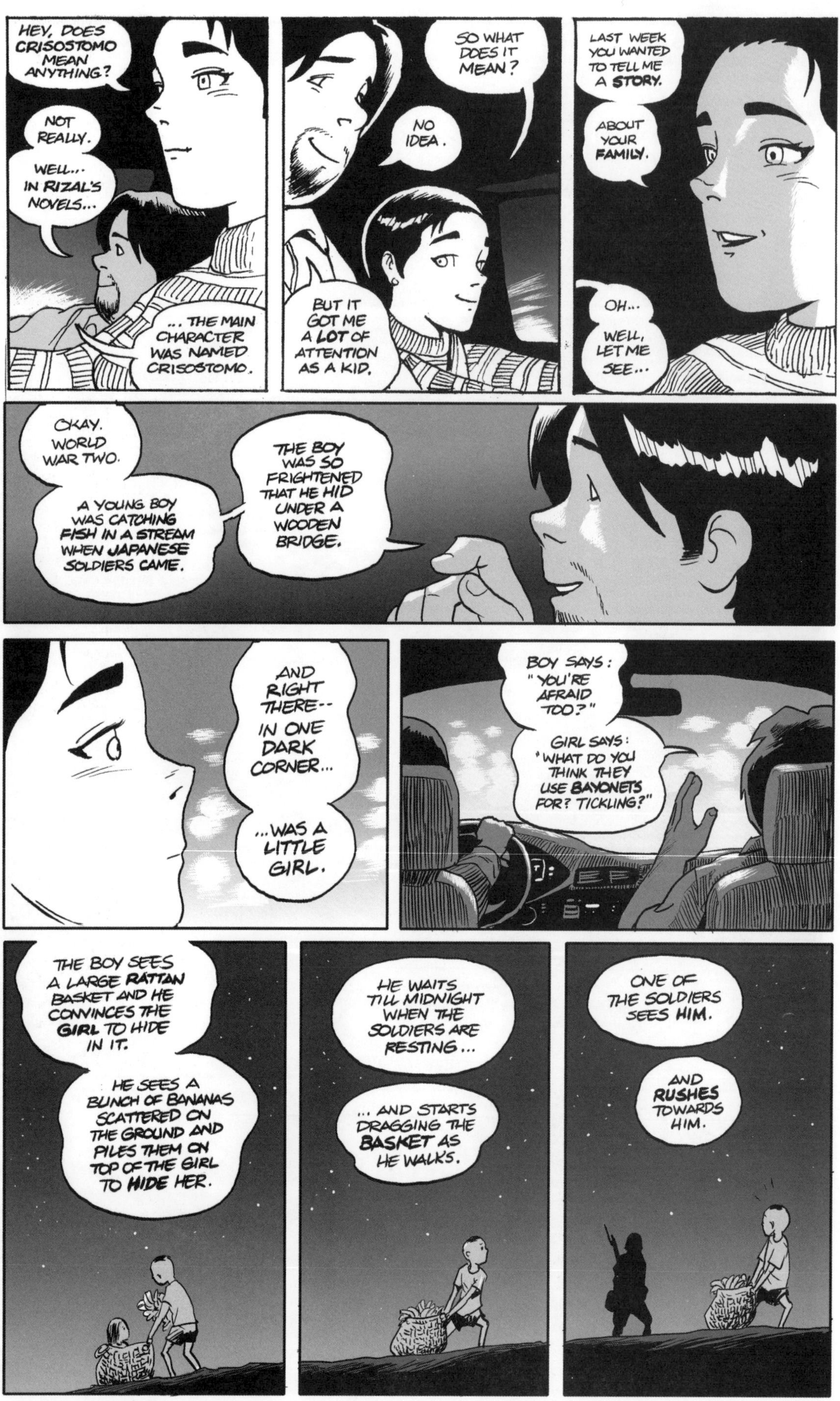
HEY, DOES CRISOSTOMO MEAN ANYTHING?
NOT REALLY.
WELL... IN RIZAL'S NOVELS...
... THE MAIN CHARACTER WAS NAMED CRISOSTOMO.
SO WHAT DOES IT MEAN?
NO IDEA.
BUT IT GOT ME A LOT OF ATTENTION AS A KID.
LAST WEEK YOU WANTED TO TELL ME A STORY.
ABOUT YOUR FAMILY.
OH...
WELL, LET ME SEE...
OKAY. WORLD WAR TWO.
A YOUNG BOY WAS CATCHING FISH IN A STREAM WHEN JAPANESE SOLDIERS CAME.
THE BOY WAS SO FRIGHTENED THAT HE HID UNDER A WOODEN BRIDGE.
AND RIGHT THERE-- IN ONE DARK CORNER...
...WAS A LITTLE GIRL.
BOY SAYS: "YOU'RE AFRAID TOO?"
GIRL SAYS: "WHAT DO YOU THINK THEY USE BAYONETS FOR? TICKLING?"
THE BOY SEES A LARGE RATTAN BASKET AND HE CONVINCES THE GIRL TO HIDE IN IT.
HE SEES A BUNCH OF BANANAS SCATTERED ON THE GROUND AND PILES THEM ON TOP OF THE GIRL TO HIDE HER.
HE WAITS TILL MIDNIGHT WHEN THE SOLDIERS ARE RESTING...
... AND STARTS DRAGGING THE BASKET AS HE WALKS.
ONE OF THE SOLDIERS SEES HIM.
AND RUSHES TOWARDS HIM.

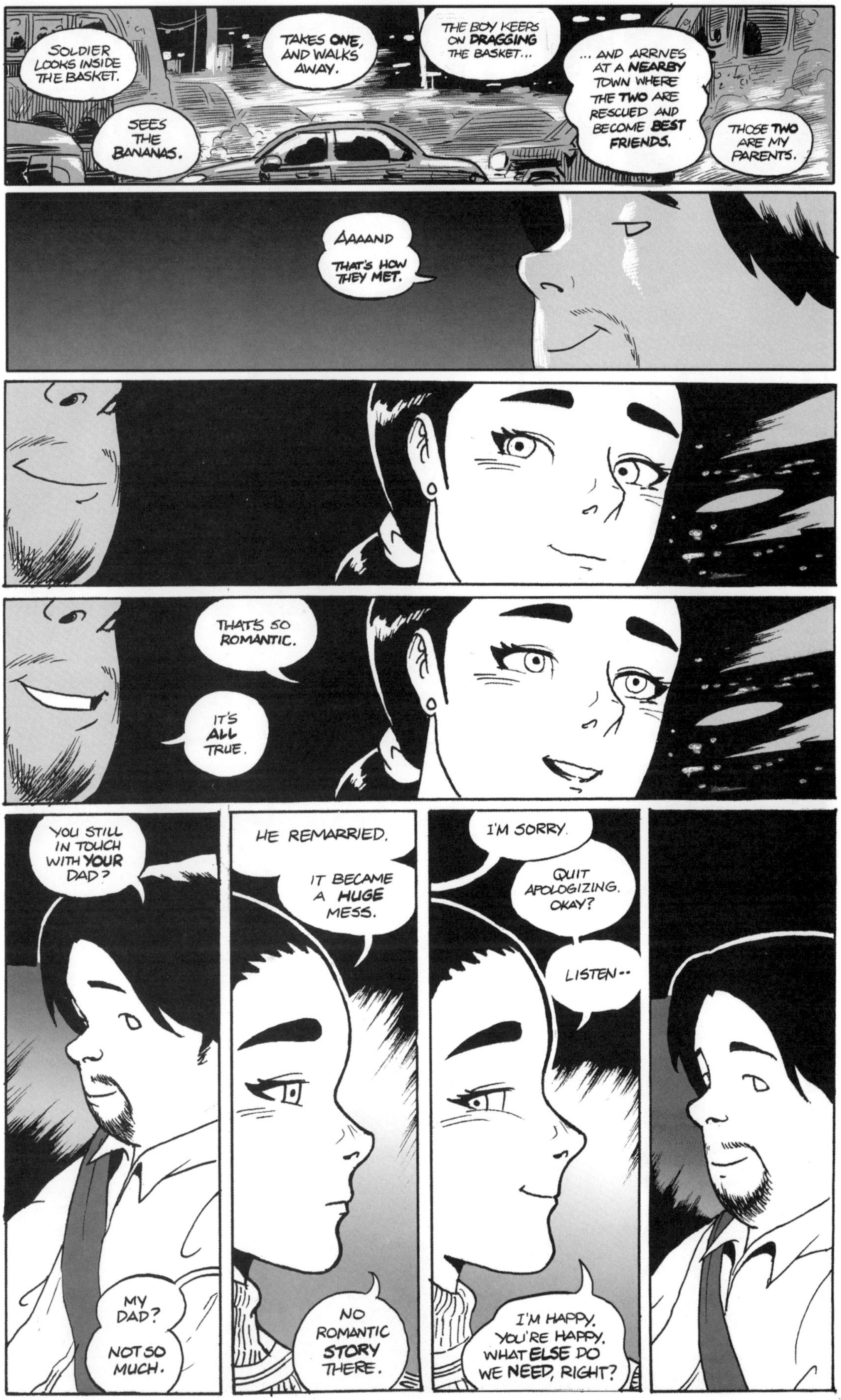
SOLDIER LOOKS INSIDE THE BASKET.
SEES THE BANANAS.
TAKES ONE, AND WALKS AWAY.
THE BOY KEEPS ON DRAGGING THE BASKET...
... AND ARRIVES AT A NEARBY TOWN WHERE THE TWO ARE RESCUED AND BECOME BEST FRIENDS.
THOSE TWO ARE MY PARENTS.
AAAAND
THAT'S HOW THEY MET.
THAT'S SO ROMANTIC.
IT'S ALL TRUE.
YOU STILL IN TOUCH WITH YOUR DAD?
MY DAD?
NOT SO MUCH.
HE REMARRIED.
IT BECAME A HUGE MESS.
NO ROMANTIC STORY THERE.
I'M SORRY.
QUIT APOLOGIZING. OKAY?
LISTEN--
I'M HAPPY. YOU'RE HAPPY. WHAT ELSE DO WE NEED, RIGHT?

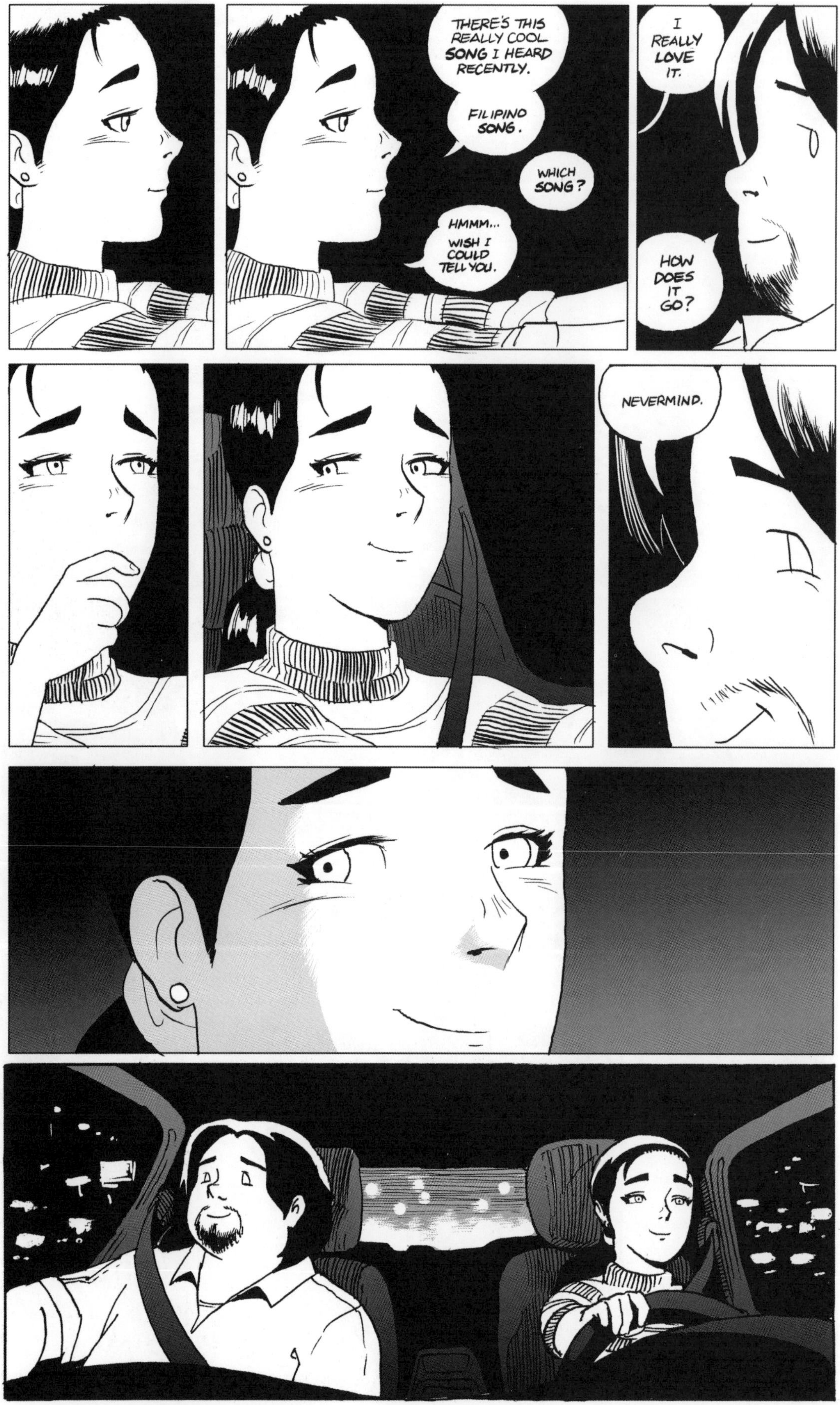
THERE'S THIS REALLY COOL SONG I HEARD RECENTLY.
FILIPINO SONG.
WHICH SONG?
HMMM... WISH I COULD TELL YOU.
I REALLY LOVE IT.
HOW DOES IT GO?
NEVERMIND.

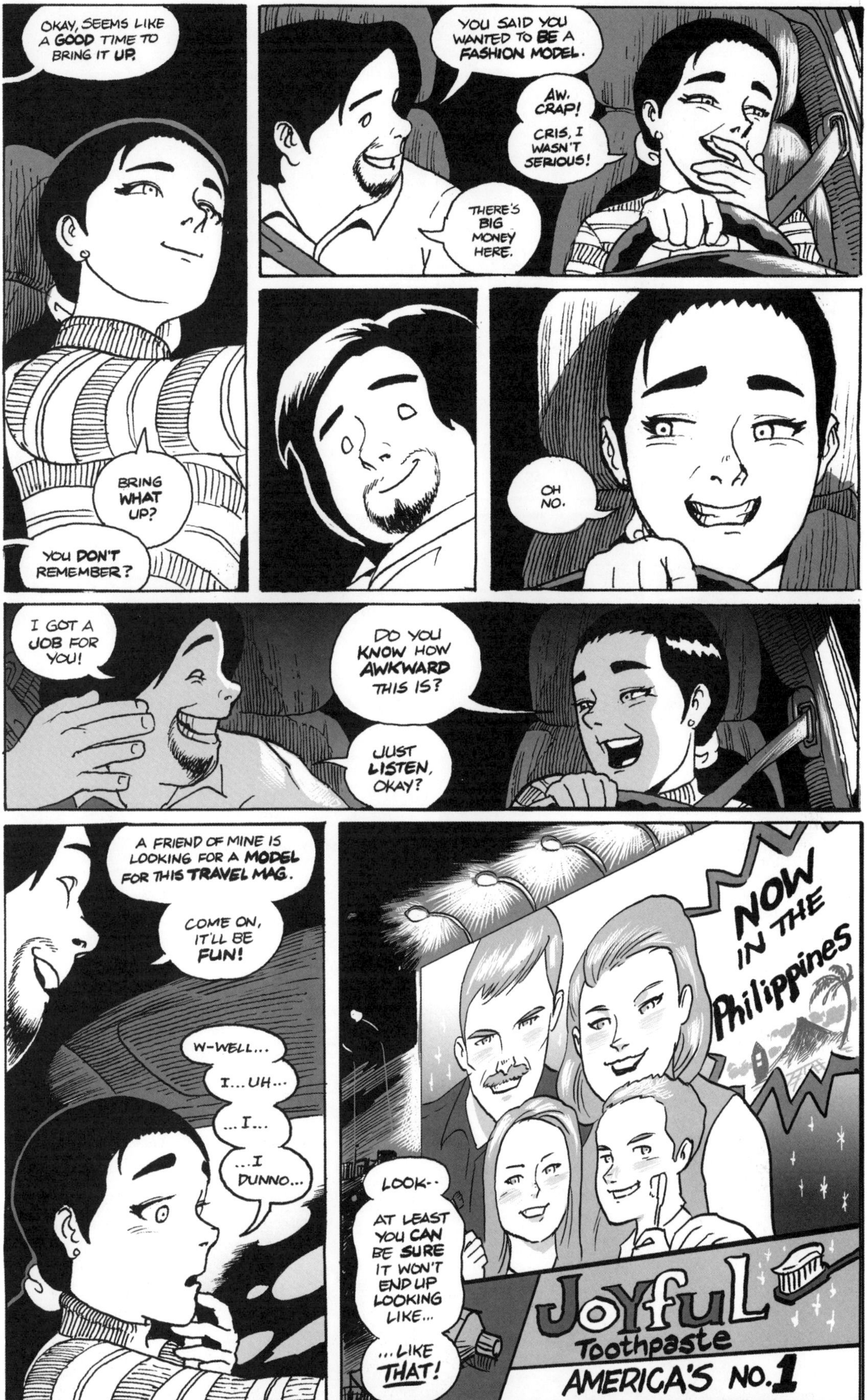
OKAY, SEEMS LIKE A GOOD TIME TO BRING IT UP.
BRING WHAT UP?
YOU DON'T REMEMBER?
YOU SAID YOU WANTED TO BE A FASHION MODEL.
AW, CRAP!
CRIS, I WASN'T SERIOUS!
THERE'S BIG MONEY HERE.
OH NO.
I GOT A JOB FOR YOU!
DO YOU KNOW HOW AWKWARD THIS IS?
JUST LISTEN, OKAY?
A FRIEND OF MINE IS LOOKING FOR A MODEL FOR THIS TRAVEL MAG.
COME ON, IT'LL BE FUN!
W-WELL...
I...UH...
...I...
...I DUNNO...
NOW IN THE Philippines
LOOK--
AT LEAST YOU CAN BE SURE IT WON'T END UP LOOKING LIKE...
...LIKE THAT!
JoYfuL Toothpaste
AMERICA'S NO.1

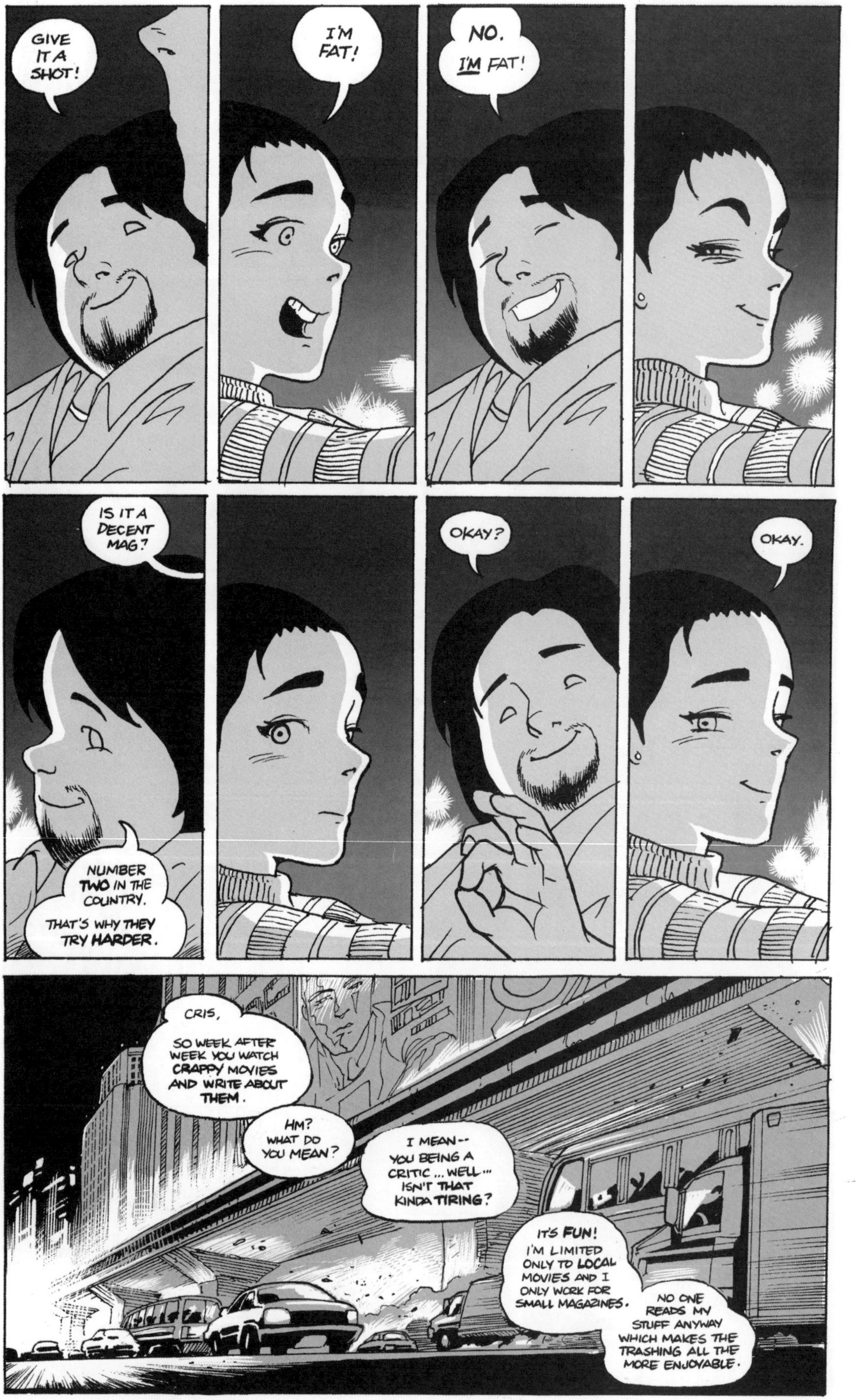
GIVE IT A SHOT!
I'M FAT!
NO. I'M FAT!
IS IT A DECENT MAG?
NUMBER TWO IN THE COUNTRY.
THAT'S WHY THEY TRY HARDER.
OKAY?
OKAY.
CRIS,
SO WEEK AFTER WEEK YOU WATCH CRAPPY MOVIES AND WRITE ABOUT THEM.
HM? WHAT DO YOU MEAN?
I MEAN-- YOU BEING A CRITIC ... WELL ... ISN'T THAT KINDA TIRING?
IT'S FUN! I'M LIMITED ONLY TO LOCAL MOVIES AND I ONLY WORK FOR SMALL MAGAZINES.
NO ONE READS MY STUFF ANYWAY WHICH MAKES THE TRASHING ALL THE MORE ENJOYABLE.

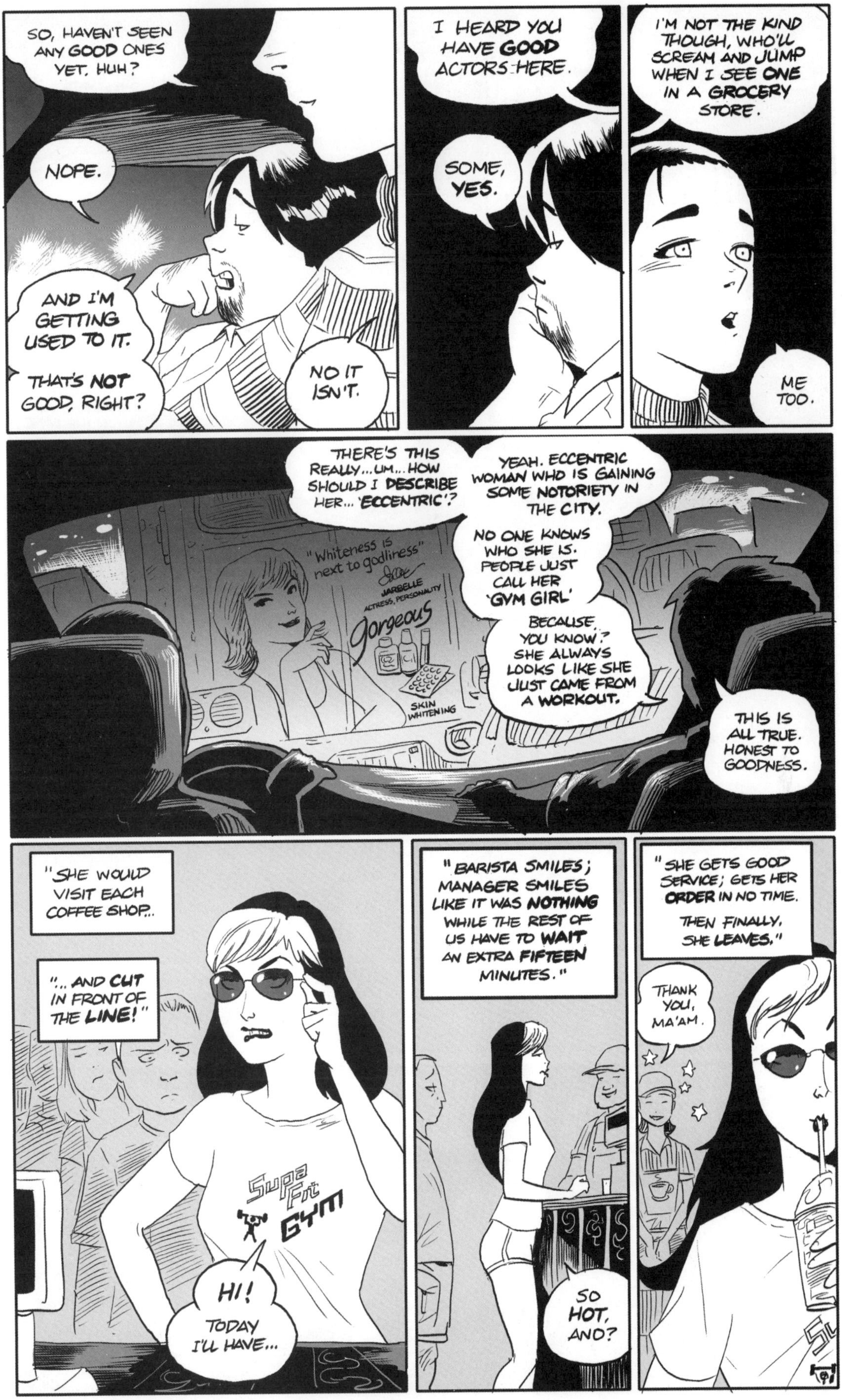
SO, HAVEN'T SEEN ANY GOOD ONES YET. HUH?
NOPE.
AND I'M GETTING USED TO IT.
THAT'S NOT GOOD, RIGHT?
NO IT ISN'T.
I HEARD YOU HAVE GOOD ACTORS HERE.
SOME, YES.
I'M NOT THE KIND THOUGH, WHO'LL SCREAM AND JUMP WHEN I SEE ONE IN A GROCERY STORE.
ME TOO.
THERE'S THIS REALLY... UM... HOW SHOULD I DESCRIBE HER... 'ECCENTRIC'?
YEAH. ECCENTRIC WOMAN WHO IS GAINING SOME NOTORIETY IN THE CITY.
NO ONE KNOWS WHO SHE IS. PEOPLE JUST CALL HER 'GYM GIRL'
BECAUSE, YOU KNOW? SHE ALWAYS LOOKS LIKE SHE JUST CAME FROM A WORKOUT.
"Whiteness is next to godliness"
JARBELLE
ACTRESS, PERSONALITY
Gorgeous
SKIN WHITENING
THIS IS ALL TRUE. HONEST TO GOODNESS.
"SHE WOULD VISIT EACH COFFEE SHOP...
"... AND CUT IN FRONT OF THE LINE!"
Supa Fit GYM
HI!
TODAY I'LL HAVE...
"BARISTA SMILES; MANAGER SMILES LIKE IT WAS NOTHING WHILE THE REST OF US HAVE TO WAIT AN EXTRA FIFTEEN MINUTES."
SO HOT, AND?
"SHE GETS GOOD SERVICE; GETS HER ORDER IN NO TIME.
THEN FINALLY, SHE LEAVES."
THANK YOU, MA'AM.

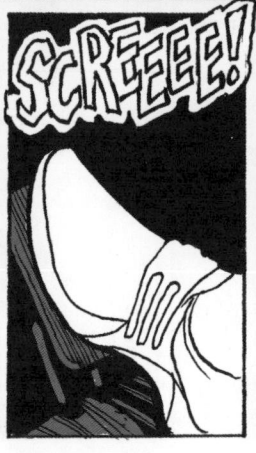

I'VE WITNESSED IT--**TWICE**!

BOY, DOES SHE **LOVE THE** ATTENTION!

SHE'LL TEST THE **LIMITS** OF YOUR TOLERANCE.

I'VE **MET** PEOPLE LIKE THAT BEFORE. I JUST STAY **CLEAR** OF THEM.

OFTENTIMES THEY'RE LONELY, UNHAPPY, UNWANTED.

NOT GETTING SOME.

NOT GETTING SOME! I WAS ABOUT TO SAY THAT! HA! HA!

SOME PEOPLE FEEL PRIVILEGED--

WHEN IN **TRUTH** THEY'RE ALL IN THE SAME **DIRT** AS EVERYONE ELSE.

VRMMNNNNNNNN

!!!

"Whiteness is next to godliness"

Gorgeous

WHOA! DAMN BUS--!

DIDN'T SEE THE SIGN...!

UH-OH! I GOT IT! I GOT IT!!!

SCREEEE!

OH NO.

I'LL HANDLE THIS. STAY COOL.

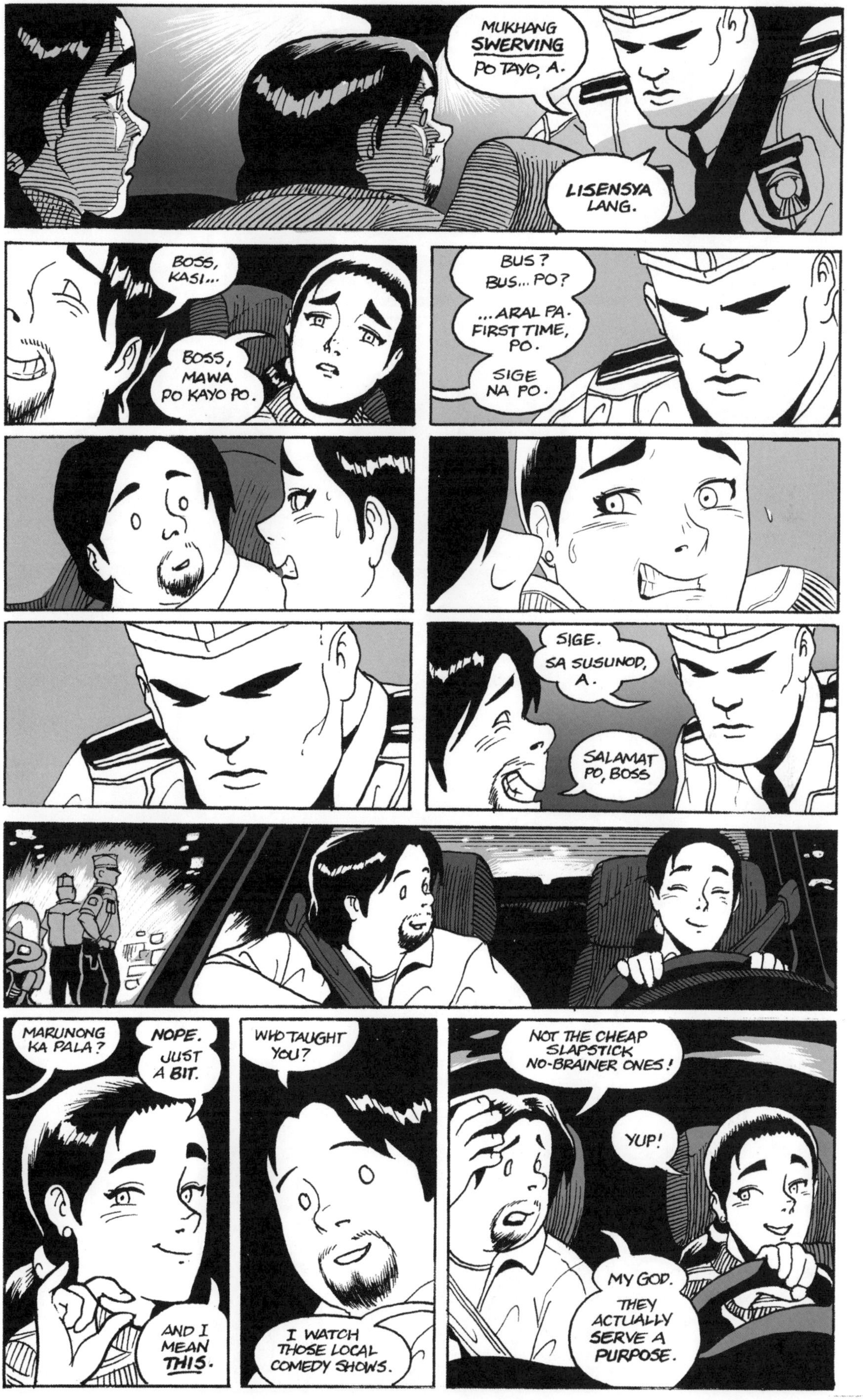
MUKHANG SWERVING PO TAYO, A.
LISENSYA LANG.
BOSS, KASI...
BOSS, MAWA PO KAYO PO.
BUS? BUS... PO?
...ARAL PA. FIRST TIME, PO.
SIGE NA PO.
SIGE. SA SUSUNOD, A.
SALAMAT PO, BOSS
MARUNONG KA PALA?
NOPE. JUST A BIT.
AND I MEAN THIS.
WHO TAUGHT YOU?
I WATCH THOSE LOCAL COMEDY SHOWS.
NOT THE CHEAP SLAPSTICK NO-BRAINER ONES!
YUP!
MY GOD.
THEY ACTUALLY SERVE A PURPOSE.

TEACH ME MORE TAGALOG, CRIS.

YOU KNOW, TAGALOG IS SUCH A FLEXIBLE LANGUAGE THAT I CAN CONSTRUCT AN ENTIRE SENTENCE WITH JUST ONE WORD?

NO!

YES.

THE WORD 'BA'.

'BA'-- AS IN 'BAH HUMBUG'?

THE WORD 'BA'. NOW LISTEN--

TWO BA'S MAKE 'BABÂ'...

...WHICH MEANS 'DOWN'.

BABÂ.

THREE BA'S BECOME AN ACTION. 'BABABA'. MEANS 'GOING DOWN' OR 'GETTING OFF' IF YOU'RE A COMMUTER.

'BABABA'. 'GETTING OFF'.

NOW WATCH. FOUR BA'S--

BABABA BA?

BABABA BA?

BABABA BA?

'ARE-YOU -GETTING -OFF-HERE?'

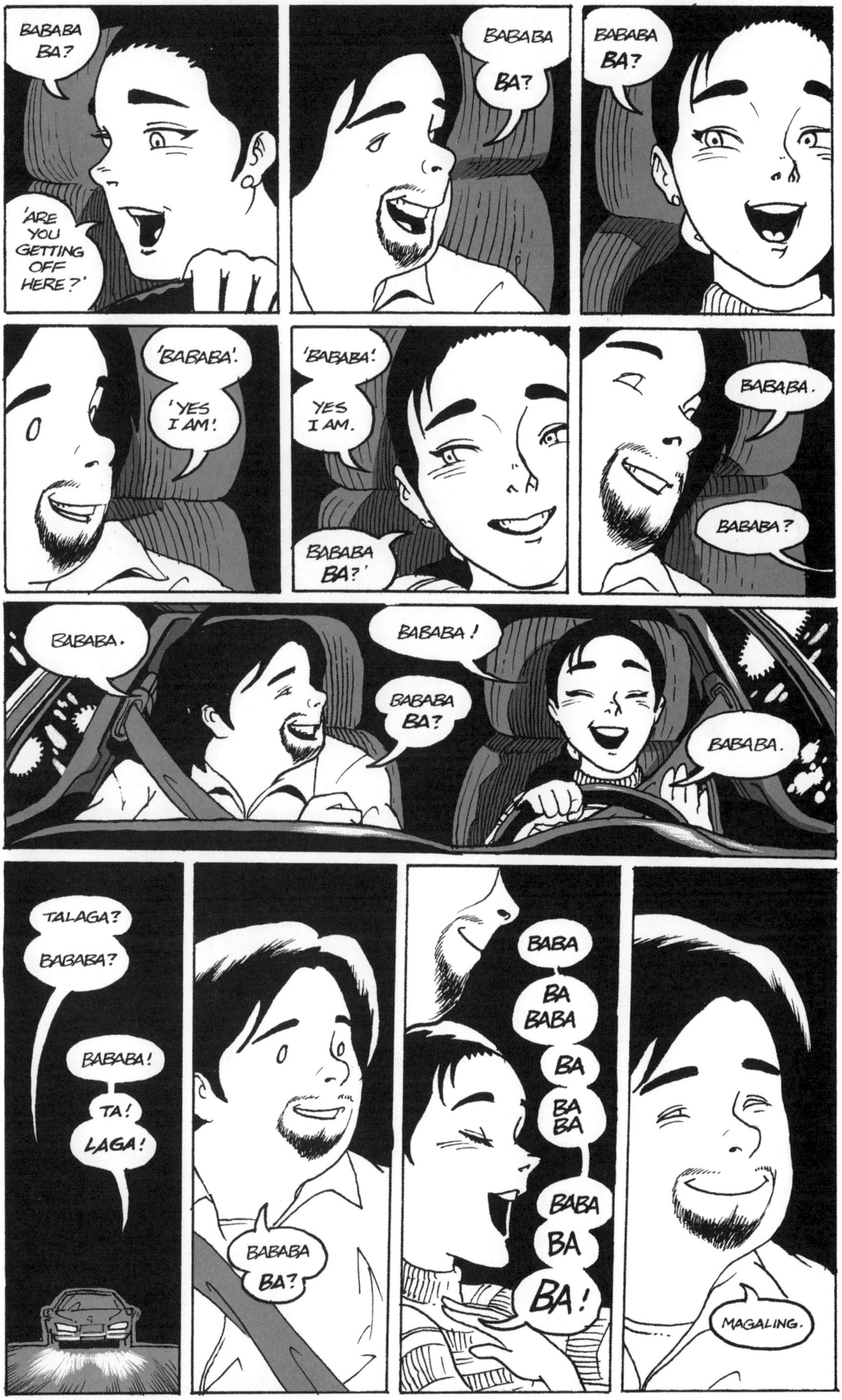
BABABA BA?
'ARE YOU GETTING OFF HERE?'
BABABA BA?
BABABA BA?
'BABABA'.
'YES I AM!
'BABABA'.
YES I AM.
BABABA BA?'
BABABA.
BABABA?
BABABA.
BABABA!
BABABA BA?
BABABA.
TALAGA?
BABABA?
BABABA!
TA!
LAGA!
BABABA BA?
BABA
BA BABA
BA
BA BA
BABA
BA
BA!
MAGALING.

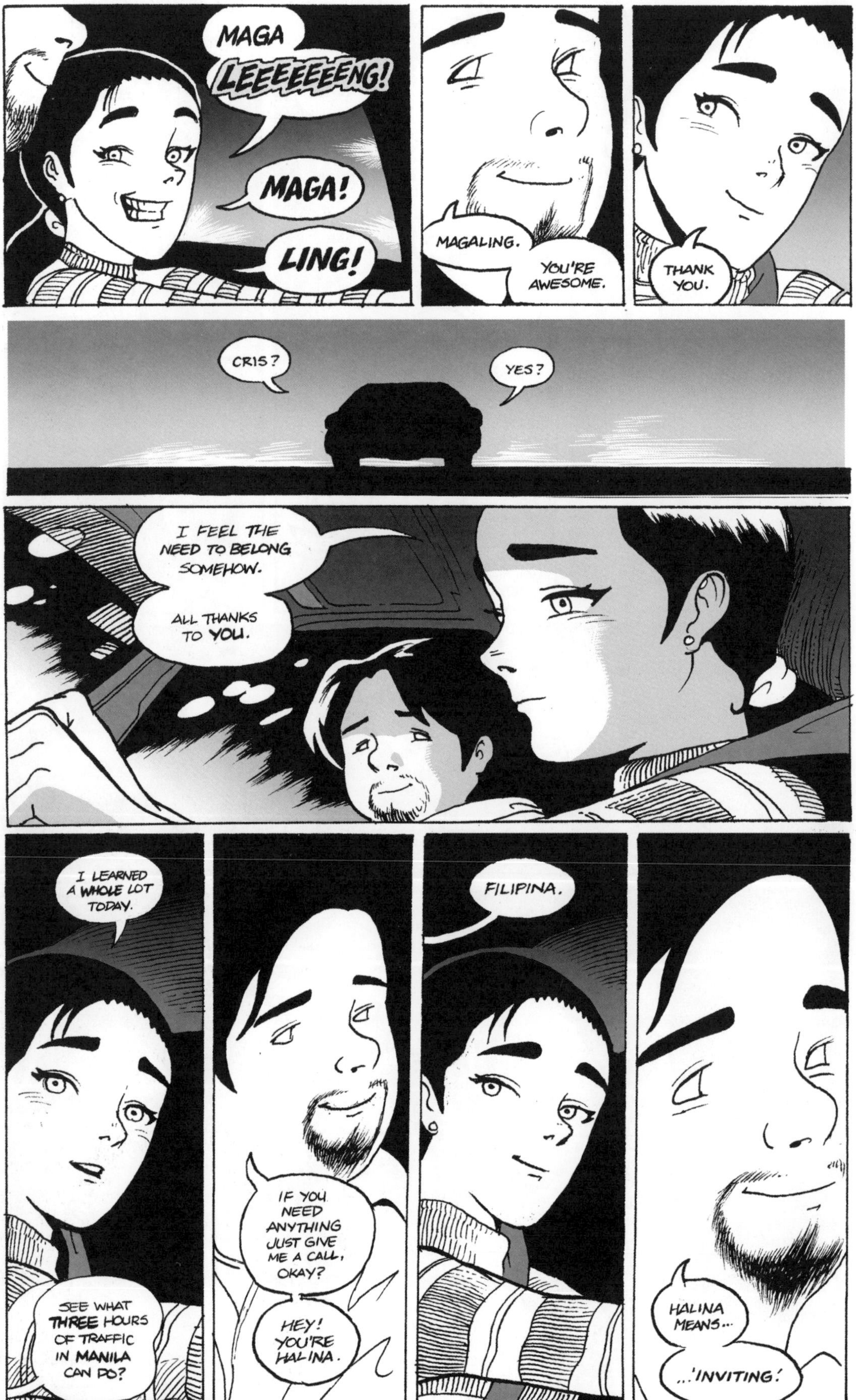
MAGA
LEEEEEEENG!
MAGA!
LING!
MAGALING.
YOU'RE AWESOME.
THANK YOU.
CRIS?
YES?
I FEEL THE NEED TO BELONG SOMEHOW.
ALL THANKS TO YOU.
I LEARNED A WHOLE LOT TODAY.
SEE WHAT THREE HOURS OF TRAFFIC IN MANILA CAN DO?
IF YOU NEED ANYTHING JUST GIVE ME A CALL, OKAY?
HEY! YOU'RE HALINA.
FILIPINA.
HALINA MEANS...
...'INVITING.'

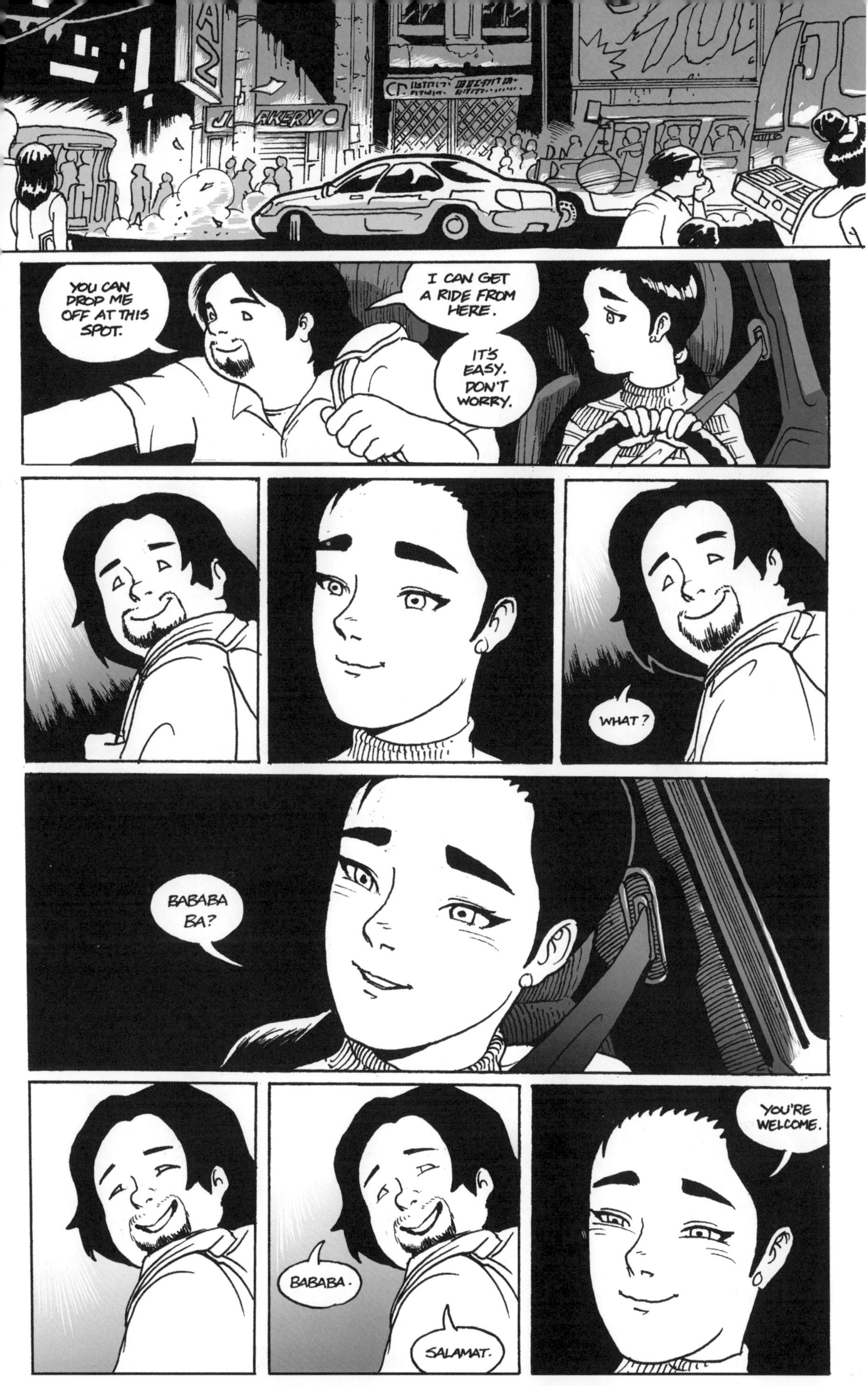
J AKERY
YOU CAN DROP ME OFF AT THIS SPOT.
I CAN GET A RIDE FROM HERE.
IT'S EASY. DON'T WORRY.
WHAT?
BABABA BA?
BABABA.
SALAMAT.
YOU'RE WELCOME.

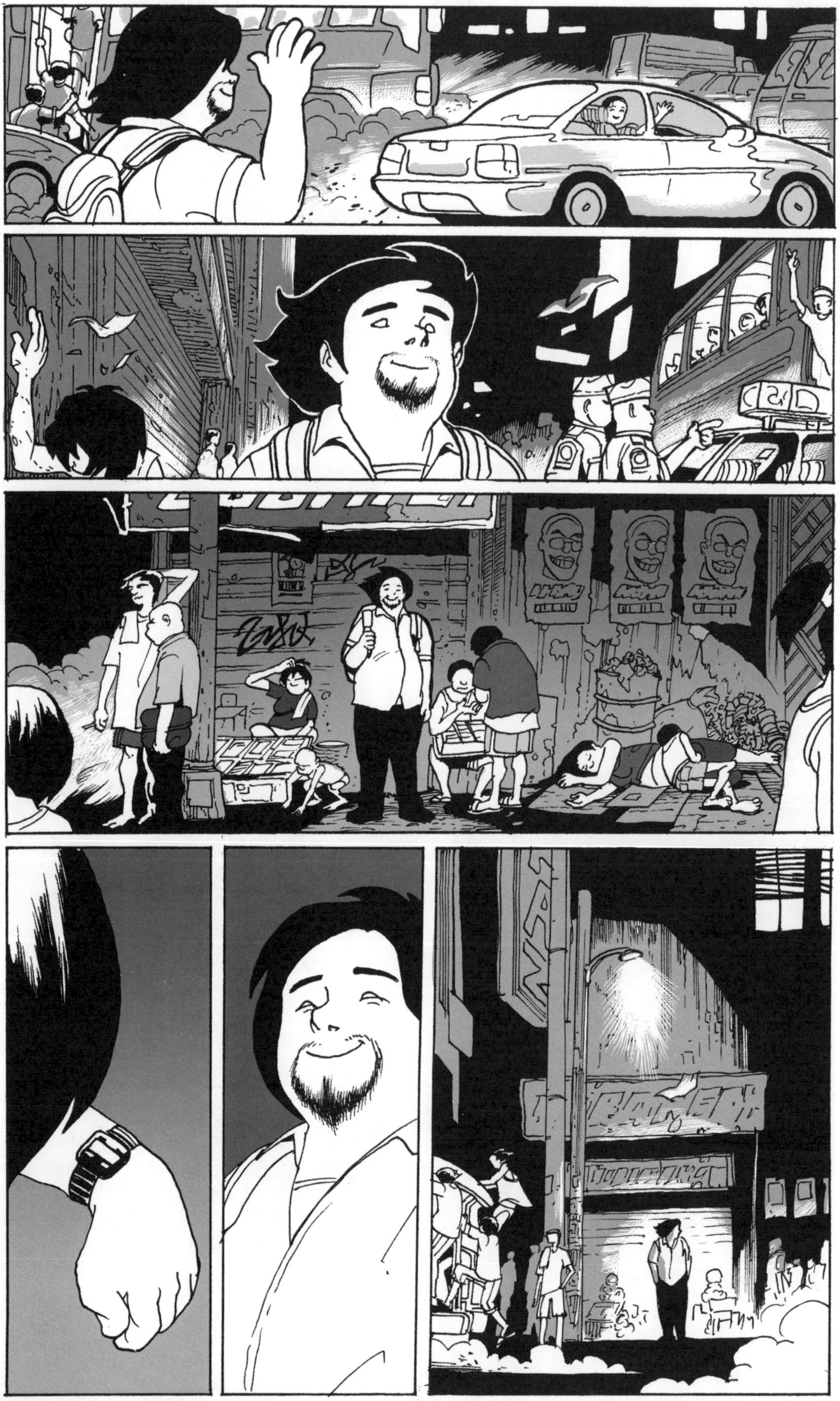

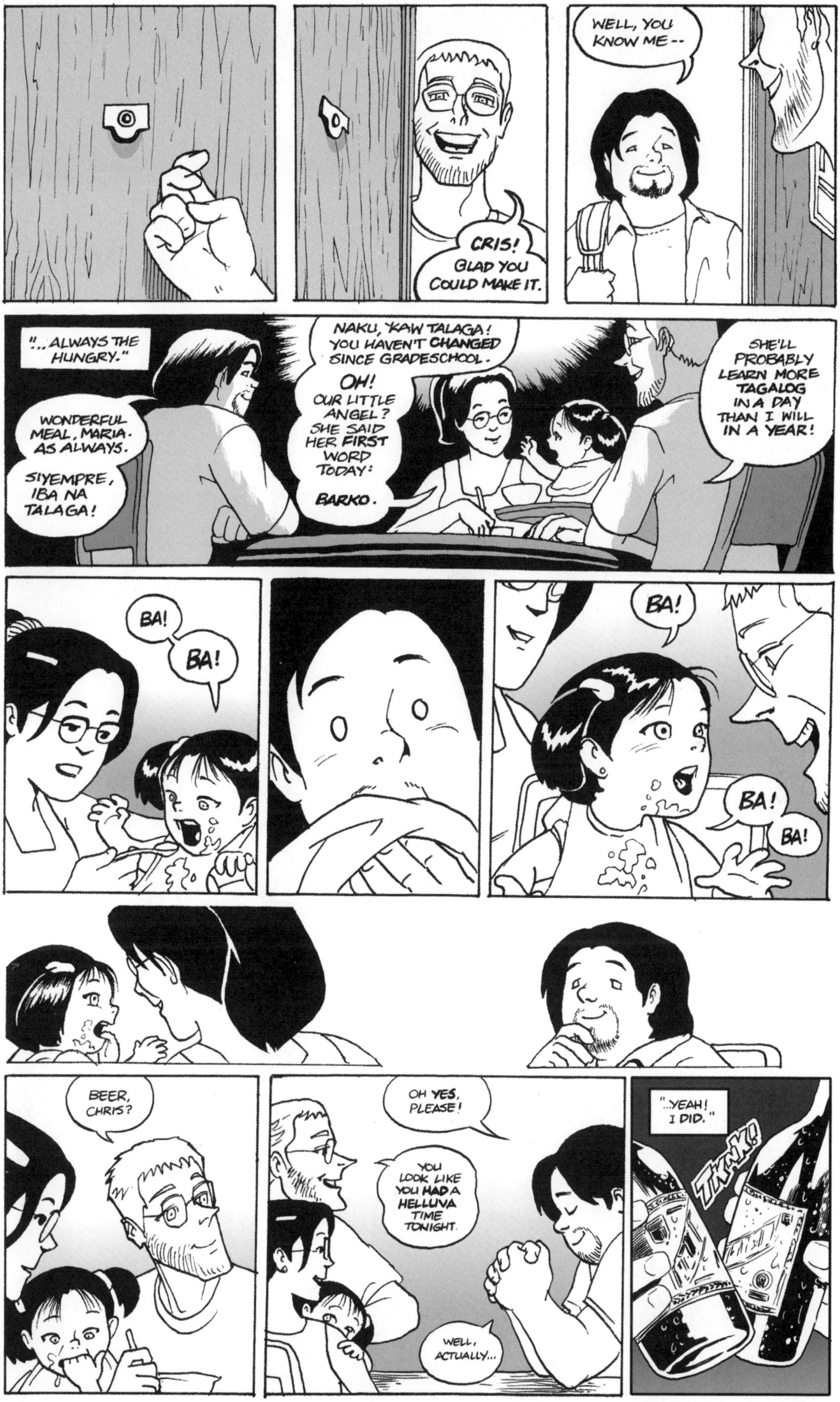
CRIS!
GLAD YOU COULD MAKE IT.
WELL, YOU KNOW ME --
"... ALWAYS THE HUNGRY."
WONDERFUL MEAL, MARIA. AS ALWAYS.
SIYEMPRE, IBA NA TALAGA!
NAKU, 'KAW TALAGA! YOU HAVEN'T CHANGED SINCE GRADESCHOOL.
OH! OUR LITTLE ANGEL? SHE SAID HER FIRST WORD TODAY:
BARKO.
SHE'LL PROBABLY LEARN MORE TAGALOG IN A DAY THAN I WILL IN A YEAR!
BA!
BA!
BA!
BA!
BA!
BEER, CHRIS?
OH YES, PLEASE!
YOU LOOK LIKE YOU HAD A HELLUVA TIME TONIGHT.
WELL, ACTUALLY...
"...YEAH! I DID."
TKNK!

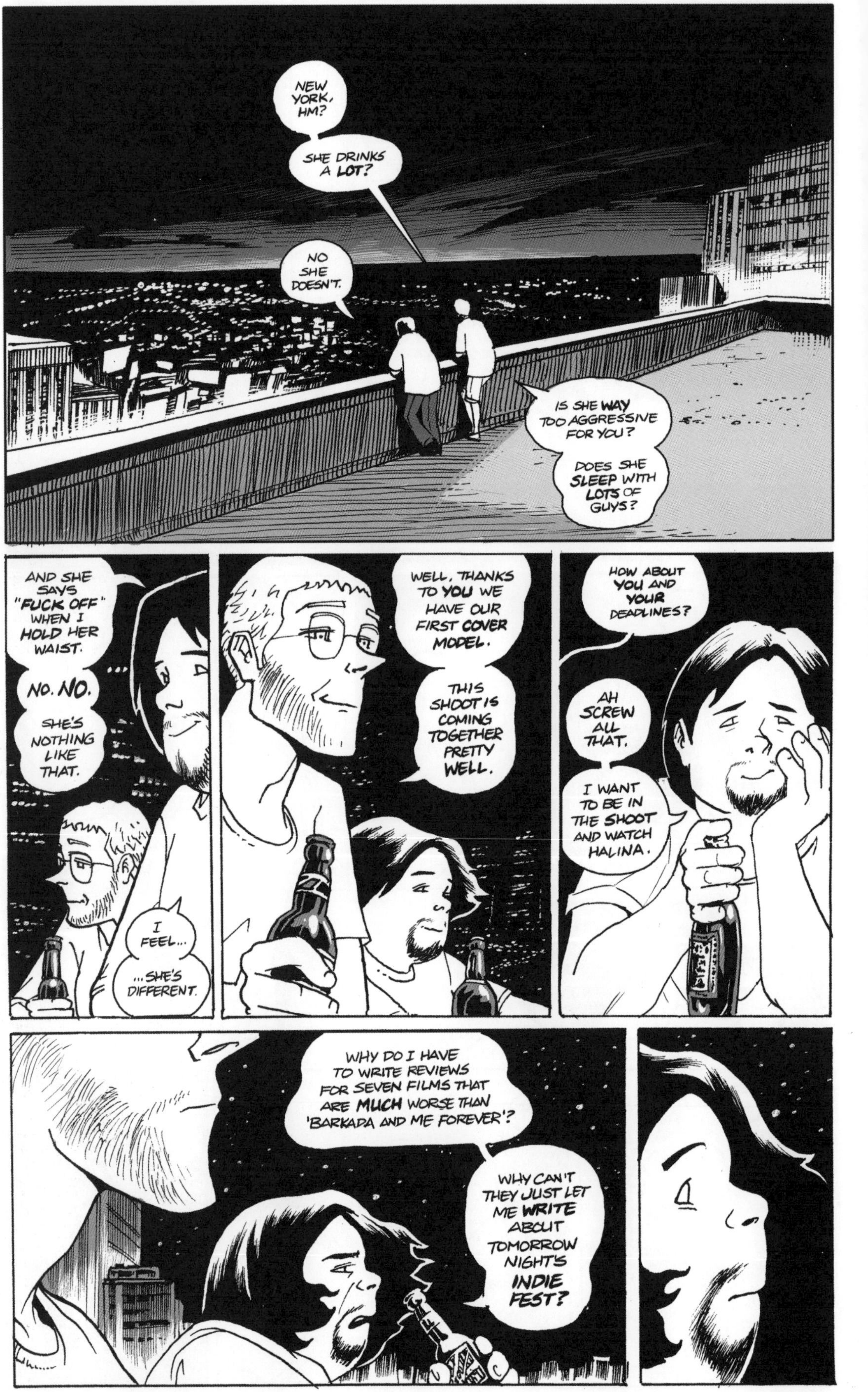
NEW YORK, HM?
SHE DRINKS A LOT?
NO SHE DOESN'T.
IS SHE WAY TOO AGGRESSIVE FOR YOU?
DOES SHE SLEEP WITH LOTS OF GUYS?
AND SHE SAYS "FUCK OFF" WHEN I HOLD HER WAIST.
NO. NO.
SHE'S NOTHING LIKE THAT.
I FEEL...
...SHE'S DIFFERENT.
WELL, THANKS TO YOU WE HAVE OUR FIRST COVER MODEL.
THIS SHOOT IS COMING TOGETHER PRETTY WELL.
HOW ABOUT YOU AND YOUR DEADLINES?
AH SCREW ALL THAT.
I WANT TO BE IN THE SHOOT AND WATCH HALINA.
WHY DO I HAVE TO WRITE REVIEWS FOR SEVEN FILMS THAT ARE MUCH WORSE THAN 'BARKADA AND ME FOREVER'?
WHY CAN'T THEY JUST LET ME WRITE ABOUT TOMORROW NIGHT'S INDIE FEST?

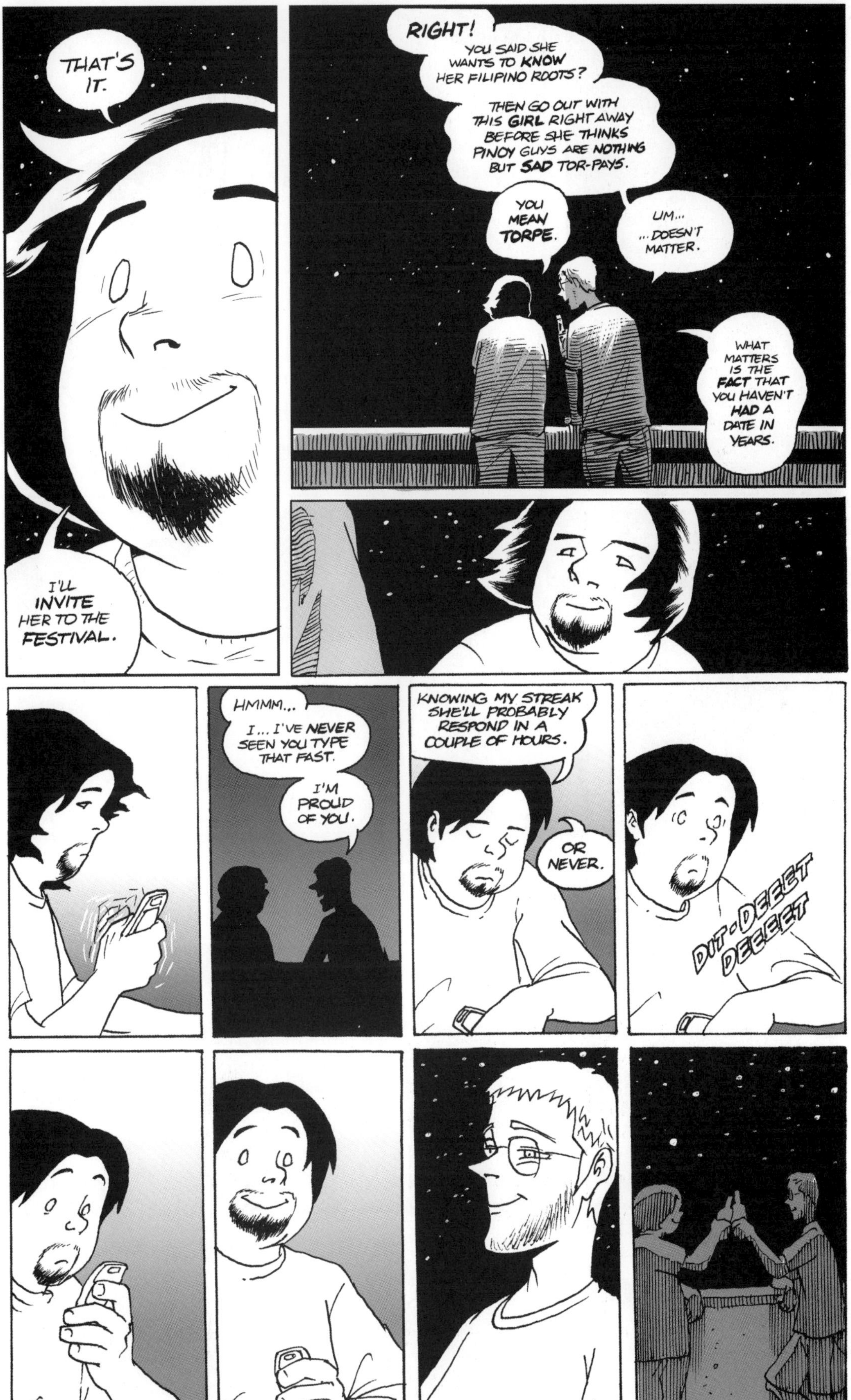
THAT'S IT.
I'LL INVITE HER TO THE FESTIVAL.
RIGHT! YOU SAID SHE WANTS TO KNOW HER FILIPINO ROOTS?
THEN GO OUT WITH THIS GIRL RIGHT AWAY BEFORE SHE THINKS PINOY GUYS ARE NOTHING BUT SAD TOR-PAYS.
YOU MEAN TORPE.
UM... ...DOESN'T MATTER.
WHAT MATTERS IS THE FACT THAT YOU HAVEN'T HAD A DATE IN YEARS.
HMMM... I... I'VE NEVER SEEN YOU TYPE THAT FAST.
I'M PROUD OF YOU.
KNOWING MY STREAK SHE'LL PROBABLY RESPOND IN A COUPLE OF HOURS.
OR NEVER.
DIT-DEEET DEEEET

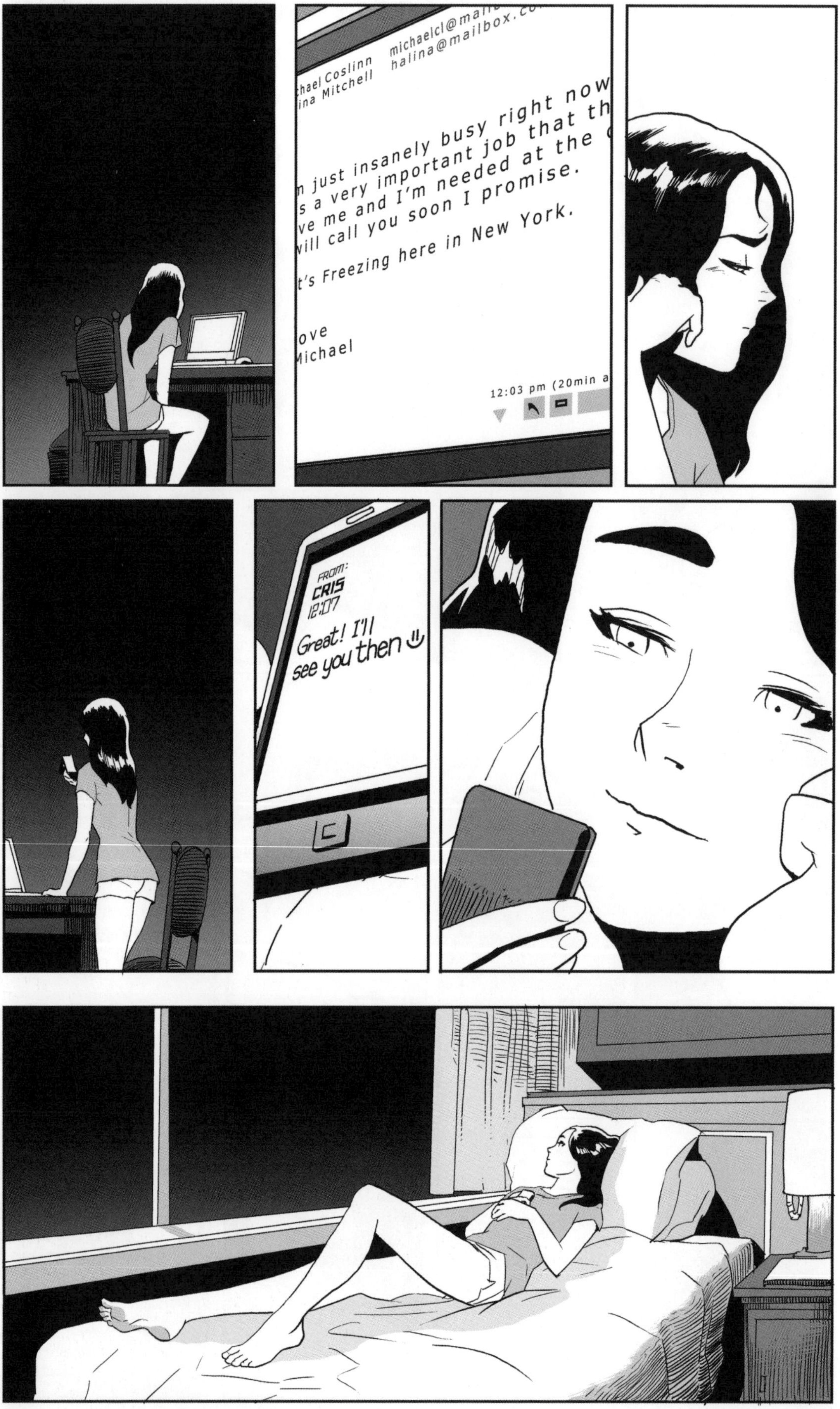
chael Coslinn michaelcl@mailb
ina Mitchell halina@mailbox.co
n just insanely busy right now
s a very important job that th
ve me and I'm needed at the
vill call you soon I promise.
t's Freezing here in New York.
ove
Michael
12:03 pm (20min a
FROM:
CRIS
12:07
Great! I'll see you then

Chapter 3
The Unspoken Language

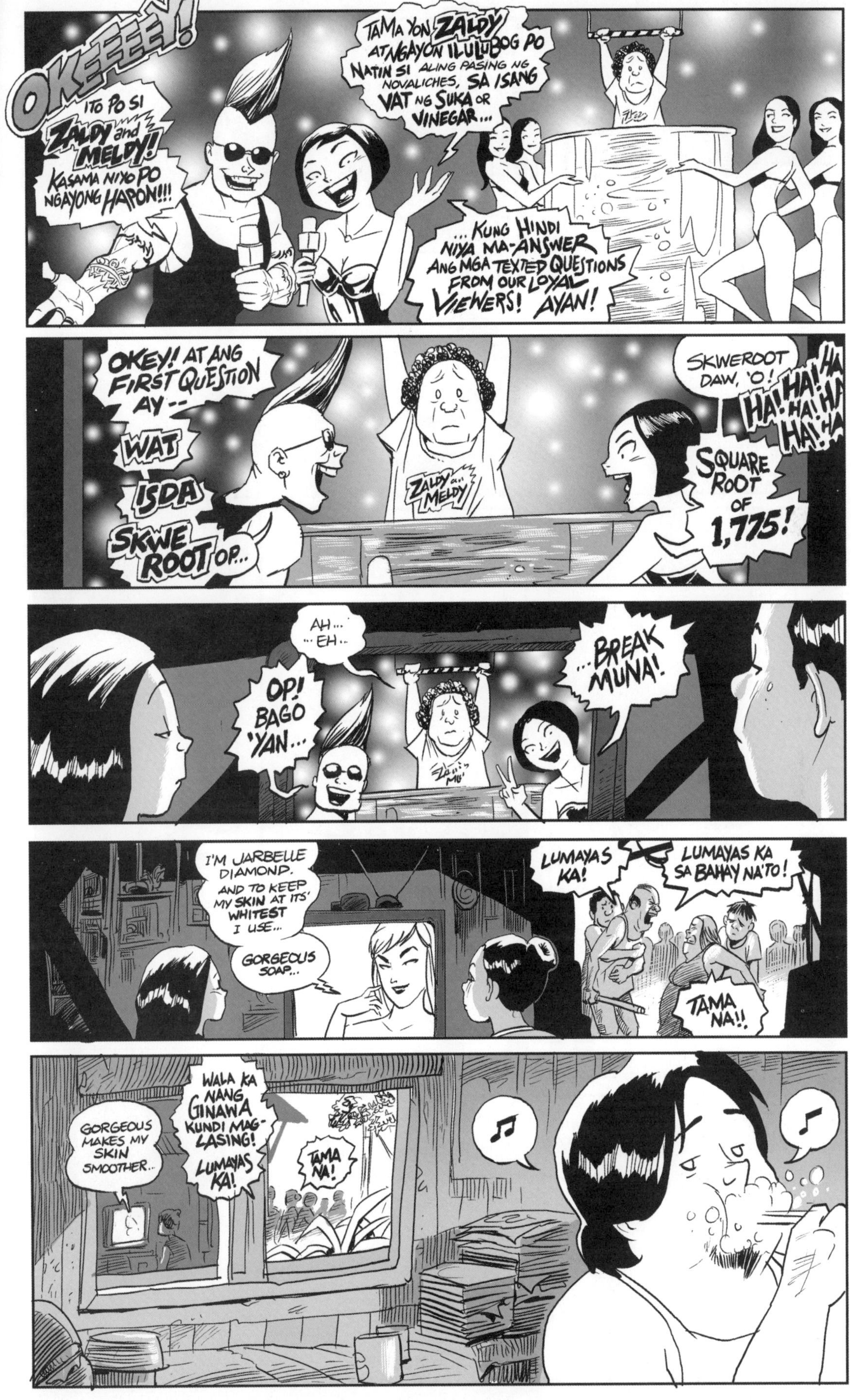
OKEEEEY!
ITO PO SI ZALDY and MELDY! KASAMA NIYO PO NGAYONG HAPON!!!
TAMA YON, ZALDY AT NGAYON ILULUBOG PO NATIN SI ALING PASING NG NOVALICHES, SA ISANG VAT NG SUKA OR VINEGAR...
...KUNG HINDI NIYA MA-ANSWER ANG MGA TEXTED QUESTIONS FROM OUR LOYAL VIEWERS! AYAN!
OKEY! AT ANG FIRST QUESTION AY --
WAT
ISDA
SKWE ROOT OP...
SKWEROOT DAW, 'O!
HA! HA! HA! HA! HA! HA! HA!
SQUARE ROOT OF 1,775!
AH... ...EH...
OP! BAGO 'YAN...
...BREAK MUNA!
I'M JARBELLE DIAMOND. AND TO KEEP MY SKIN AT ITS' WHITEST I USE...
GORGEOUS SOAP...
LUMAYAS KA!
LUMAYAS KA SA BAHAY NA'TO!
TAMA NA!!
GORGEOUS MAKES MY SKIN SMOOTHER...
WALA KA NANG GINAWA KUNDI MAG-LASING! LUMAYAS KA!
TAMA NA!
♪
♪

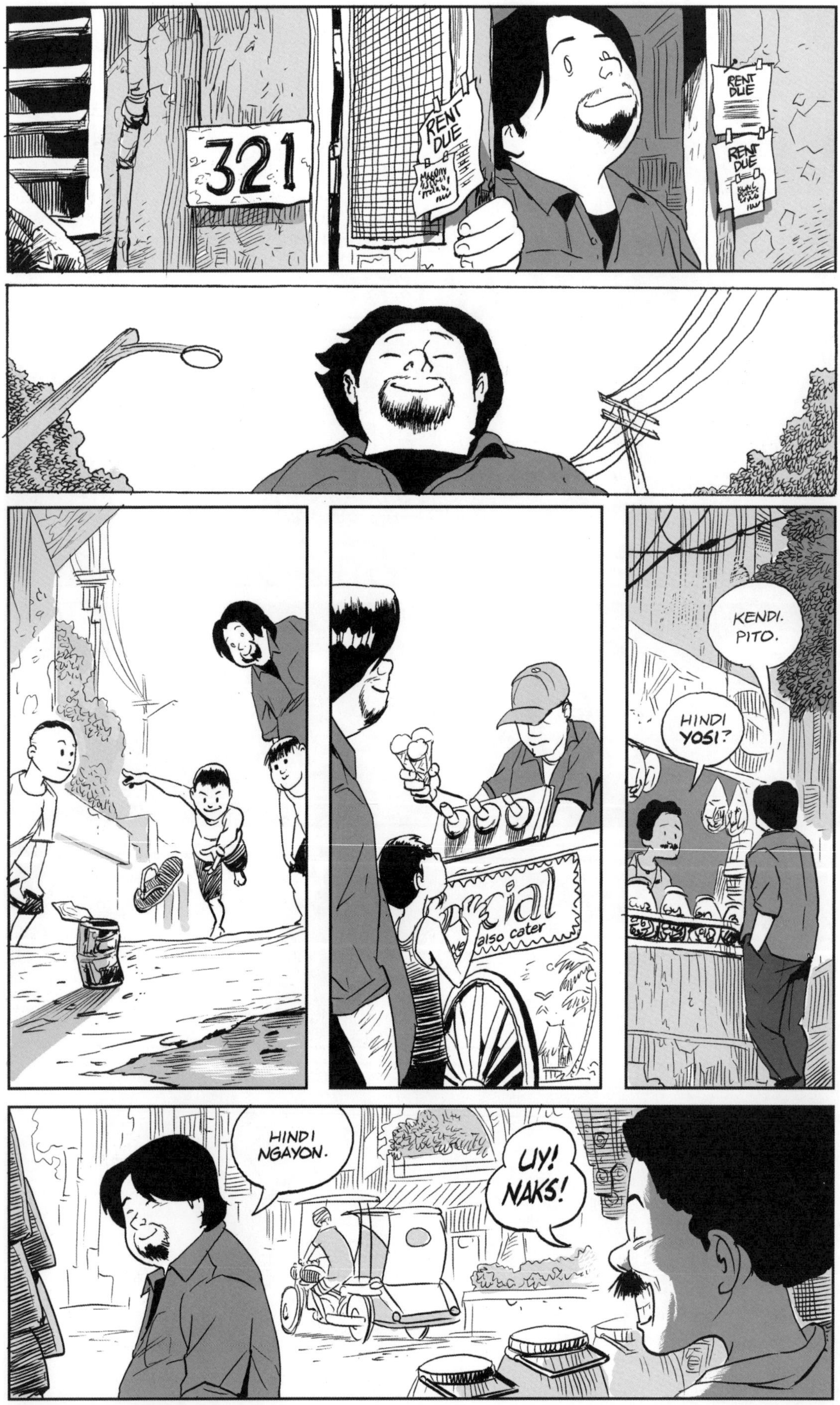
321
RENT DUE
RENT DUE
RENT DUE
cial
also cater
KENDI. PITO.
HINDI YOSI?
HINDI NGAYON.
UY! NAKS!

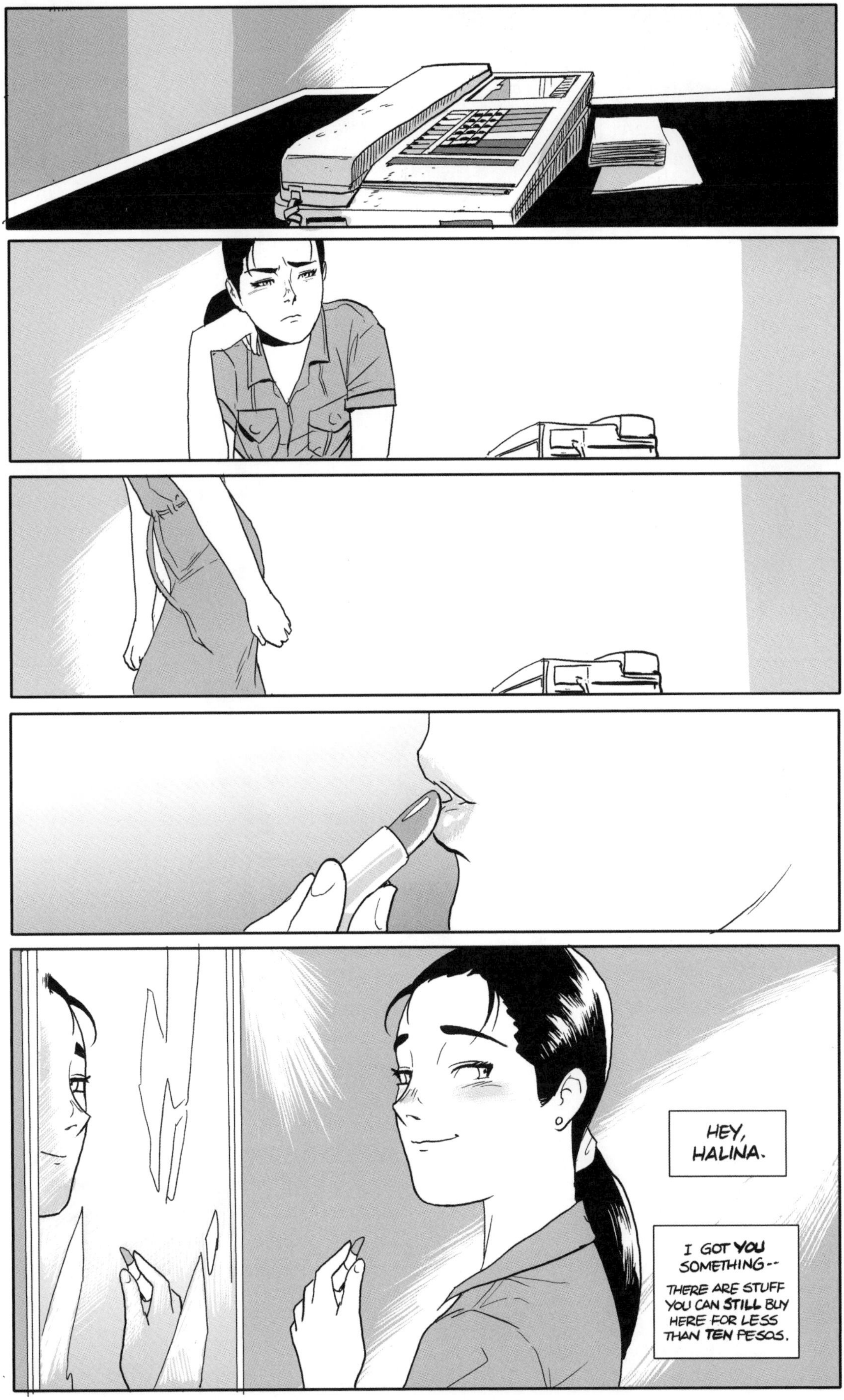
HEY, HALINA.
I GOT YOU SOMETHING--
THERE ARE STUFF YOU CAN STILL BUY HERE FOR LESS THAN TEN PESOS.

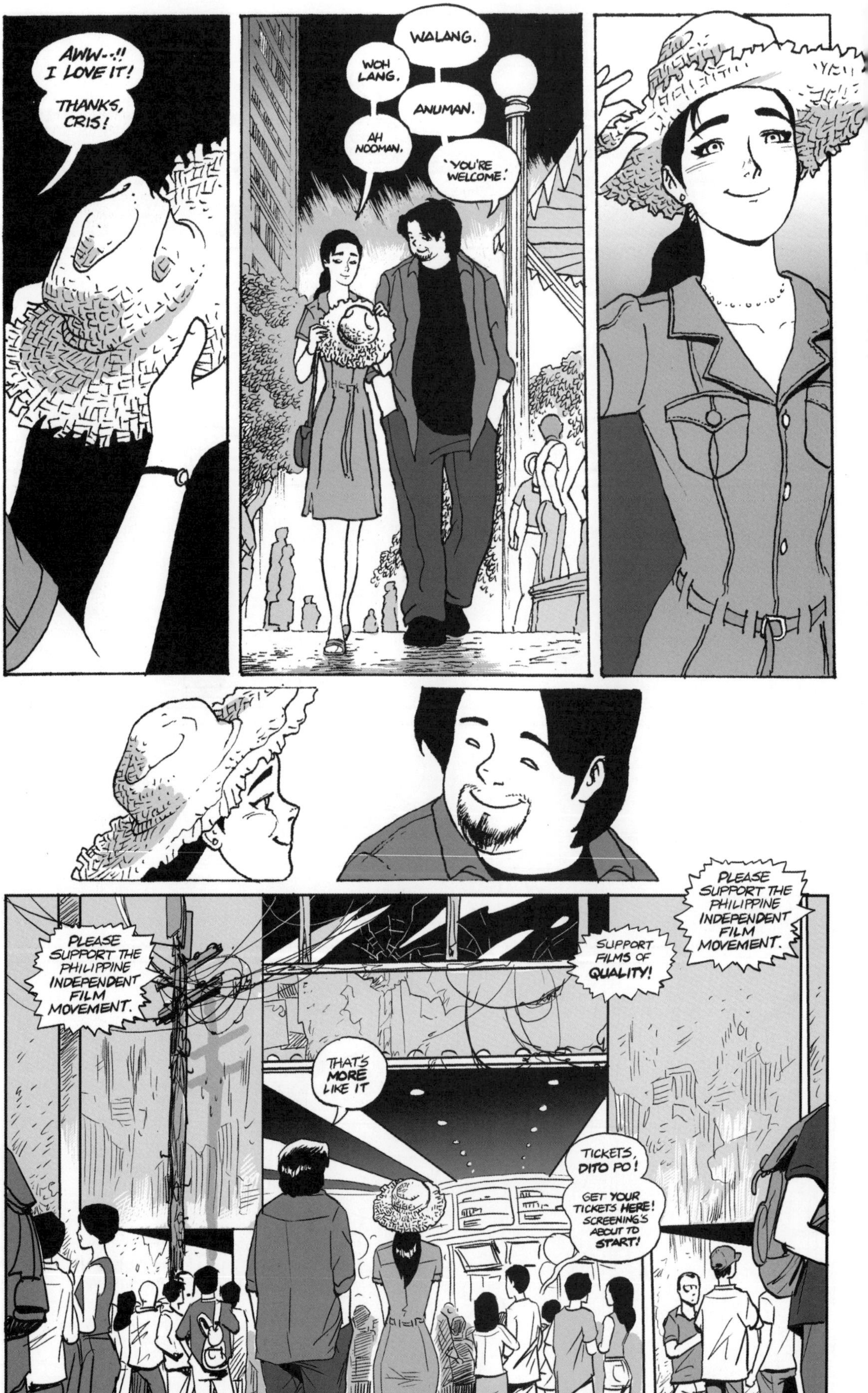
AWW--!! I LOVE IT!
THANKS, CRIS!
WALANG.
WOH LANG.
ANUMAN.
AH NOOMAN.
'YOU'RE WELCOME.'
PLEASE SUPPORT THE PHILIPPINE INDEPENDENT FILM MOVEMENT.
SUPPORT FILMS OF QUALITY!
PLEASE SUPPORT THE PHILIPPINE INDEPENDENT FILM MOVEMENT.
THAT'S MORE LIKE IT
TICKETS, DITO PO!
GET YOUR TICKETS HERE! SCREENING'S ABOUT TO START!

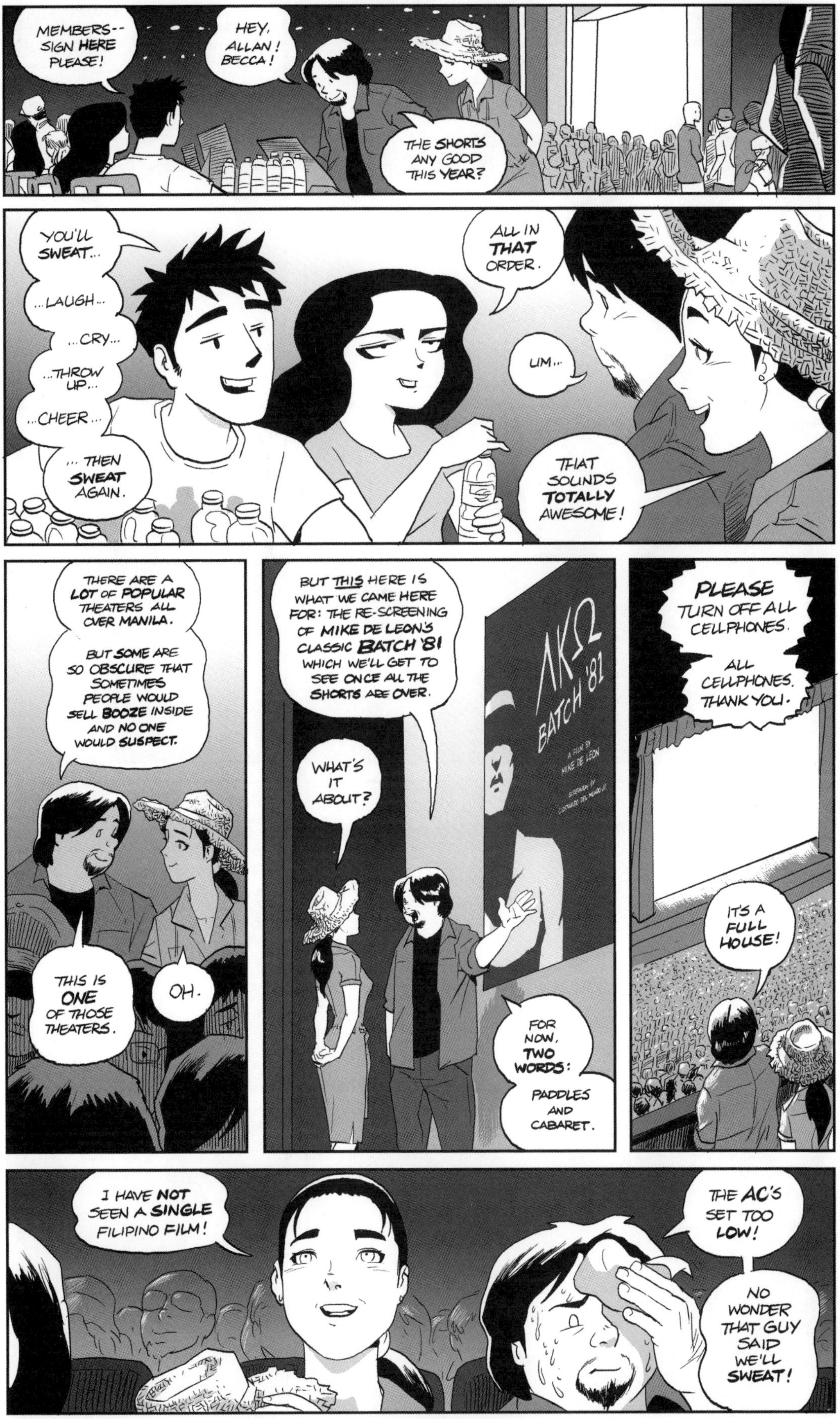
MEMBERS-- SIGN HERE PLEASE!
HEY, ALLAN! BECCA!
THE SHORTS ANY GOOD THIS YEAR?
YOU'LL SWEAT...
...LAUGH...
...CRY...
...THROW UP...
...CHEER...
... THEN SWEAT AGAIN.
ALL IN THAT ORDER.
UM...
THAT SOUNDS TOTALLY AWESOME!
THERE ARE A LOT OF POPULAR THEATERS ALL OVER MANILA.
BUT SOME ARE SO OBSCURE THAT SOMETIMES PEOPLE WOULD SELL BOOZE INSIDE AND NO ONE WOULD SUSPECT.
THIS IS ONE OF THOSE THEATERS.
OH.
BUT THIS HERE IS WHAT WE CAME HERE FOR: THE RE-SCREENING OF MIKE DE LEON'S CLASSIC BATCH '81 WHICH WE'LL GET TO SEE ONCE ALL THE SHORTS ARE OVER.
ΛΚΩ
BATCH '81
A FILM BY MIKE DE LEON
WHAT'S IT ABOUT?
FOR NOW, TWO WORDS:
PADDLES AND CABARET.
PLEASE TURN OFF ALL CELLPHONES.
ALL CELLPHONES. THANK YOU.
IT'S A FULL HOUSE!
I HAVE NOT SEEN A SINGLE FILIPINO FILM!
THE AC'S SET TOO LOW!
NO WONDER THAT GUY SAID WE'LL SWEAT!

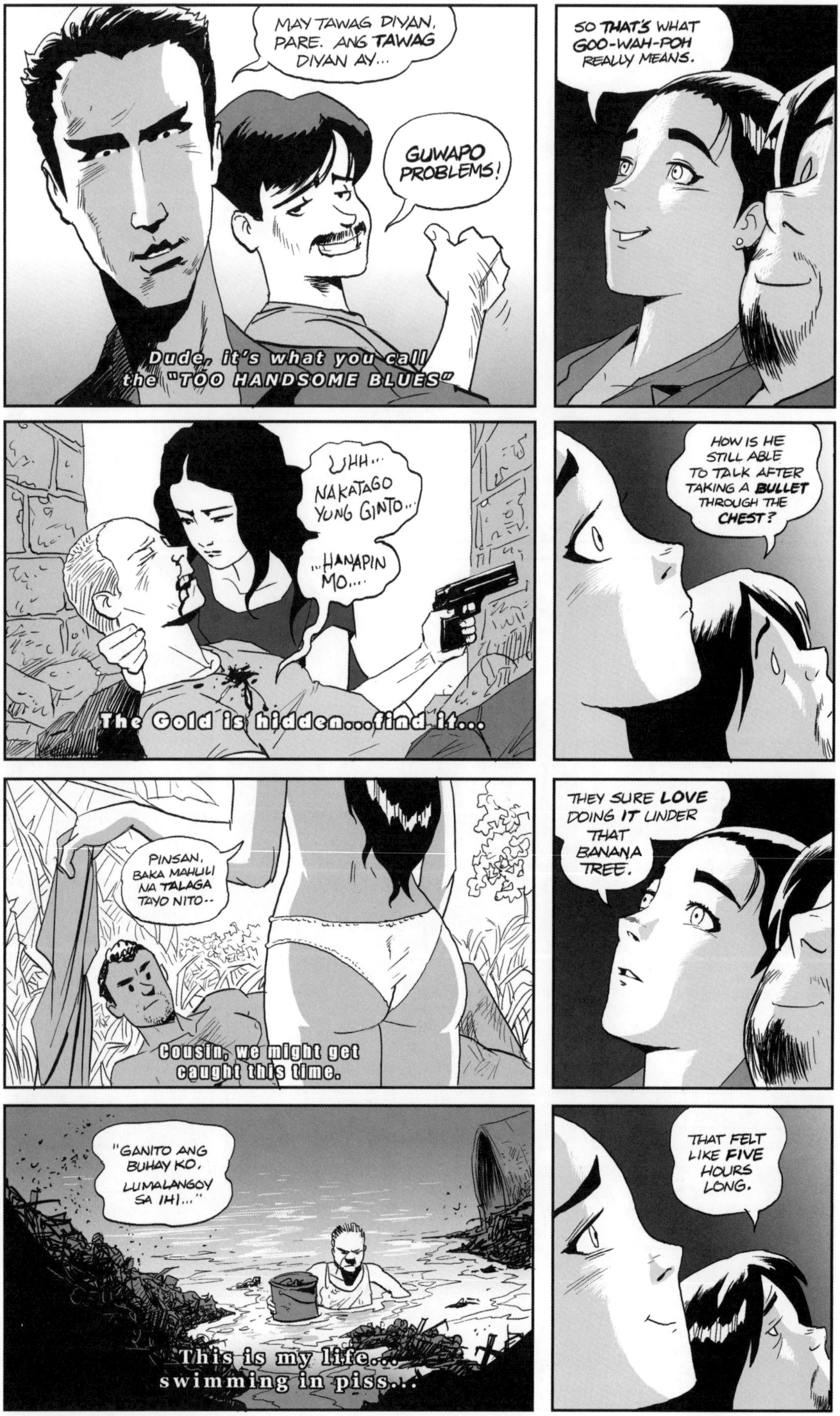
MAY TAWAG DIYAN, PARE. ANG TAWAG DIYAN AY...
GUWAPO PROBLEMS!
Dude, it's what you call the "TOO HANDSOME BLUES"
SO THAT'S WHAT GOO-WAH-POH REALLY MEANS.
UHH... NAKATAGO YUNG GINTO...
...HANAPIN MO....
The Gold is hidden...find it...
HOW IS HE STILL ABLE TO TALK AFTER TAKING A BULLET THROUGH THE CHEST?
PINSAN, BAKA MAHULI NA TALAGA TAYO NITO..
Cousin, we might get caught this time.
THEY SURE LOVE DOING IT UNDER THAT BANANA TREE.
"GANITO ANG BUHAY KO, LUMALANGOY SA IHI..."
This is my life... swimming in piss...
THAT FELT LIKE FIVE HOURS LONG.

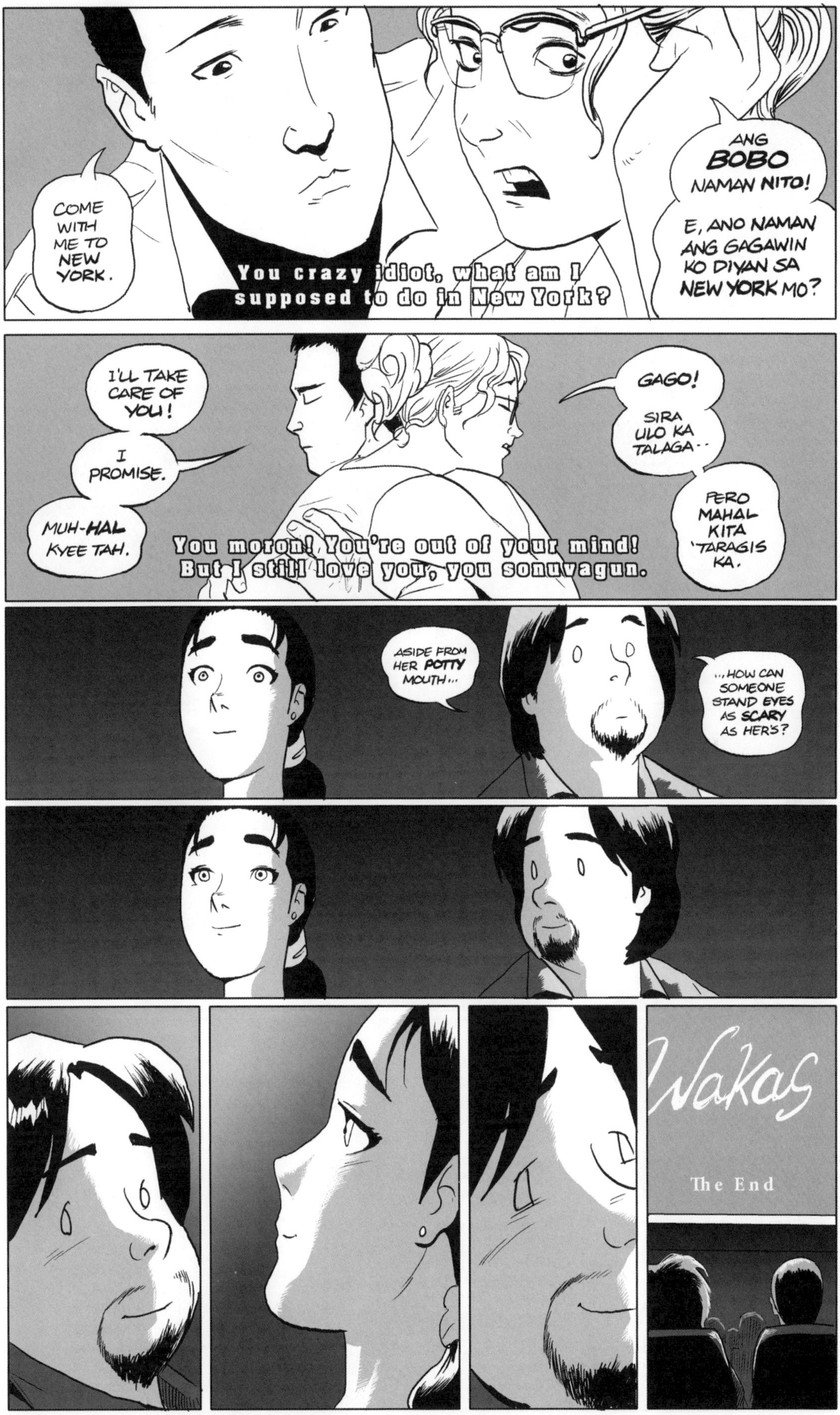
COME WITH ME TO NEW YORK.
ANG BOBO NAMAN NITO!
E, ANO NAMAN ANG GAGAWIN KO DIYAN SA NEW YORK MO?
You crazy idiot, what am I supposed to do in New York?
I'LL TAKE CARE OF YOU!
I PROMISE.
MUH-HAL KYEE TAH.
GAGO!
SIRA ULO KA TALAGA...
PERO MAHAL KITA 'TARAGIS KA.
You moron! You're out of your mind! But I still love you, you sonuvagun.
ASIDE FROM HER POTTY MOUTH...
...HOW CAN SOMEONE STAND EYES AS SCARY AS HER'S?
Wakas
The End

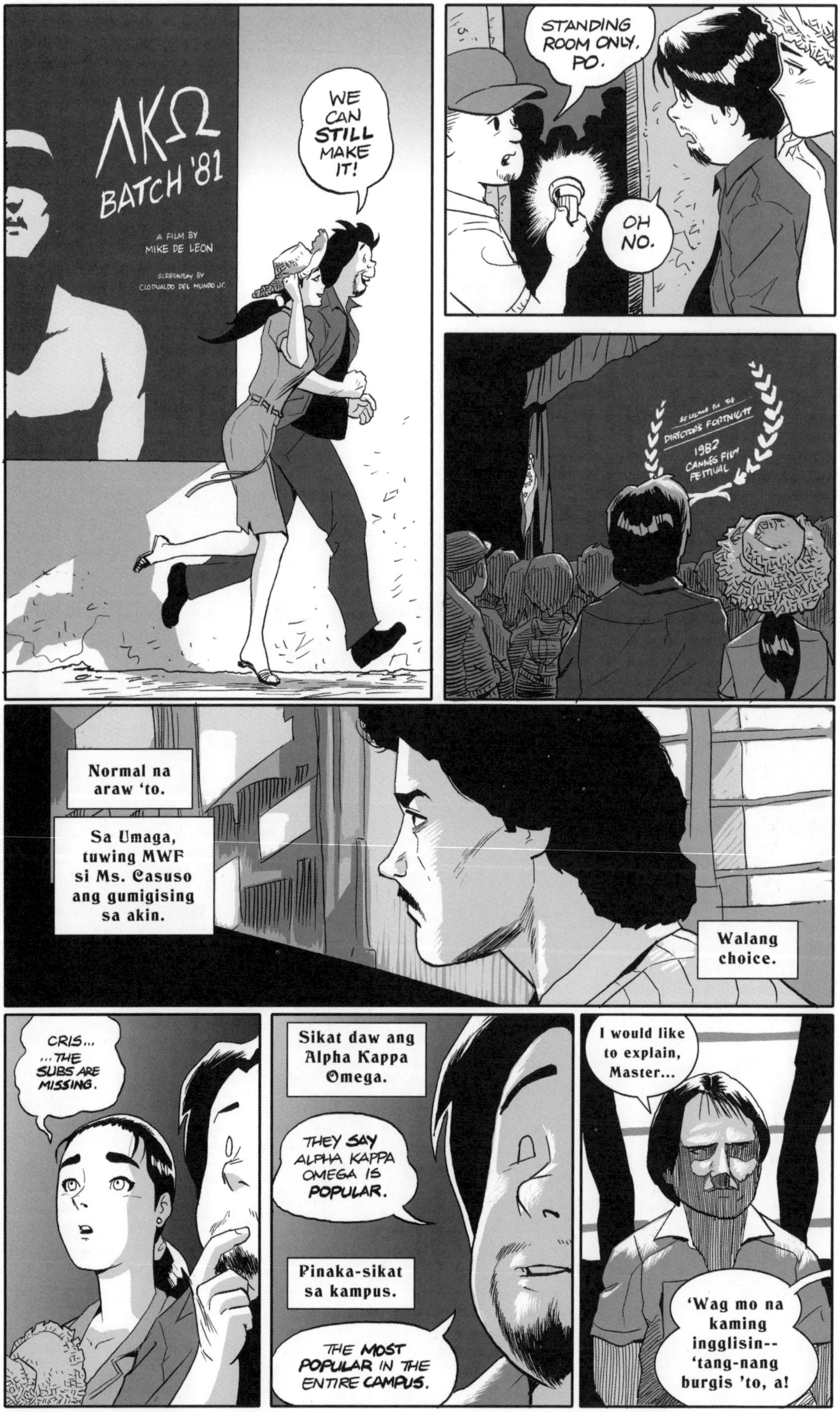
ΛΚΩ
BATCH '81
A FILM BY
MIKE DE LEON
SCREENPLAY BY
CLODUALDO DEL MUNDO JR.
WE CAN STILL MAKE IT!
STANDING ROOM ONLY, PO.
OH NO.
DIRECTOR'S FORTNIGHT
1982
CANNES FILM FESTIVAL
Normal na araw 'to.
Sa Umaga, tuwing MWF si Ms. Casuso ang gumigising sa akin.
Walang choice.
CRIS... ...THE SUBS ARE MISSING.
Sikat daw ang Alpha Kappa Omega.
THEY SAY ALPHA KAPPA OMEGA IS POPULAR.
Pinaka-sikat sa kampus.
THE MOST POPULAR IN THE ENTIRE CAMPUS.
I would like to explain, Master...
'Wag mo na kaming inggglisin-- 'tang-nang burgis 'to, a!

| Amerikano ka ba? Ba't mo kami ini-ingles? | ARE YOU AMERICAN? WHY DO YOU KEEP TALKIN' TO US IN ENGLISH? |

'Di naman po. / I DON'T, SIR.

SHUT UP!!!

O! Ingglis 'yon, Master. / WASN'T THAT ENGLISH, MASTER?

HA! HA! HA!

E ang legs? Maganda ba? Baka puros peklat legs ng syota mo. / AND YOUR GIRLFRIEND'S LEGS? ARE THEY HOT? OR MAYBE THEY'RE FULL OF SCARS.

Wala hong peklat. / NO SCARS, SIR.

Alam na alam mo, ha? / YOU SURE ARE CERTAIN.

Alpha Kappa Omega...

Ang simula at wakas... / THE BEGINNING AND THE END...

...ay kapatiran. / IS BROTHERHOOD.

Brads! / BROTHERS.

Brads na kami. / WE ARE NOW BROTHERS.

Masters na kami. / AS WELL AS MASTERS.

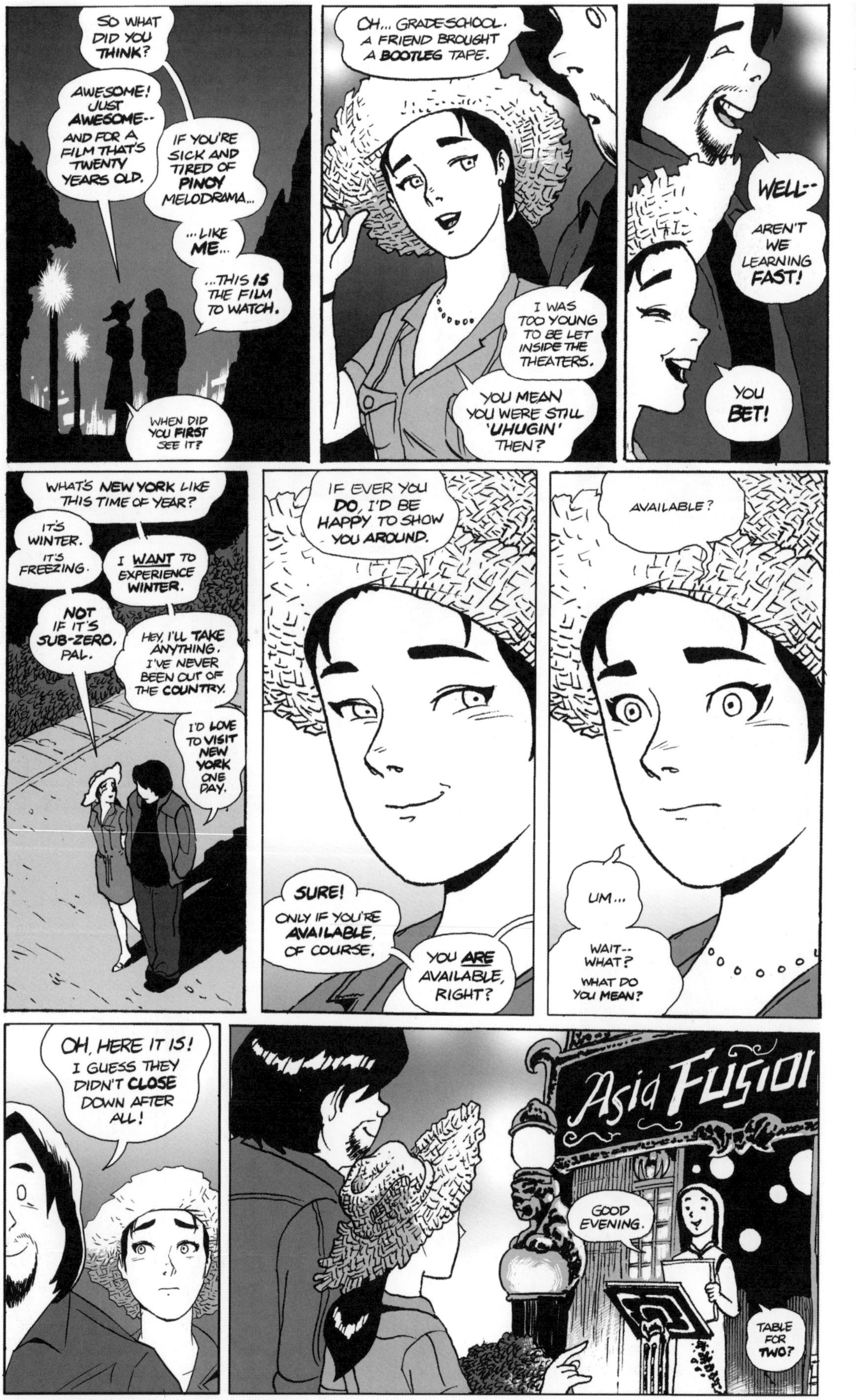
SO WHAT DID YOU THINK?
AWESOME! JUST AWESOME-- AND FOR A FILM THAT'S TWENTY YEARS OLD.
IF YOU'RE SICK AND TIRED OF PINOY MELODRAMA...
...LIKE ME...
...THIS IS THE FILM TO WATCH.
WHEN DID YOU FIRST SEE IT?
OH... GRADESCHOOL. A FRIEND BROUGHT A BOOTLEG TAPE.
I WAS TOO YOUNG TO BE LET INSIDE THE THEATERS.
YOU MEAN YOU WERE STILL 'UHUGIN' THEN?
WELL--
AREN'T WE LEARNING FAST!
YOU BET!
WHAT'S NEW YORK LIKE THIS TIME OF YEAR?
IT'S WINTER. IT'S FREEZING.
I WANT TO EXPERIENCE WINTER.
NOT IF IT'S SUB-ZERO, PAL.
HEY, I'LL TAKE ANYTHING. I'VE NEVER BEEN OUT OF THE COUNTRY.
I'D LOVE TO VISIT NEW YORK ONE DAY.
IF EVER YOU DO, I'D BE HAPPY TO SHOW YOU AROUND.
SURE! ONLY IF YOU'RE AVAILABLE, OF COURSE.
YOU ARE AVAILABLE, RIGHT?
AVAILABLE?
UM...
WAIT-- WHAT? WHAT DO YOU MEAN?
OH, HERE IT IS! I GUESS THEY DIDN'T CLOSE DOWN AFTER ALL!
Asia Fusion
GOOD EVENING.
TABLE FOR TWO?

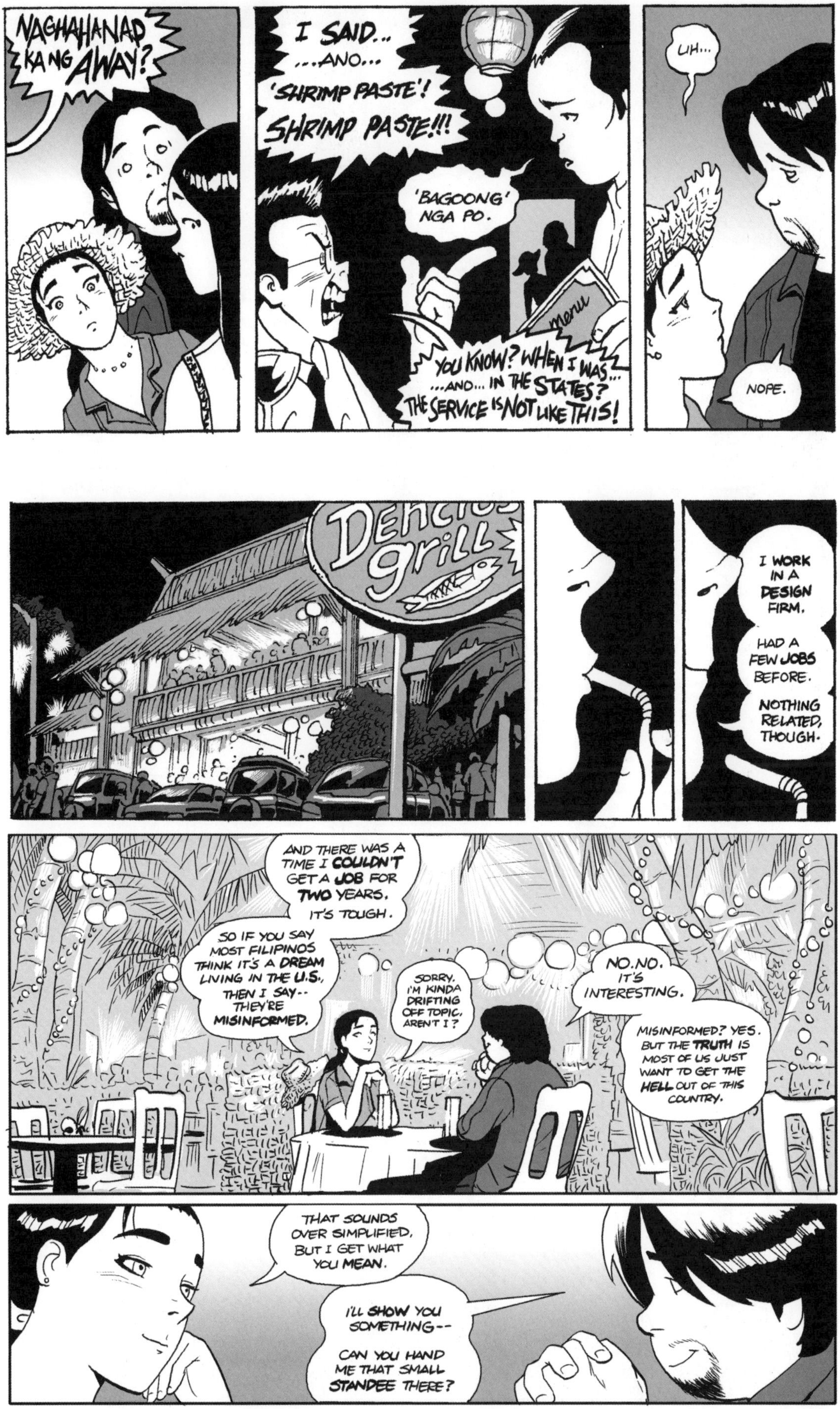
NAGHAHANAP KA NG AWAY?
I SAID... ...ANO... 'SHRIMP PASTE'! SHRIMP PASTE!!!
'BAGOONG' NGA PO.
menu
YOU KNOW? WHEN I WAS... ...AND... IN THE STATES? THE SERVICE IS NOT LIKE THIS!
UH...
NOPE.
Delicios grill
I WORK IN A DESIGN FIRM.
HAD A FEW JOBS BEFORE.
NOTHING RELATED, THOUGH.
AND THERE WAS A TIME I COULDN'T GET A JOB FOR TWO YEARS. IT'S TOUGH.
SO IF YOU SAY MOST FILIPINOS THINK IT'S A DREAM LIVING IN THE U.S., THEN I SAY-- THEY'RE MISINFORMED.
SORRY. I'M KINDA DRIFTING OFF TOPIC, AREN'T I?
NO. NO. IT'S INTERESTING.
MISINFORMED? YES. BUT THE TRUTH IS MOST OF US JUST WANT TO GET THE HELL OUT OF THIS COUNTRY.
THAT SOUNDS OVER SIMPLIFIED, BUT I GET WHAT YOU MEAN.
I'LL SHOW YOU SOMETHING--
CAN YOU HAND ME THAT SMALL STANDEE THERE?

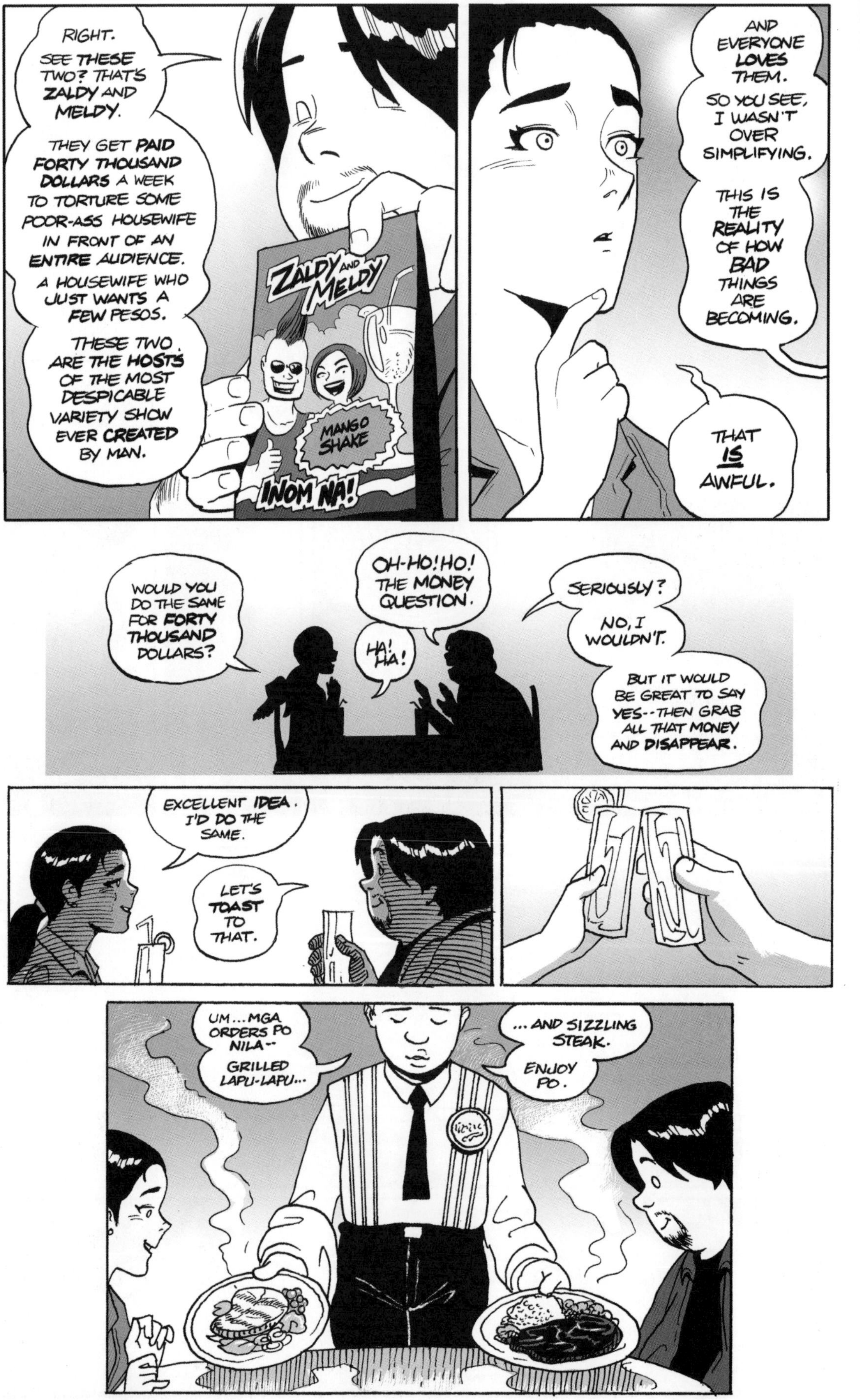
RIGHT.
SEE THESE TWO? THAT'S ZALDY AND MELDY.
THEY GET PAID FORTY THOUSAND DOLLARS A WEEK TO TORTURE SOME POOR-ASS HOUSEWIFE IN FRONT OF AN ENTIRE AUDIENCE.
A HOUSEWIFE WHO JUST WANTS A FEW PESOS.
THESE TWO ARE THE HOSTS OF THE MOST DESPICABLE VARIETY SHOW EVER CREATED BY MAN.
ZALDY AND MELDY
MANGO SHAKE
INOM NA!
AND EVERYONE LOVES THEM.
SO YOU SEE, I WASN'T OVER SIMPLIFYING.
THIS IS THE REALITY OF HOW BAD THINGS ARE BECOMING.
THAT IS AWFUL.
WOULD YOU DO THE SAME FOR FORTY THOUSAND DOLLARS?
OH-HO! HO! THE MONEY QUESTION.
HA! HA!
SERIOUSLY?
NO, I WOULDN'T.
BUT IT WOULD BE GREAT TO SAY YES--THEN GRAB ALL THAT MONEY AND DISAPPEAR.
EXCELLENT IDEA. I'D DO THE SAME.
LET'S TOAST TO THAT.
UM... MGA ORDERS PO NILA--
GRILLED LAPU-LAPU...
... AND SIZZLING STEAK.
ENJOY PO.

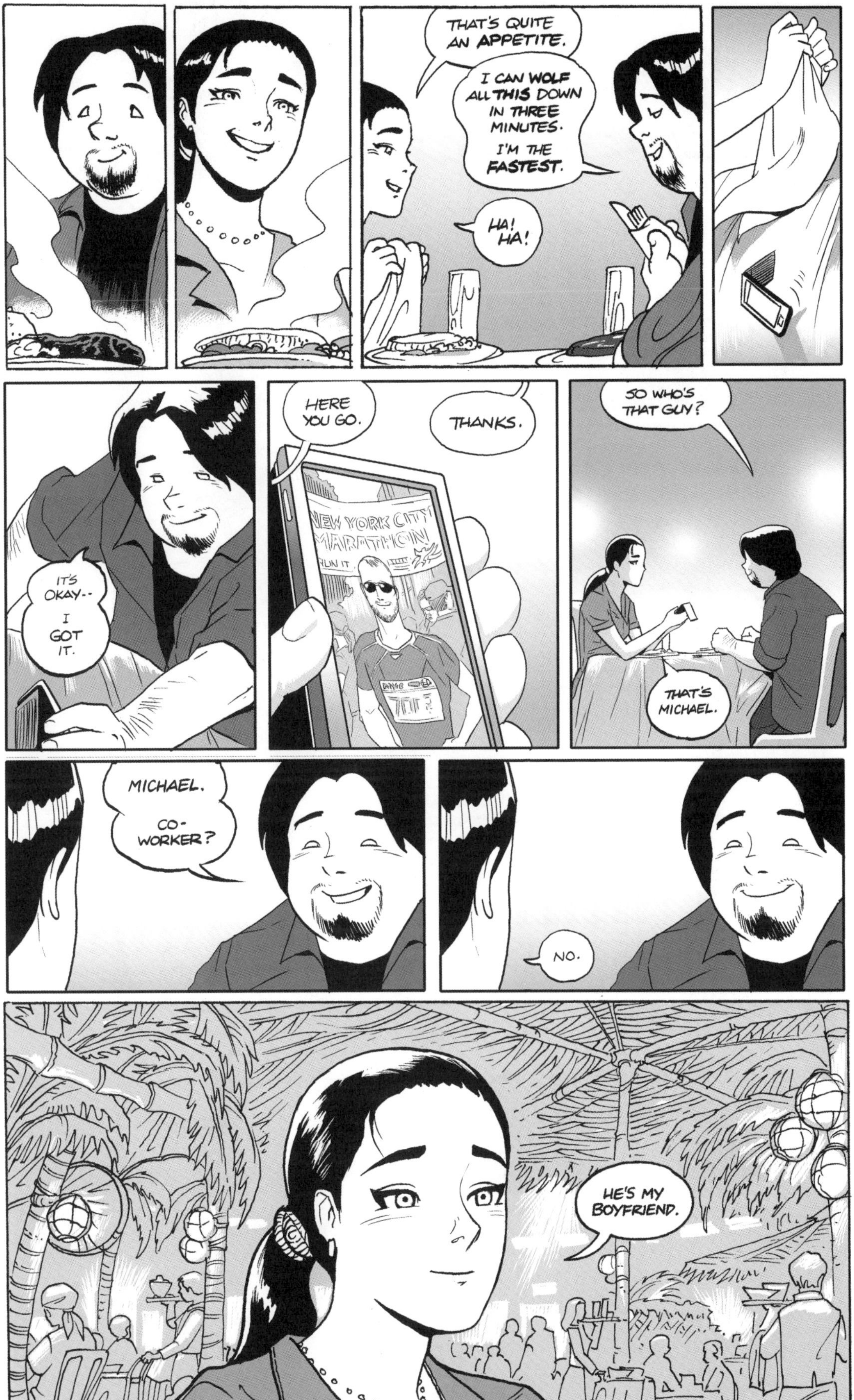
THAT'S QUITE AN APPETITE.
I CAN WOLF ALL THIS DOWN IN THREE MINUTES. I'M THE FASTEST.
HA! HA!
IT'S OKAY-- I GOT IT.
HERE YOU GO.
THANKS.
NEW YORK CITY MARATHON
SO WHO'S THAT GUY?
THAT'S MICHAEL.
MICHAEL. CO-WORKER?
NO.
HE'S MY BOYFRIEND.

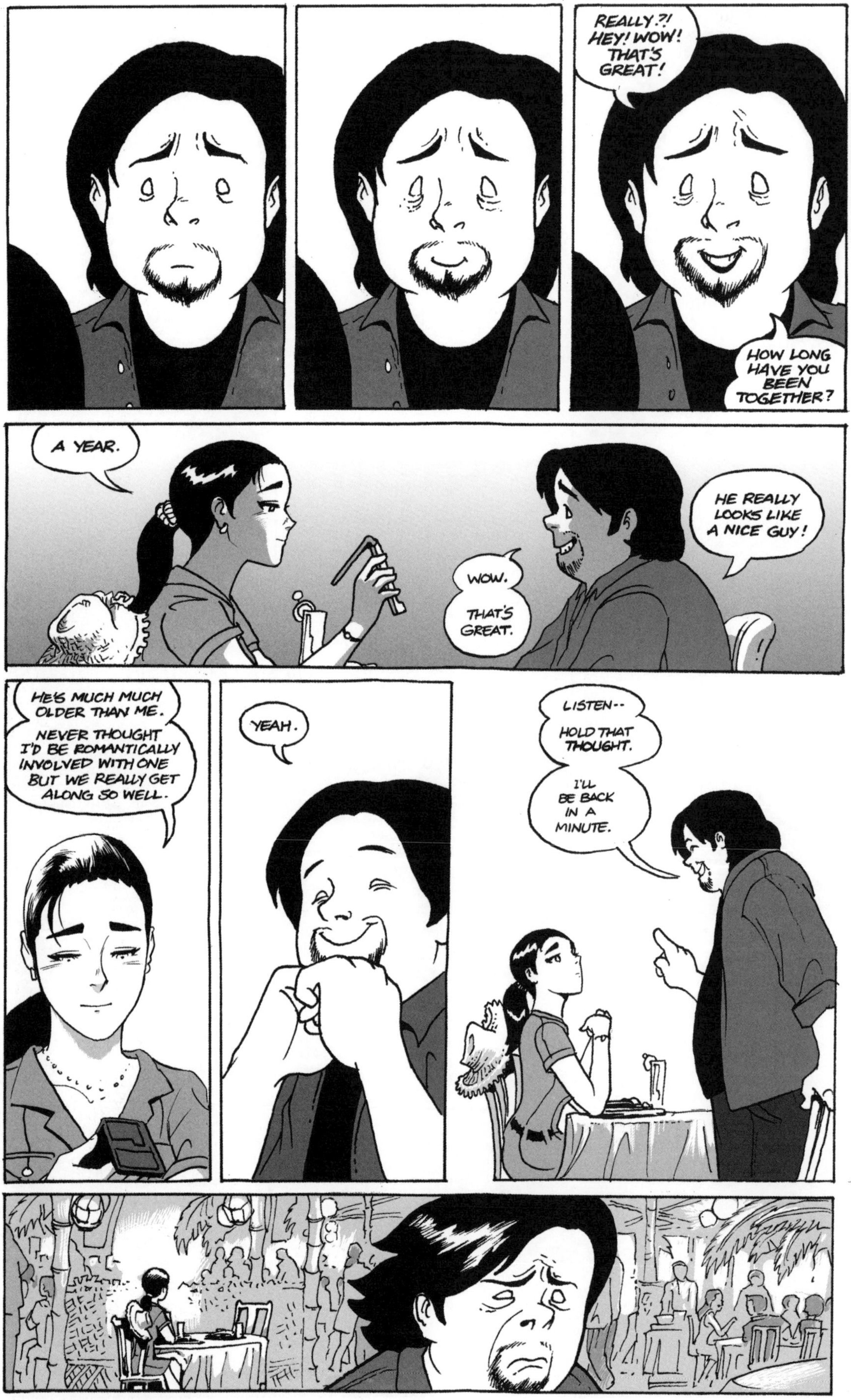
REALLY?! HEY! WOW! THAT'S GREAT!
HOW LONG HAVE YOU BEEN TOGETHER?
A YEAR.
HE REALLY LOOKS LIKE A NICE GUY!
WOW.
THAT'S GREAT.
HE'S MUCH MUCH OLDER THAN ME.
NEVER THOUGHT I'D BE ROMANTICALLY INVOLVED WITH ONE BUT WE REALLY GET ALONG SO WELL.
YEAH.
LISTEN--
HOLD THAT THOUGHT.
I'LL BE BACK IN A MINUTE.

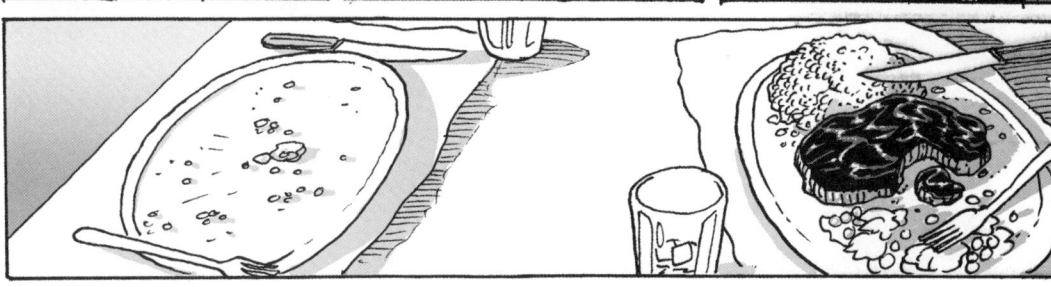

I'M BACK! HA! HA!

LOOK AT ME -- I'M PRACTICALLY **CLEANING** THE PLATE!

I'M SO EMBARRASSED.

HA! HA!

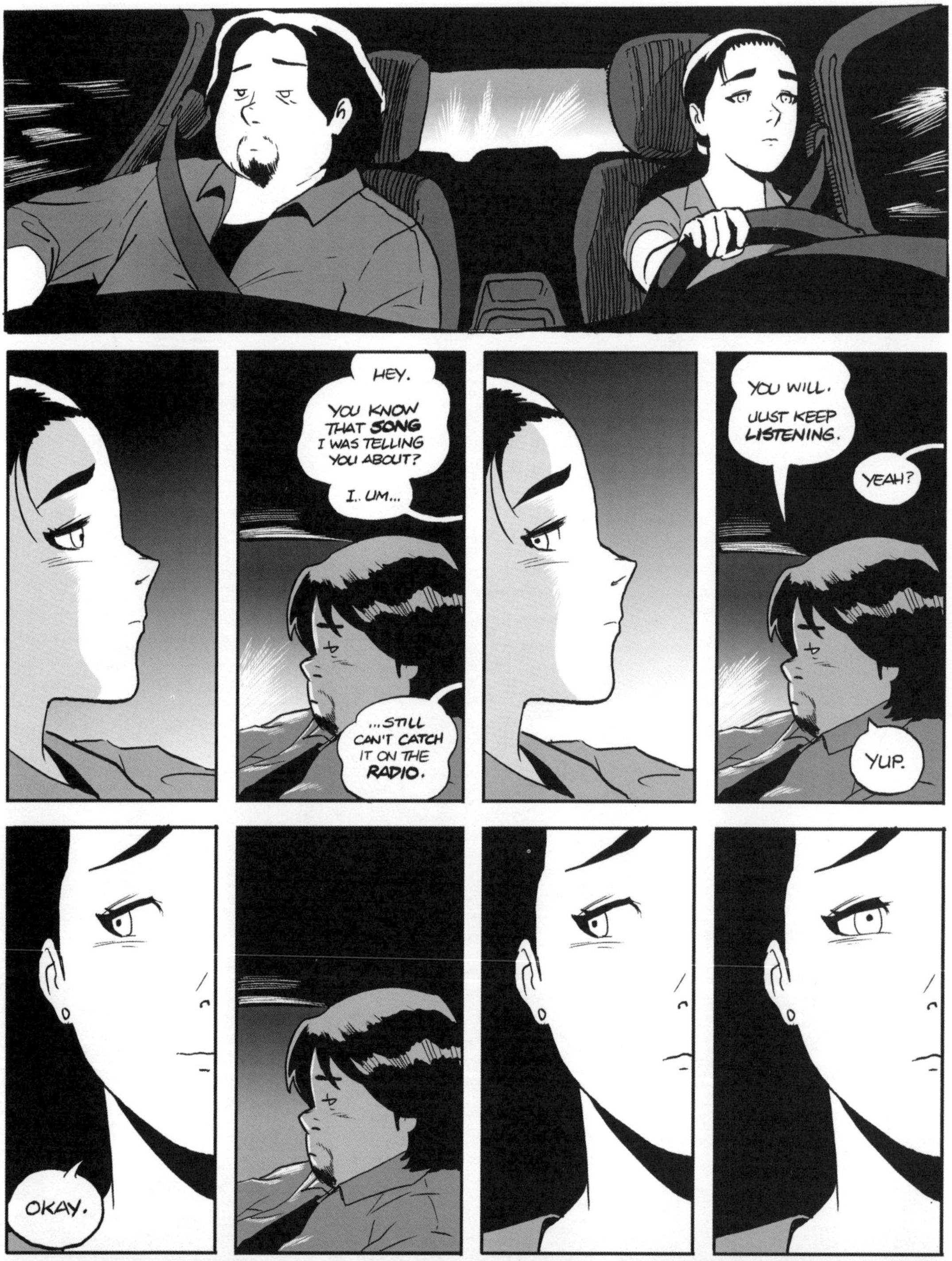
HEY.
YOU KNOW THAT SONG I WAS TELLING YOU ABOUT?
I.. UM...
...STILL CAN'T CATCH IT ON THE RADIO.
YOU WILL. JUST KEEP LISTENING.
YEAH?
YUP.
OKAY.

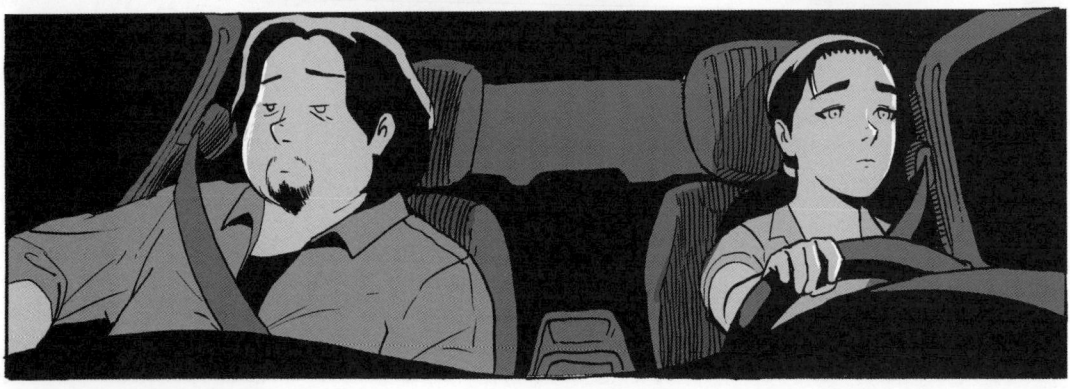

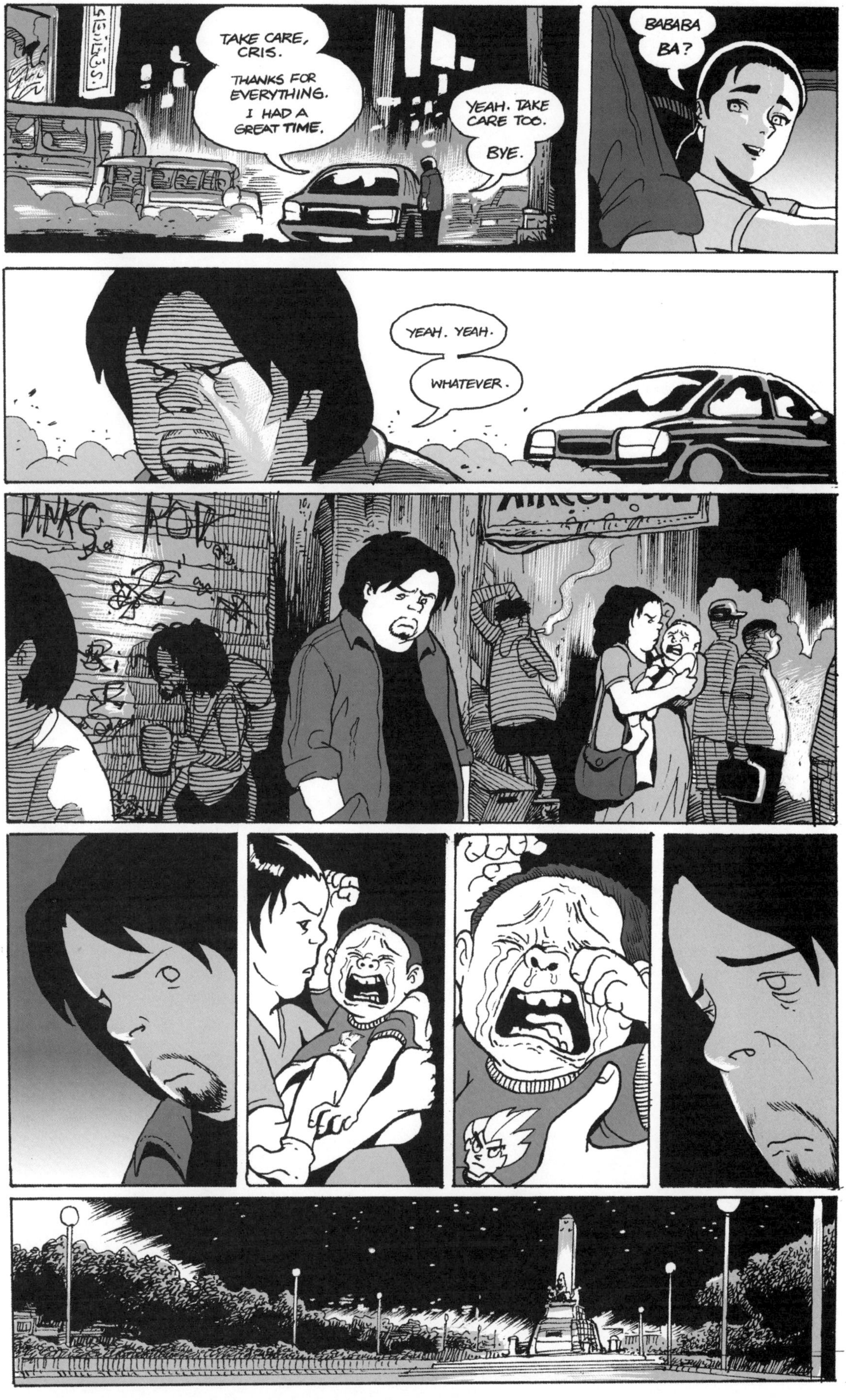
TAKE CARE, CRIS.
THANKS FOR EVERYTHING.
I HAD A GREAT TIME.
YEAH. TAKE CARE TOO.
BYE.
BABABA BA?
YEAH. YEAH.
WHATEVER.

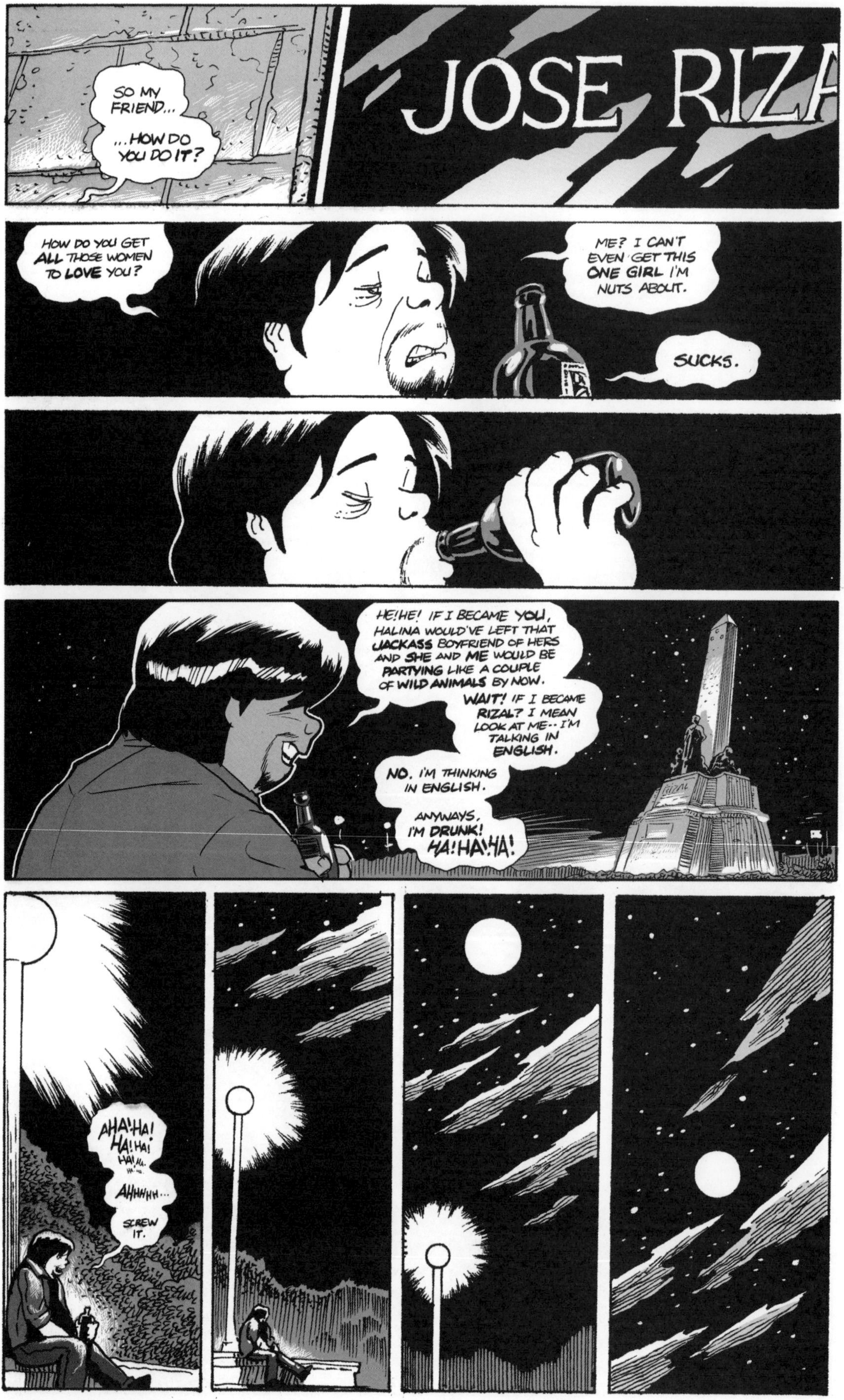
SO MY FRIEND...
...HOW DO YOU DO IT?
JOSE RIZA
HOW DO YOU GET ALL THOSE WOMEN TO LOVE YOU?
ME? I CAN'T EVEN GET THIS ONE GIRL I'M NUTS ABOUT.
SUCKS.
HE!HE! IF I BECAME YOU, HALINA WOULD'VE LEFT THAT JACKASS BOYFRIEND OF HERS AND SHE AND ME WOULD BE PARTYING LIKE A COUPLE OF WILD ANIMALS BY NOW.
WAIT! IF I BECAME RIZAL? I MEAN LOOK AT ME-- I'M TALKING IN ENGLISH.
NO. I'M THINKING IN ENGLISH.
ANYWAYS, I'M DRUNK! HA!HA!HA!
RIZAL
AHA!HA! HA!HA! HA!HA. HA.HA.
AHHHHH...
SCREW IT.

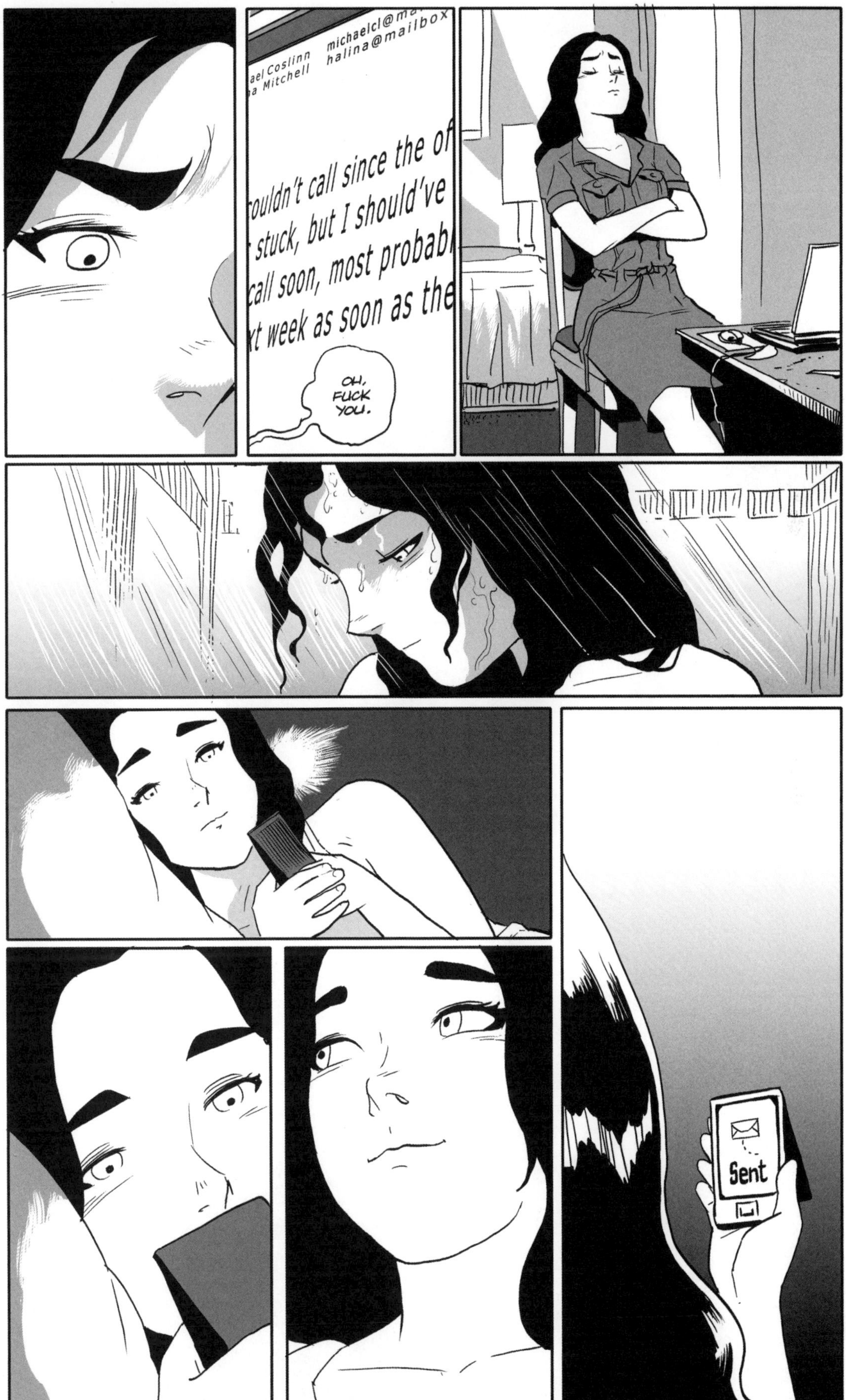
ael Coslinn michaelcl@ma
a Mitchell halina@mailbox
ouldn't call since the of
t stuck, but I should've
call soon, most probab
xt week as soon as the
OH, FUCK YOU.
Sent

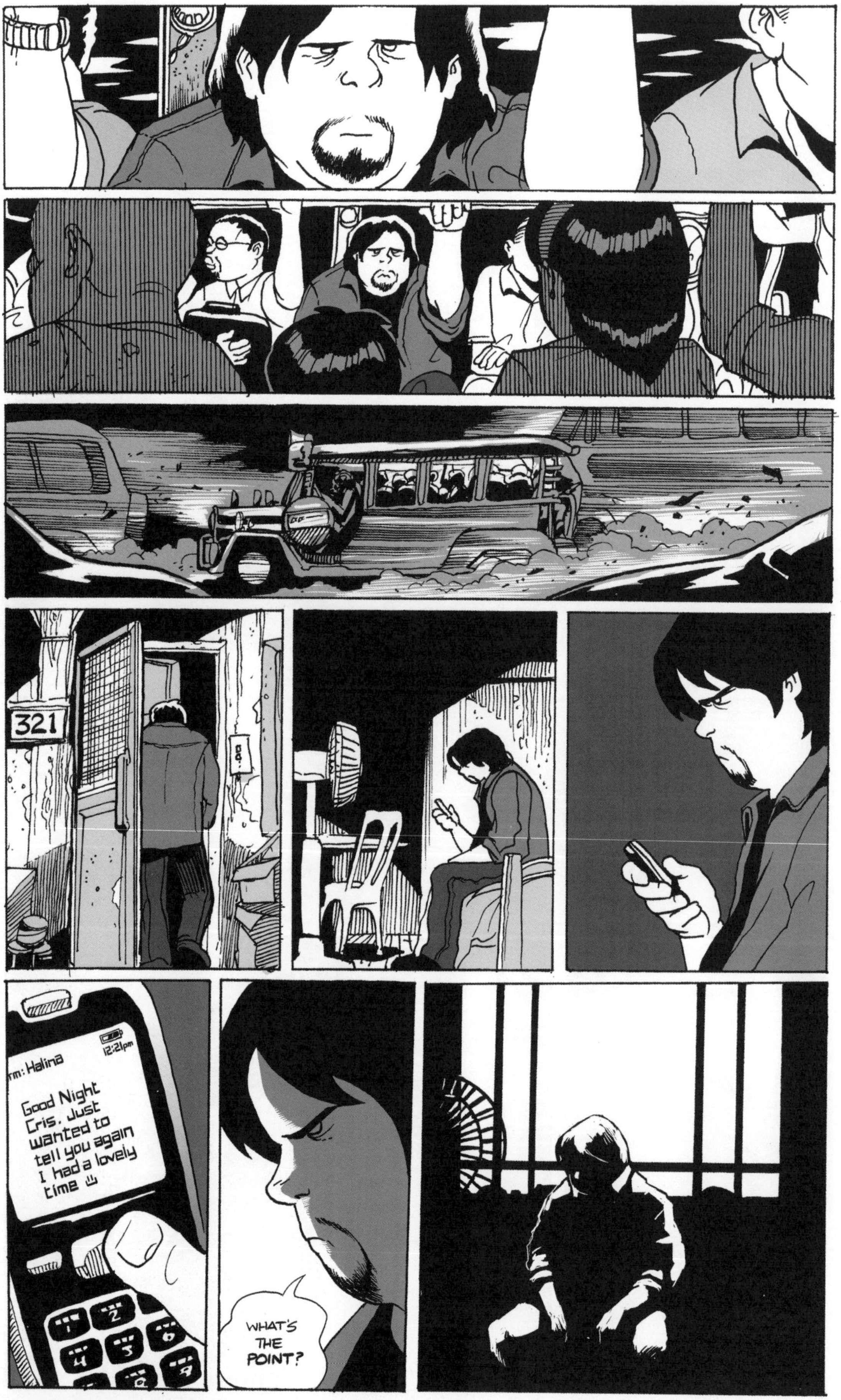
321
rm: Halina
12:21pm
Good Night Cris. Just wanted to tell you again I had a lovely time
WHAT'S THE POINT?

Chapter 4
Connections

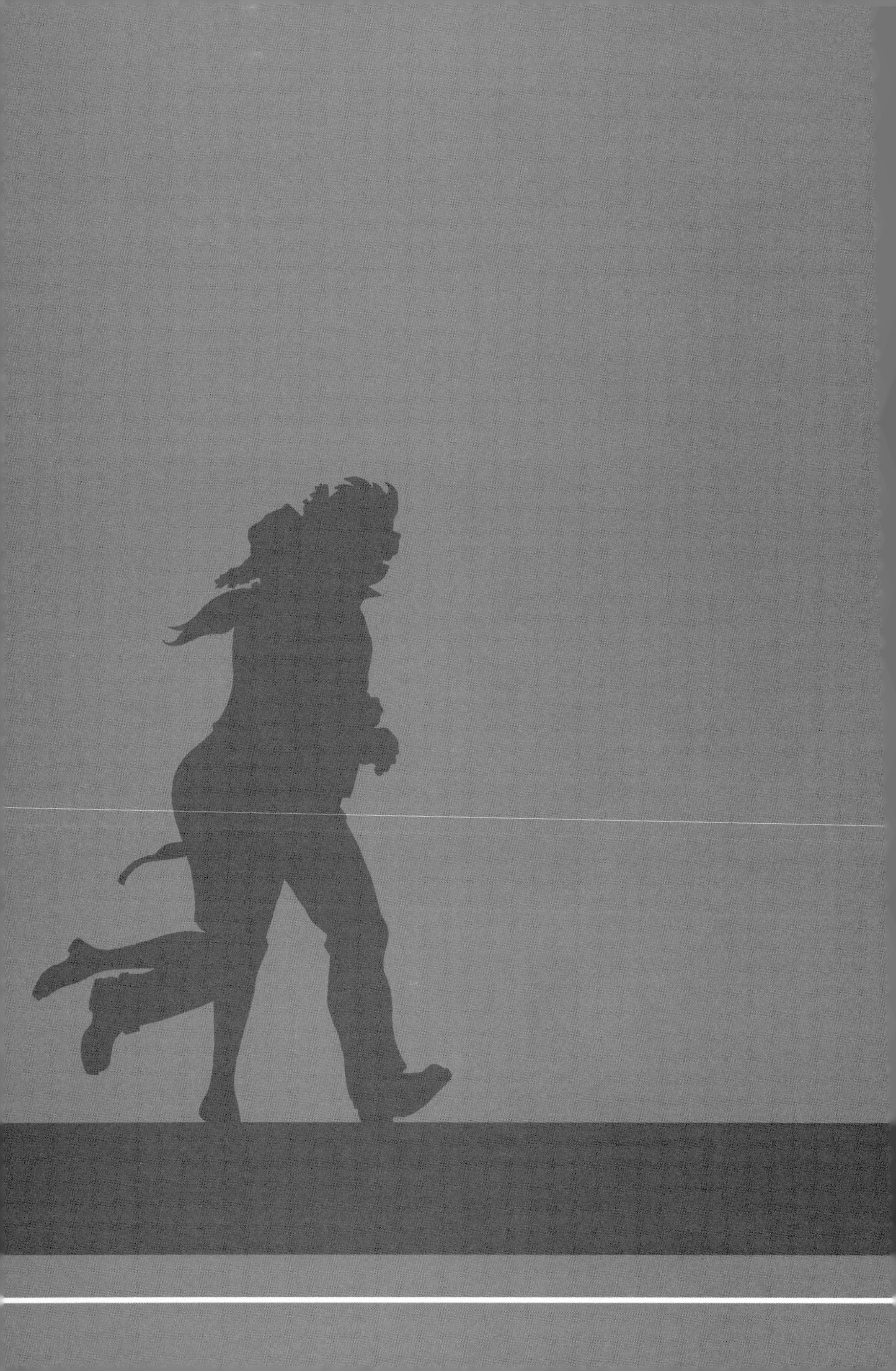

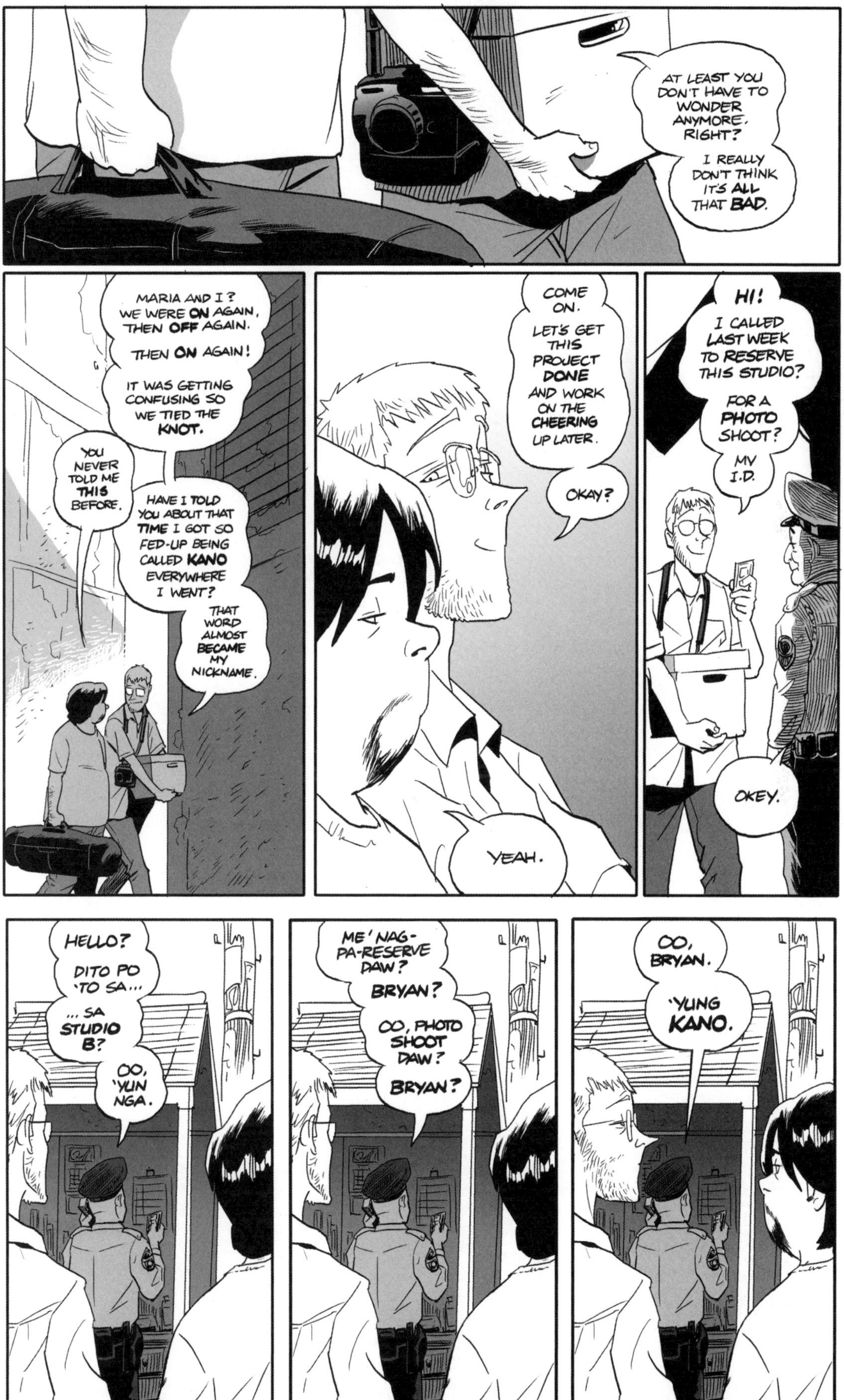
AT LEAST YOU DON'T HAVE TO WONDER ANYMORE, RIGHT?
I REALLY DON'T THINK IT'S **ALL** THAT **BAD**.
MARIA AND I? WE WERE **ON** AGAIN, THEN **OFF** AGAIN.
THEN **ON** AGAIN!
IT WAS GETTING CONFUSING SO WE TIED THE **KNOT**.
YOU NEVER TOLD ME **THIS** BEFORE.
HAVE I **TOLD** YOU ABOUT THAT **TIME** I GOT SO FED-UP BEING CALLED **KANO** EVERYWHERE I WENT?
THAT WORD ALMOST **BECAME** MY NICKNAME.
COME ON.
LET'S GET THIS PROJECT **DONE** AND WORK ON THE **CHEERING** UP LATER.
OKAY?
YEAH.
HI!
I CALLED **LAST WEEK TO RESERVE** THIS STUDIO?
FOR A **PHOTO** SHOOT?
MY I.D.
OKEY.
HELLO?
DITO PO 'TO SA...
... SA **STUDIO B**?
OO, 'YUN NGA.
ME' NAG-PA-RESERVE DAW?
BRYAN?
OO, PHOTO SHOOT DAW?
BRYAN?
OO, BRYAN.
'YUNG **KANO.**

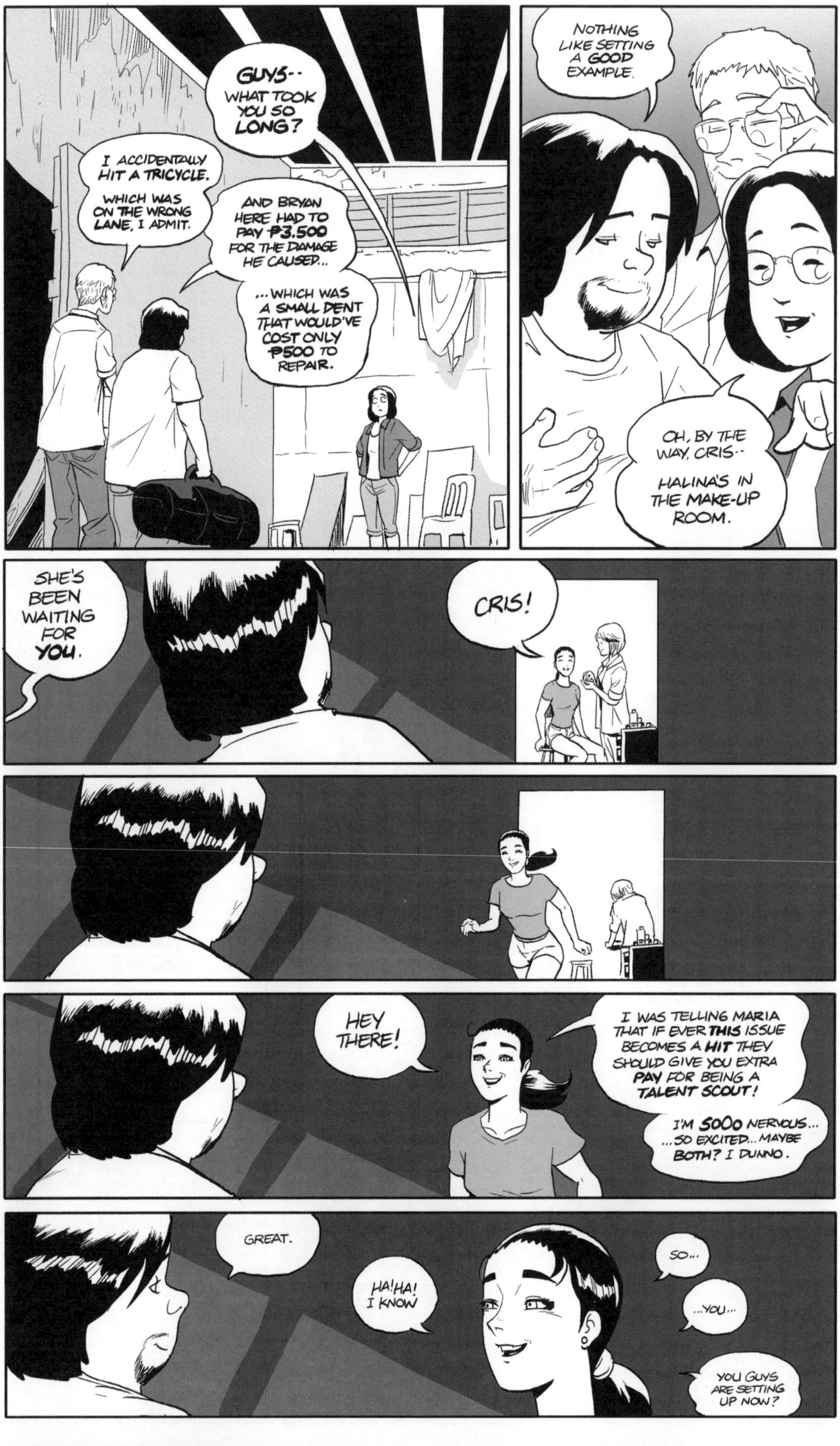
GUYS-- WHAT TOOK YOU SO LONG?
I ACCIDENTALLY HIT A TRICYCLE.
WHICH WAS ON THE WRONG LANE, I ADMIT.
AND BRYAN HERE HAD TO PAY ₱3.500 FOR THE DAMAGE HE CAUSED...
...WHICH WAS A SMALL DENT THAT WOULD'VE COST ONLY ₱500 TO REPAIR.
NOTHING LIKE SETTING A GOOD EXAMPLE.
OH, BY THE WAY, CRIS--
HALINA'S IN THE MAKE-UP ROOM.
SHE'S BEEN WAITING FOR YOU.
CRIS!
HEY THERE!
I WAS TELLING MARIA THAT IF EVER THIS ISSUE BECOMES A HIT THEY SHOULD GIVE YOU EXTRA PAY FOR BEING A TALENT SCOUT!
I'M SOOO NERVOUS... ...SO EXCITED... MAYBE BOTH? I DUNNO.
GREAT.
HA! HA! I KNOW
SO...
...YOU...
YOU GUYS ARE SETTING UP NOW?

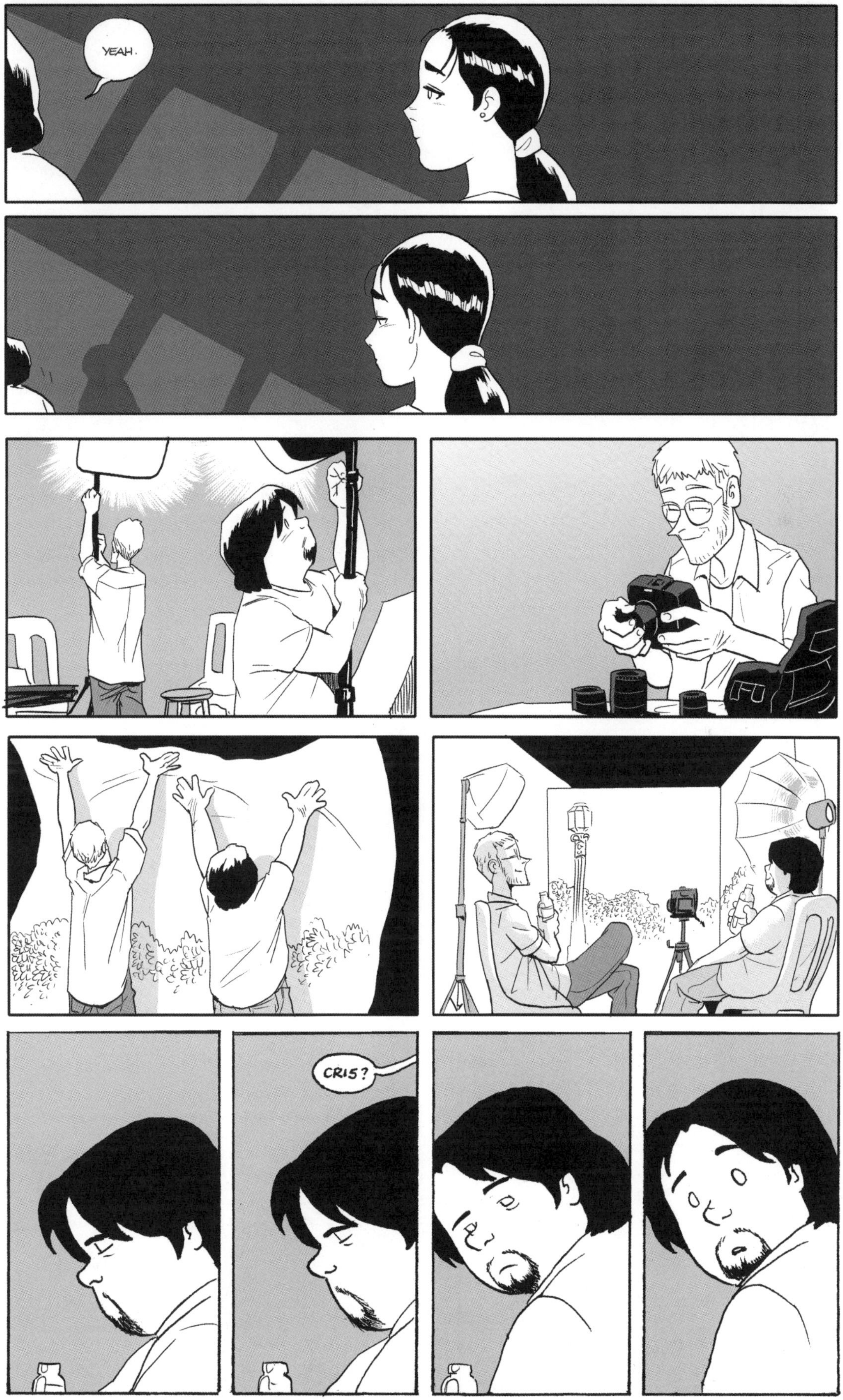
YEAH.
CRIS?

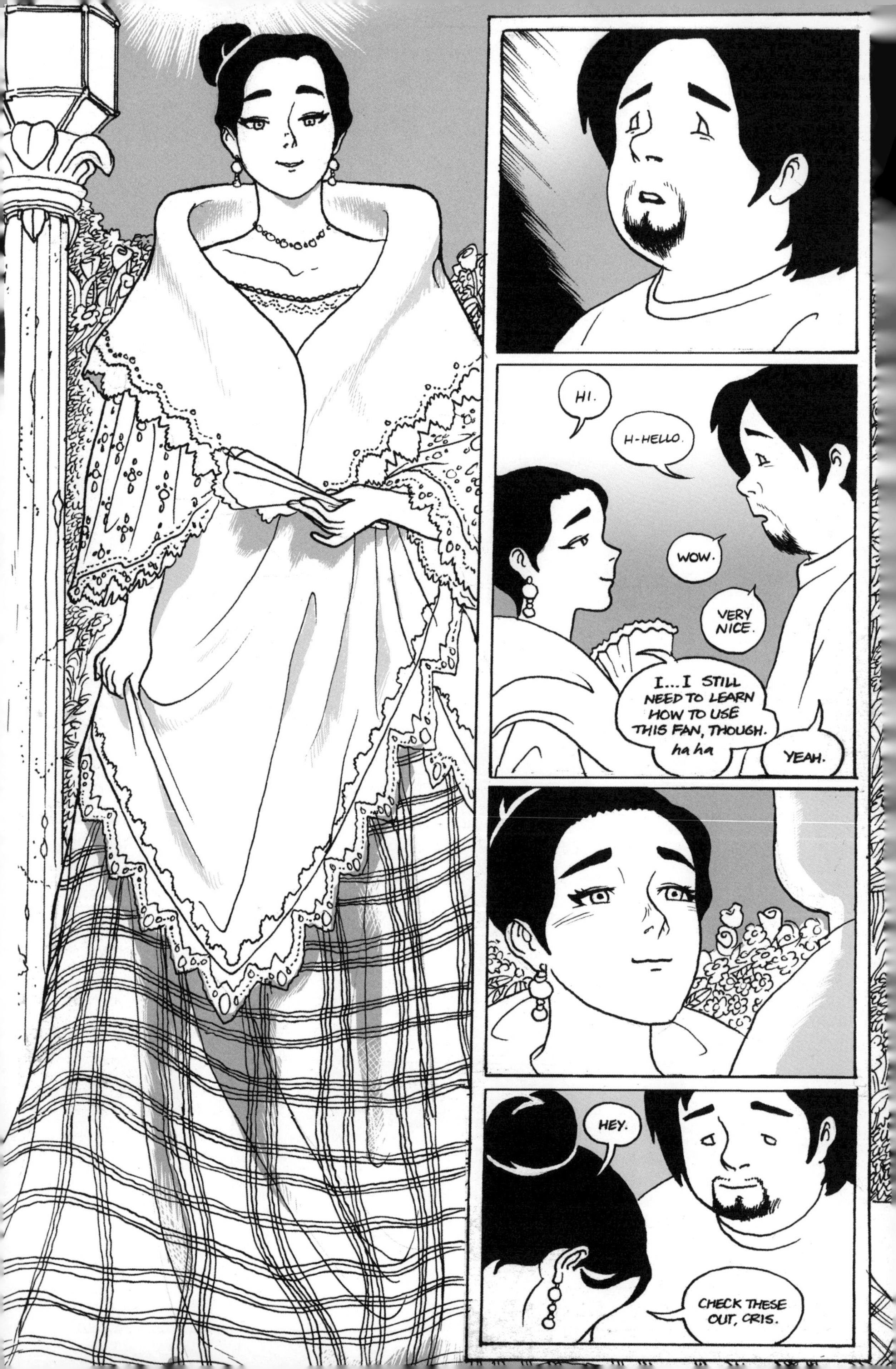
HI.
H-HELLO.
WOW.
VERY NICE.
I... I STILL NEED TO LEARN HOW TO USE THIS FAN, THOUGH. ha ha
YEAH.
HEY.
CHECK THESE OUT, CRIS.

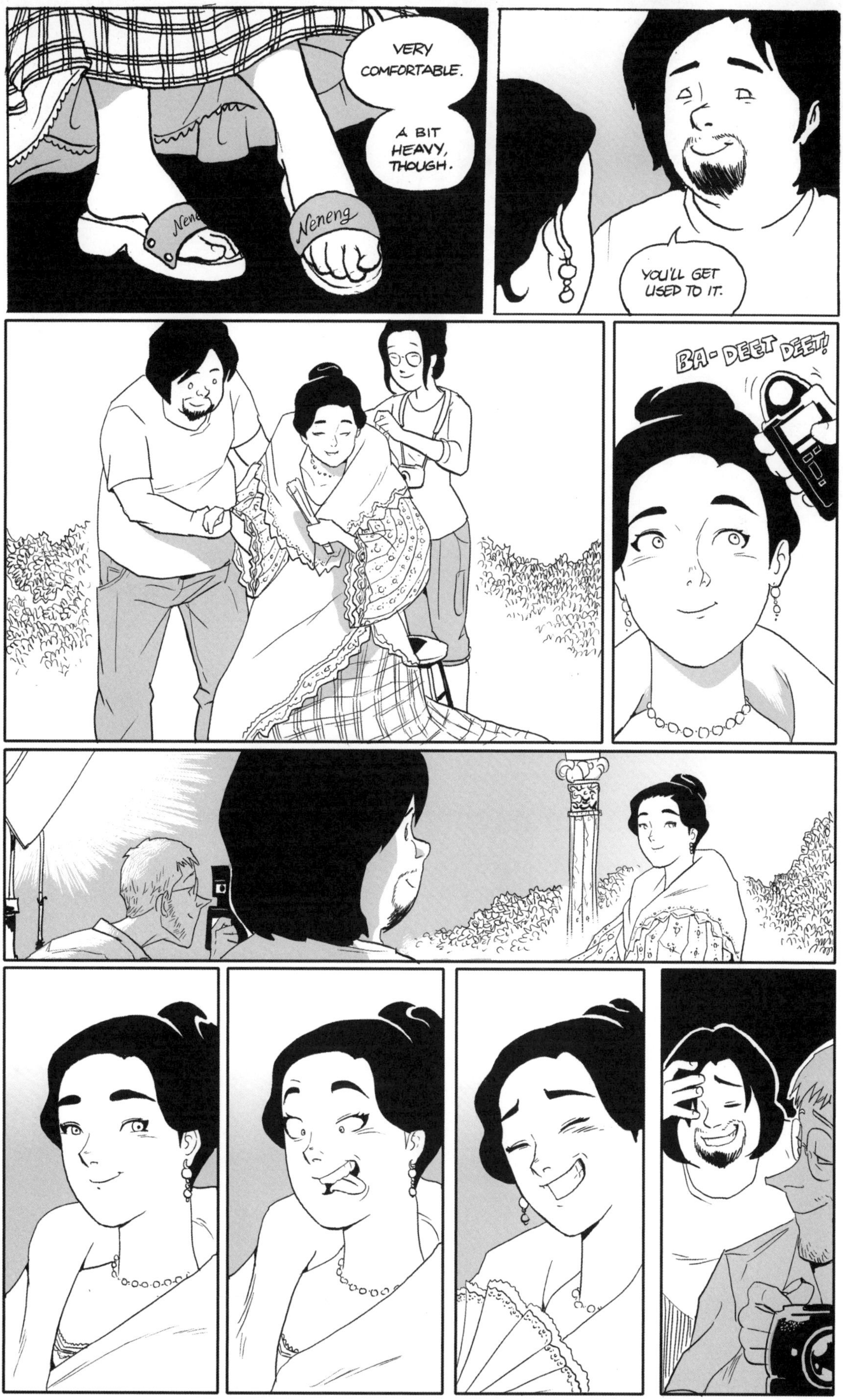
Neneng
Neneng
VERY COMFORTABLE.
A BIT HEAVY, THOUGH.
YOU'LL GET USED TO IT.
BA-DEET DEET!

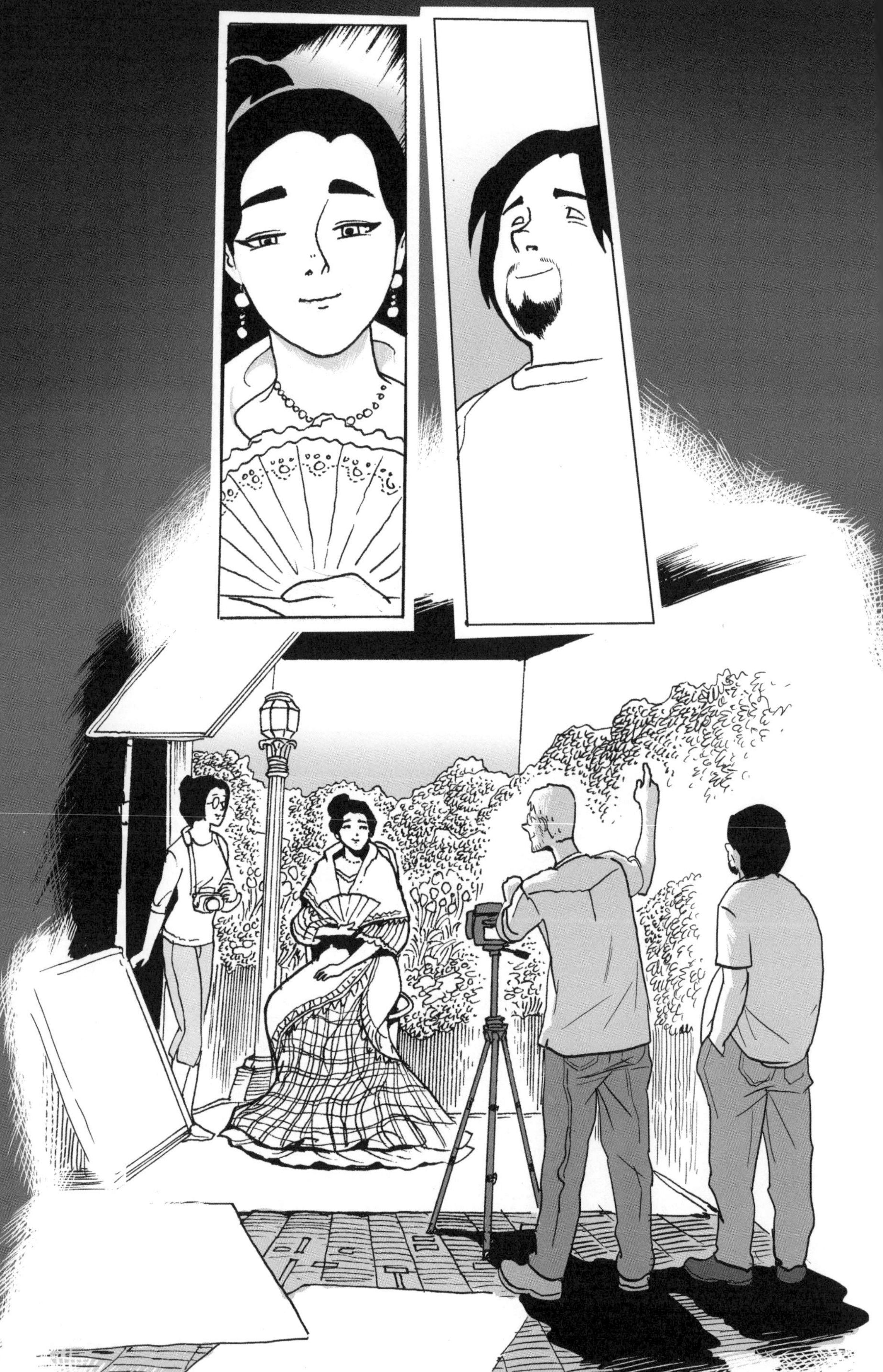

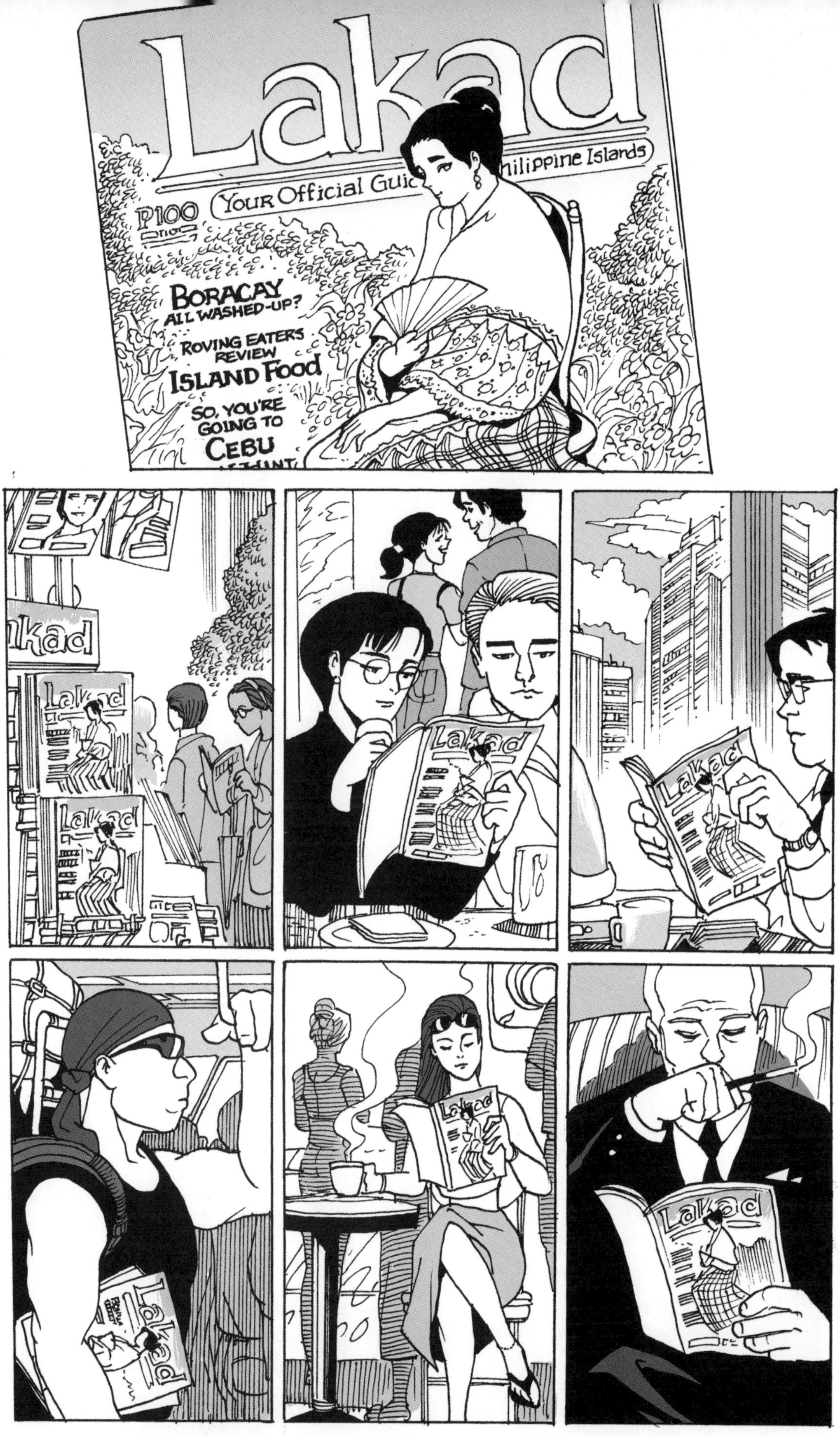
Lakad
Your Official Guic
hilippine Islands
P100
BORACAY
ALL WASHED-UP?
ROVING EATERS
REVIEW
ISLAND Food
SO, YOU'RE
GOING TO
CEBU

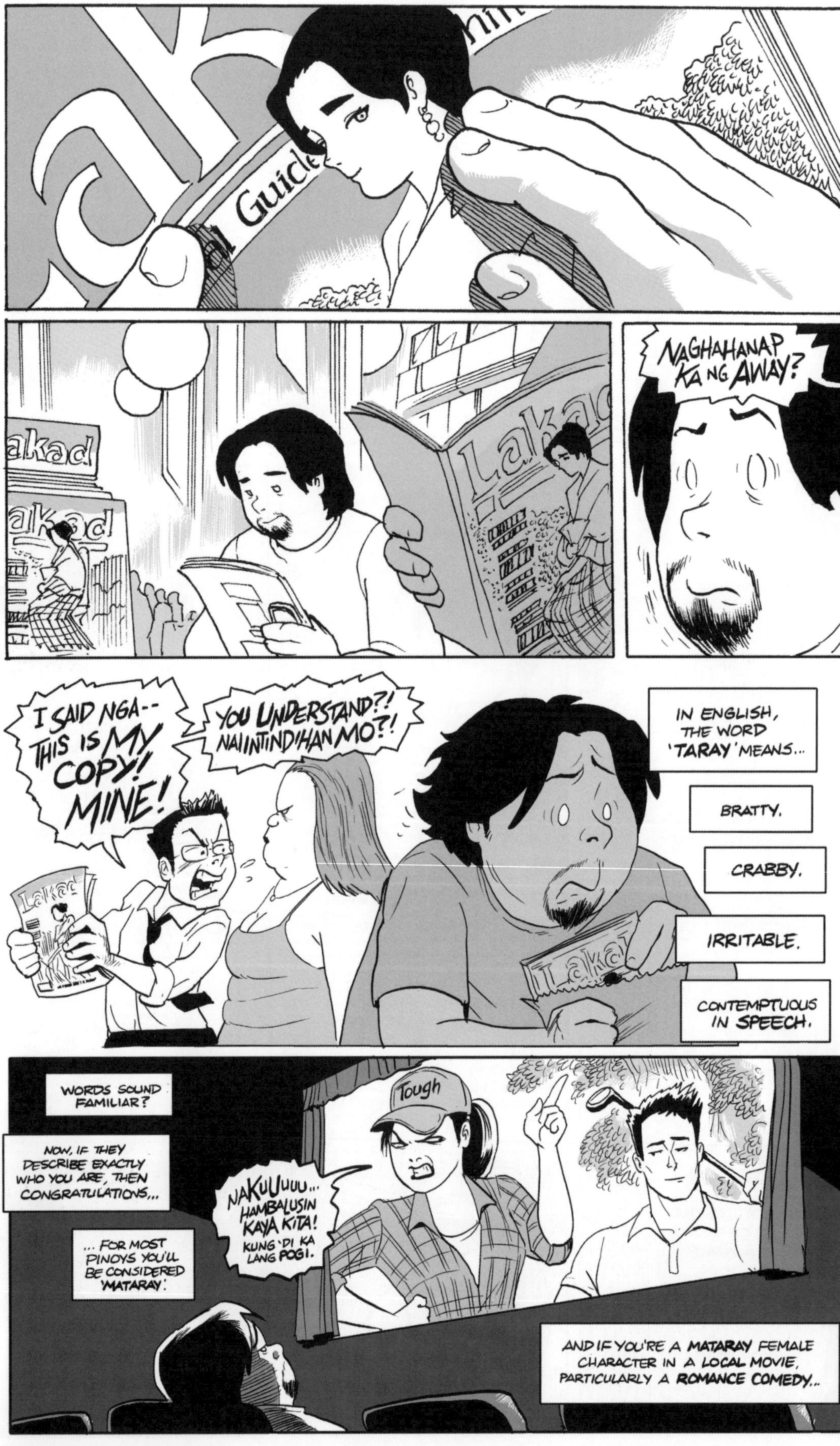
Guide
Lakad
NAGHAHANAP KA NG AWAY?
I SAID NGA-- THIS IS MY COPY! MINE!
YOU UNDERSTAND?! NAIINTINDIHAN MO?!
IN ENGLISH, THE WORD 'TARAY' MEANS...
BRATTY.
CRABBY.
IRRITABLE.
CONTEMPTUOUS IN SPEECH.
WORDS SOUND FAMILIAR?
NOW, IF THEY DESCRIBE EXACTLY WHO YOU ARE, THEN CONGRATULATIONS...
... FOR MOST PINOYS YOU'LL BE CONSIDERED 'MATARAY'.
Tough
NAKUUuuu... HAMBALUSIN KAYA KITA! KUNG 'DI KA LANG POGI.
AND IF YOU'RE A MATARAY FEMALE CHARACTER IN A LOCAL MOVIE, PARTICULARLY A ROMANCE COMEDY...

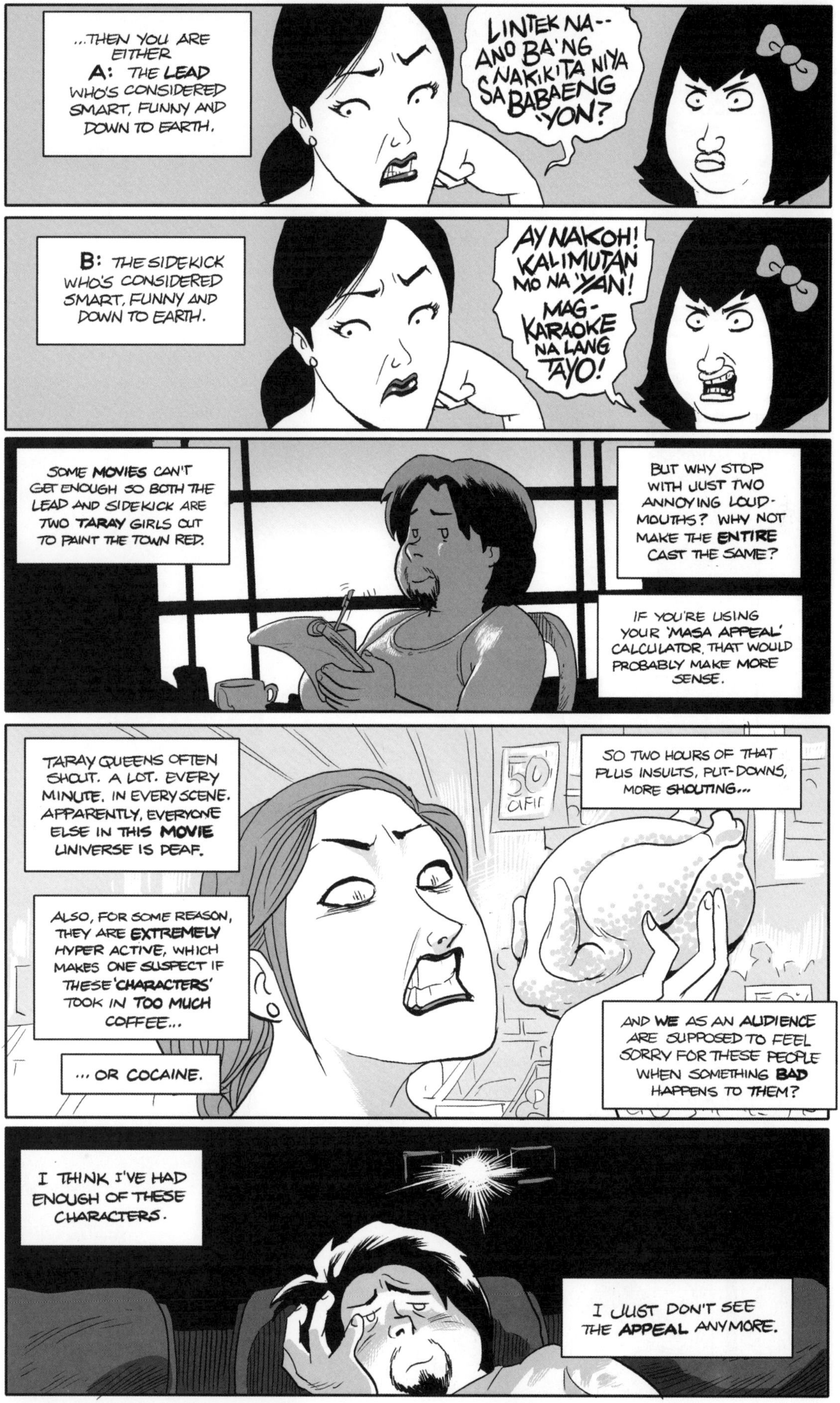
...THEN YOU ARE EITHER A: THE LEAD WHO'S CONSIDERED SMART, FUNNY AND DOWN TO EARTH.
LINTEK NA-- ANO BA'NG NAKIKITA NIYA SA BABAENG 'YON?
B: THE SIDEKICK WHO'S CONSIDERED SMART, FUNNY AND DOWN TO EARTH.
AY NAKOH! KALIMUTAN MO NA 'YAN! MAG-KARAOKE NA LANG TAYO!
SOME MOVIES CAN'T GET ENOUGH SO BOTH THE LEAD AND SIDEKICK ARE TWO TARAY GIRLS OUT TO PAINT THE TOWN RED.
BUT WHY STOP WITH JUST TWO ANNOYING LOUD-MOUTHS? WHY NOT MAKE THE ENTIRE CAST THE SAME?
IF YOU'RE USING YOUR 'MASA APPEAL' CALCULATOR, THAT WOULD PROBABLY MAKE MORE SENSE.
TARAY QUEENS OFTEN SHOUT. A LOT. EVERY MINUTE. IN EVERY SCENE. APPARENTLY, EVERYONE ELSE IN THIS MOVIE UNIVERSE IS DEAF.
SO TWO HOURS OF THAT PLUS INSULTS, PUT-DOWNS, MORE SHOUTING...
ALSO, FOR SOME REASON, THEY ARE EXTREMELY HYPER ACTIVE, WHICH MAKES ONE SUSPECT IF THESE 'CHARACTERS' TOOK IN TOO MUCH COFFEE...
...OR COCAINE.
AND WE AS AN AUDIENCE ARE SUPPOSED TO FEEL SORRY FOR THESE PEOPLE WHEN SOMETHING BAD HAPPENS TO THEM?
I THINK I'VE HAD ENOUGH OF THESE CHARACTERS.
I JUST DON'T SEE THE APPEAL ANYMORE.

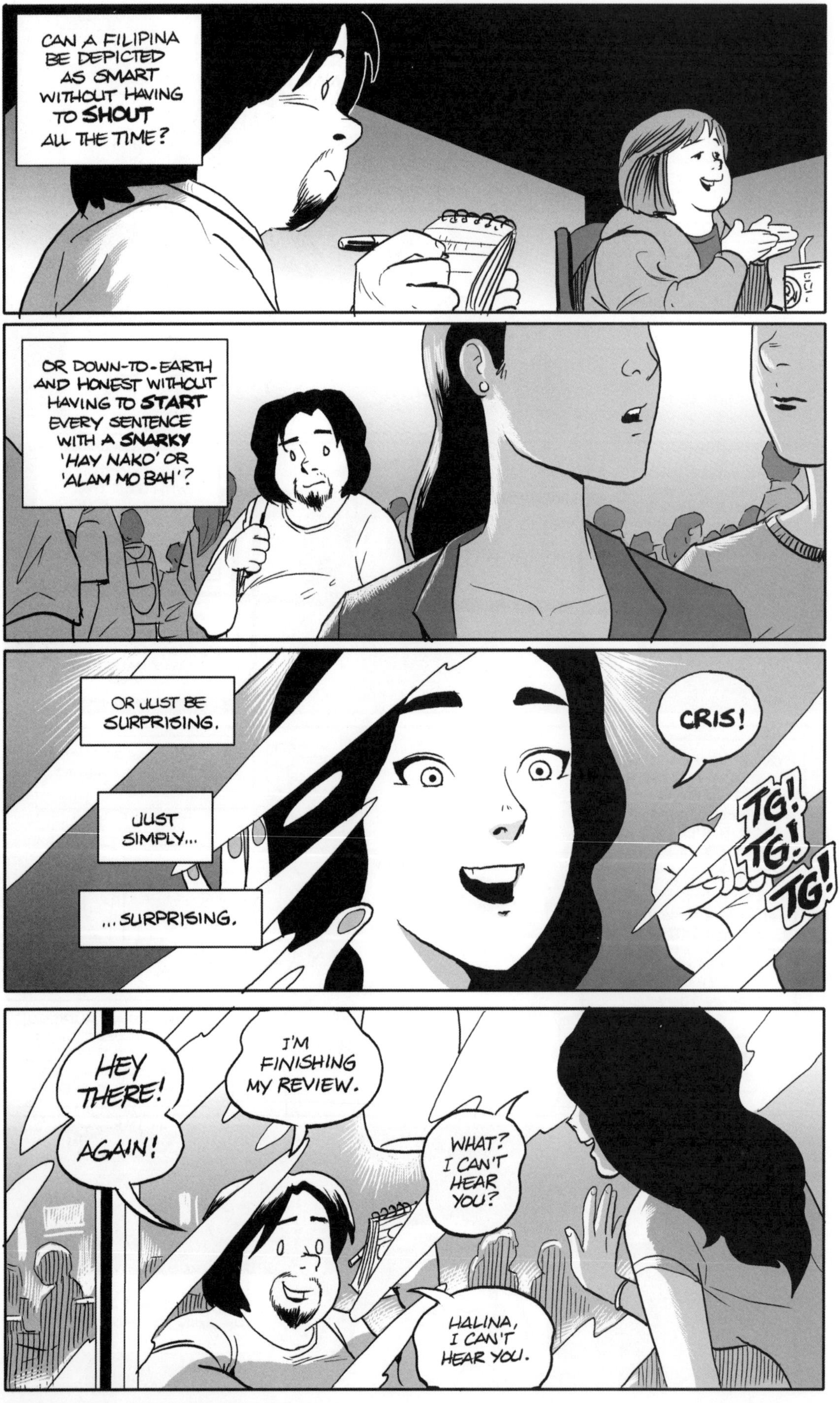
CAN A FILIPINA BE DEPICTED AS SMART WITHOUT HAVING TO SHOUT ALL THE TIME?
OR DOWN-TO-EARTH AND HONEST WITHOUT HAVING TO START EVERY SENTENCE WITH A SNARKY 'HAY NAKO' OR 'ALAM MO BAH'?
OR JUST BE SURPRISING.
JUST SIMPLY...
...SURPRISING.
CRIS!
TG! TG! TG!
HEY THERE! AGAIN!
I'M FINISHING MY REVIEW.
WHAT? I CAN'T HEAR YOU?
HALINA, I CAN'T HEAR YOU.

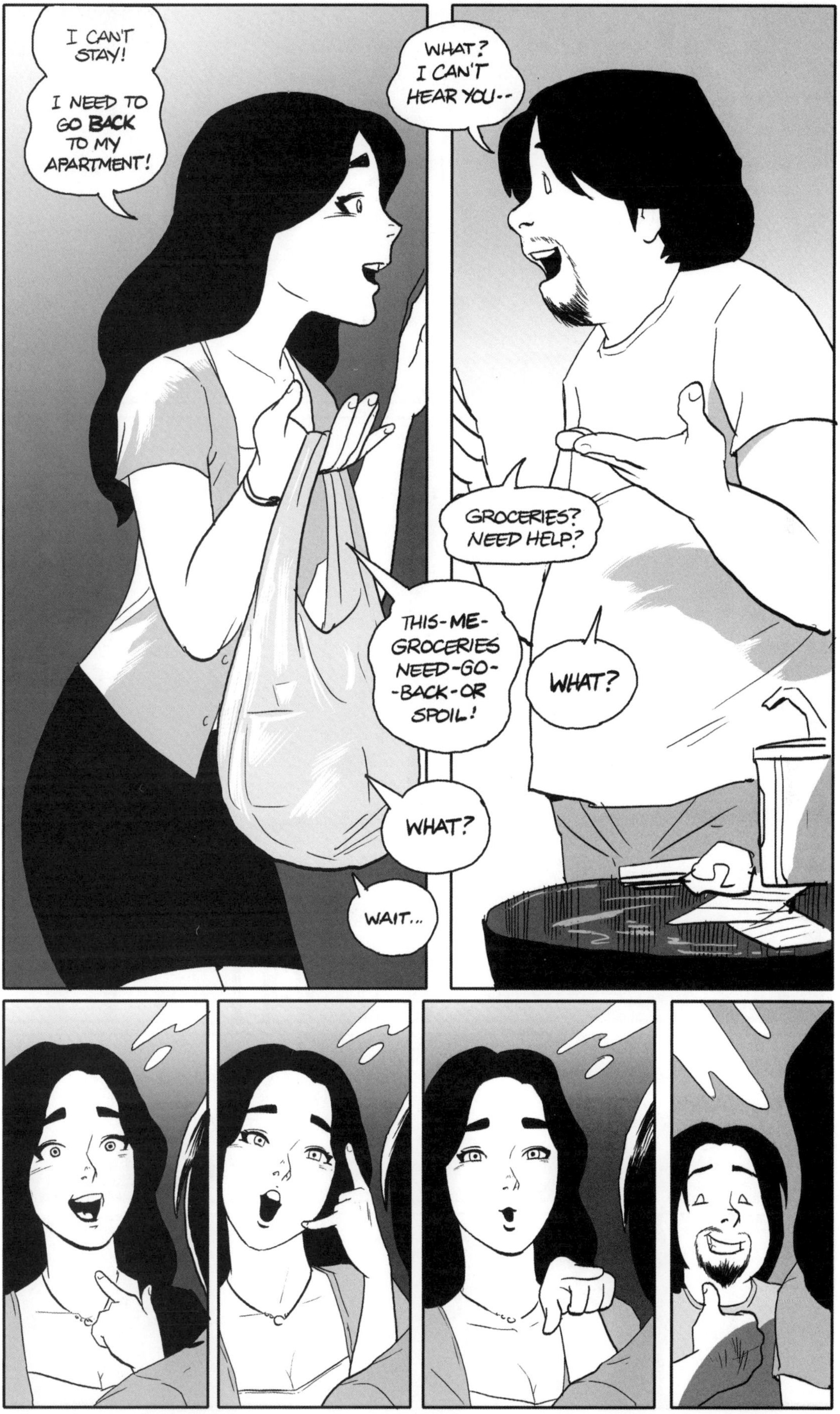

I CAN'T STAY!
I NEED TO GO BACK TO MY APARTMENT!
WHAT? I CAN'T HEAR YOU--
GROCERIES? NEED HELP?
THIS-ME-GROCERIES NEED-GO--BACK-OR SPOIL!
WHAT?
WHAT?
WAIT...

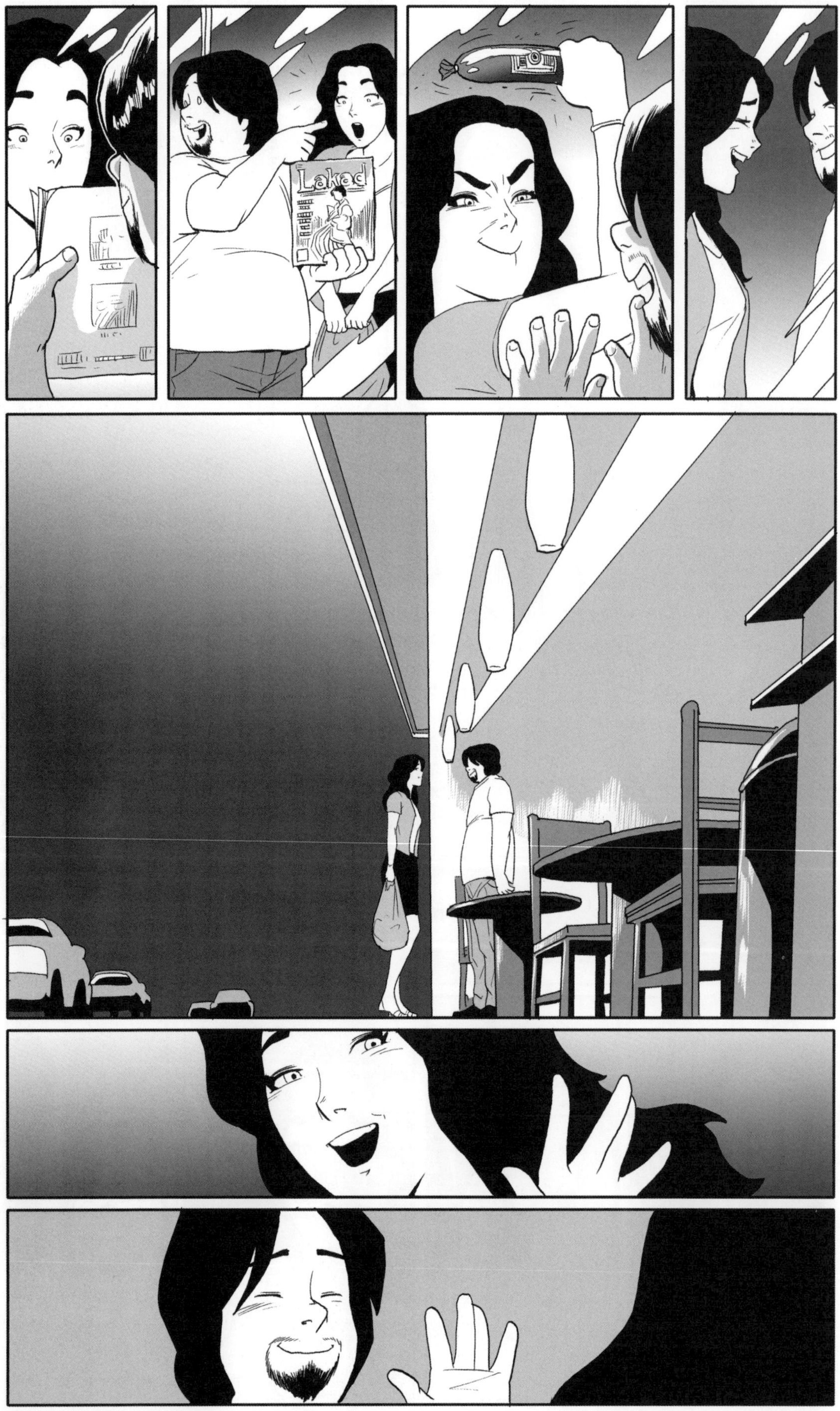
Lakad

OH NO--

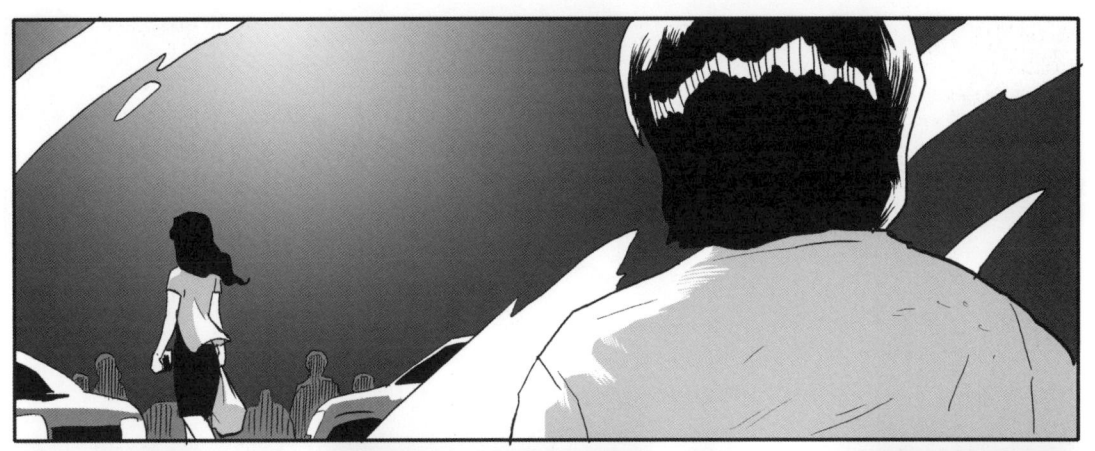

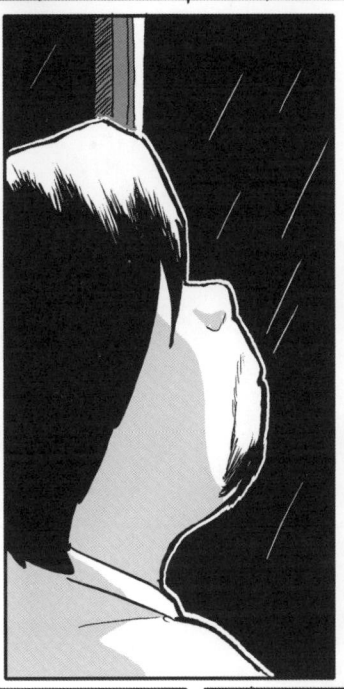

SHIT.

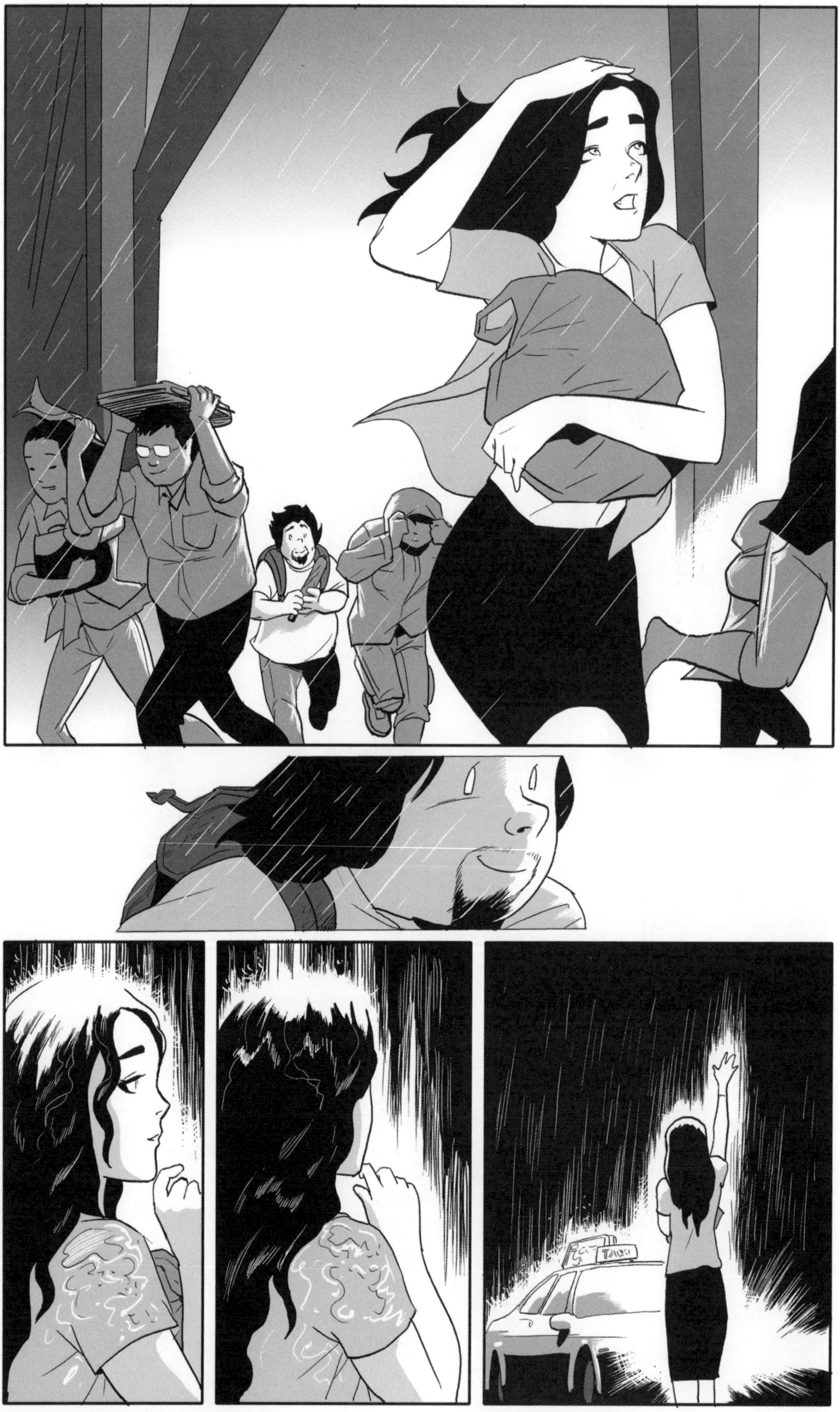

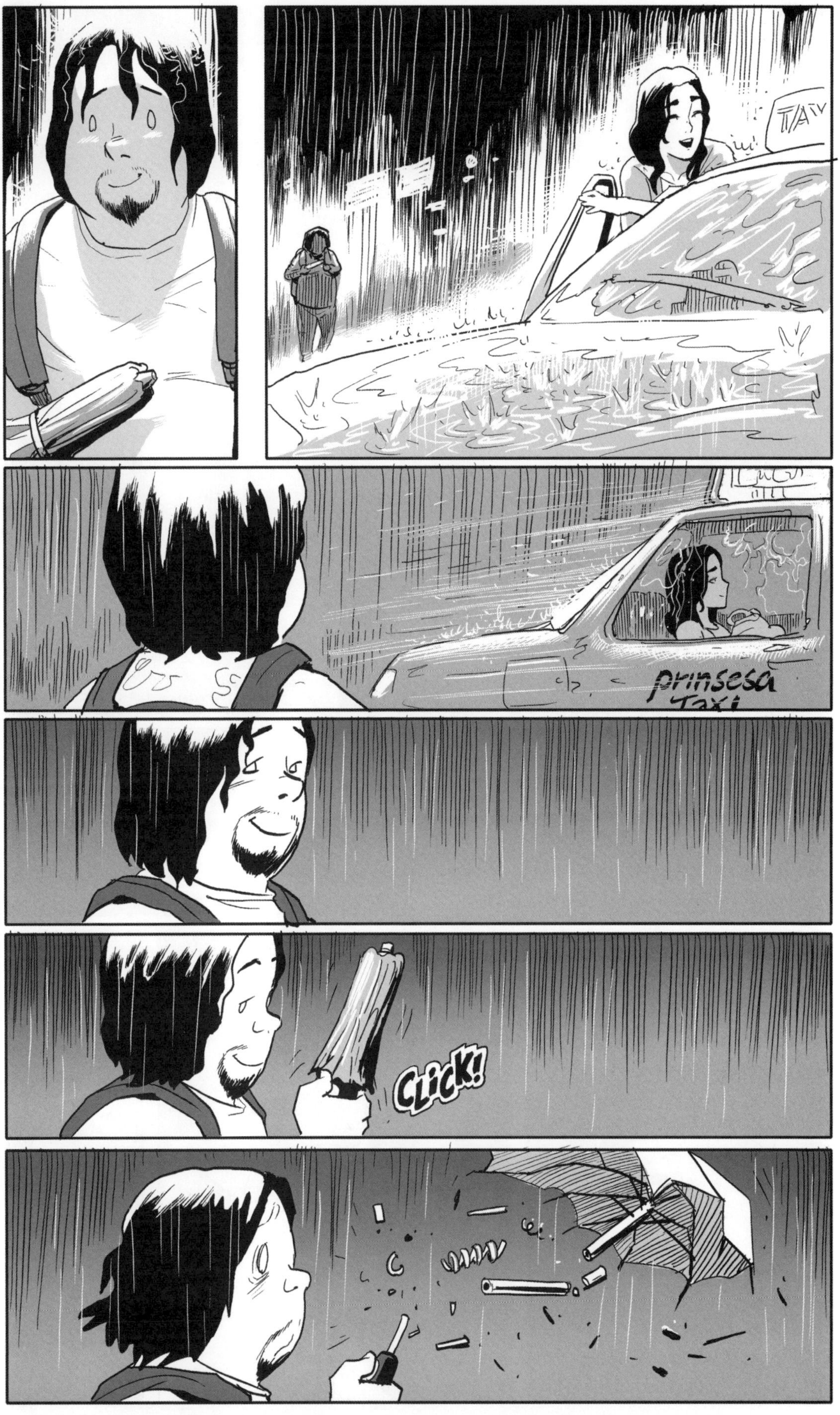

prinsesa Taxi
CLICK!

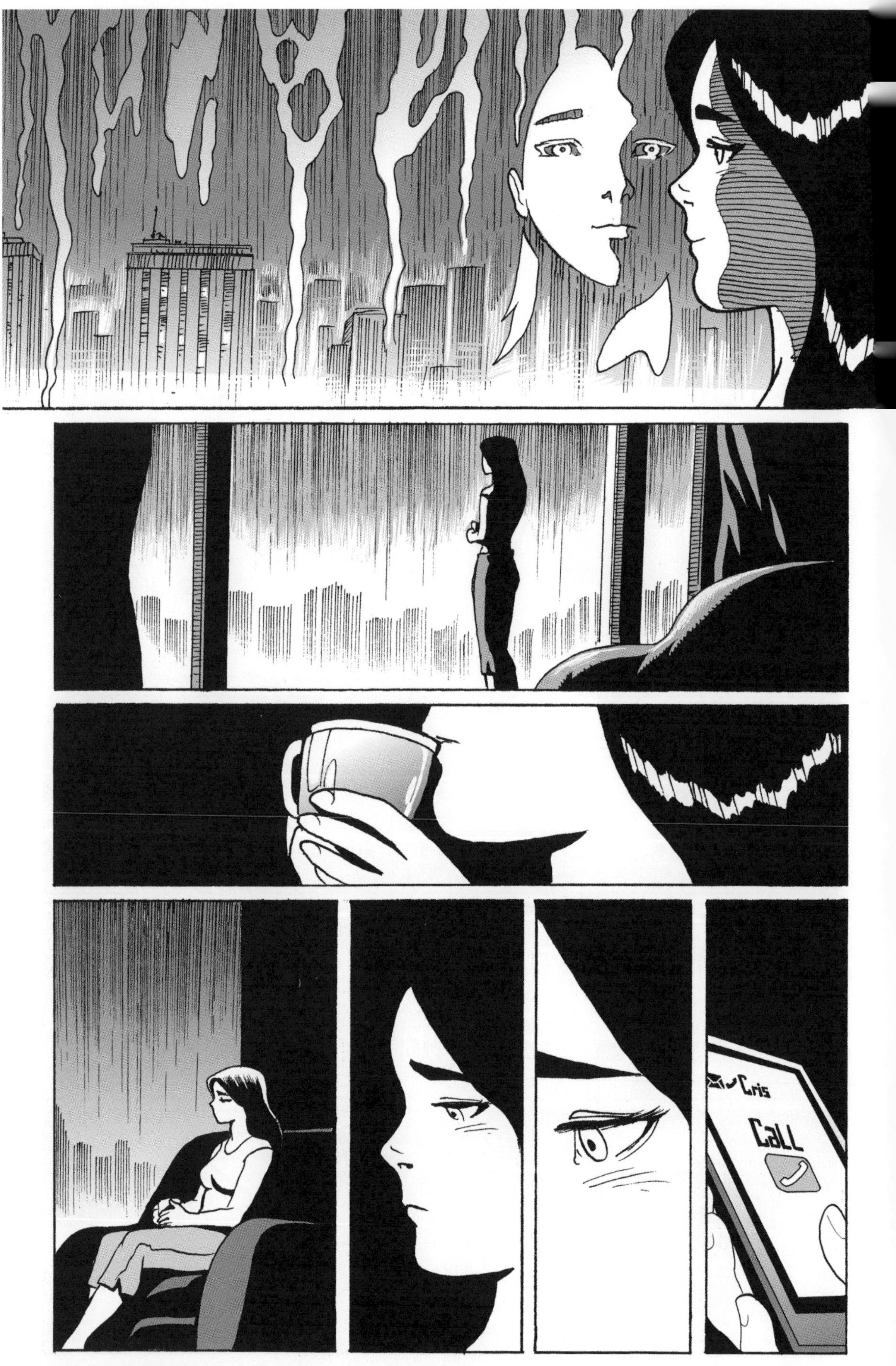
Cris
CaLL

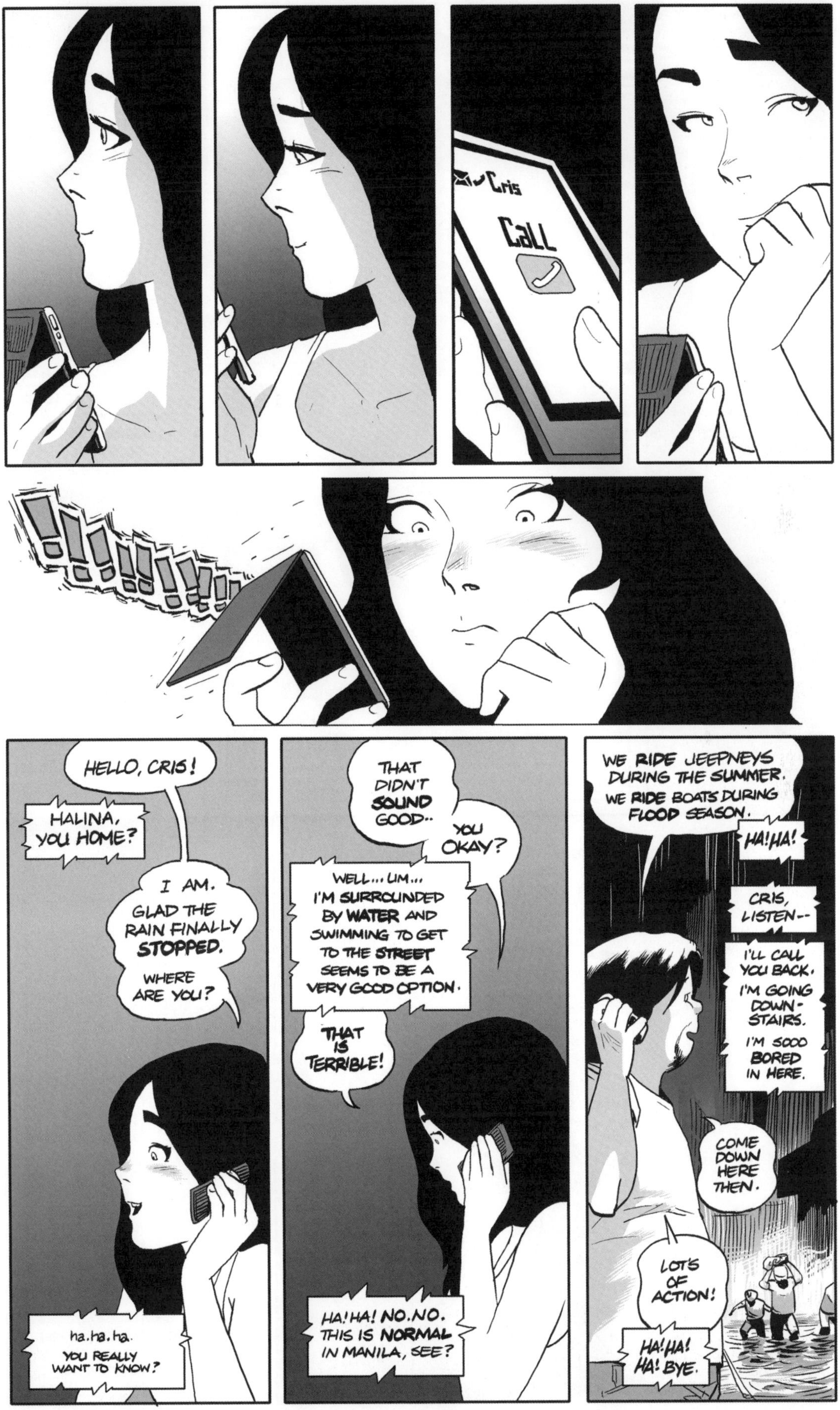
Cris
CALL
HELLO, CRIS!
HALINA, YOU HOME?
I AM.
GLAD THE RAIN FINALLY STOPPED.
WHERE ARE YOU?
ha. ha. ha.
YOU REALLY WANT TO KNOW?
THAT DIDN'T SOUND GOOD..
YOU OKAY?
WELL... UM... I'M SURROUNDED BY WATER AND SWIMMING TO GET TO THE STREET SEEMS TO BE A VERY GOOD OPTION.
THAT IS TERRIBLE!
HA! HA! NO. NO. THIS IS NORMAL IN MANILA, SEE?
WE RIDE JEEPNEYS DURING THE SUMMER.
WE RIDE BOATS DURING FLOOD SEASON.
HA! HA!
CRIS, LISTEN--
I'LL CALL YOU BACK.
I'M GOING DOWN-STAIRS.
I'M SOOO BORED IN HERE.
COME DOWN HERE THEN.
LOT'S OF ACTION!
HA! HA! HA! BYE.

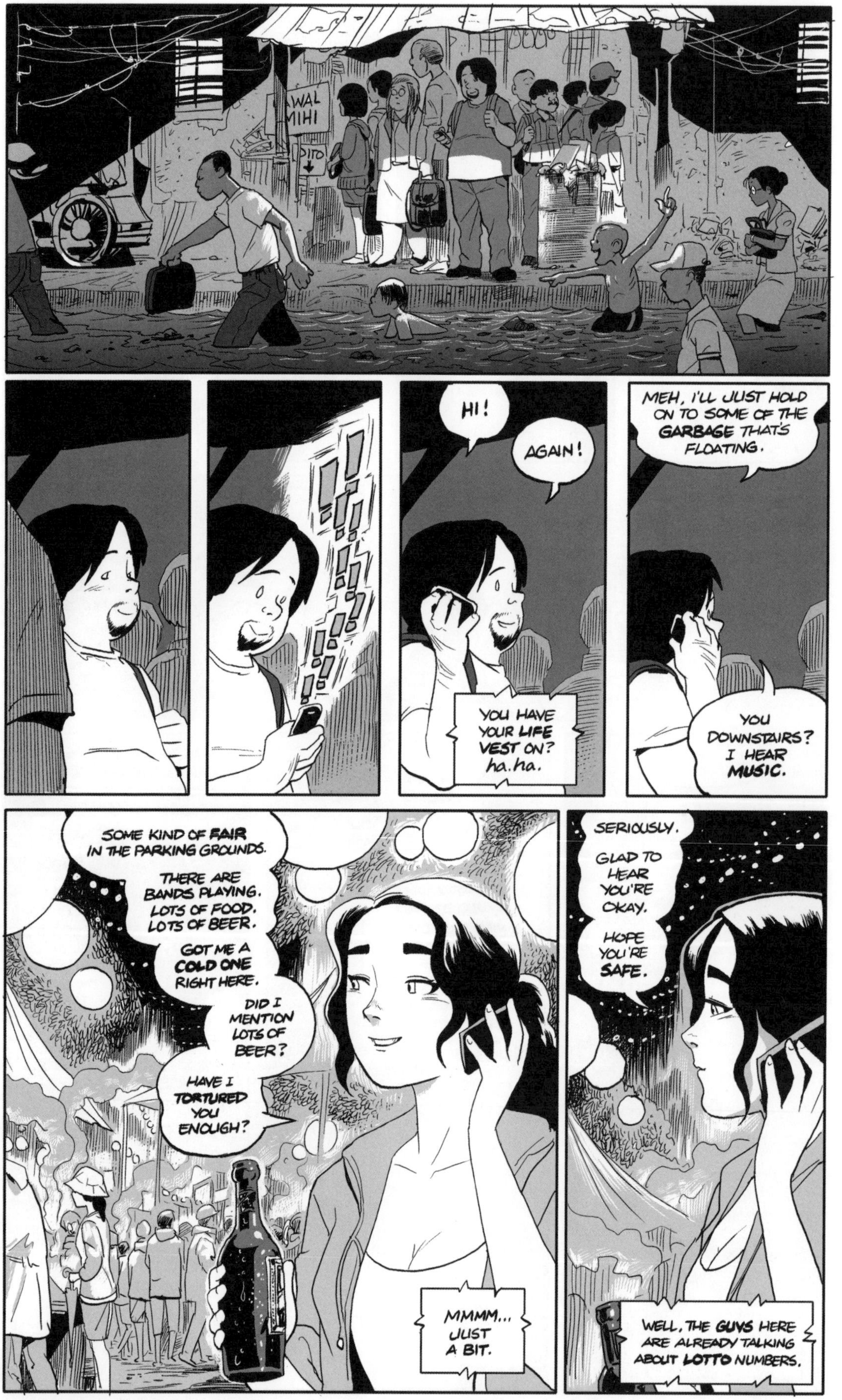
DITO
HI!
AGAIN!
YOU HAVE YOUR LIFE VEST ON? ha.ha.
MEH, I'LL JUST HOLD ON TO SOME OF THE GARBAGE THAT'S FLOATING.
YOU DOWNSTAIRS? I HEAR MUSIC.
SOME KIND OF FAIR IN THE PARKING GROUNDS.
THERE ARE BANDS PLAYING. LOTS OF FOOD. LOTS OF BEER.
GOT ME A COLD ONE RIGHT HERE.
DID I MENTION LOTS OF BEER?
HAVE I TORTURED YOU ENOUGH?
MMMM... JUST A BIT.
SERIOUSLY.
GLAD TO HEAR YOU'RE OKAY.
HOPE YOU'RE SAFE.
WELL, THE GUYS HERE ARE ALREADY TALKING ABOUT LOTTO NUMBERS.

ANYWAY, I FEEL LIKE JOINING YOU--

ISANG BEER.

NO FANCY ATMOSPHERE HERE THOUGH. JUST THE FRESH SMELL OF RAW SEWAGE.

HA! HA! SO IT *IS* TRUE WHAT I'VE READ ABOUT THE FILIPINO RESILIENCE-- ABOUT NOT TAKING LIFE TOO SERIOUSLY.

JUST SMILING AND NOT LETTING ANYTHING GET YOU DOWN.

THAT'S NICE.

NOT ALL THE TIME.

YOU READ ABOUT CRAB MENTALITY?

UM... LIKE-- THE PLEASURE OF SEEING A PERSON'S MISFORTUNE?

LIKE SCHADENFREUDE, YOU MEAN?

KINDA.

IT'S: 'LET'S PULL THAT LUCKY SON-OF-A-BITCH DOWN TO OUR LEVEL OF MISERY.'

HAPPENS EVERYWHERE, CRIS. LIKE, I KNOW SEVERAL IN MANHATTAN WHO ARE MUCH WORSE THAN WHAT YOU DESCRIBED.

YOU KNOW SEVERAL CRABS IN MANHATTAN?

HA! HA! HA! LADIES AND GENTLEMEN, 'STAND UP NEW YORK' BRINGS YOU THE FUNNIEST MAN IN MANILA--!

YOU KNOW-- ALL THIS TALK ABOUT CRABS IS ACTUALLY MAKING ME HUNGRY.

HUNGRY? LET'S SEE WHAT WE GOT HERE, THEN.

OOOH! THIS LOOKS INTERESTING!

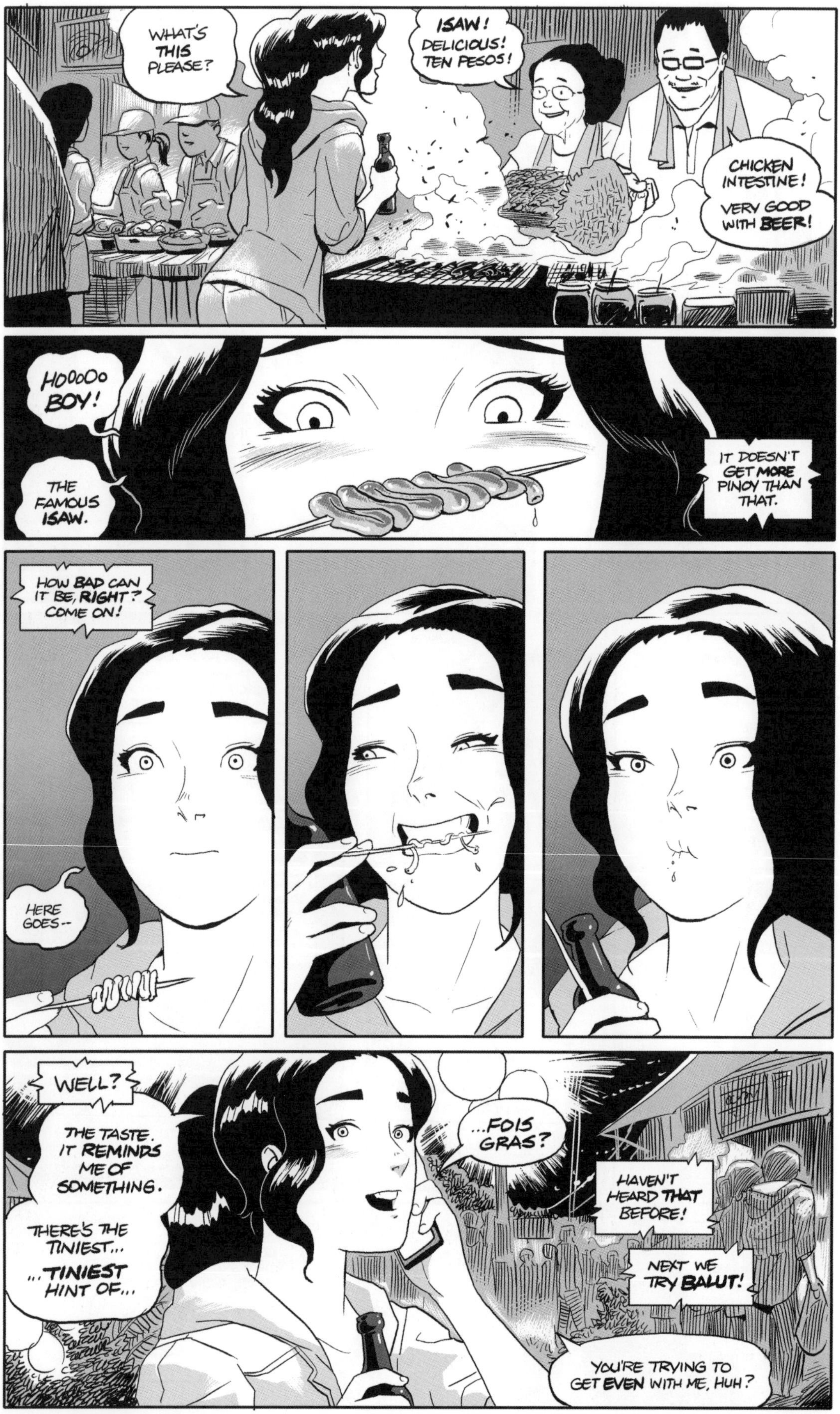
WHAT'S THIS PLEASE?
ISAW! DELICIOUS! TEN PESOS!
CHICKEN INTESTINE!
VERY GOOD WITH BEER!
HOOOOO BOY!
THE FAMOUS ISAW.
IT DOESN'T GET MORE PINOY THAN THAT.
HOW BAD CAN IT BE, RIGHT? COME ON!
HERE GOES--
WELL?
THE TASTE. IT REMINDS ME OF SOMETHING.
THERE'S THE TINIEST...
...TINIEST HINT OF...
...FOIS GRAS?
HAVEN'T HEARD THAT BEFORE!
NEXT WE TRY BALUT!
YOU'RE TRYING TO GET EVEN WITH ME, HUH?

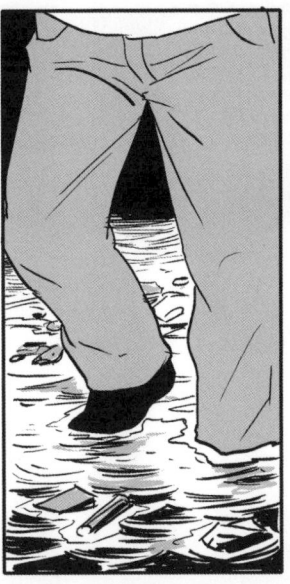

TUMATAAS 'YUNG TUBIG! AY!! BASA NA AKO!

HELLO? CRIS?

CRIS? HELLO? EVERYTHING OKAY THERE? WHAT'S HAPPENING?

OH, NOTHING.

YOU? FIND ANYTHING THAT ATTRACTS YOUR FANCY?

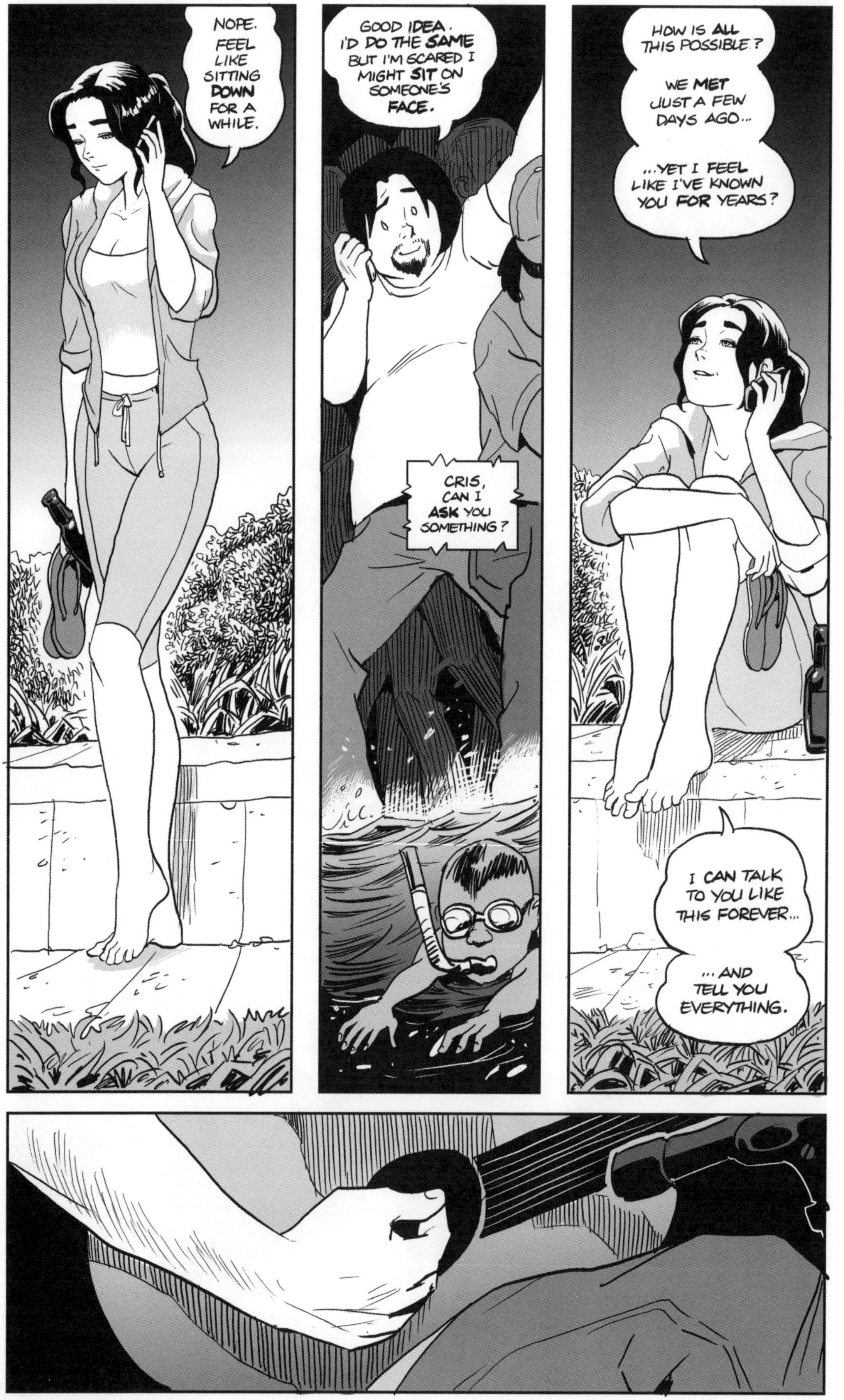
NOPE. FEEL LIKE SITTING DOWN FOR A WHILE.
GOOD IDEA. I'D DO THE SAME BUT I'M SCARED I MIGHT SIT ON SOMEONE'S FACE.
CRIS, CAN I ASK YOU SOMETHING?
HOW IS ALL THIS POSSIBLE?
WE MET JUST A FEW DAYS AGO...
...YET I FEEL LIKE I'VE KNOWN YOU FOR YEARS?
I CAN TALK TO YOU LIKE THIS FOREVER...
... AND TELL YOU EVERYTHING.

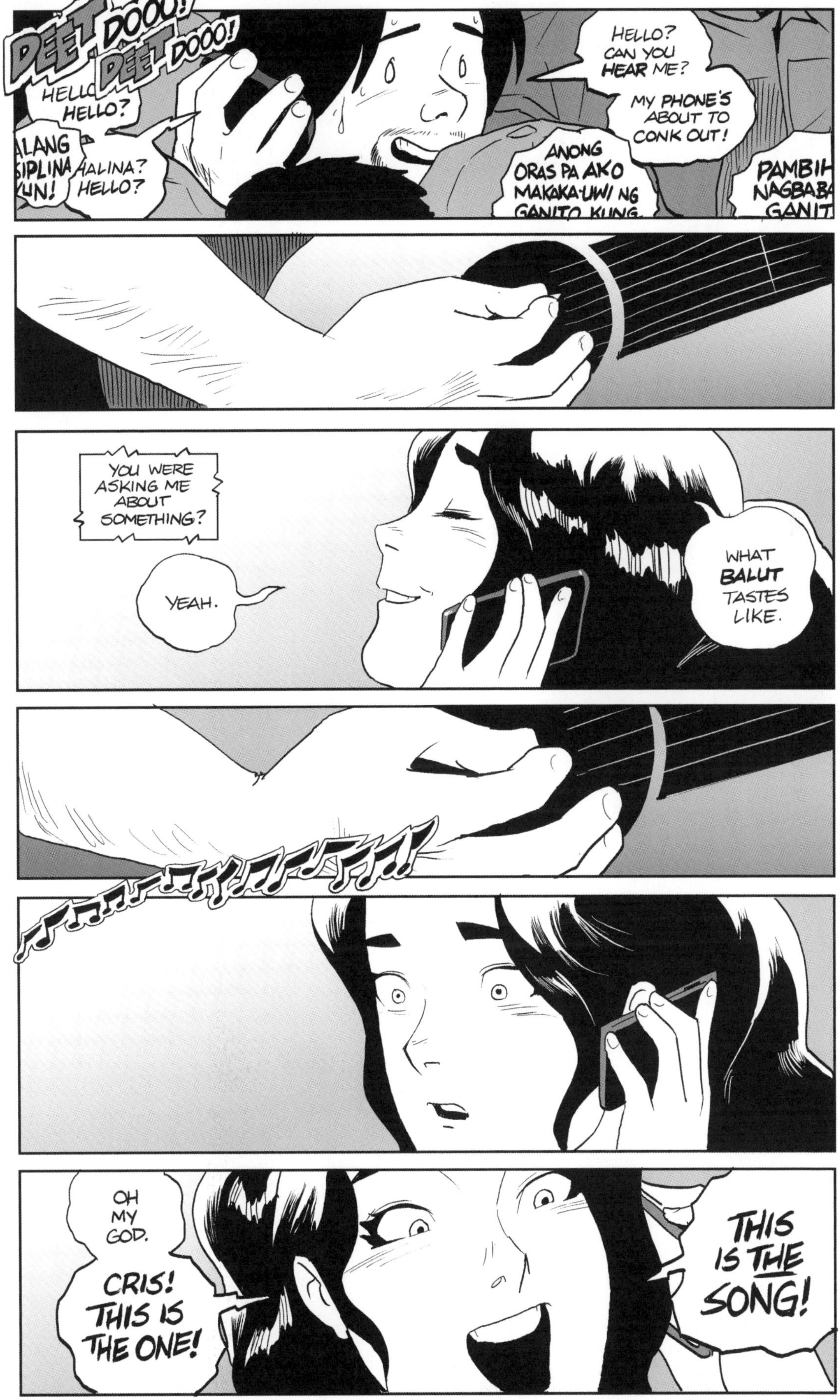
DEET DOOO! DEET DOOO!
HELLO?
HELLO?
HELLO? CAN YOU HEAR ME?
MY PHONE'S ABOUT TO CONK OUT!
ANONG ORAS PA AKO MAKAKA-UWI NG
YOU WERE ASKING ME ABOUT SOMETHING?
YEAH.
WHAT BALUT TASTES LIKE.
OH MY GOD.
CRIS! THIS IS THE ONE!
THIS IS THE SONG!

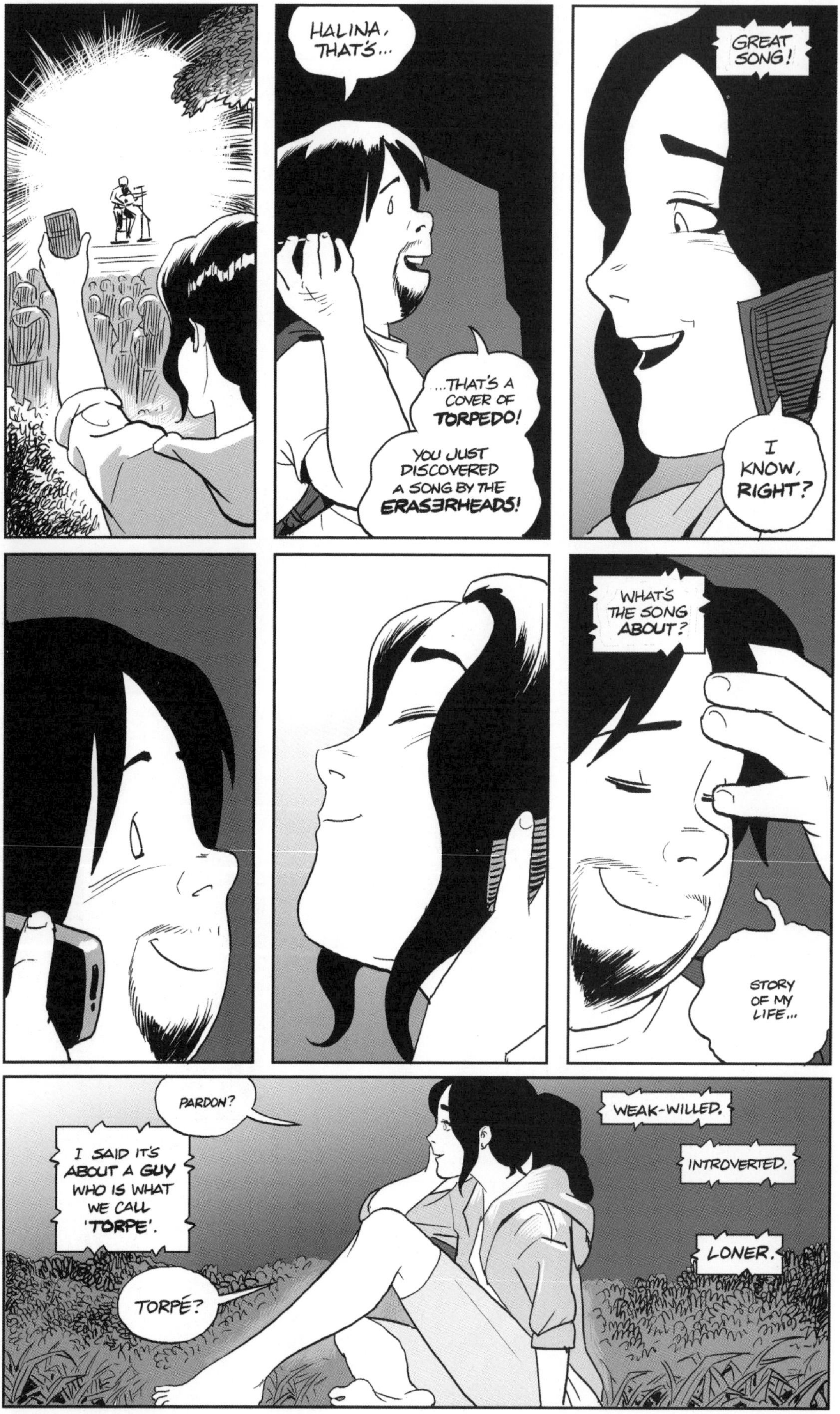
HALINA, THAT'S...
...THAT'S A COVER OF TORPEDO!
YOU JUST DISCOVERED A SONG BY THE ERASERHEADS!
GREAT SONG!
I KNOW, RIGHT?
WHAT'S THE SONG ABOUT?
STORY OF MY LIFE...
PARDON?
I SAID IT'S ABOUT A GUY WHO IS WHAT WE CALL 'TORPE'.
TORPÉ?
WEAK-WILLED.
INTROVERTED.
LONER.

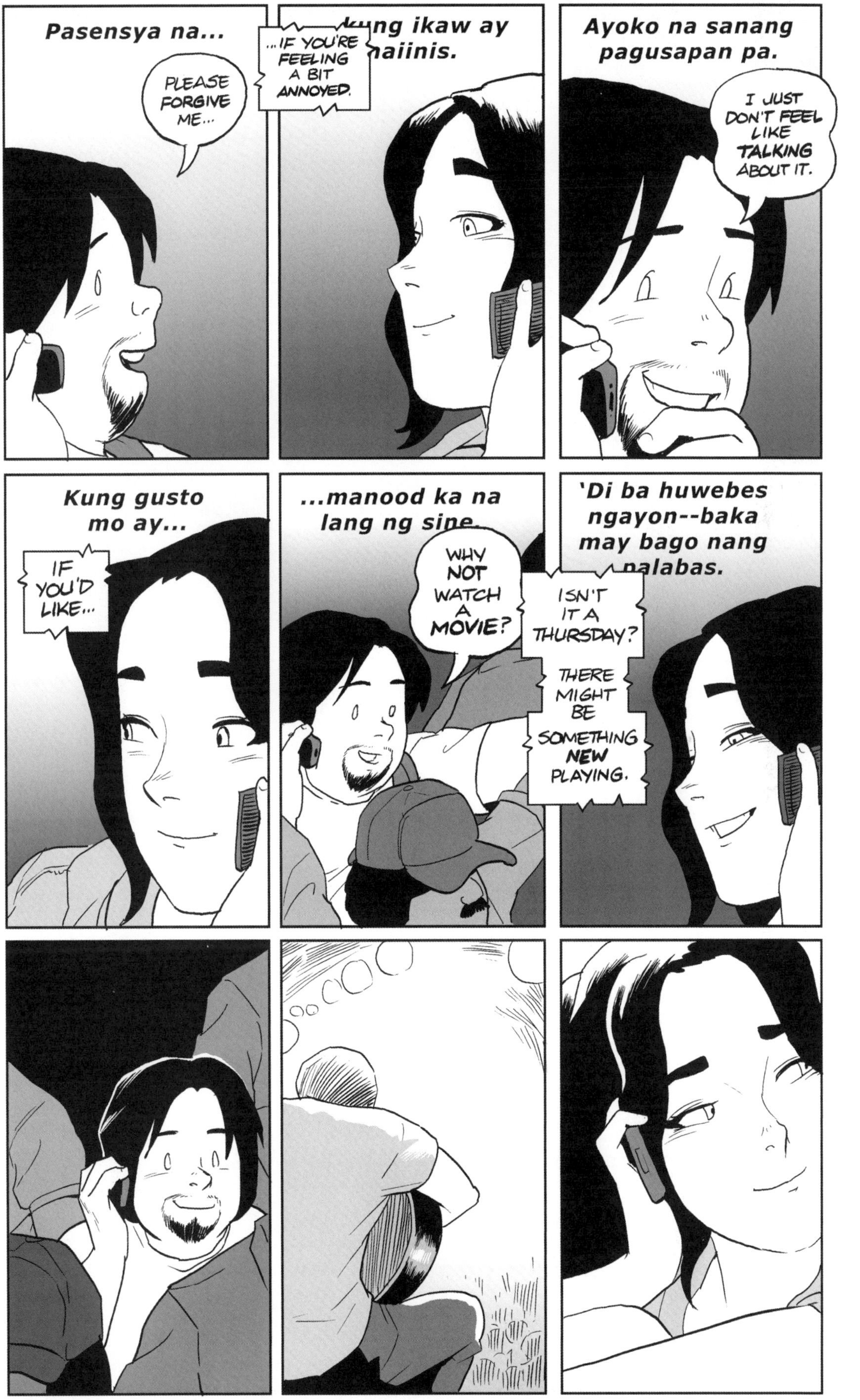
Pasensya na...
PLEASE FORGIVE ME...
...IF YOU'RE FEELING A BIT ANNOYED.
...kung ikaw ay naiinis.
Ayoko na sanang pagusapan pa.
I JUST DON'T FEEL LIKE TALKING ABOUT IT.
Kung gusto mo ay...
IF YOU'D LIKE...
...manood ka na lang ng sine.
WHY NOT WATCH A MOVIE?
'Di ba huwebes ngayon--baka may bago nang palabas.
ISN'T IT A THURSDAY?
THERE MIGHT BE SOMETHING NEW PLAYING.

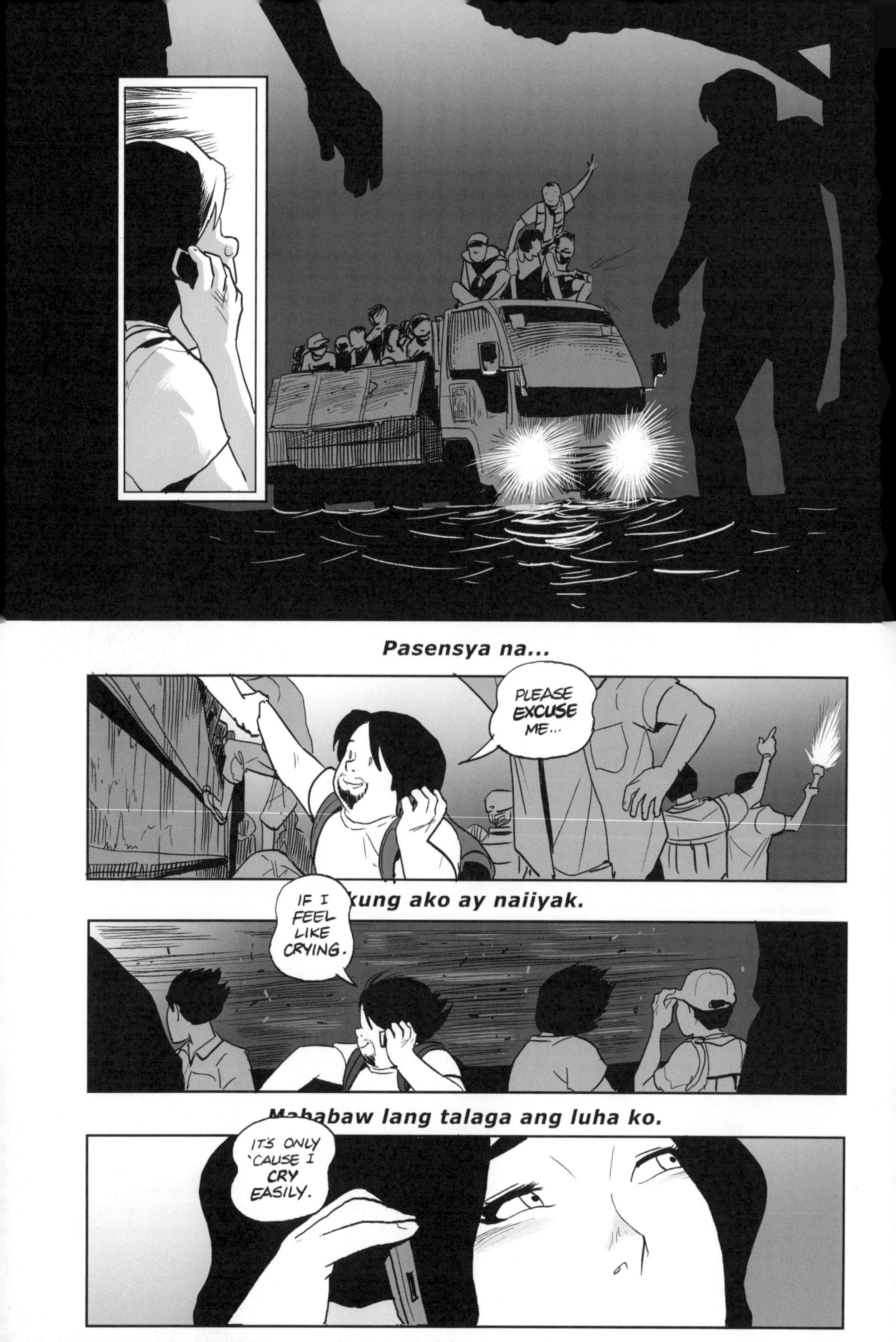

Pasensya na...
PLEASE EXCUSE ME...
kung ako ay naiiyak.
IF I FEEL LIKE CRYING.
Mababaw lang talaga ang luha ko.
IT'S ONLY 'CAUSE I CRY EASILY.

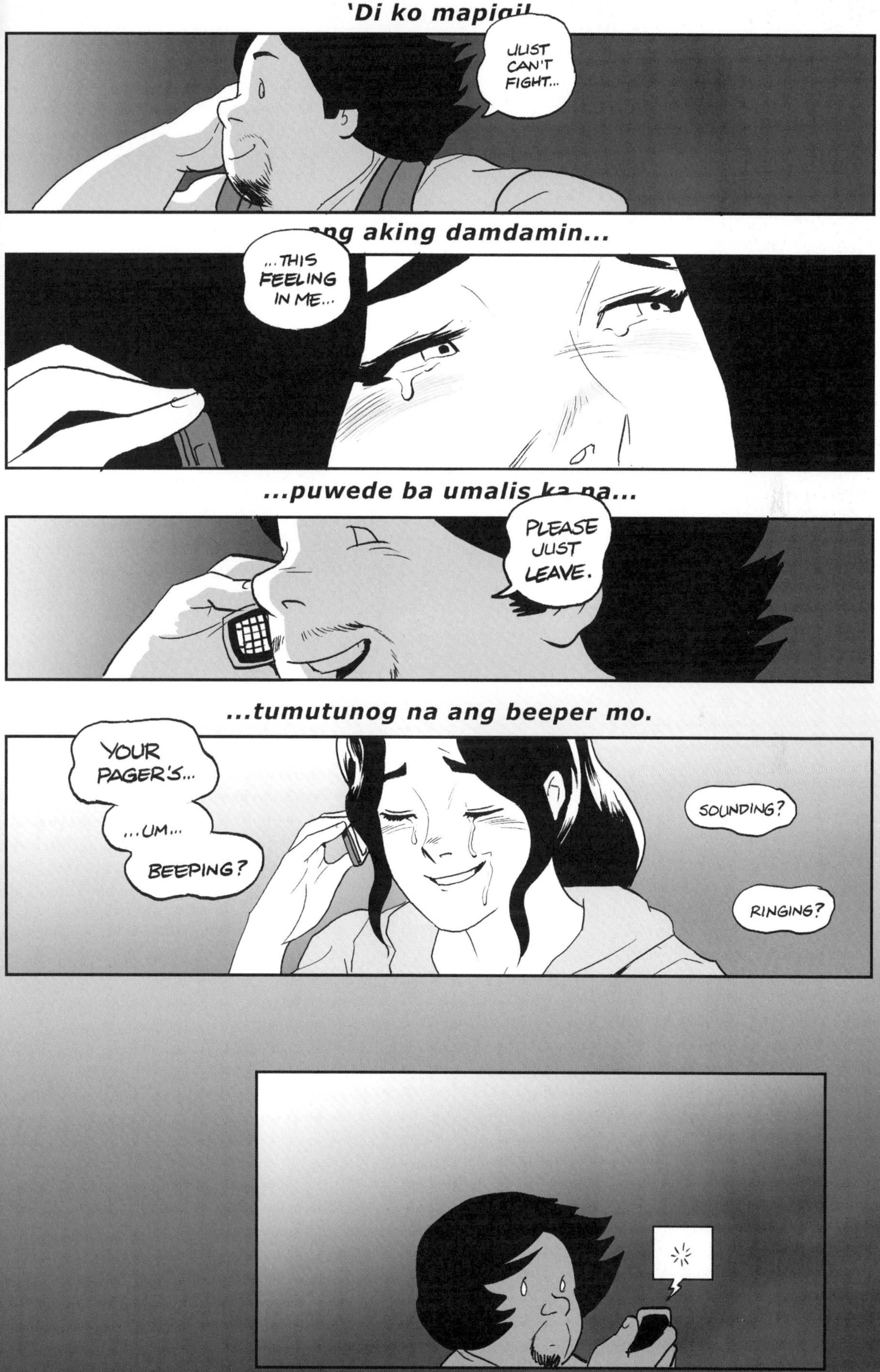
'Di ko mapigil
JUST CAN'T FIGHT...
ang aking damdamin...
...THIS FEELING IN ME...
...puwede ba umalis ka na...
PLEASE JUST LEAVE.
...tumutunog na ang beeper mo.
YOUR PAGER'S...
...UM...
BEEPING?
SOUNDING?
RINGING?

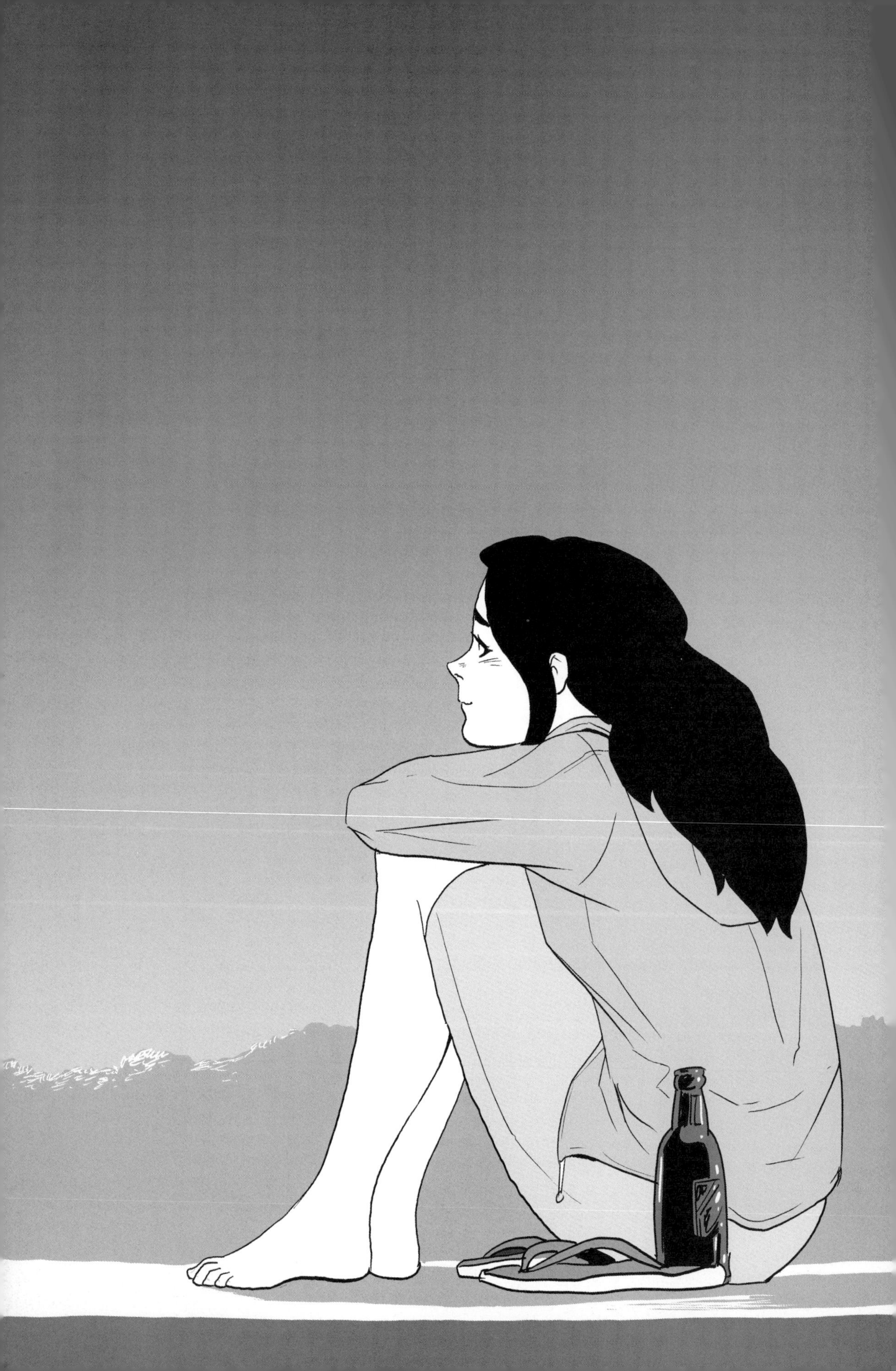

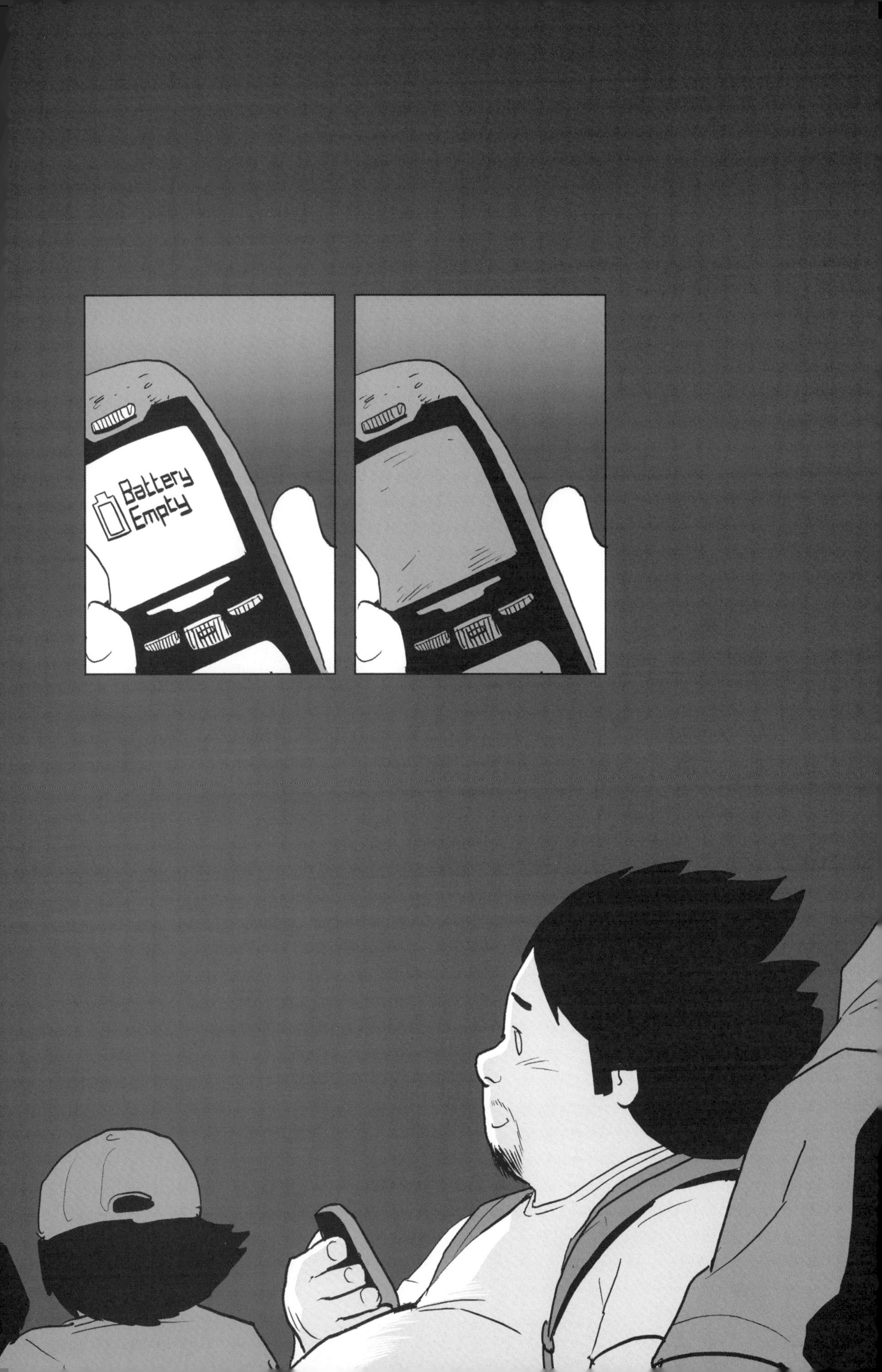
Battery
Empty

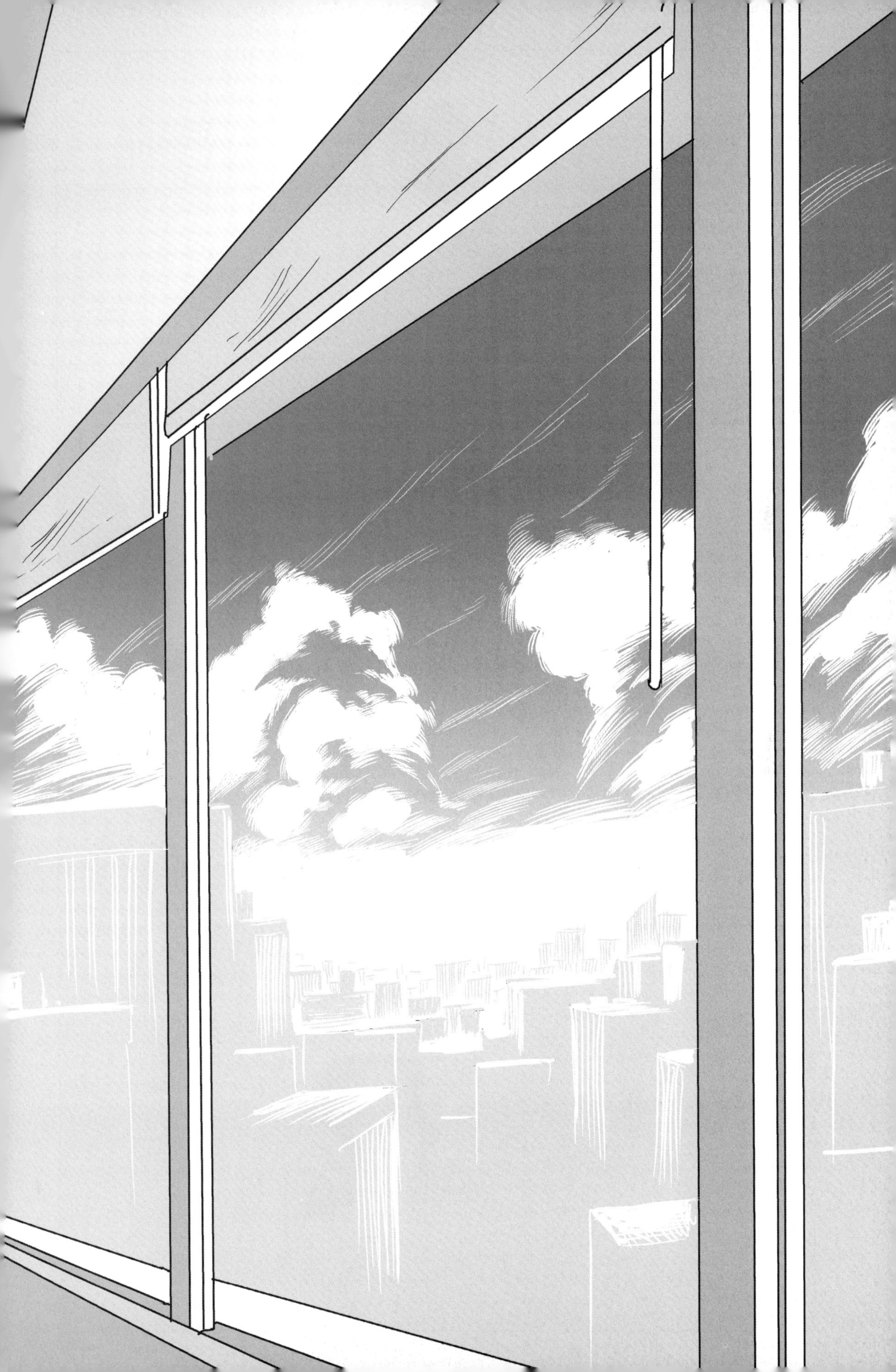

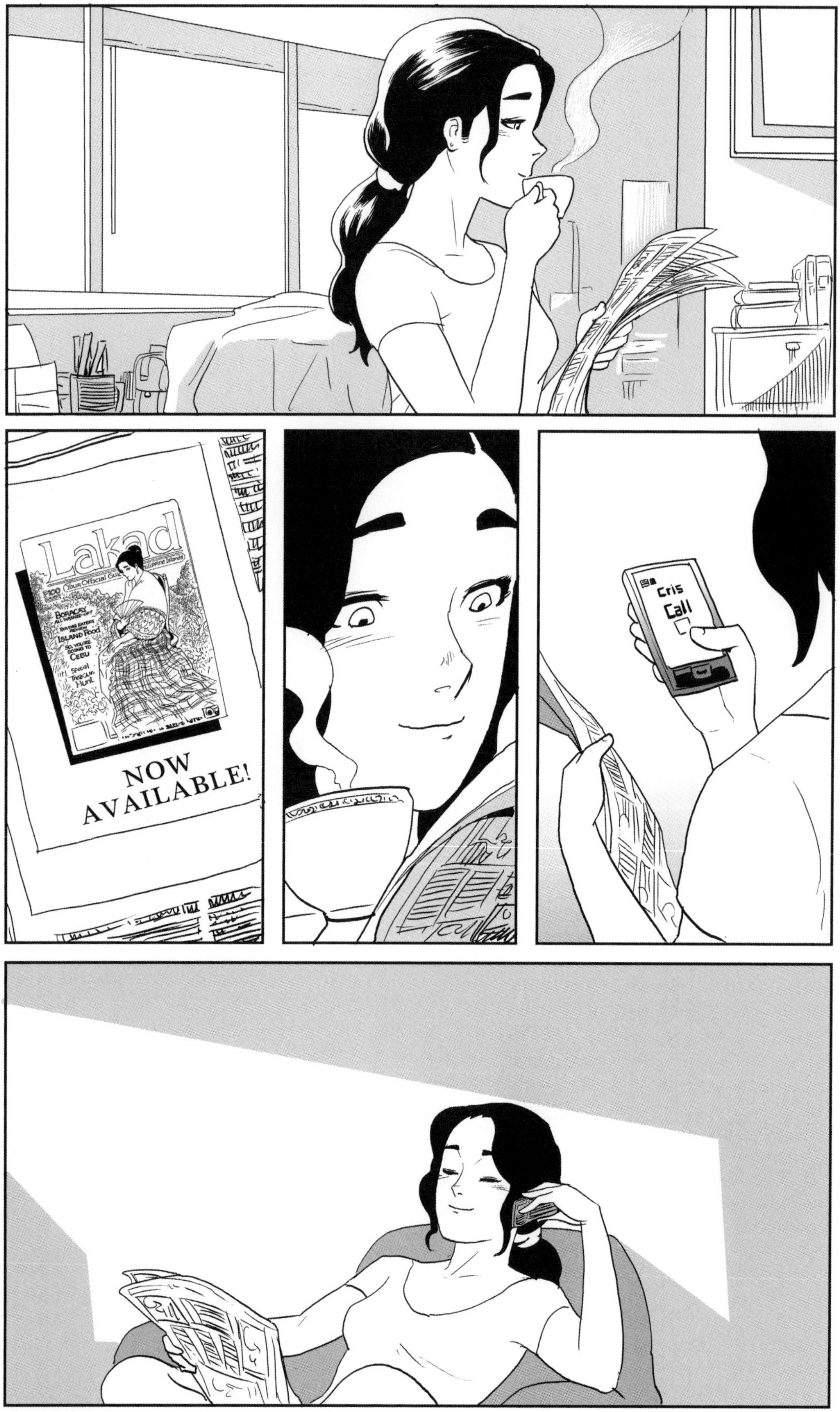
Lakad
Your Official Gui
hilippine Islands
P100
Boracay All Washed-Up?
Roving Eaters Review Island Food
So, You're Going to Cebu
Special Treasur. Hunt
NOW AVAILABLE!
Cris
Call

YES?

OH.

OH, OKAY.

NO. I'LL MEET THEM IN THE LOBBY. MARAMI SALAMAT PO.

TNNG!

SI ATE HALINA!

HEEEY! WHAT A SURPRISE!

AUNTIES! SO NICE TO SEE YOU GUYS AGAIN!

THE GANG'S ALL HERE!

WE PLANNED A SPECIAL SURPRISE.

LIKE A DISPID-- DISPIDI-- DISPIDIDA!

'GOING AWAY PARTY'

ANG ENGLISH, TANGE!

HEEEY! I KNOW WHAT '**TANGE**' MEANS.

SO YOU BETTER APOLOGIZE TO **HER** NOW, OKAY?

HI! HI! HI! H!

A GOING AWAY PARTY?

YES. YOUR AUNTIE HERE TALKED TO A PRODUCER.

PLEASE! PLEASE ATE HALINA, SAY YES!

UM... ...A PRODUCER?

PLEASE ATE HALINA!

YES! COME, LET'S TALK OVER TANGHALIAN.

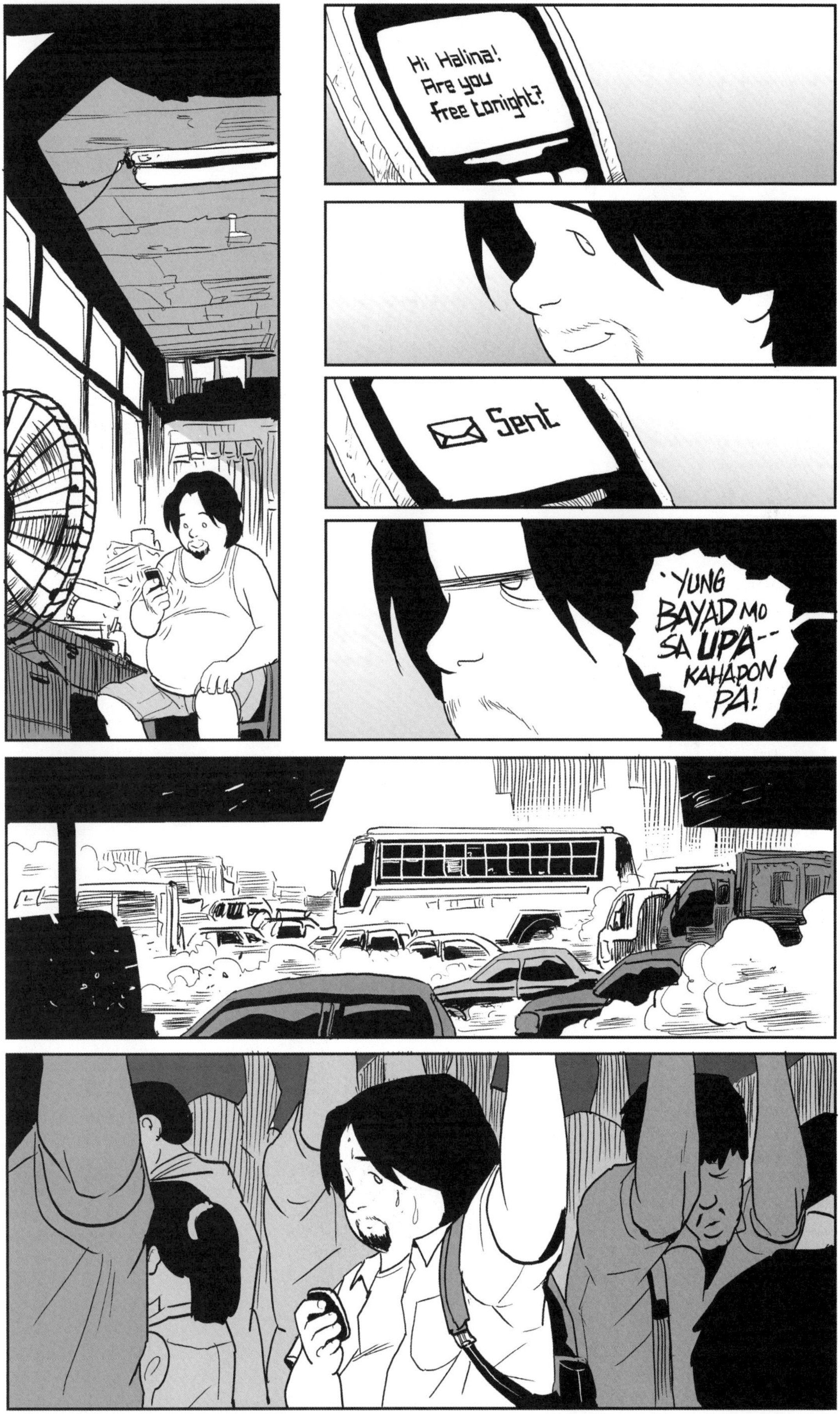
Hi Halina!
Are you
free tonight?
Sent
'YUNG BAYAD MO SA UPA-- KAHAPON PA!

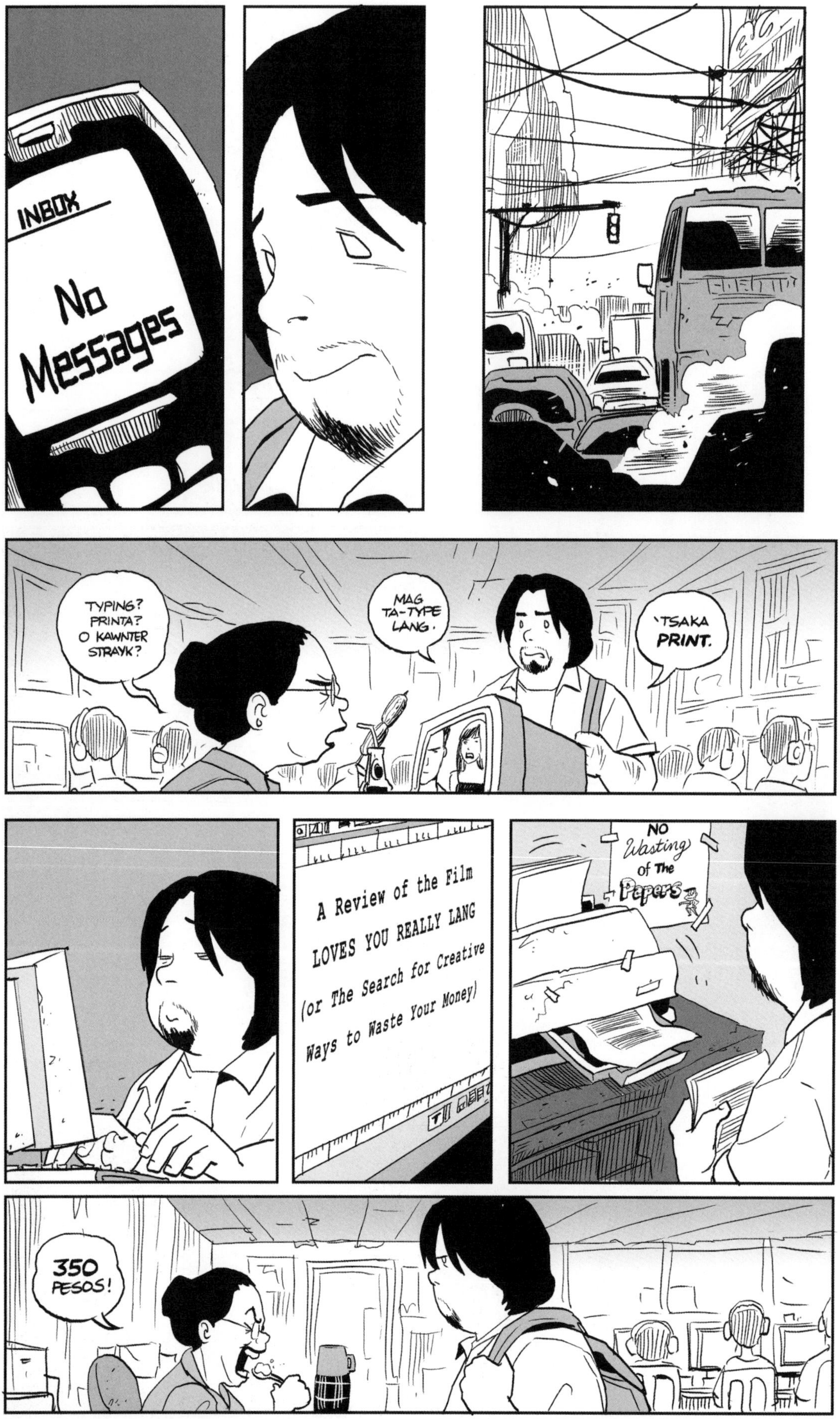
INBOX
No Messages
TYPING? PRINTA? O KAWNTER STRAYK?
MAG TA-TYPE LANG.
`TSAKA PRINT.
A Review of the Film
LOVES YOU REALLY LANG
(or The Search for Creative
Ways to Waste Your Money)
NO Wasting of The Papers
350 PESOS!

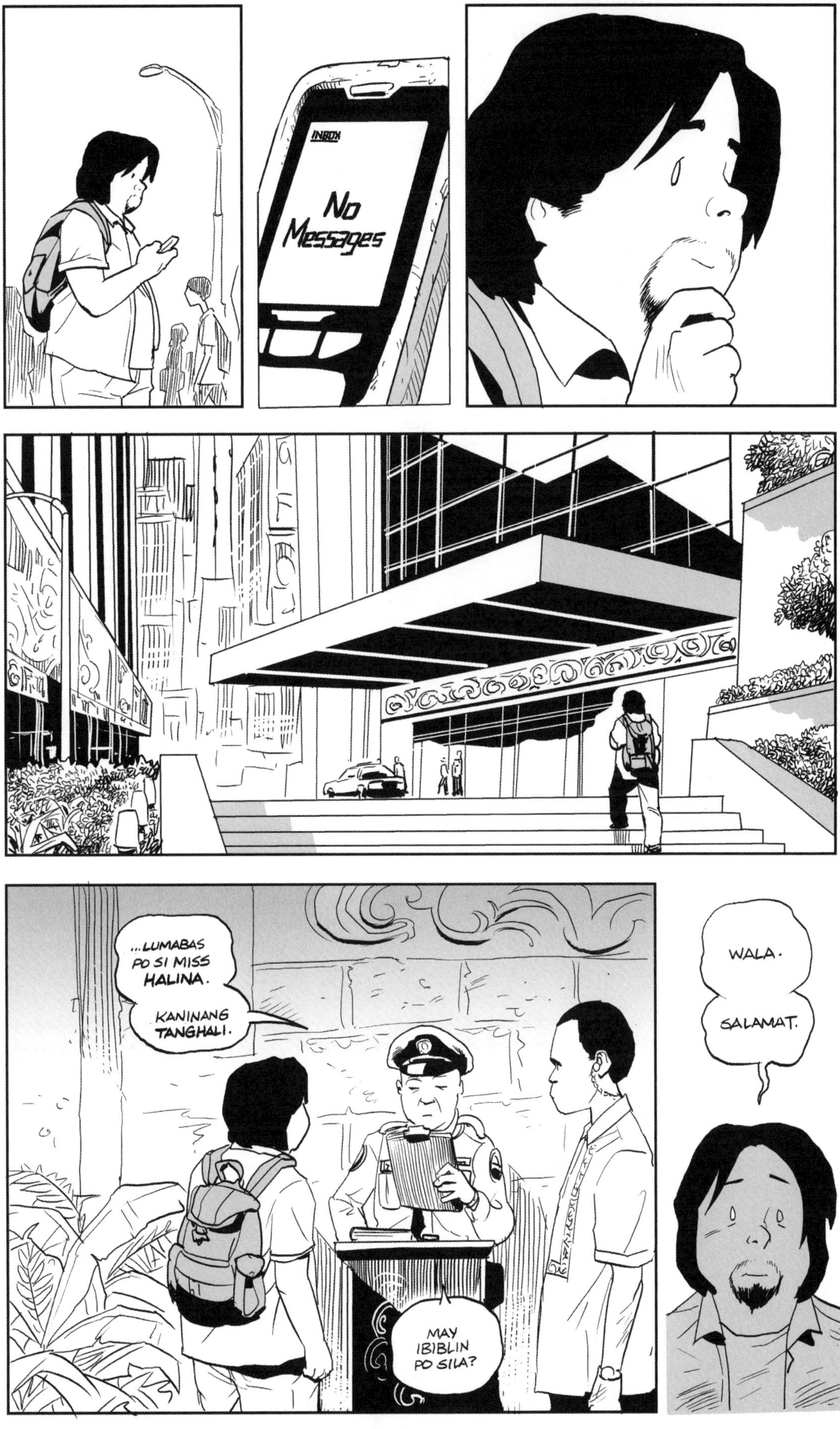
INBOX
No Messages
...LUMABAS PO SI MISS HALINA.
KANINANG TANGHALI.
MAY IBIBLIN PO SILA?
WALA.
SALAMAT.

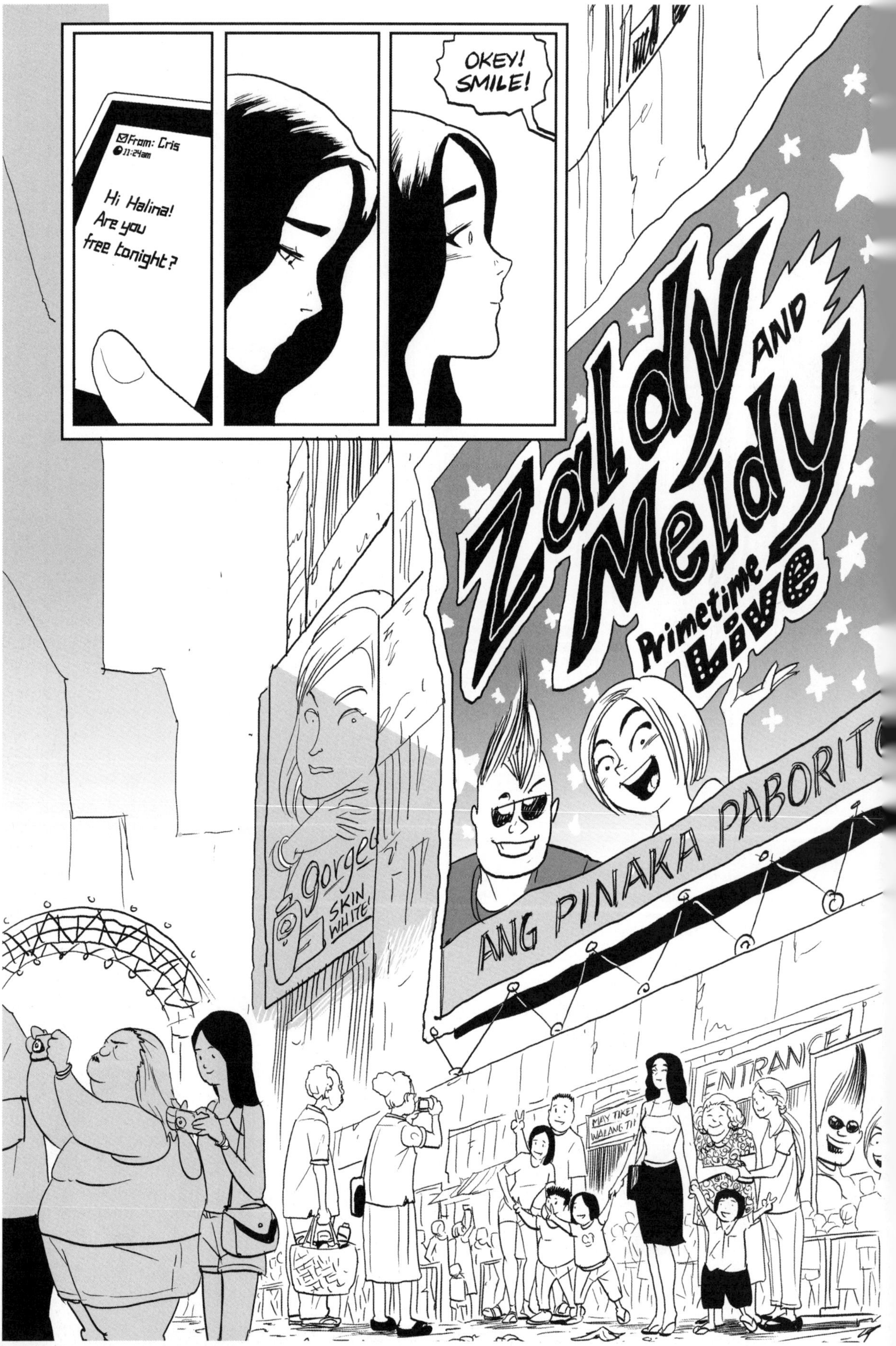
From: Cris
11:24am
Hi Halina! Are you free tonight?
OKEY! SMILE!
Zaldy AND Meldy
Primetime Live
ANG PINAKA PABORIT
gorge
SKIN WHITE
ENTRANCE
MAY TIKET
WALANG TI

Chapter 5
All Mixed Up

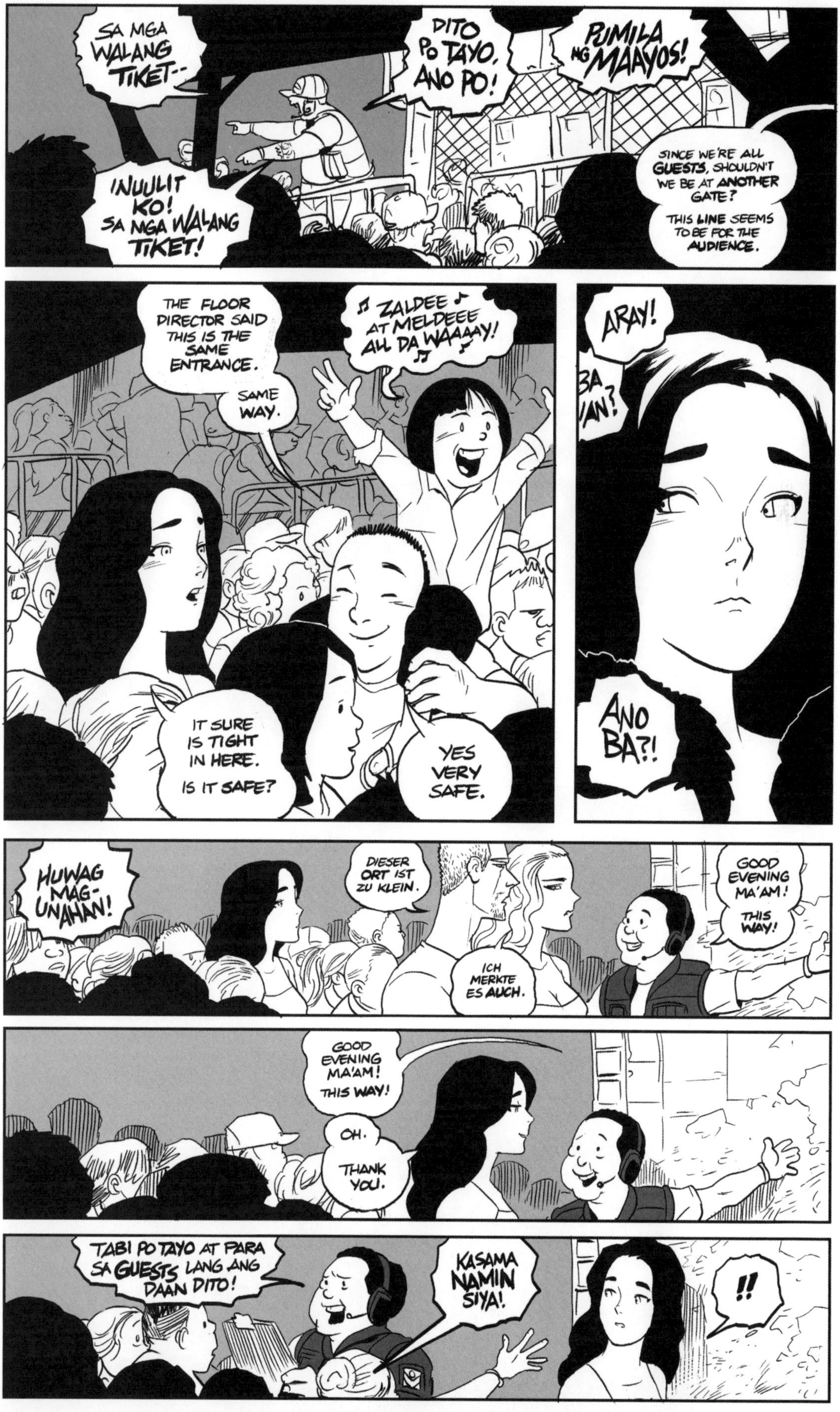
SA MGA WALANG TIKET--
DITO PO TAYO, ANO PO!
PUMILA NG MAAYOS!
INUULIT KO! SA NGA WALANG TIKET!
SINCE WE'RE ALL GUESTS, SHOULDN'T WE BE AT ANOTHER GATE?
THIS LINE SEEMS TO BE FOR THE AUDIENCE.
THE FLOOR DIRECTOR SAID THIS IS THE SAME ENTRANCE.
SAME WAY.
ZALDEE AT MELDEEE ALL DA WAAAAY!
IT SURE IS TIGHT IN HERE.
IS IT SAFE?
YES VERY SAFE.
ARAY!
BA ...AN?
ANO BA?!
HUWAG MAG-UNAHAN!
DIESER ORT IST ZU KLEIN.
ICH MERKTE ES AUCH.
GOOD EVENING MA'AM! THIS WAY!
GOOD EVENING MA'AM! THIS WAY!
OH.
THANK YOU.
TABI PO TAYO AT PARA SA GUESTS LANG ANG DAAN DITO!
KASAMA NAMIN SIYA!
!!

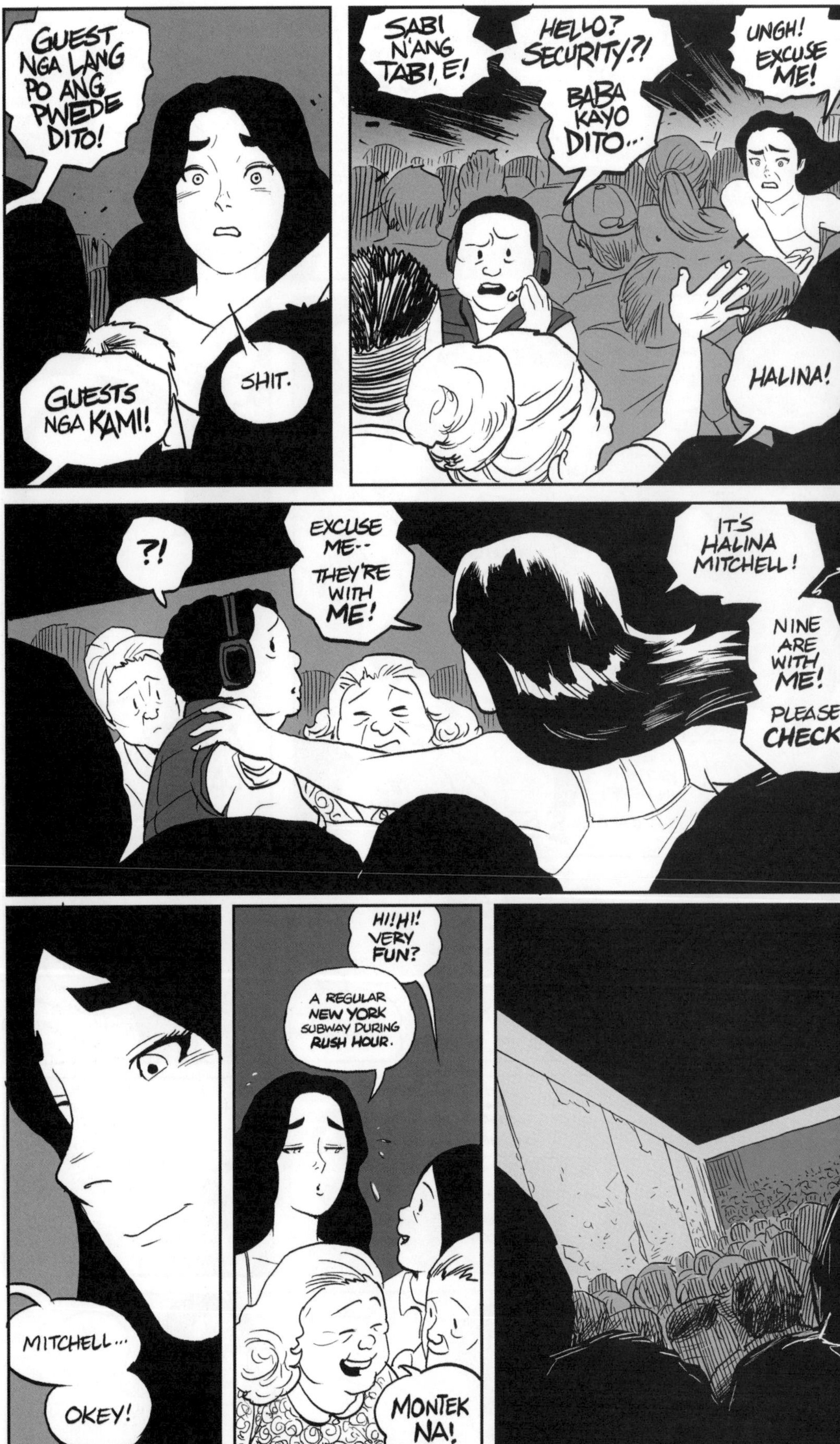
GUEST NGA LANG PO ANG PWEDE DITO!
GUESTS NGA KAMI!
SHIT.
SABI N'ANG TABI, E!
HELLO? SECURITY?!
BABA KAYO DITO...
UNGH! EXCUSE ME!
HALINA!
?!
EXCUSE ME-- THEY'RE WITH ME!
IT'S HALINA MITCHELL!
NINE ARE WITH ME!
PLEASE CHECK!
MITCHELL...
OKEY!
HI!HI! VERY FUN?
A REGULAR NEW YORK SUBWAY DURING RUSH HOUR.
MONTEK NA!

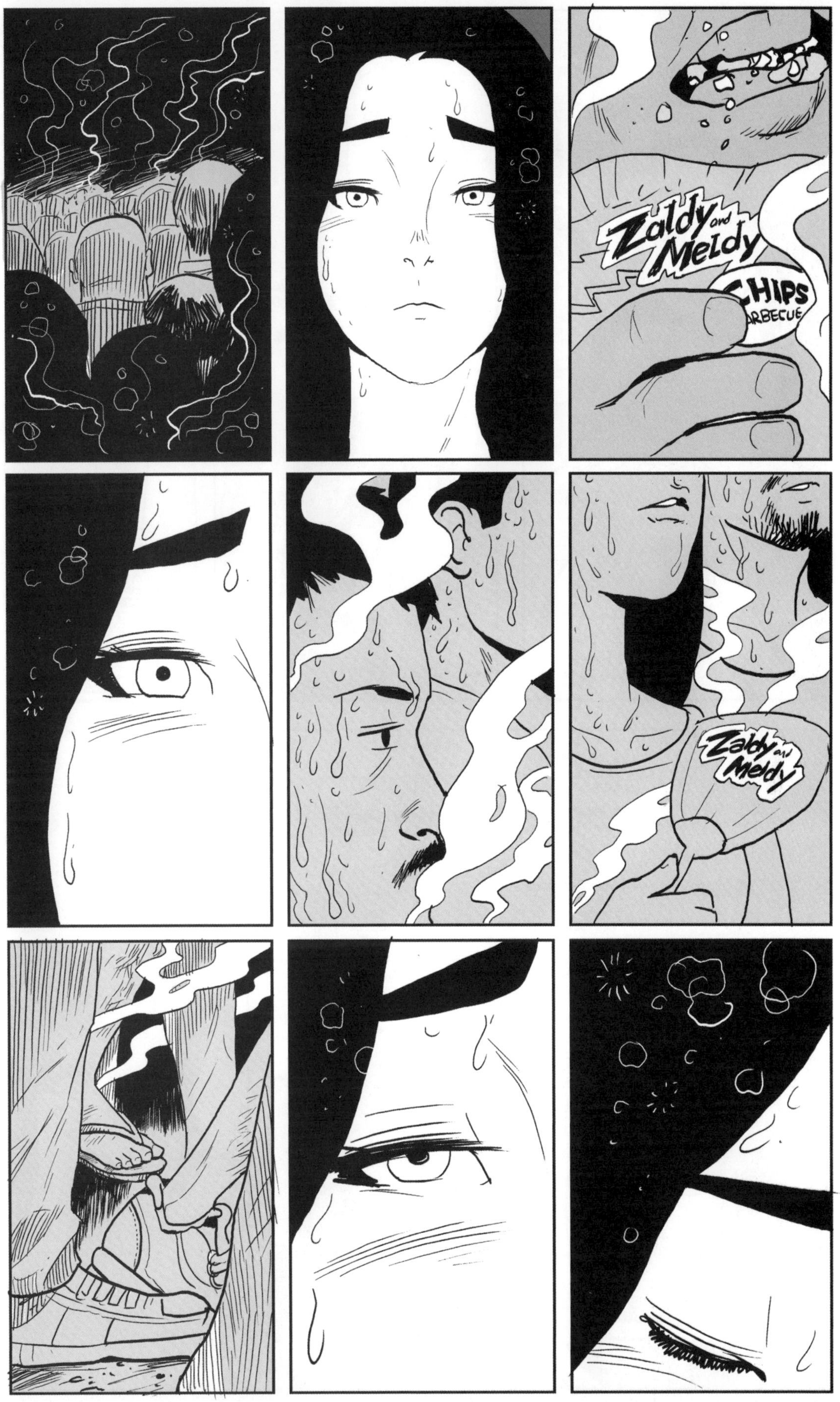
Zaldy and Meldy
CHIPS
ARBECUE
Zaldy and Meldy

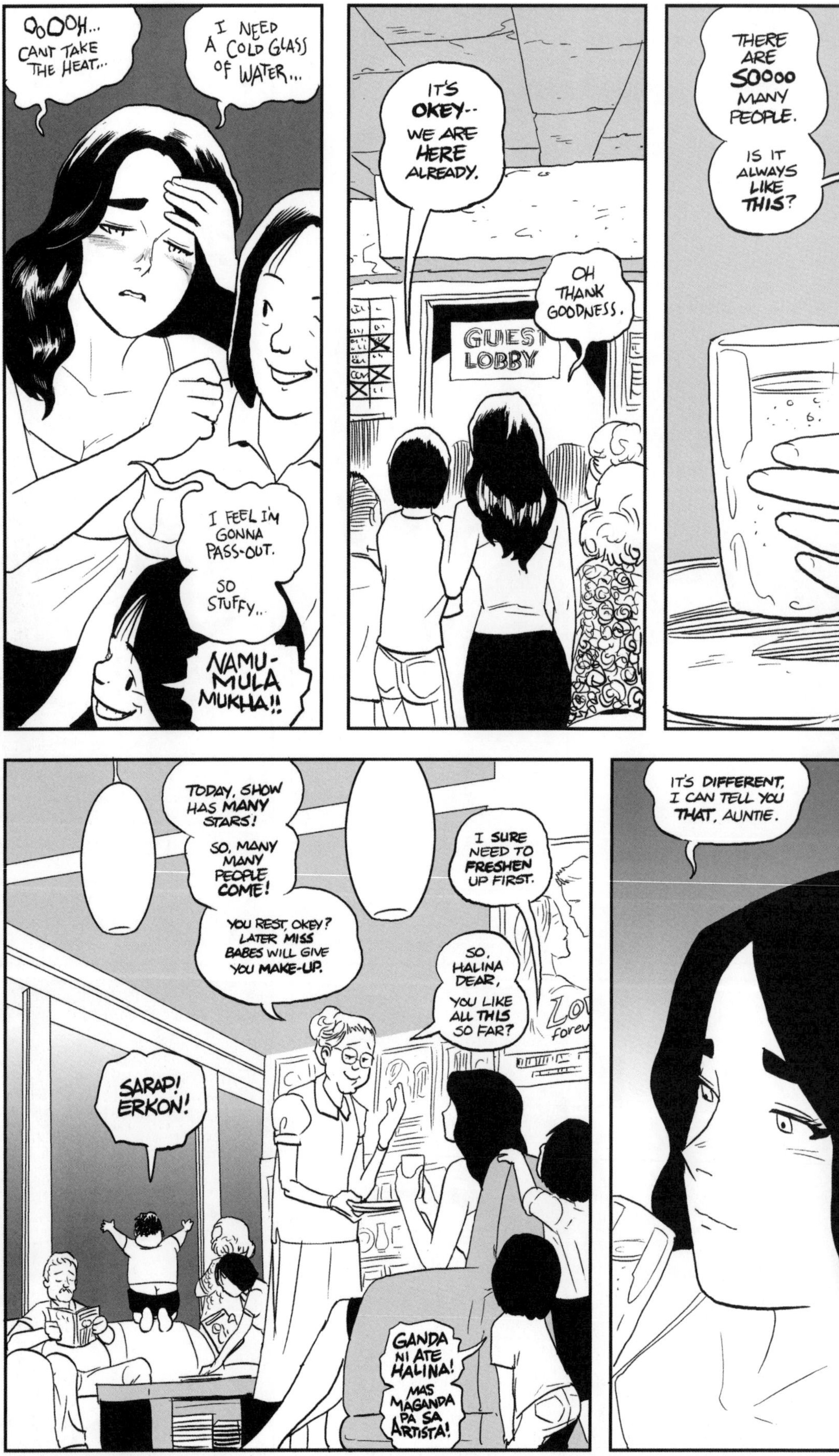
OoOOH... CANT TAKE THE HEAT...
I NEED A COLD GLASS OF WATER...
I FEEL I'M GONNA PASS-OUT.
SO STUFFY...
NAMU-MULA MUKHA!!
IT'S OKEY.. WE ARE HERE ALREADY.
GUEST LOBBY
OH THANK GOODNESS.
THERE ARE SOooo MANY PEOPLE.
IS IT ALWAYS LIKE THIS?
TODAY, SHOW HAS MANY STARS!
SO, MANY MANY PEOPLE COME!
YOU REST, OKEY? LATER MISS BABES WILL GIVE YOU MAKE-UP.
I SURE NEED TO FRESHEN UP FIRST.
SO, HALINA DEAR, YOU LIKE ALL THIS SO FAR?
SARAP! ERKON!
GANDA NI ATE HALINA! MAS MAGANDA PA SA ARTISTA!
IT'S DIFFERENT, I CAN TELL YOU THAT, AUNTIE.

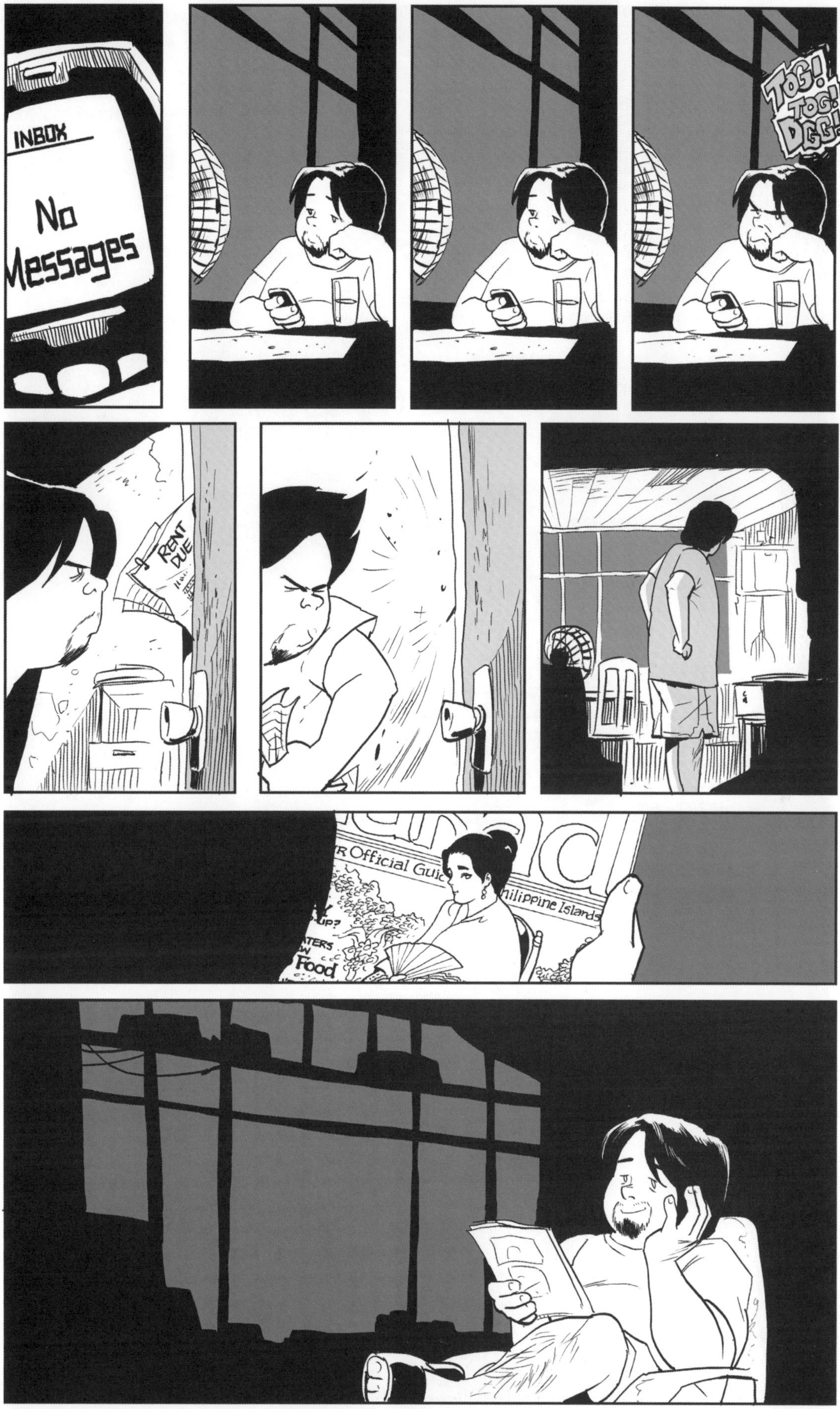
INBOX
No Messages
TOG! TOG! DGG!
RENT DUE
Official Guide
Philippine Islands
Food

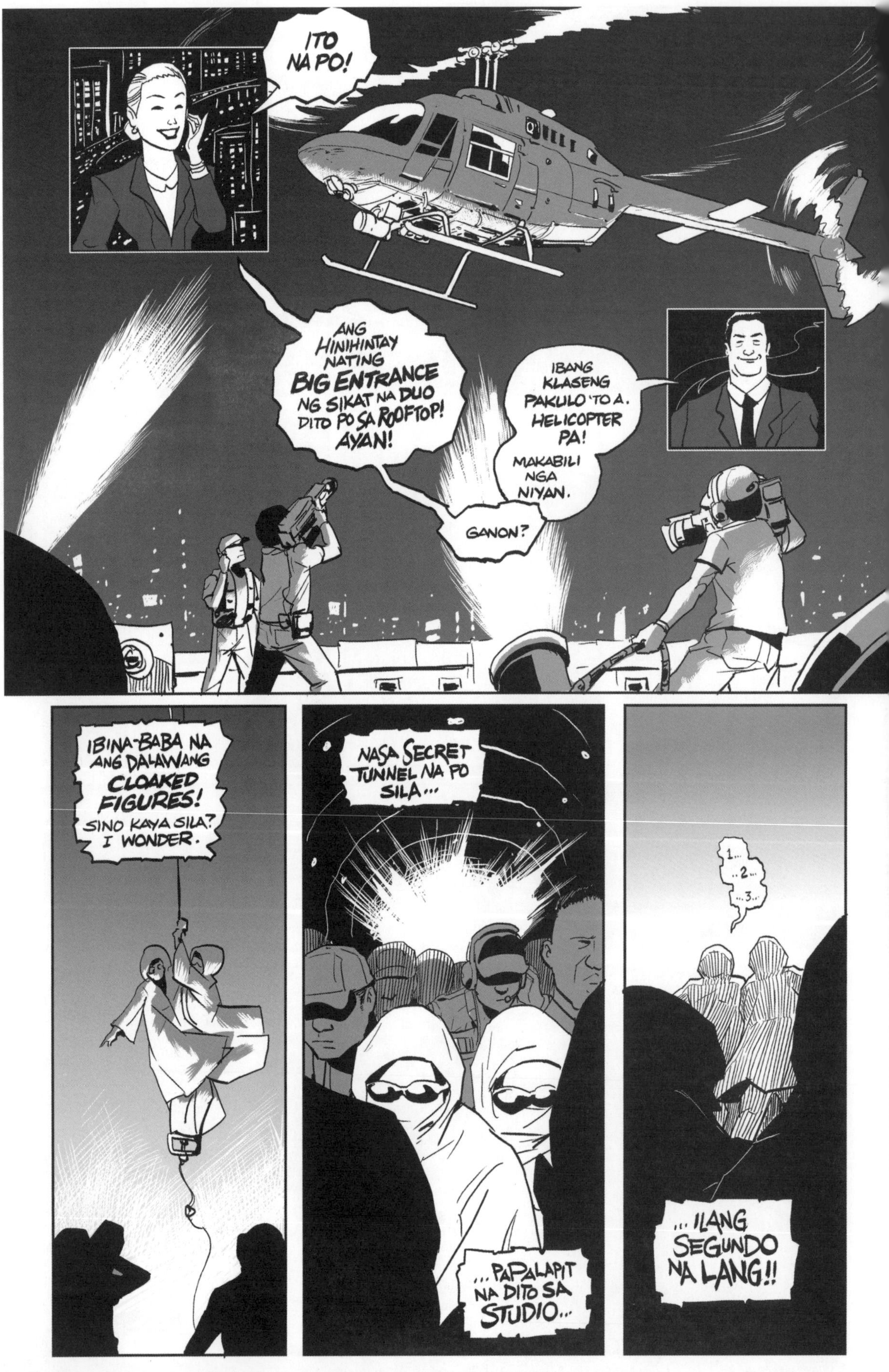
ITO NA PO!
ANG HINIHINTAY NATING BIG ENTRANCE NG SIKAT NA DUO DITO PO SA ROOFTOP! AYAN!
IBANG KLASENG PAKULO 'TO A. HELICOPTER PA!
MAKABILI NGA NIYAN.
GANON?
IBINA-BABA NA ANG DALAWANG CLOAKED FIGURES! SINO KAYA SILA? I WONDER.
NASA SECRET TUNNEL NA PO SILA...
...PAPALAPIT NA DITO SA STUDIO...
1...
..2...
...3...
...ILANG SEGUNDO NA LANG!!

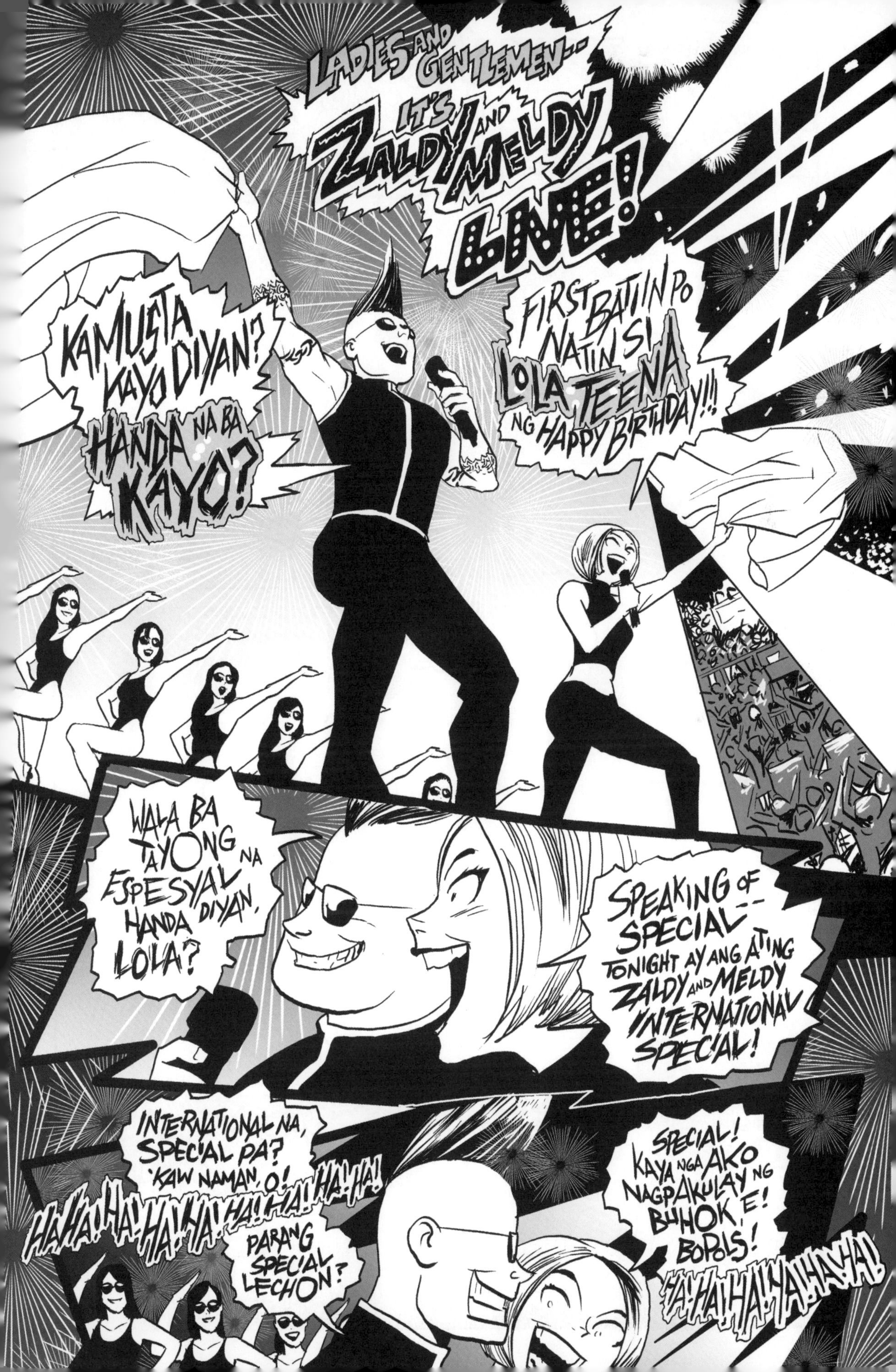

LADIES AND GENTLEMEN--
IT'S ZALDY AND MELDY LIVE!
KAMUSTA KAYO DIYAN? HANDA NA BA KAYO?
FIRST BATIIN PO NATIN SI LOLA TEENA NG HAPPY BIRTHDAY!!!
WALA BA TAYONG ESPESYAL NA HANDA DIYAN, LOLA?
SPEAKING OF SPECIAL-- SPECIAL TONIGHT AY ANG ATING ZALDY AND MELDY INTERNATIONAL SPECIAL!
INTERNATIONAL NA, SPECIAL PA? 'KAW NAMAN, O!
HA HA! HA! HA! HA! HA! HA! HA! HA!
PARANG SPECIAL LECHON?
SPECIAL! KAYA NGA AKO NAGPAKULAY NG BUHOK E! BOPOLS!
HA! HA! HA! HA! HA!

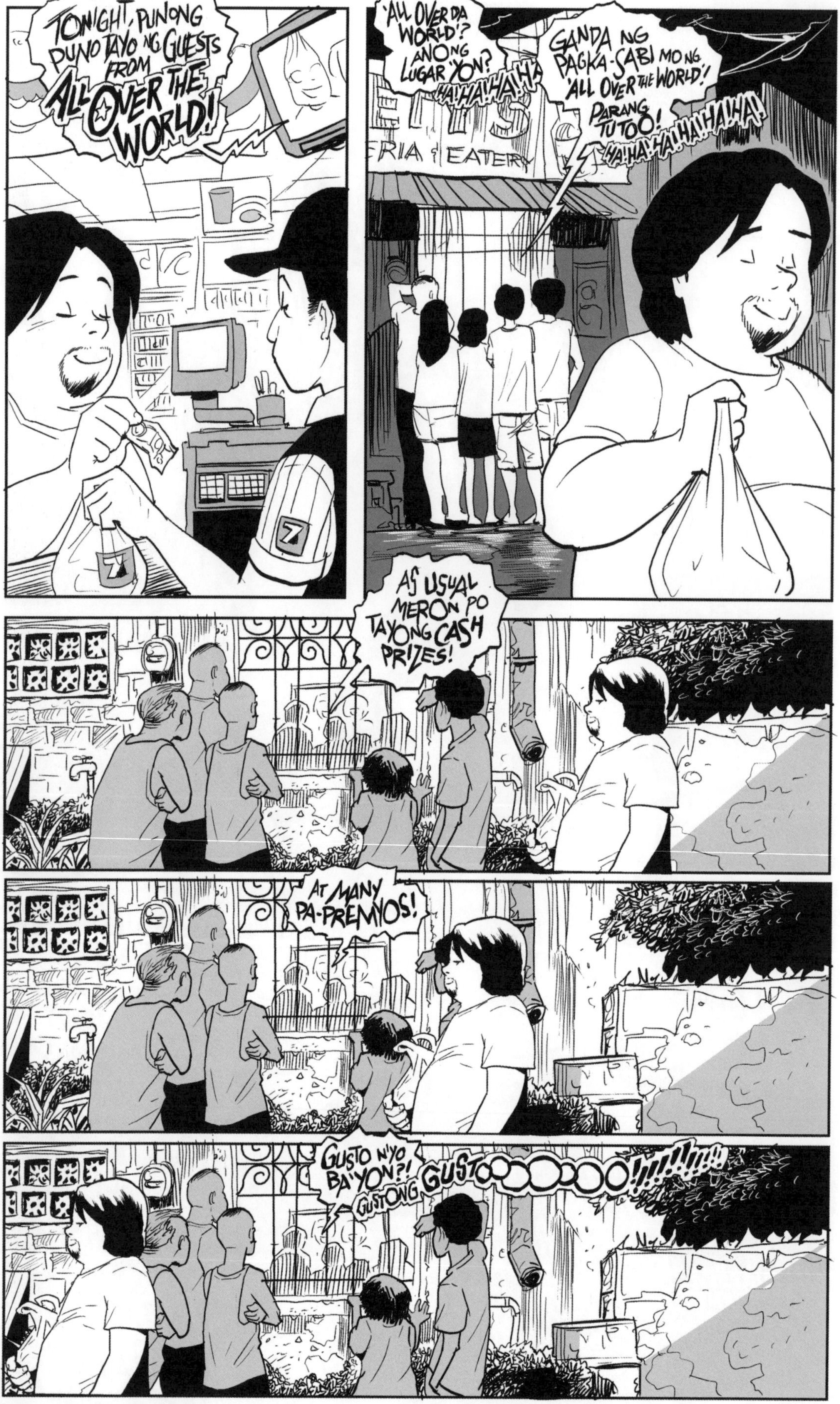
TONIGHT, PUNONG PUNO TAYO NG GUESTS FROM ALL OVER THE WORLD!
'ALL OVER DA WORLD'? ANONG LUGAR 'YON?
HA! HA! HA! HA
GANDA NG PAGKA-SABI MO NG 'ALL OVER THE WORLD'! PARANG TUTOO!
HA! HA! HA! HA! HA! HA!
AS USUAL MERON PO TAYONG CASH PRIZES!
AT MANY PA-PREMYOS!
GUSTO N'YO BA 'YON?!
GUSTONG GUSTOOOOOOOOO!!!!!!!!!

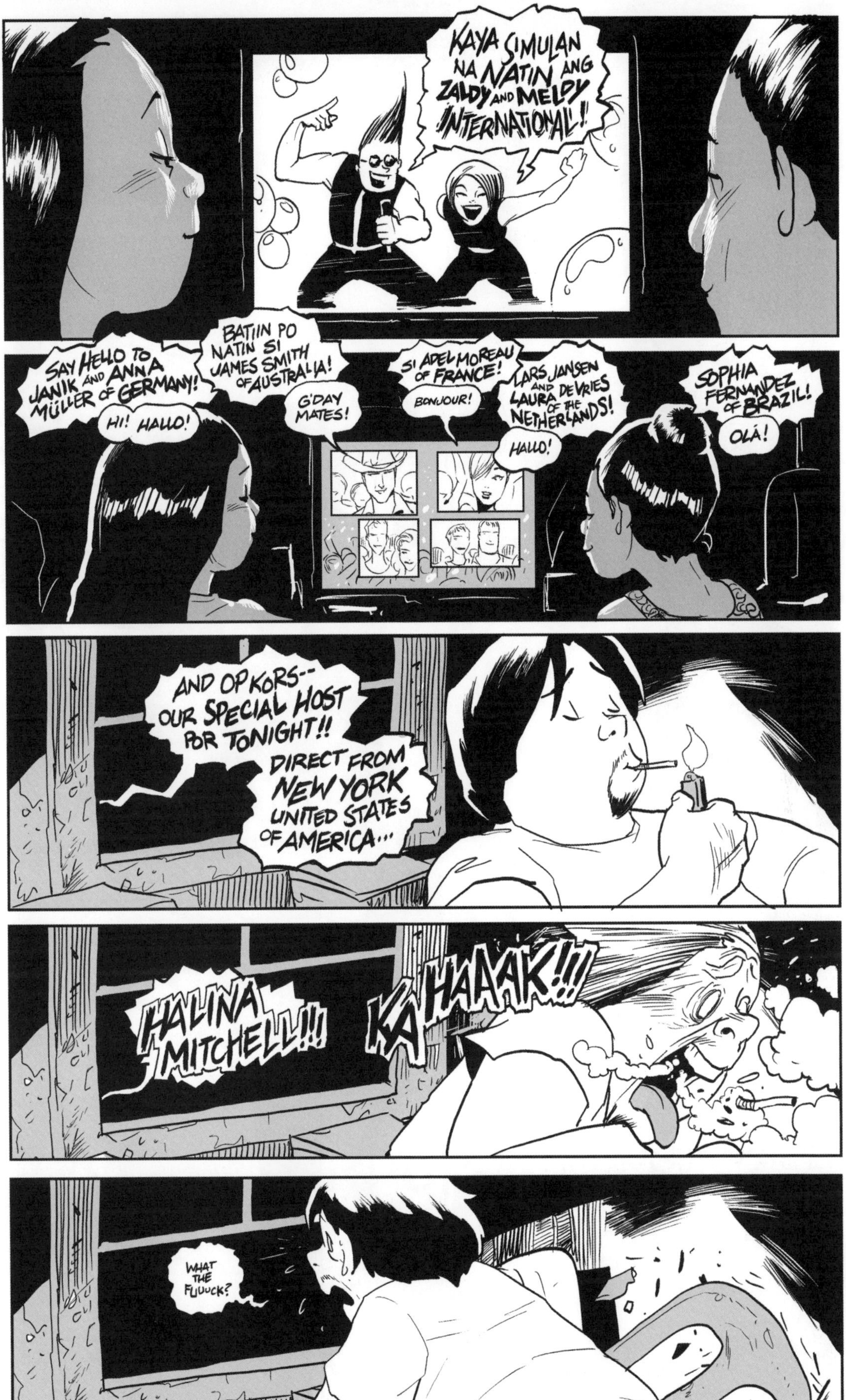
KAYA SIMULAN NA NATIN ANG ZALDY AND MELODY INTERNATIONAL!
SAY HELLO TO JANIK AND ANNA MÜLLER OF GERMANY!
HI! HALLO!
BATIIN PO NATIN SI JAMES SMITH OF AUSTRALIA!
G'DAY MATES!
SI ADEL MOREAU OF FRANCE!
BONJOUR!
LARS JANSEN AND LAURA DEVRIES OF THE NETHERLANDS!
HALLO!
SOPHIA FERNANDEZ OF BRAZIL!
OLÁ!
AND OP KORS-- OUR SPECIAL HOST POR TONIGHT!!
DIRECT FROM NEW YORK UNITED STATES OF AMERICA...
HALINA MITCHELL!!!
KAHAAAK!!!
WHAT THE FUUUCK?

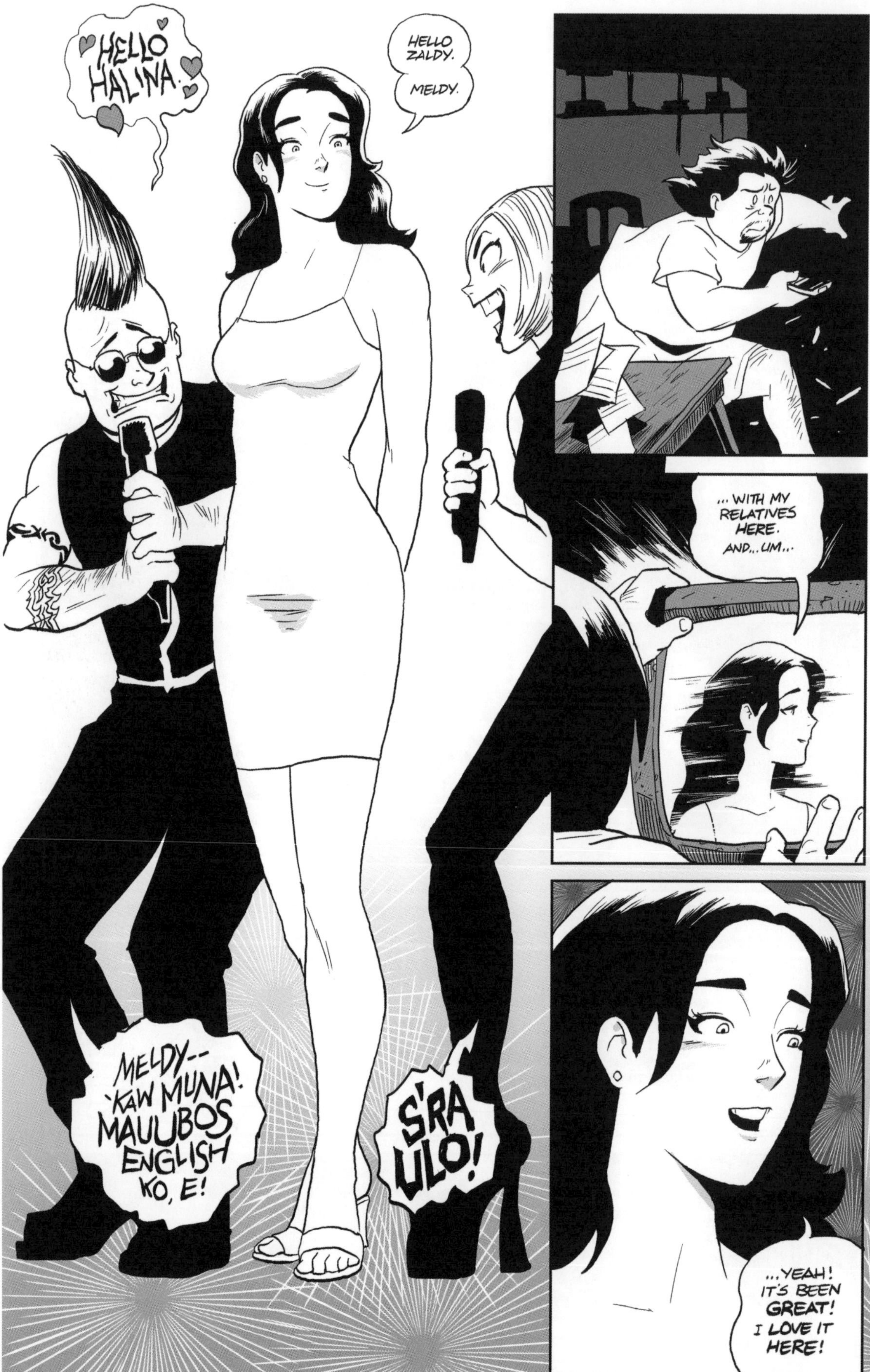
HELLO HALINA.
HELLO ZALDY.
MELDY.
... WITH MY RELATIVES HERE. AND... UM...
MELDY-- 'KAW MUNA! MAUUBOS ENGLISH KO, E!
S'RA ULO!
... YEAH! IT'S BEEN GREAT! I LOVE IT HERE!

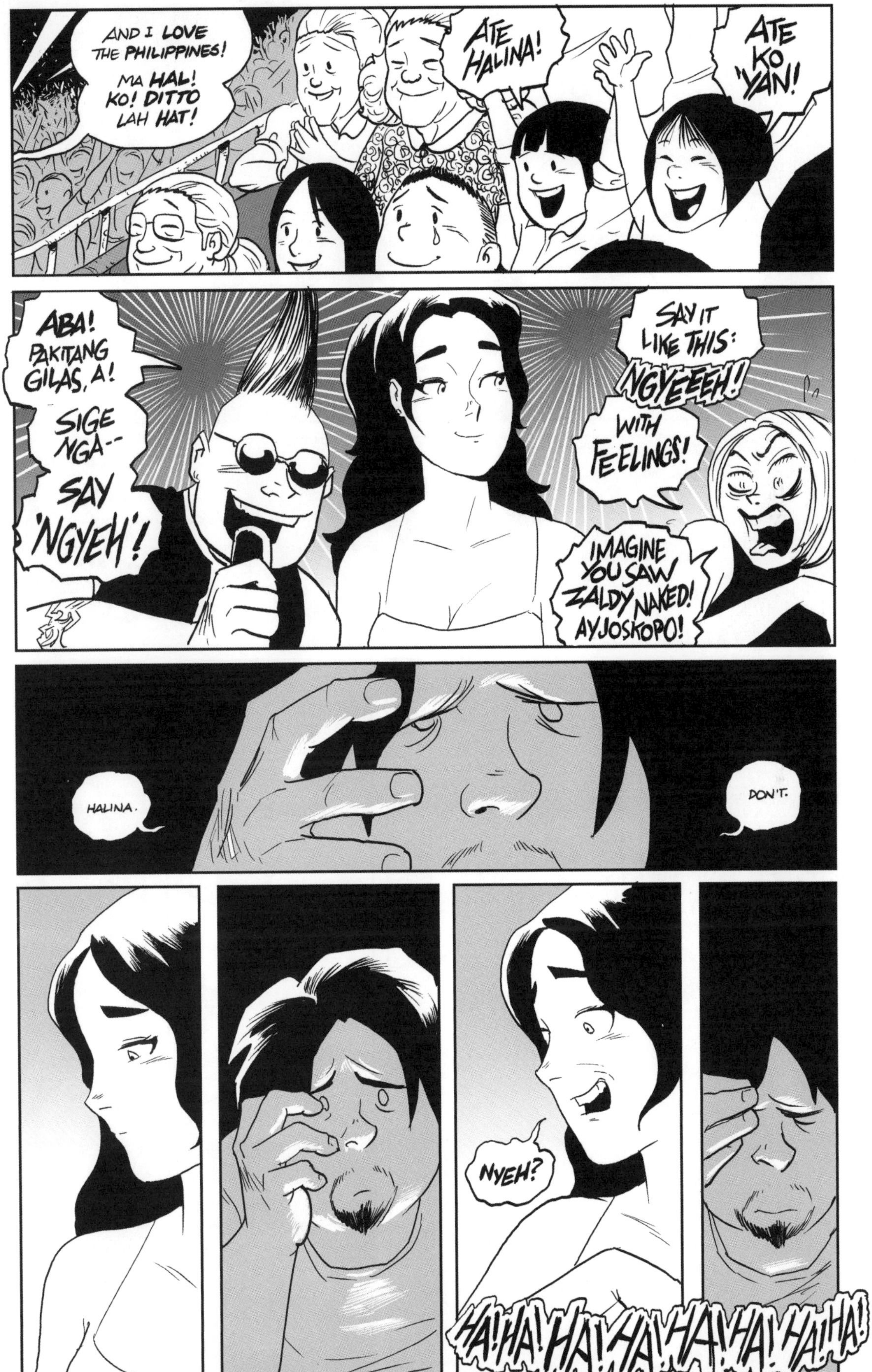

AND I LOVE THE PHILIPPINES!
MA HAL! KO! DITTO LAH HAT!
ATE HALINA!
ATE KO 'YAN!
ABA! PAKITANG GILAS, A!
SIGE NGA-- SAY 'NGYEH'!
SAY IT LIKE THIS: NGYEEEH!
WITH FEELINGS!
IMAGINE YOU SAW ZALDY NAKED! AYJOSKOPO!
HALINA.
DON'T.
NYEH?
HA! HA! HA! HA! HA! HA! HA! HA!

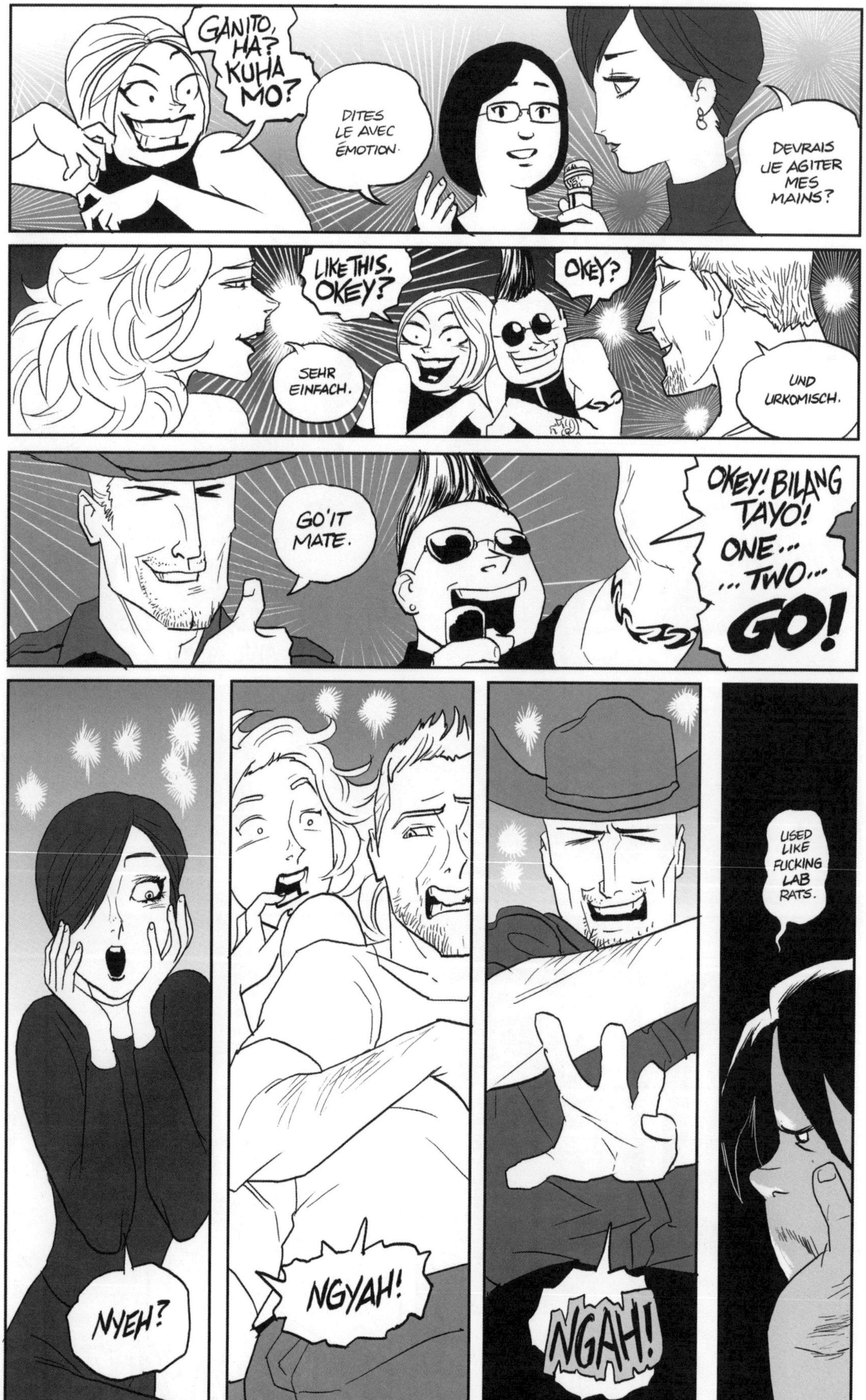
GANITO, HA? KUHA MO?
DITES LE AVEC ÉMOTION.
DEVRAIS UE AGITER MES MAINS?
LIKE THIS, OKEY?
OKEY?
SEHR EINFACH.
UND URKOMISCH.
GO'IT MATE.
OKEY! BILANG TAYO! ONE... ...TWO... GO!
NYEH?
NGYAH!
NGAH!
USED LIKE FUCKING LAB RATS.

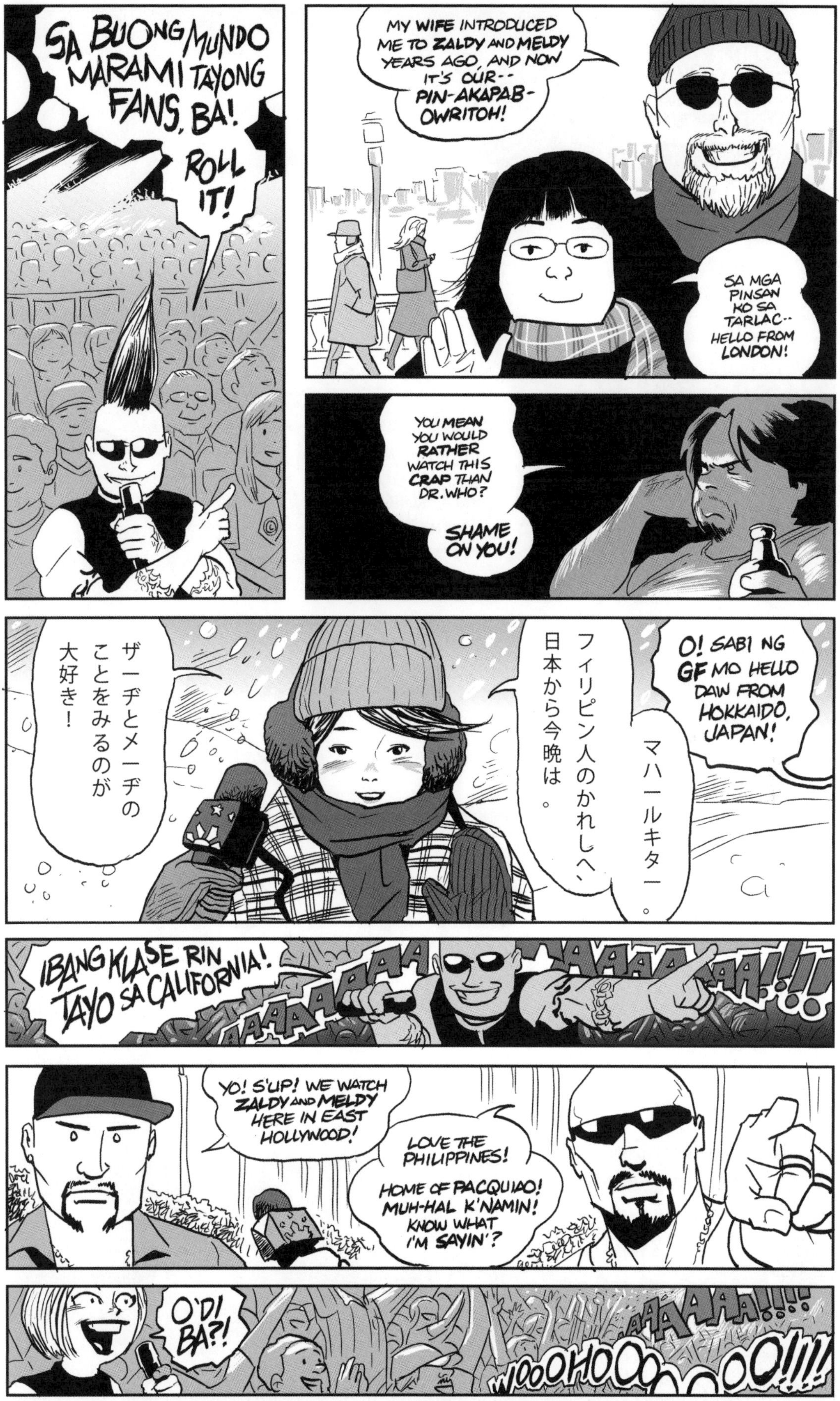
SA BUONG MUNDO MARAMI TAYONG FANS, BA!
ROLL IT!
MY WIFE INTRODUCED ME TO ZALDY AND MELDY YEARS AGO, AND NOW IT'S OUR-- PIN-AKAPAB-OWRITOH!
SA MGA PINSAN KO SA TARLAC-- HELLO FROM LONDON!
YOU MEAN YOU WOULD RATHER WATCH THIS CRAP THAN DR. WHO?
SHAME ON YOU!
O! SABI NG GF MO HELLO DAW FROM HOKKAIDO, JAPAN!
マハールキター。
フィリピン人のかれしへ、日本から今晩は。
ザーヂとメーヂのことをみるのが大好き！
IBANG KLASE RIN TAYO SA CALIFORNIA!
AAAAAAAAAAAAAAAAA!!!
YO! S'UP! WE WATCH ZALDY AND MELDY HERE IN EAST HOLLYWOOD!
LOVE THE PHILIPPINES!
HOME OF PACQUIAO! MUH-HAL K'NAMIN! KNOW WHAT I'M SAYIN'?
O'DI BA?!
AAAAAA!!!!
WOOOHOOOOOOOOO!!!!

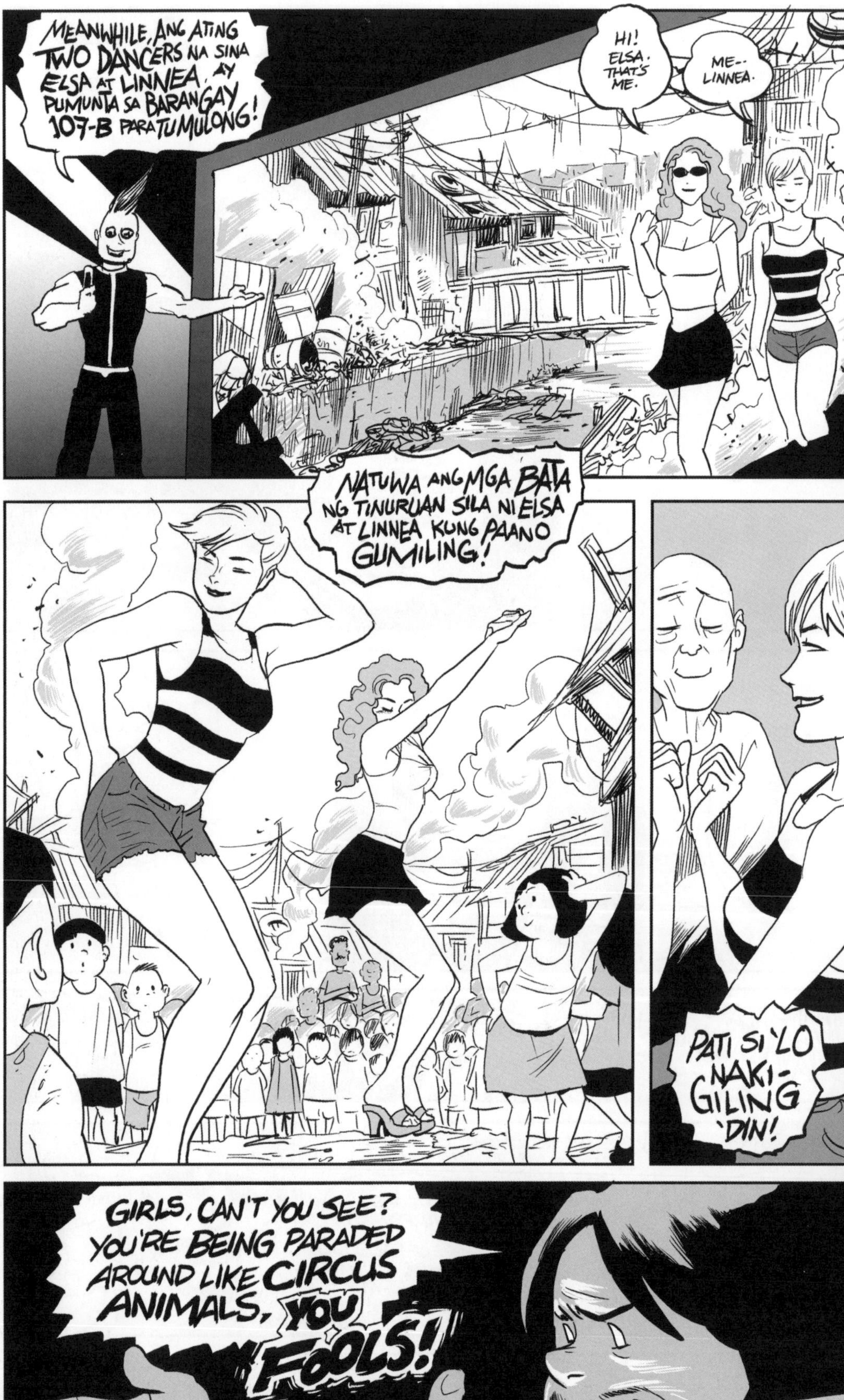
MEANWHILE, ANG ATING TWO DANCERS NA SINA ELSA AT LINNEA AY PUMUNTA SA BARANGAY 107-B PARA TUMULONG!
HI! ELSA. THAT'S ME.
ME-- LINNEA.
NATUWA ANG MGA BATA NG TINURUAN SILA NI ELSA AT LINNEA KUNG PAANO GUMILING!
PATI SI 'LO NAKI-GILING 'DIN!
GIRLS, CAN'T YOU SEE? YOU'RE BEING PARADED AROUND LIKE CIRCUS ANIMALS, YOU FOOLS!

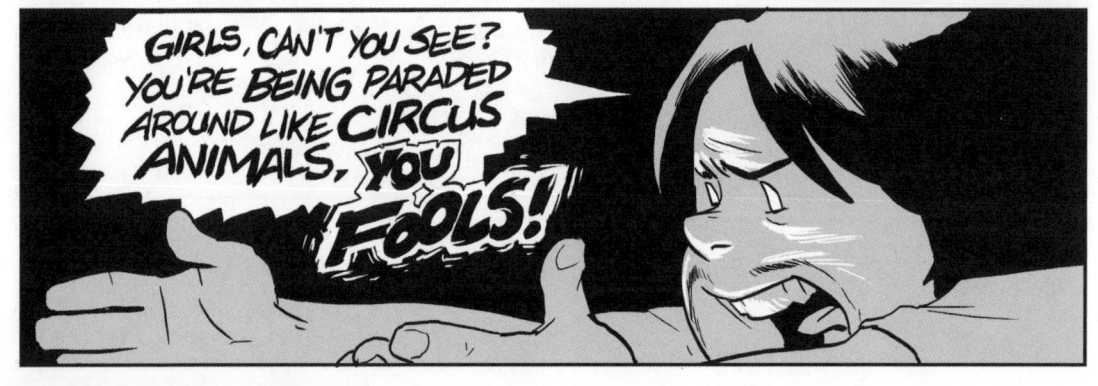

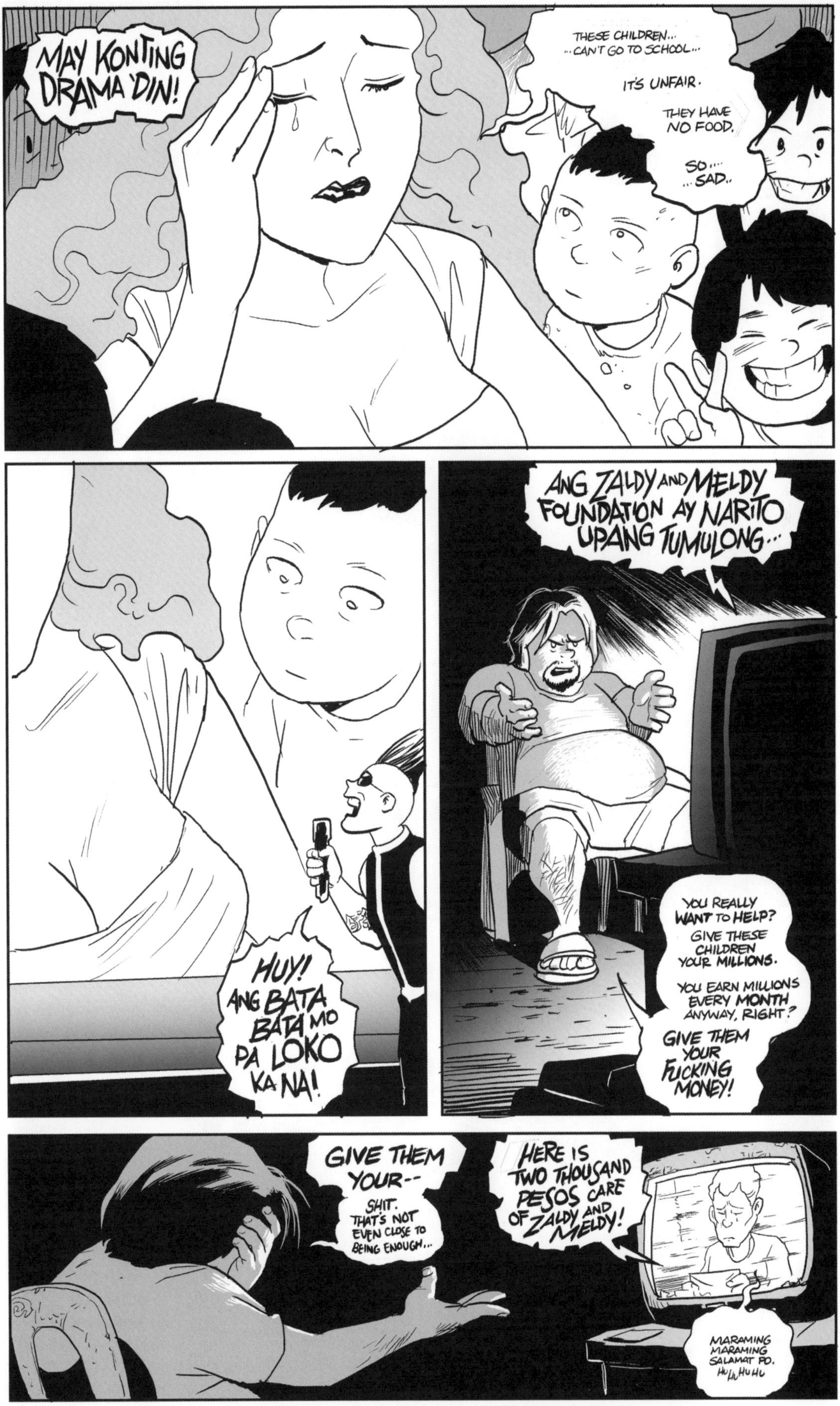
MAY KONTING DRAMA 'DIN!
THESE CHILDREN... ...CAN'T GO TO SCHOOL...
IT'S UNFAIR.
THEY HAVE NO FOOD.
SO.... ...SAD..
HUY! ANG BATA BATA MO PA LOKO KA NA!
ANG ZALDY AND MELDY FOUNDATION AY NARITO UPANG TUMULONG...
YOU REALLY WANT TO HELP? GIVE THESE CHILDREN YOUR MILLIONS.
YOU EARN MILLIONS EVERY MONTH ANYWAY, RIGHT?
GIVE THEM YOUR FUCKING MONEY!
GIVE THEM YOUR--
SHIT. THAT'S NOT EVEN CLOSE TO BEING ENOUGH...
HERE IS TWO THOUSAND PESOS CARE OF ZALDY AND MELDY!
MARAMING MARAMING SALAMAT PO. HU HU HU HU

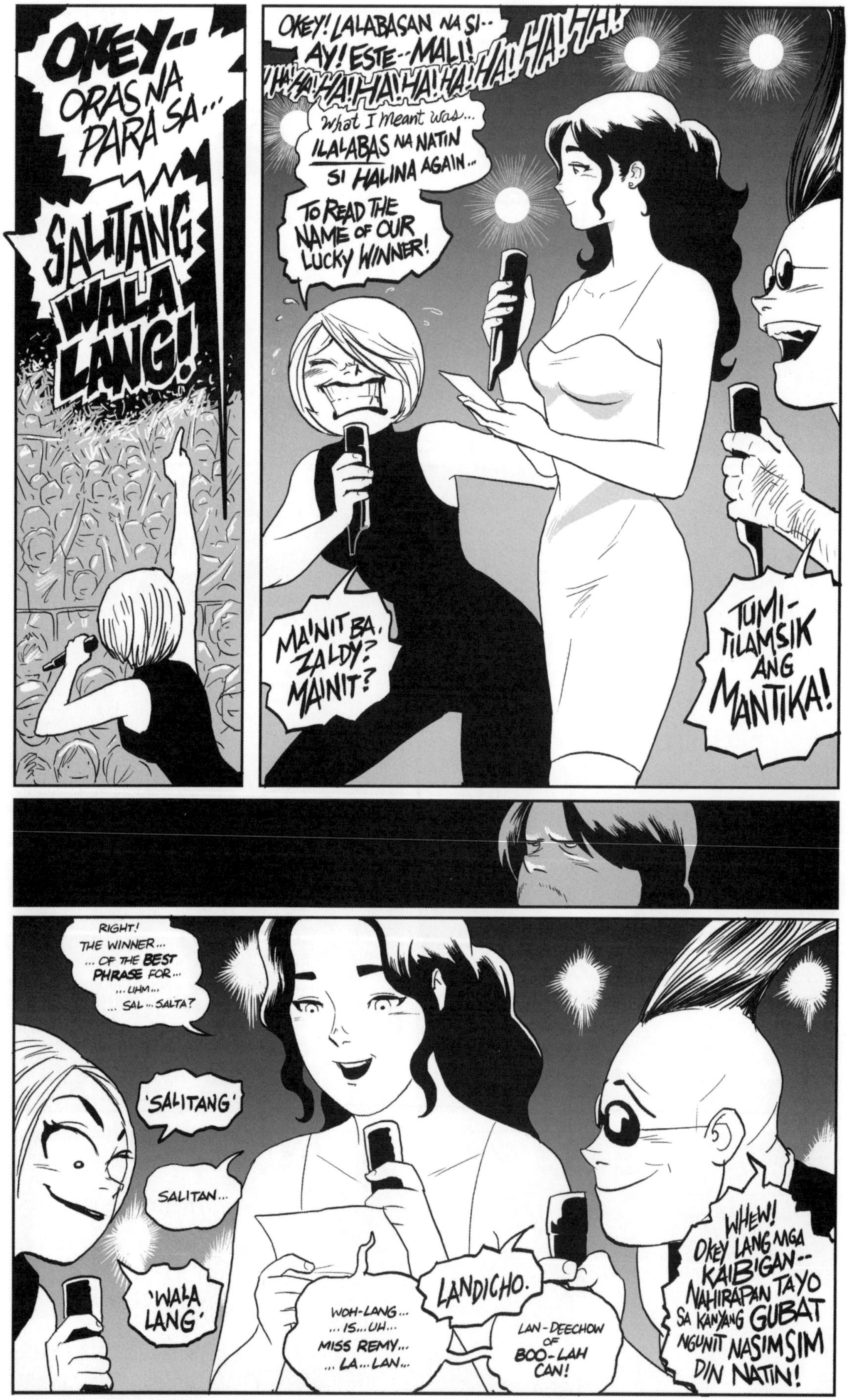
OKEY-- ORAS NA PARA SA...
SALITANG WALA LANG!
OKEY! LALABASAN NA SI-- AY! ESTE--MALI!
HA! HA! HA! HA! HA! HA! HA! HA! HA!
What I meant was... ILALABAS NA NATIN SI HALINA AGAIN...
TO READ THE NAME OF OUR LUCKY WINNER!
MA'INIT BA, ZALDY? MAINIT?
TUMI-TILAMSIK ANG MANTIKA!
RIGHT! THE WINNER... ...OF THE BEST PHRASE FOR... ...UHM... ...SAL...SALTA?
'SALITANG'
SALITAN...
'WALA LANG'
WOH-LANG... ...IS...UH... MISS REMY... ...LA...LAN...
LANDICHO.
LAN-DEECHOW OF BOO-LAH CAN!
WHEW! OKEY LANG MGA KAIBIGAN-- NAHIRAPAN TAYO SA KANYANG GUBAT NGUNIT NASIMSIM DIN NATIN!

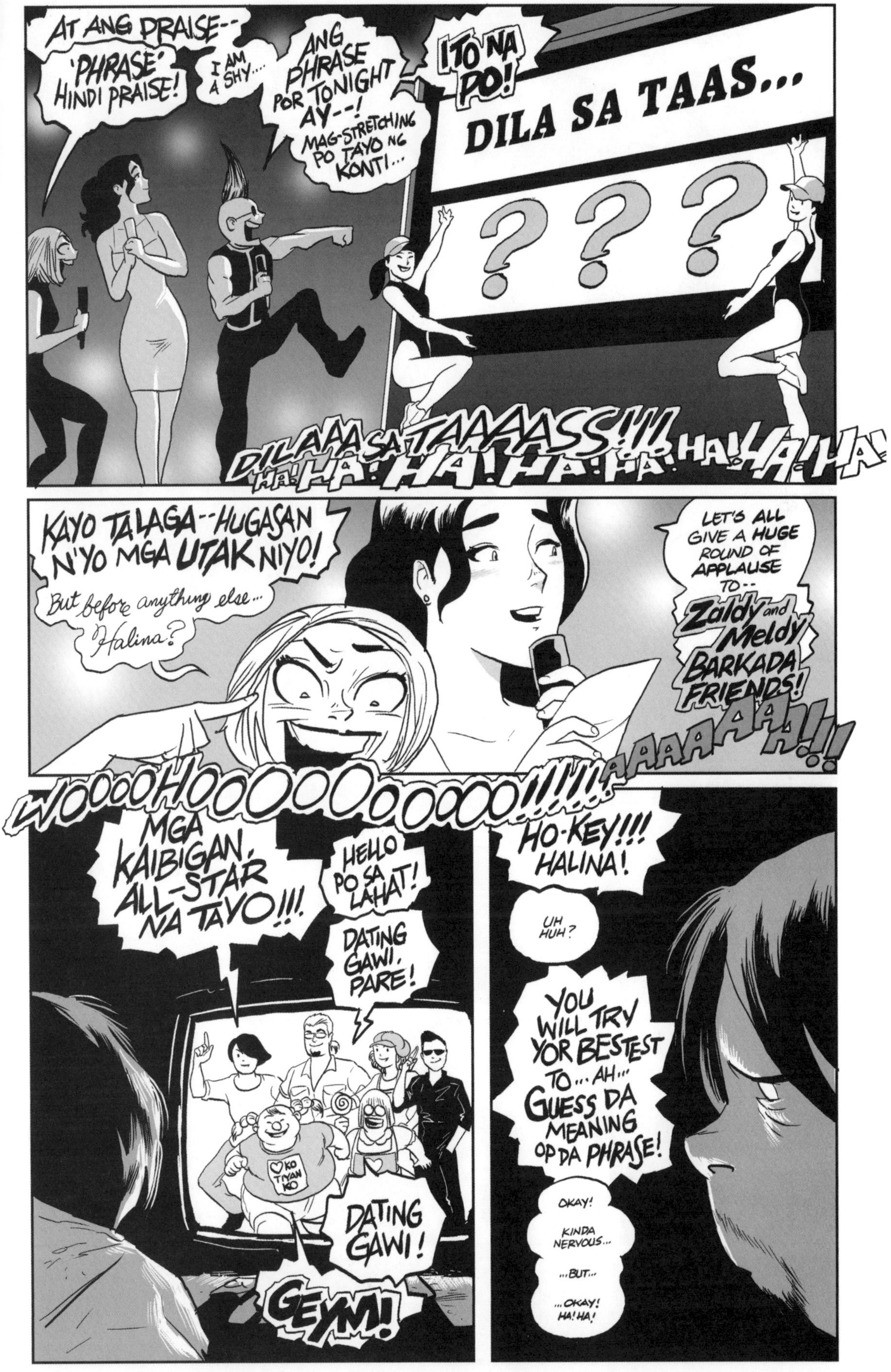
AT ANG PRAISE--
'PHRASE' HINDI PRAISE!
I AM A SHY...
ANG PHRASE POR TONIGHT AY--!
MAG-STRETCHING PO TAYO NG KONTI...
ITO NA PO!
DILA SA TAAS...
???
DILAAA SA TAAAAASS!!!!
HA! HA! HA! HA! HA! HA! HA! HA! HA!
KAYO TALAGA--HUGASAN N'YO MGA UTAK NIYO!
But before anything else... Halina?
LET'S ALL GIVE A HUGE ROUND OF APPLAUSE TO--
Zaldy and Meldy BARKADA FRIENDS!
AAAAAAH!!!
WOOOOHOOOOOOOOOOO!!!!!...
MGA KAIBIGAN, ALL-STAR NA TAYO!!!
HELLO PO SA LAHAT!
DATING GAWI, PARE!
KO TIYAN KO
DATING GAWI!
GEYM!
HO-KEY!!! HALINA!
UH HUH?
YOU WILL TRY YOR BESTEST TO... AH... GUESS DA MEANING OP DA PHRASE!
OKAY!
KINDA NERVOUS...
...BUT...
...OKAY! HA! HA!

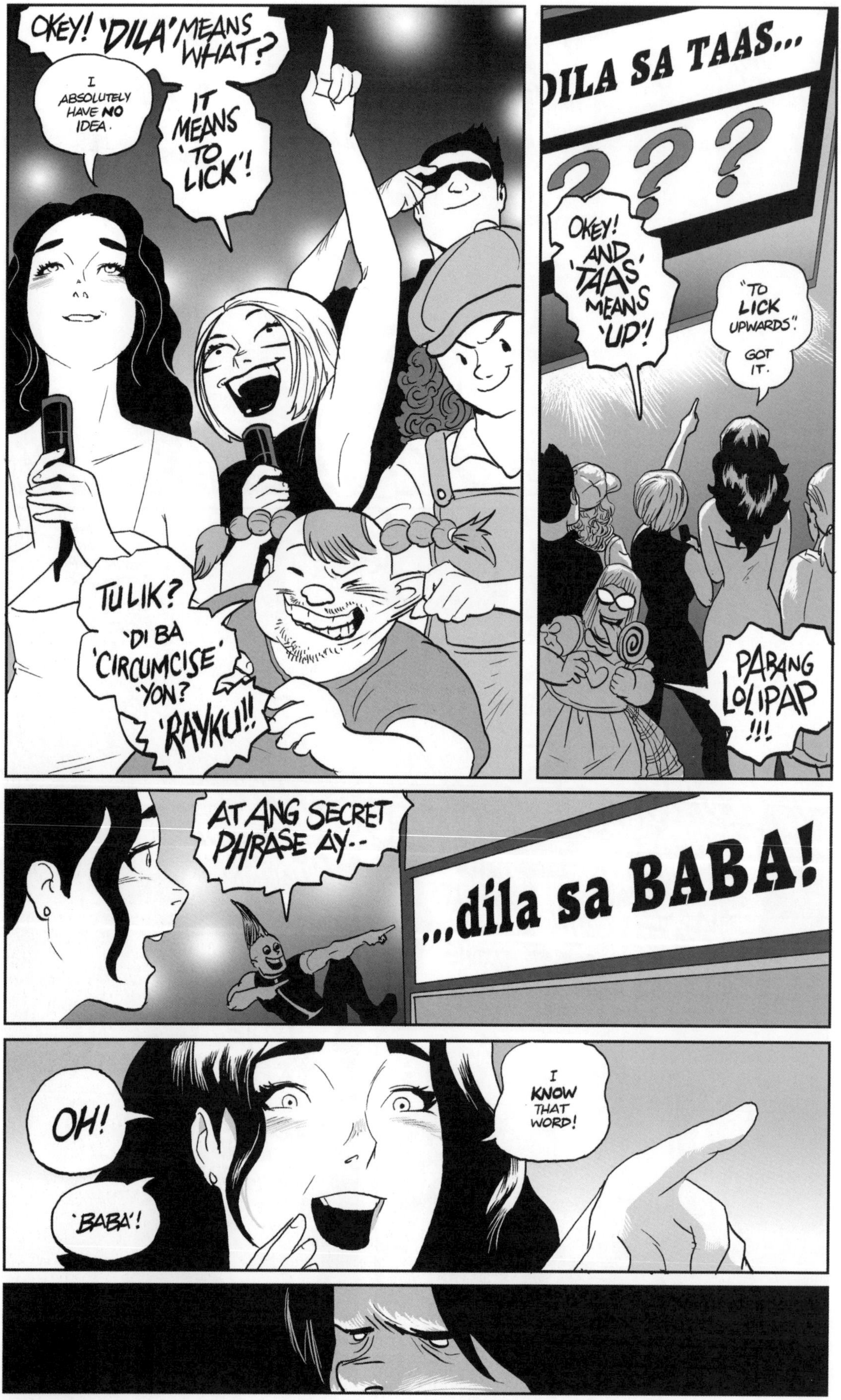
OKEY! 'DILA' MEANS WHAT?
I ABSOLUTELY HAVE NO IDEA.
IT MEANS 'TO LICK'!
TULIK? 'DI BA 'CIRCUMCISE' 'YON? 'RAYKU!!
DILA SA TAAS...
???
OKEY! AND 'TAAS' MEANS 'UP'!
"TO LICK UPWARDS". GOT IT.
PARANG LOLIPAP!!!
AT ANG SECRET PHRASE AY--
...dila sa BABA!
OH!
'BABA'!
I KNOW THAT WORD!

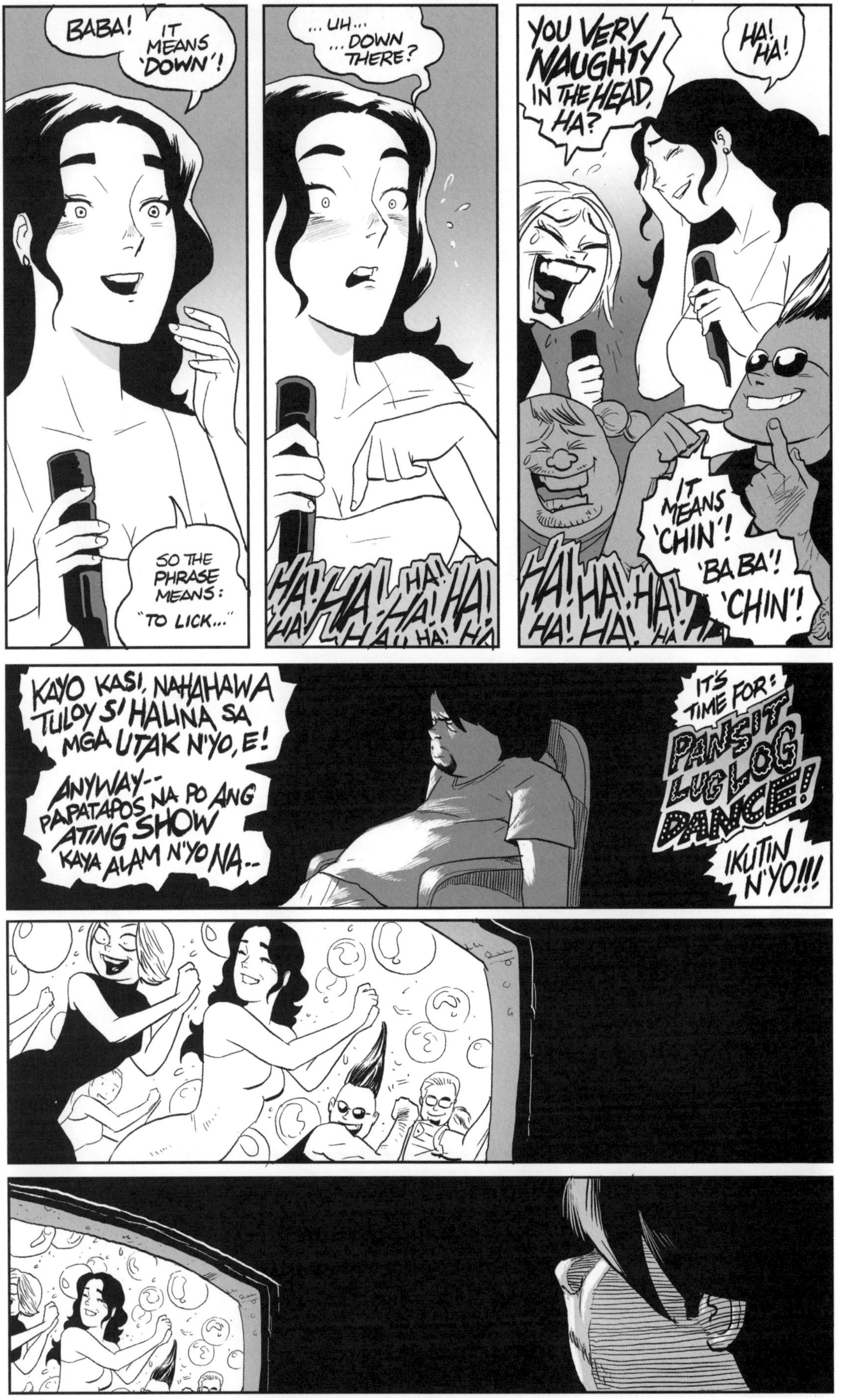
BABA!
IT MEANS 'DOWN'!
SO THE PHRASE MEANS: "TO LICK..."
...UH... ...DOWN THERE?
HA! HA! HA! HA! HA! HA! HA! HA!
YOU VERY NAUGHTY IN THE HEAD, HA?
HA! HA!
IT MEANS 'CHIN'!
'BA BA'! 'CHIN'!
HA! HA! HA! HA! HA!
KAYO KASI, NAHAHAWA TULOY S'I HALINA SA MGA UTAK N'YO, E!
ANYWAY-- PAPATAPOS NA PO ANG ATING SHOW KAYA ALAM N'YO NA--
IT'S TIME FOR: PANSIT LUG LOG DANCE!
IKUTIN N'YO!!!

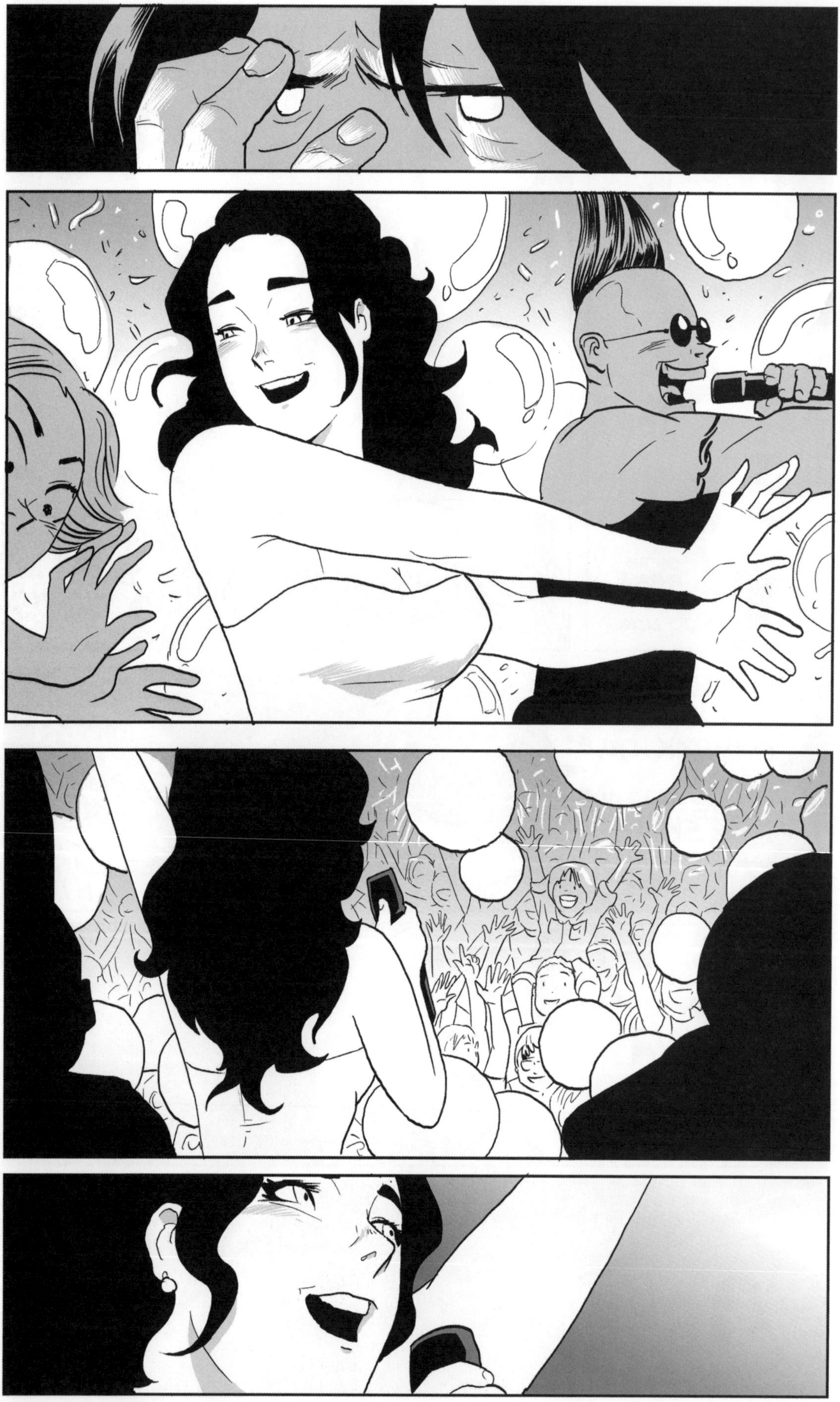

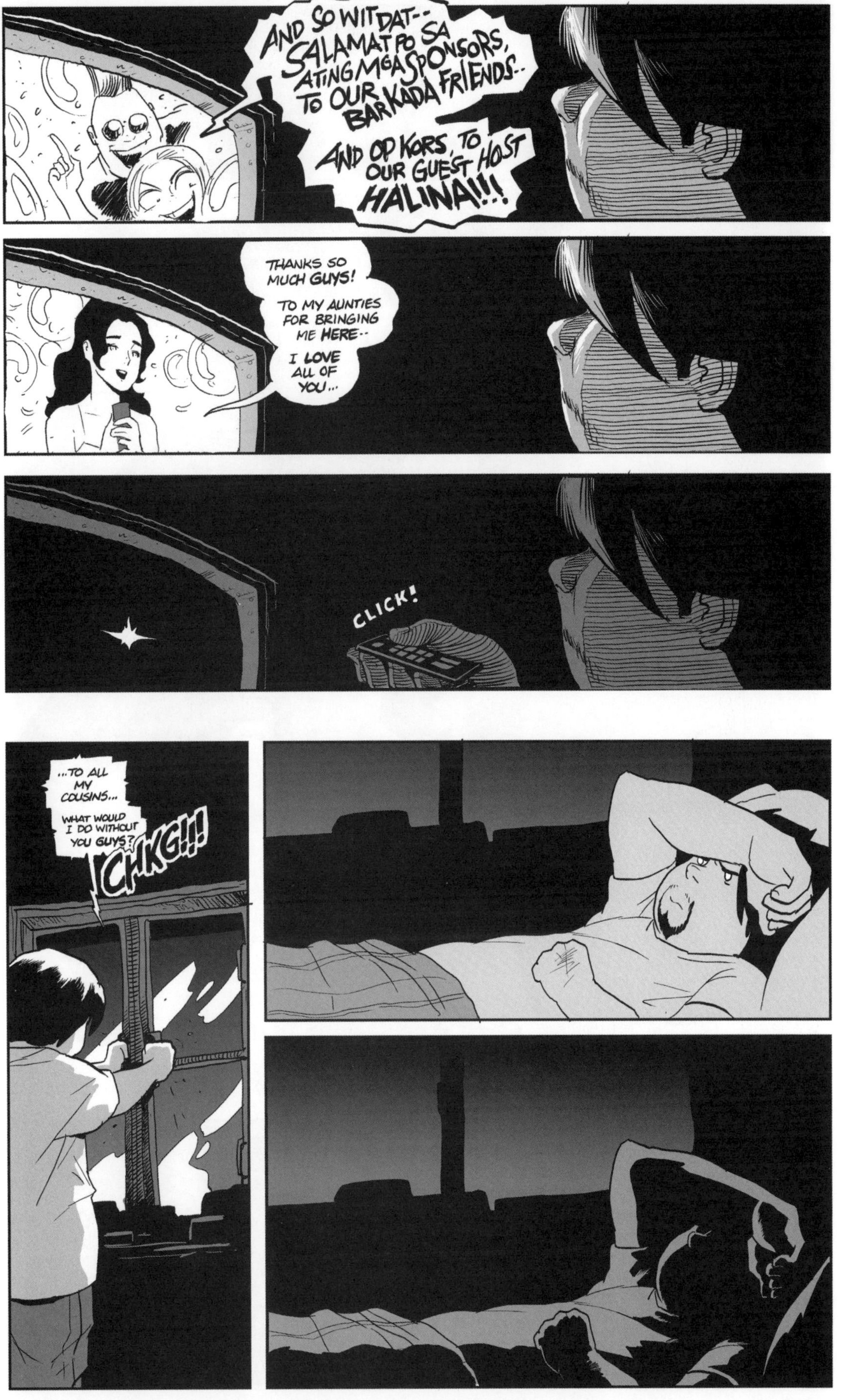
AND SO WIT DAT-- SALAMAT PO SA ATING MGA SPONSORS, TO OUR BARKADA FRIENDS--
AND OP KORS, TO OUR GUEST HOST HALINA!!!
THANKS SO MUCH GUYS!
TO MY AUNTIES FOR BRINGING ME HERE--
I LOVE ALL OF YOU...
CLICK!
...TO ALL MY COUSINS...
WHAT WOULD I DO WITHOUT YOU GUYS?
CHKG!!!

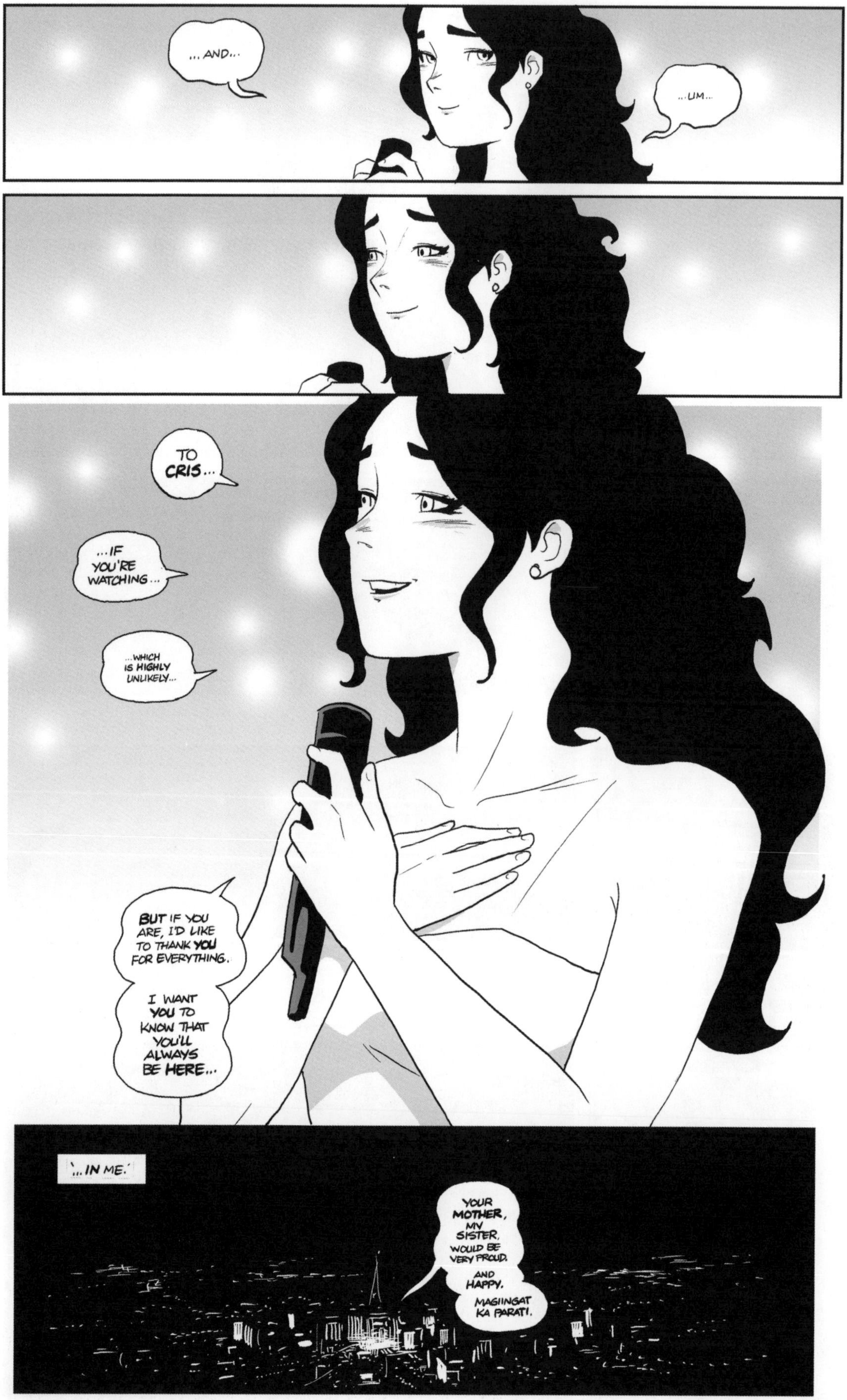
...AND...
...UM...
TO CRIS...
...IF YOU'RE WATCHING...
...WHICH IS HIGHLY UNLIKELY...
BUT IF YOU ARE, I'D LIKE TO THANK YOU FOR EVERYTHING.
I WANT YOU TO KNOW THAT YOU'LL ALWAYS BE HERE...
'...IN ME.'
YOUR MOTHER, MY SISTER, WOULD BE VERY PROUD.
AND HAPPY.
MAGIINGAT KA PARATI.

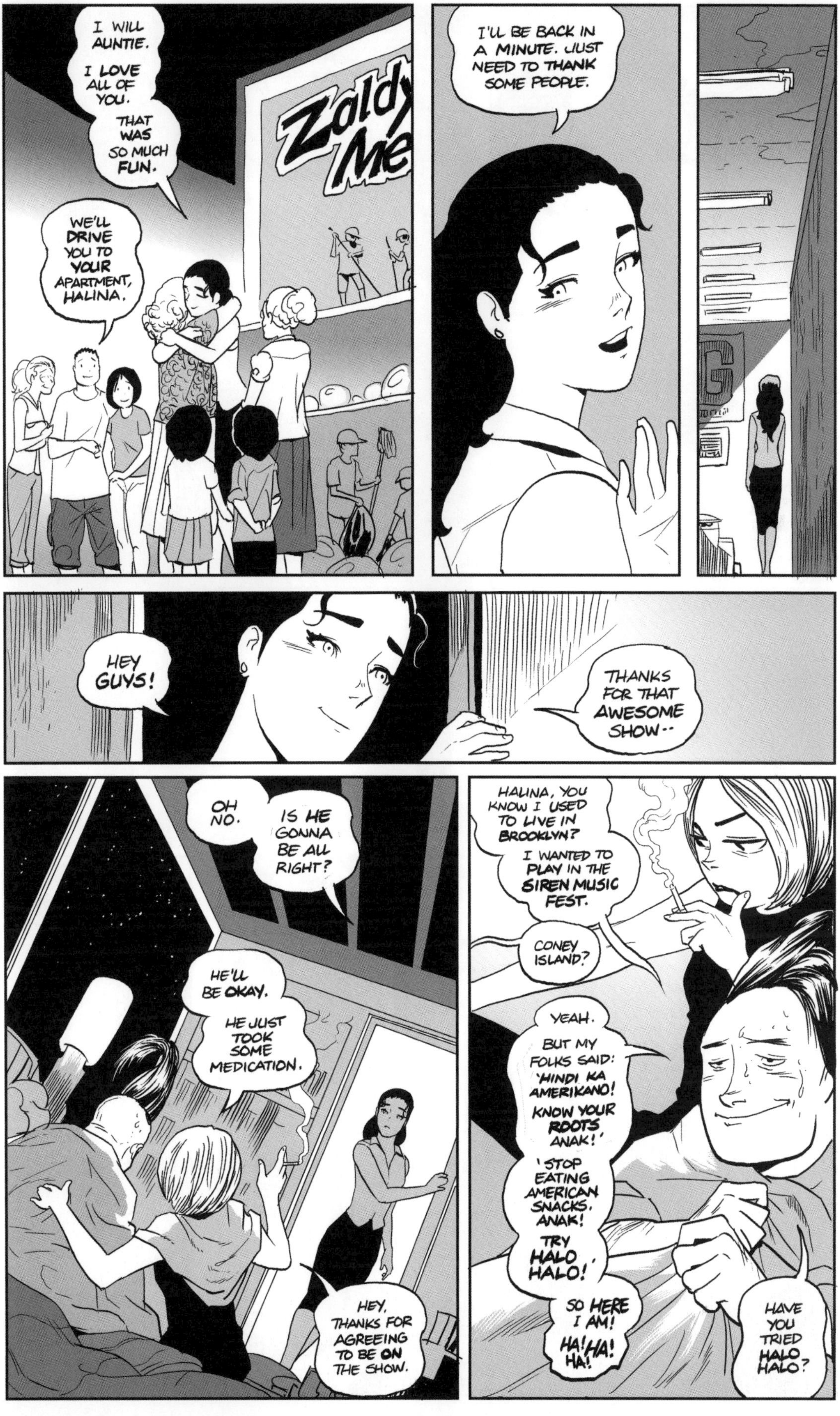
I WILL AUNTIE.
I LOVE ALL OF YOU.
THAT WAS SO MUCH FUN.
WE'LL DRIVE YOU TO YOUR APARTMENT, HALINA.
I'LL BE BACK IN A MINUTE. JUST NEED TO THANK SOME PEOPLE.
HEY GUYS!
THANKS FOR THAT AWESOME SHOW--
OH NO.
IS HE GONNA BE ALL RIGHT?
HE'LL BE OKAY.
HE JUST TOOK SOME MEDICATION.
HEY, THANKS FOR AGREEING TO BE ON THE SHOW.
HALINA, YOU KNOW I USED TO LIVE IN BROOKLYN?
I WANTED TO PLAY IN THE SIREN MUSIC FEST.
CONEY ISLAND?
YEAH.
BUT MY FOLKS SAID: 'HINDI KA AMERIKANO! KNOW YOUR ROOTS, ANAK!'
'STOP EATING AMERICAN SNACKS, ANAK! TRY HALO HALO!'
SO HERE I AM!
HA! HA! HA!
HAVE YOU TRIED HALO HALO?

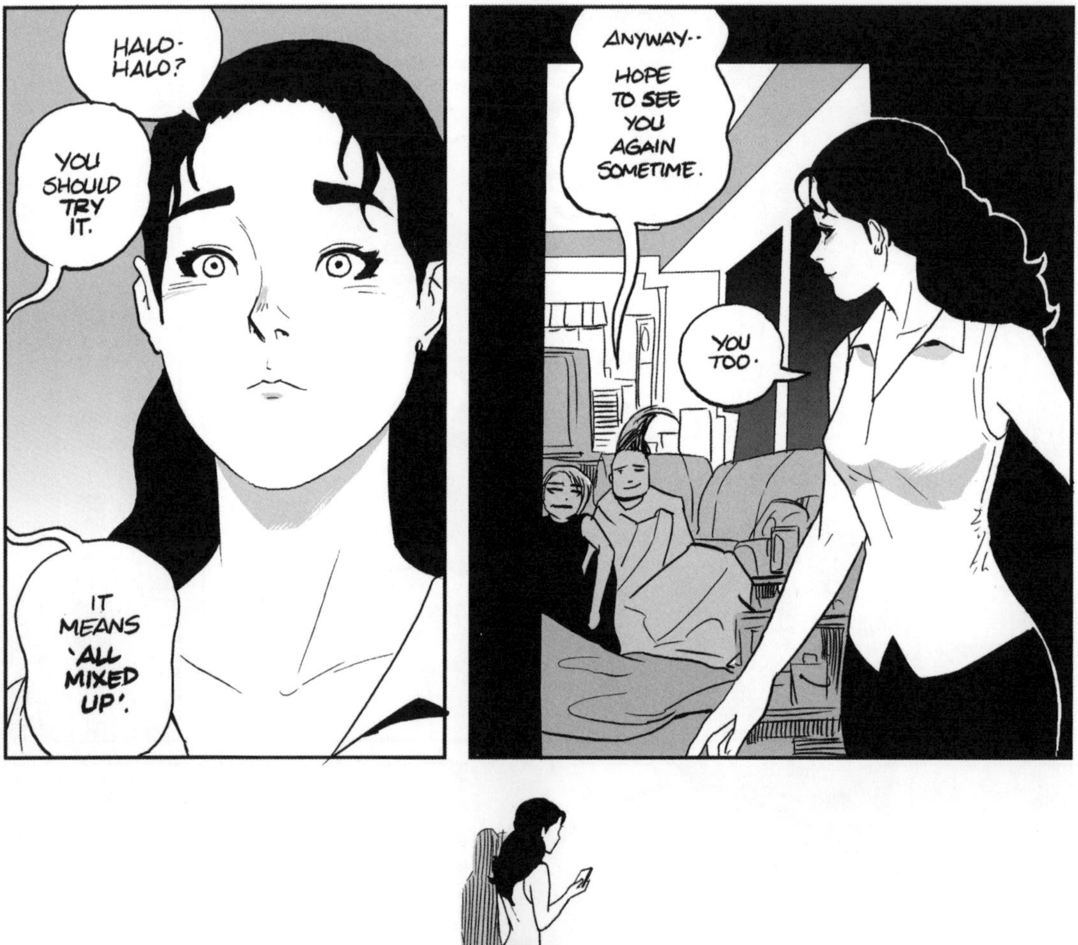
HALO-HALO?
YOU SHOULD TRY IT.
IT MEANS 'ALL MIXED UP'.
ANYWAY..
HOPE TO SEE YOU AGAIN SOMETIME.
YOU TOO.
HALO-HALO.
ALL MIXED UP.
AREN'T WE ALL?
Cris
Call

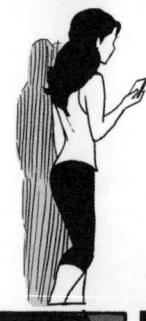

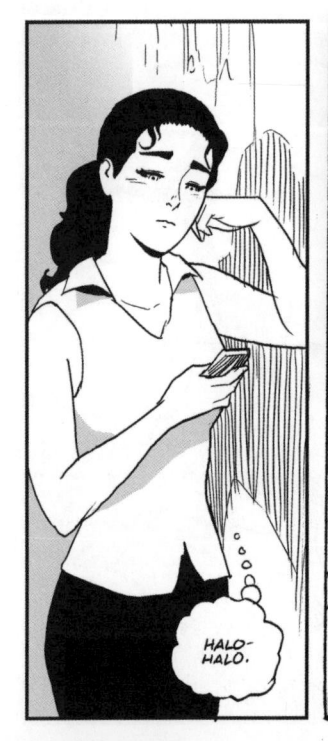

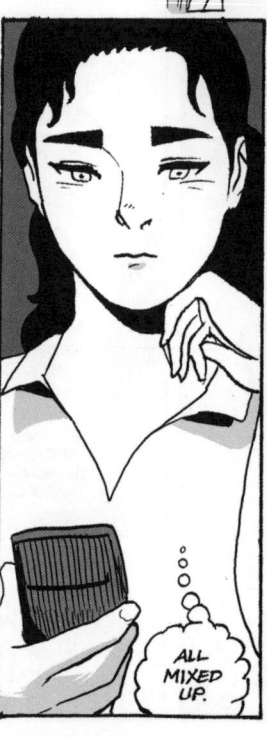

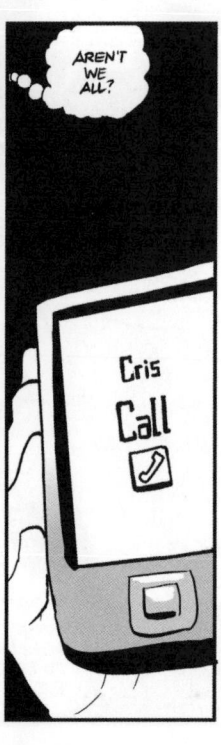

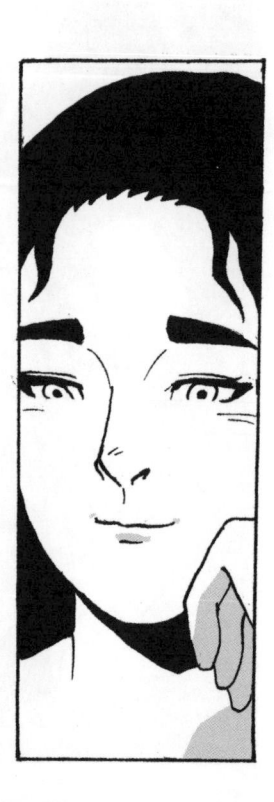

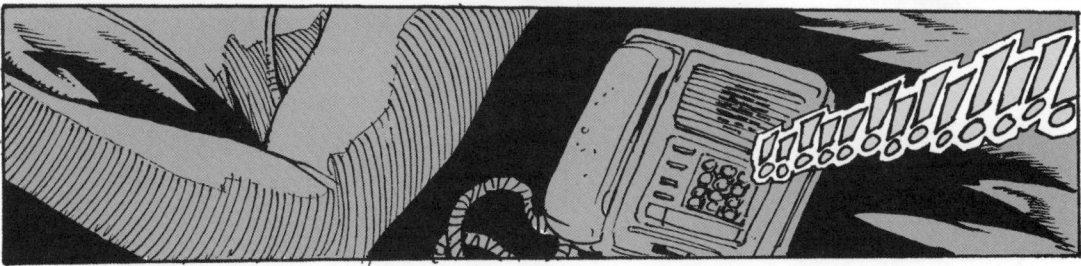

SUBSCRIBER CANNOT BE REACHED. PLEASE TRY TO-- DEEEET

UH... ...GUYS?

I WAS WONDERING IF I COULD USE YOUR PHONE...?

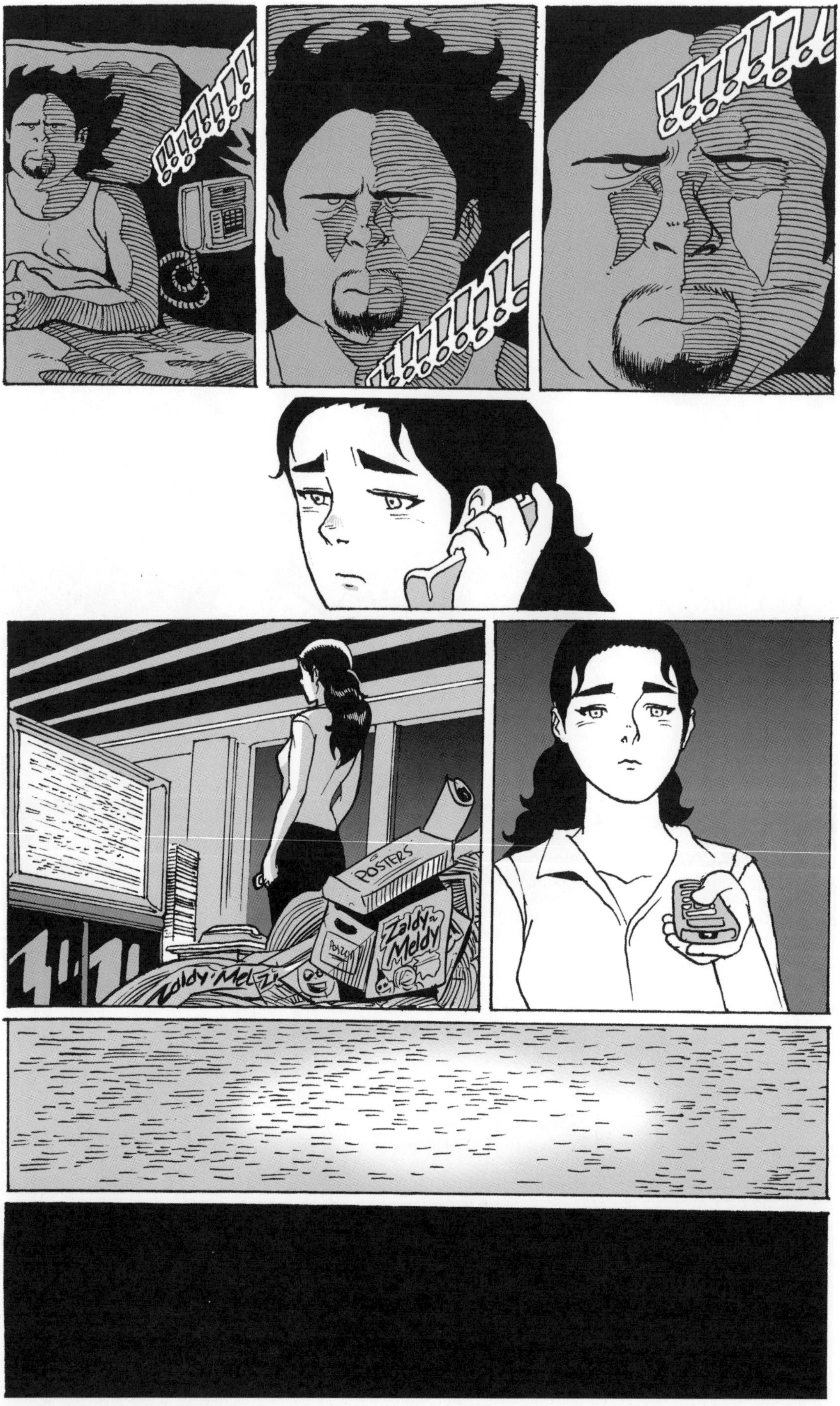
POSTERS
Zaldy Meldy

Chapter 6
Lost Signal

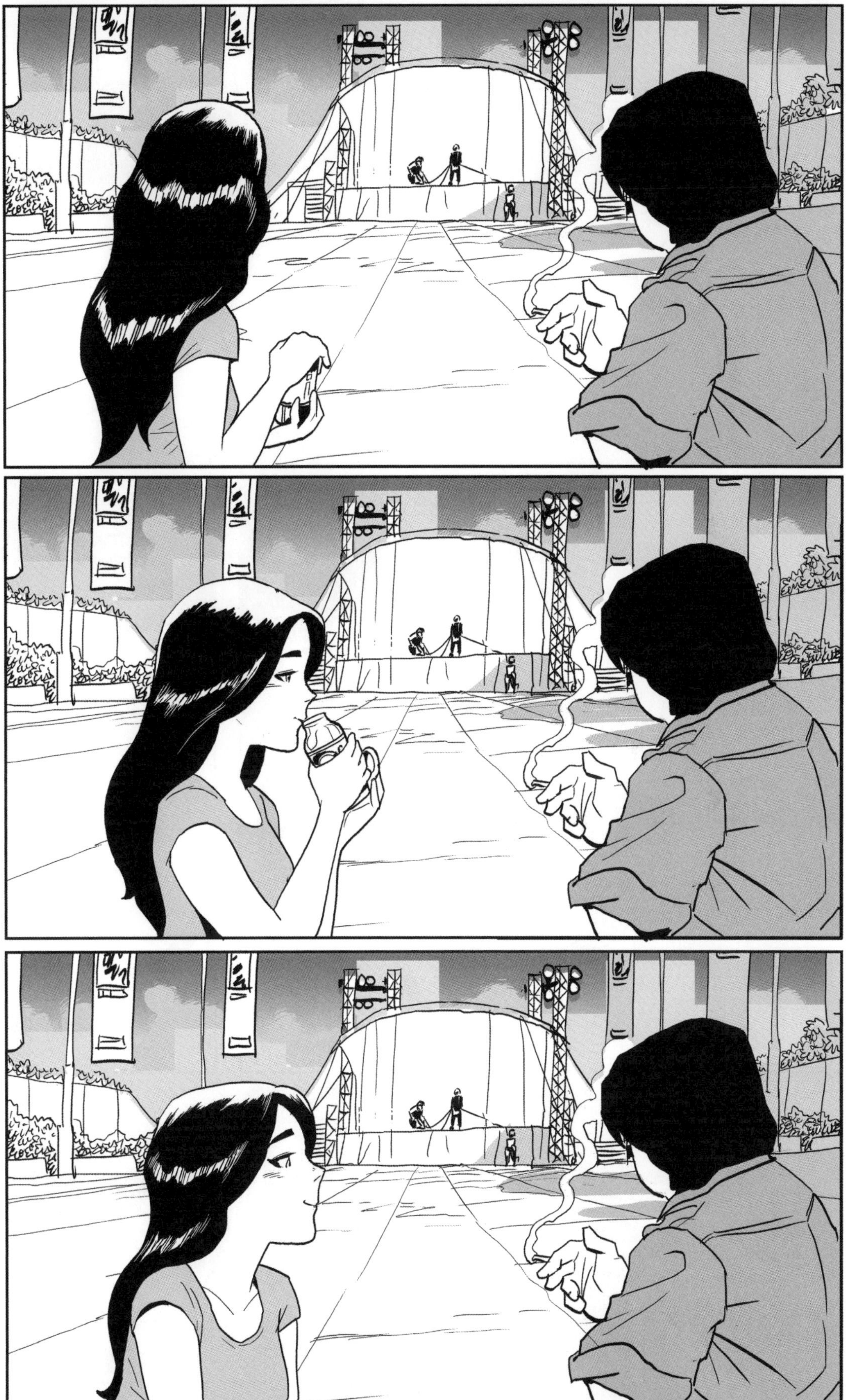

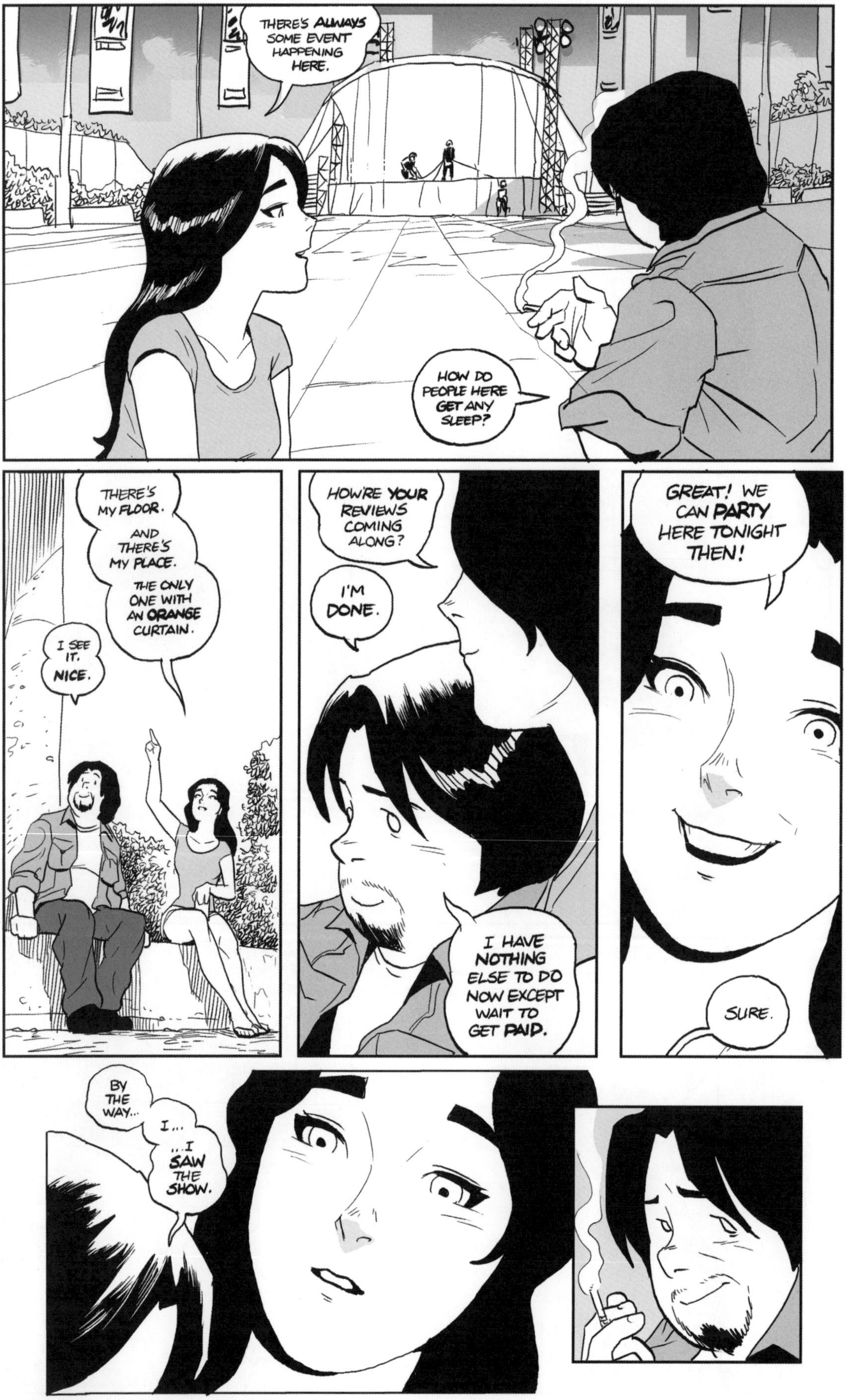
THERE'S ALWAYS SOME EVENT HAPPENING HERE.
HOW DO PEOPLE HERE GET ANY SLEEP?
THERE'S MY FLOOR.
AND THERE'S MY PLACE.
THE ONLY ONE WITH AN ORANGE CURTAIN.
I SEE IT. NICE.
HOW'RE YOUR REVIEWS COMING ALONG?
I'M DONE.
I HAVE NOTHING ELSE TO DO NOW EXCEPT WAIT TO GET PAID.
GREAT! WE CAN PARTY HERE TONIGHT THEN!
SURE.
BY THE WAY...
I...
...I SAW THE SHOW.

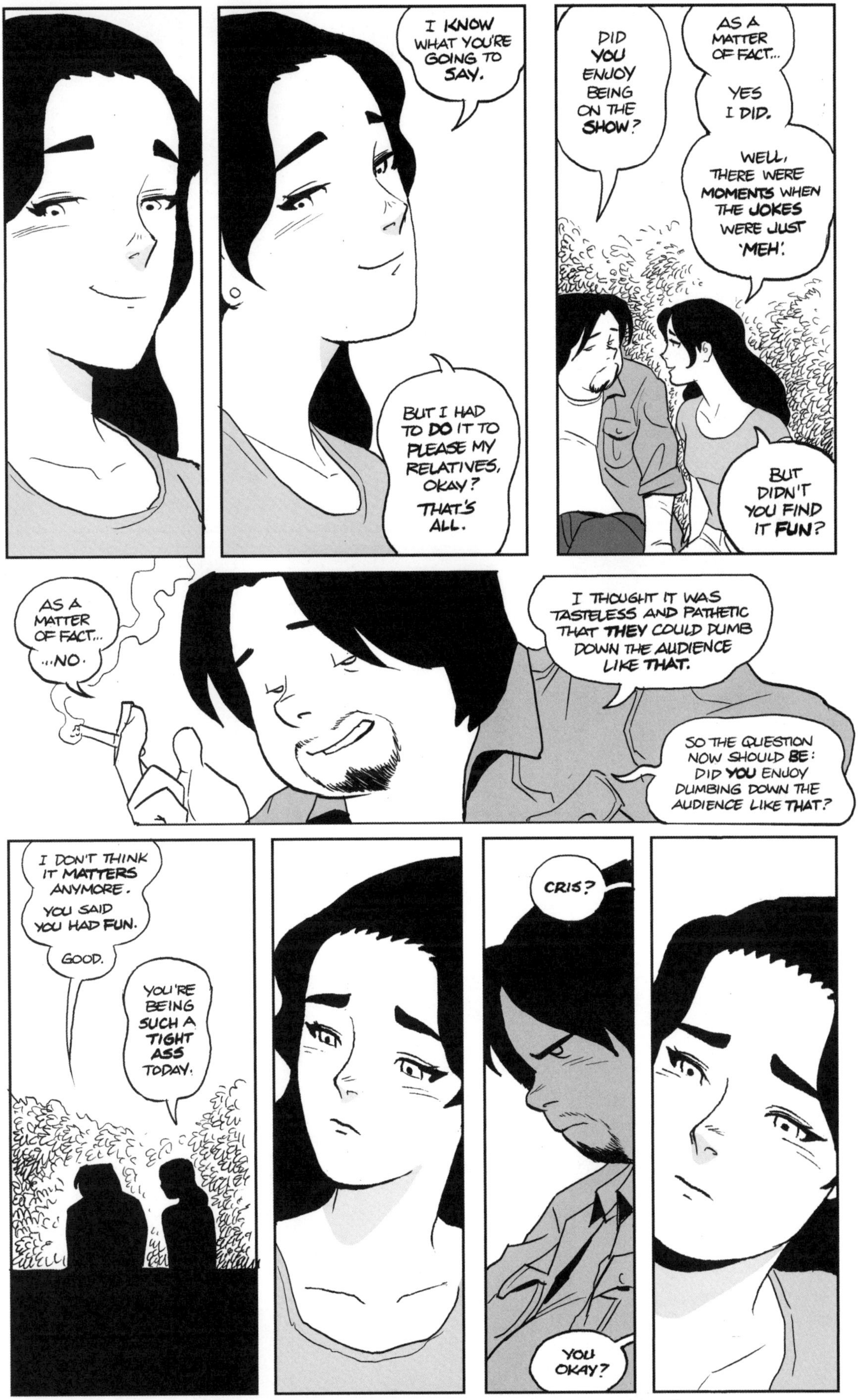
I KNOW WHAT YOU'RE GOING TO SAY.
BUT I HAD TO DO IT TO PLEASE MY RELATIVES, OKAY? THAT'S ALL.
DID YOU ENJOY BEING ON THE SHOW?
AS A MATTER OF FACT... YES I DID.
WELL, THERE WERE MOMENTS WHEN THE JOKES WERE JUST 'MEH'.
BUT DIDN'T YOU FIND IT FUN?
AS A MATTER OF FACT... ...NO.
I THOUGHT IT WAS TASTELESS AND PATHETIC THAT THEY COULD DUMB DOWN THE AUDIENCE LIKE THAT.
SO THE QUESTION NOW SHOULD BE: DID YOU ENJOY DUMBING DOWN THE AUDIENCE LIKE THAT?
I DON'T THINK IT MATTERS ANYMORE. YOU SAID YOU HAD FUN. GOOD.
YOU'RE BEING SUCH A TIGHT ASS TODAY.
CRIS?
YOU OKAY?

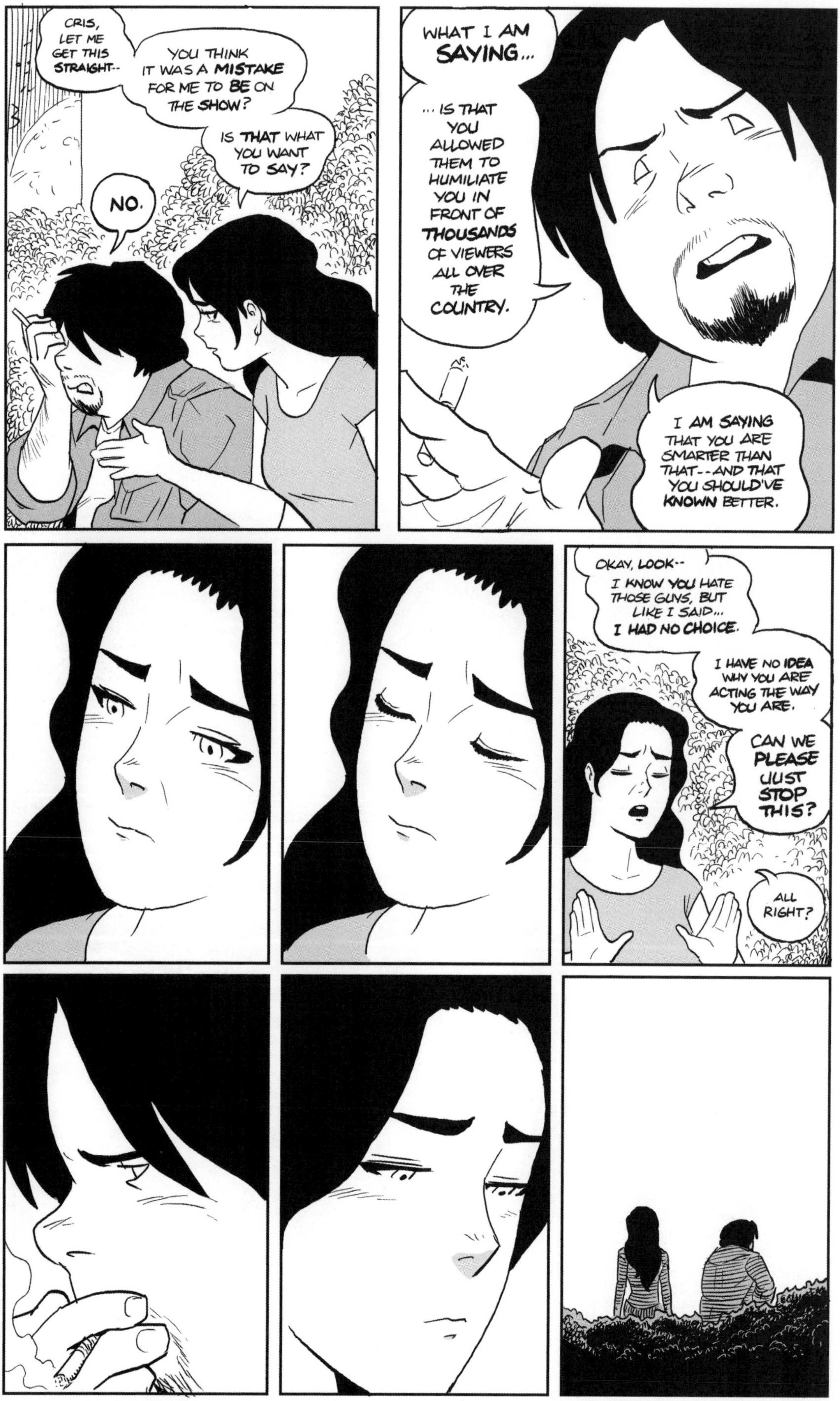
CRIS, LET ME GET THIS STRAIGHT--
YOU THINK IT WAS A MISTAKE FOR ME TO BE ON THE SHOW?
IS THAT WHAT YOU WANT TO SAY?
NO.
WHAT I AM SAYING...
... IS THAT YOU ALLOWED THEM TO HUMILIATE YOU IN FRONT OF THOUSANDS OF VIEWERS ALL OVER THE COUNTRY.
I AM SAYING THAT YOU ARE SMARTER THAN THAT--AND THAT YOU SHOULD'VE KNOWN BETTER.
OKAY, LOOK--
I KNOW YOU HATE THOSE GUYS, BUT LIKE I SAID... I HAD NO CHOICE.
I HAVE NO IDEA WHY YOU ARE ACTING THE WAY YOU ARE.
CAN WE PLEASE JUST STOP THIS?
ALL RIGHT?

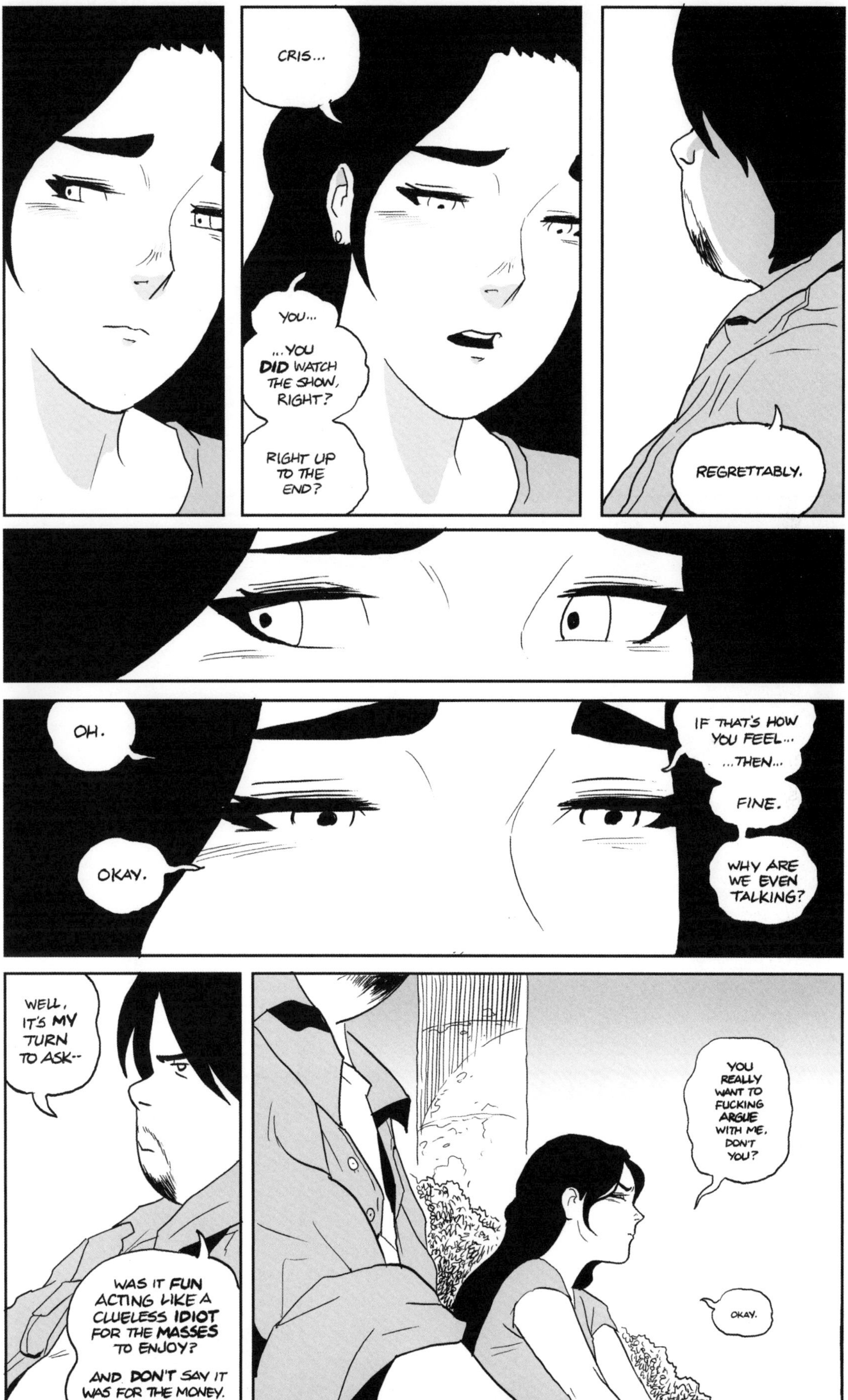
CRIS...
YOU...
...YOU **DID** WATCH THE SHOW, RIGHT?
RIGHT UP TO THE END?
REGRETTABLY.
OH.
OKAY.
IF THAT'S HOW YOU FEEL...
...THEN...
FINE.
WHY ARE WE EVEN TALKING?
WELL, IT'S **MY** TURN TO ASK--
WAS IT **FUN** ACTING LIKE A CLUELESS **IDIOT** FOR THE **MASSES** TO ENJOY?
AND **DON'T** SAY IT WAS FOR THE MONEY.
YOU REALLY WANT TO FUCKING ARGUE WITH ME, DON'T YOU?
OKAY.

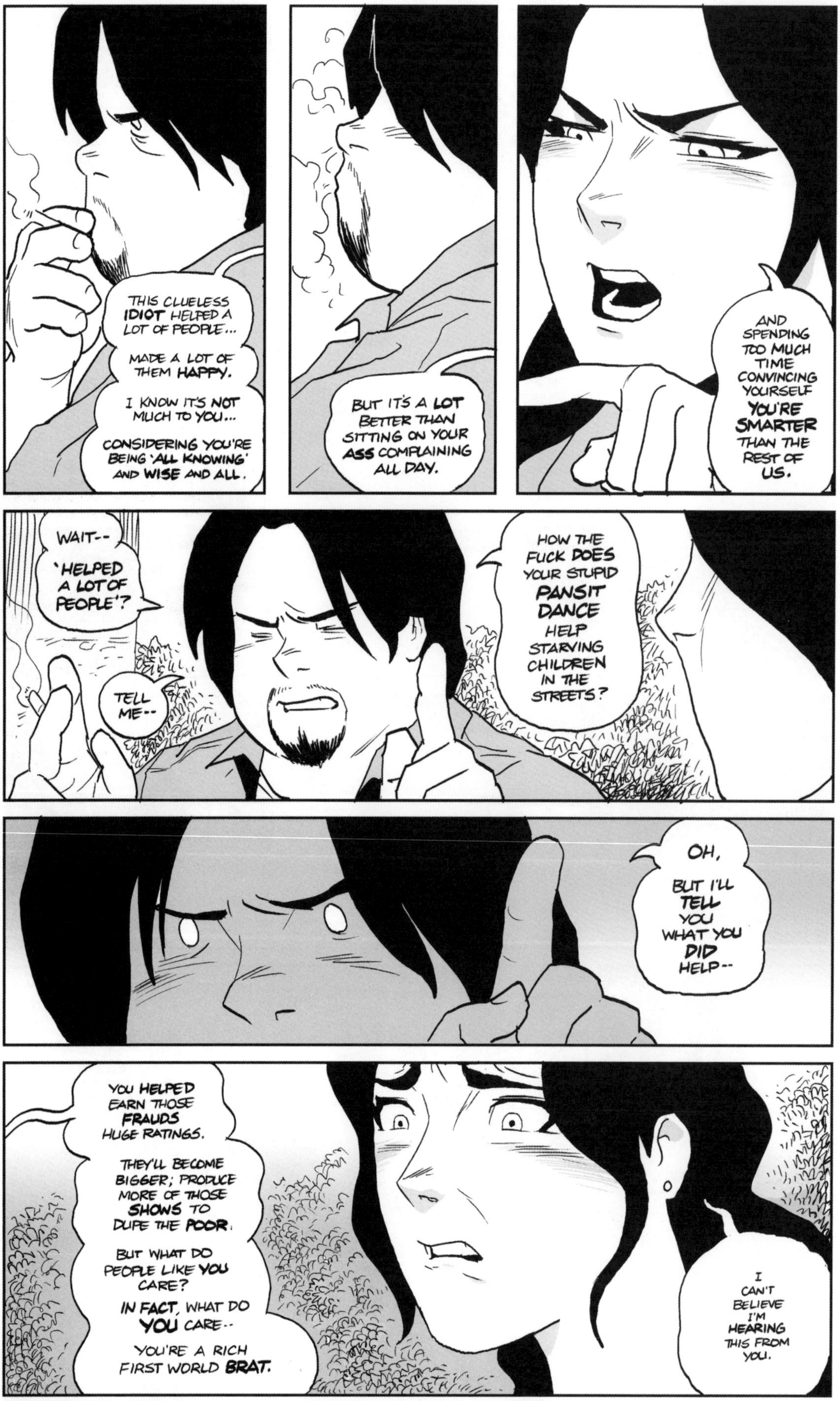

THIS CLUELESS IDIOT HELPED A LOT OF PEOPLE...
MADE A LOT OF THEM HAPPY.
I KNOW IT'S NOT MUCH TO YOU...
CONSIDERING YOU'RE BEING 'ALL KNOWING' AND WISE AND ALL.
BUT IT'S A LOT BETTER THAN SITTING ON YOUR ASS COMPLAINING ALL DAY.
AND SPENDING TOO MUCH TIME CONVINCING YOURSELF YOU'RE SMARTER THAN THE REST OF US.
WAIT--
'HELPED A LOT OF PEOPLE'?
TELL ME--
HOW THE FUCK DOES YOUR STUPID PANSIT DANCE HELP STARVING CHILDREN IN THE STREETS?
OH,
BUT I'LL TELL YOU WHAT YOU DID HELP--
YOU HELPED EARN THOSE FRAUDS HUGE RATINGS.
THEY'LL BECOME BIGGER; PRODUCE MORE OF THOSE SHOWS TO DUPE THE POOR.
BUT WHAT DO PEOPLE LIKE YOU CARE?
IN FACT, WHAT DO YOU CARE--
YOU'RE A RICH FIRST WORLD BRAT.
I CAN'T BELIEVE I'M HEARING THIS FROM YOU.

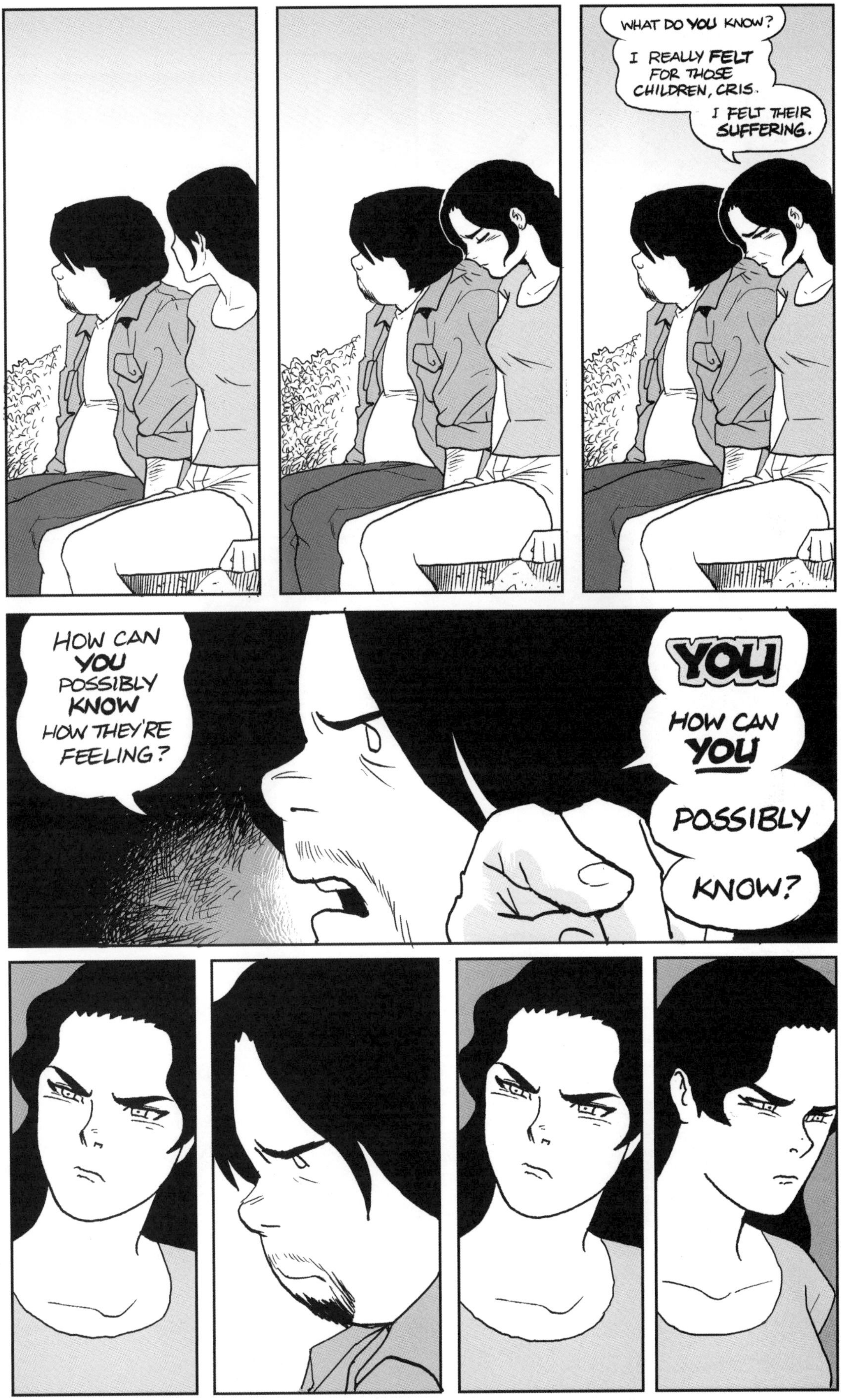
WHAT DO YOU KNOW?
I REALLY FELT FOR THOSE CHILDREN, CRIS.
I FELT THEIR SUFFERING.
HOW CAN YOU POSSIBLY KNOW HOW THEY'RE FEELING?
YOU
HOW CAN YOU
POSSIBLY
KNOW?

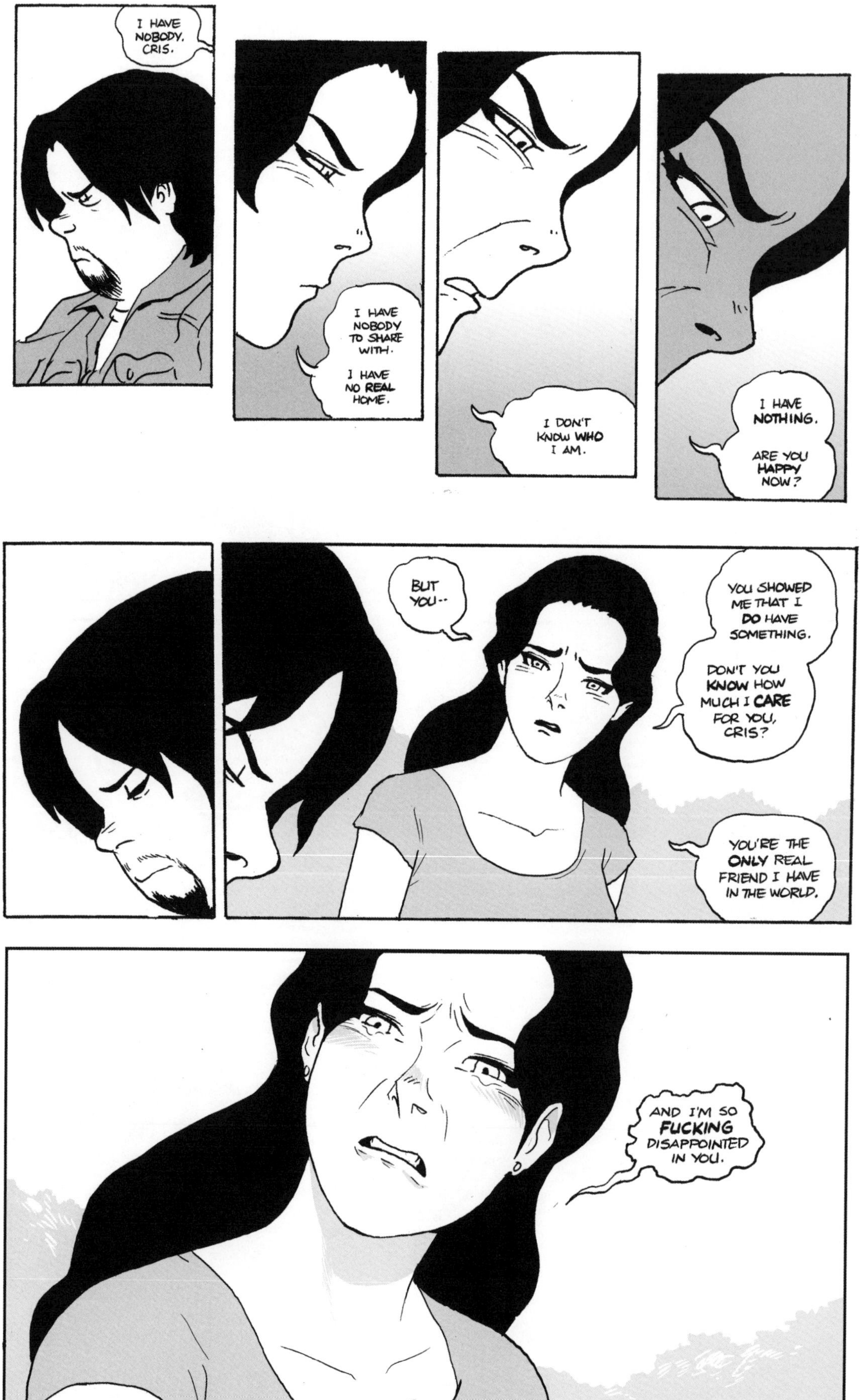
I HAVE NOBODY, CRIS.
I HAVE NOBODY TO SHARE WITH.
I HAVE NO REAL HOME.
I DON'T KNOW WHO I AM.
I HAVE NOTHING.
ARE YOU HAPPY NOW?
BUT YOU--
YOU SHOWED ME THAT I DO HAVE SOMETHING.
DON'T YOU KNOW HOW MUCH I CARE FOR YOU, CRIS?
YOU'RE THE ONLY REAL FRIEND I HAVE IN THE WORLD.
AND I'M SO FUCKING DISAPPOINTED IN YOU.

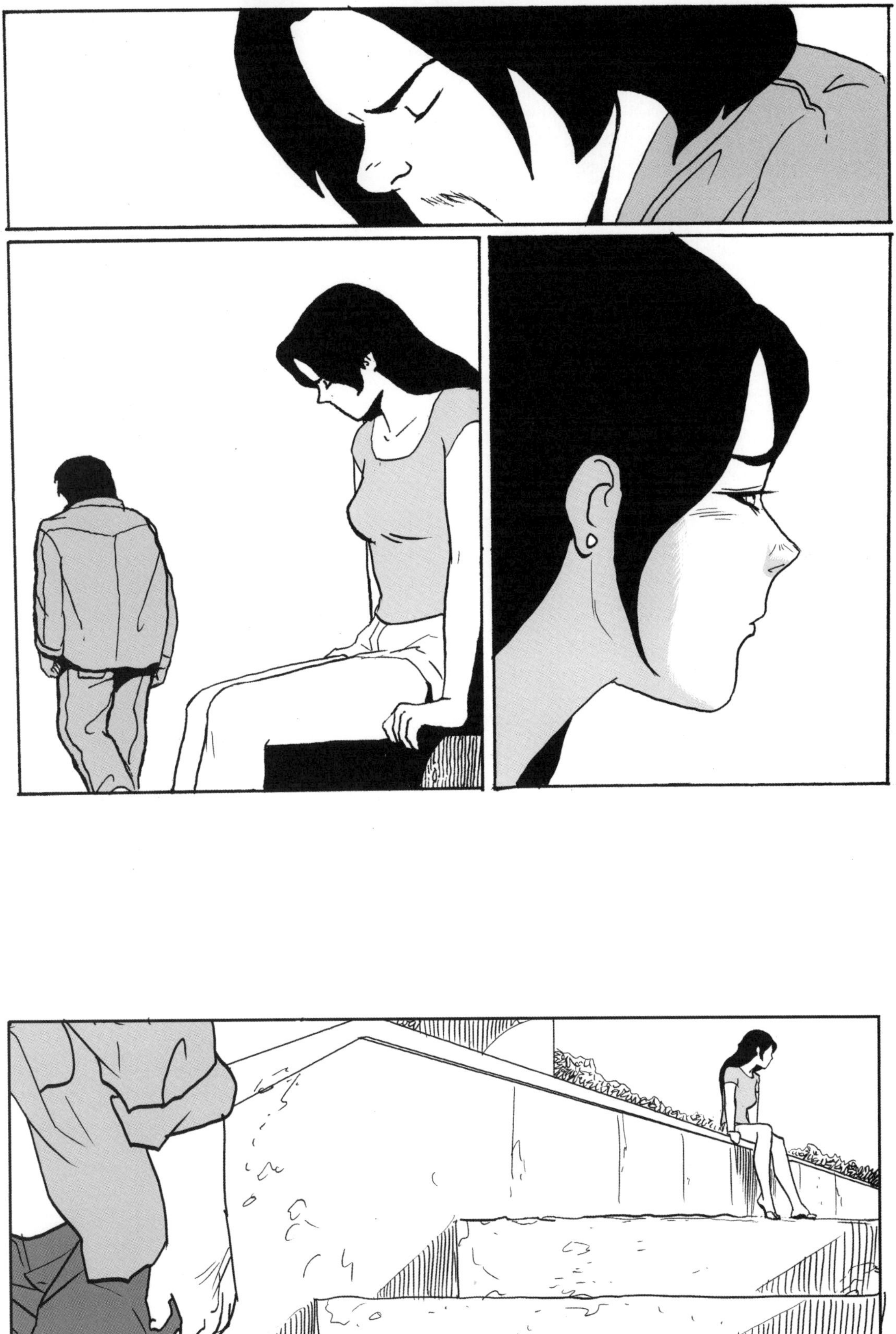

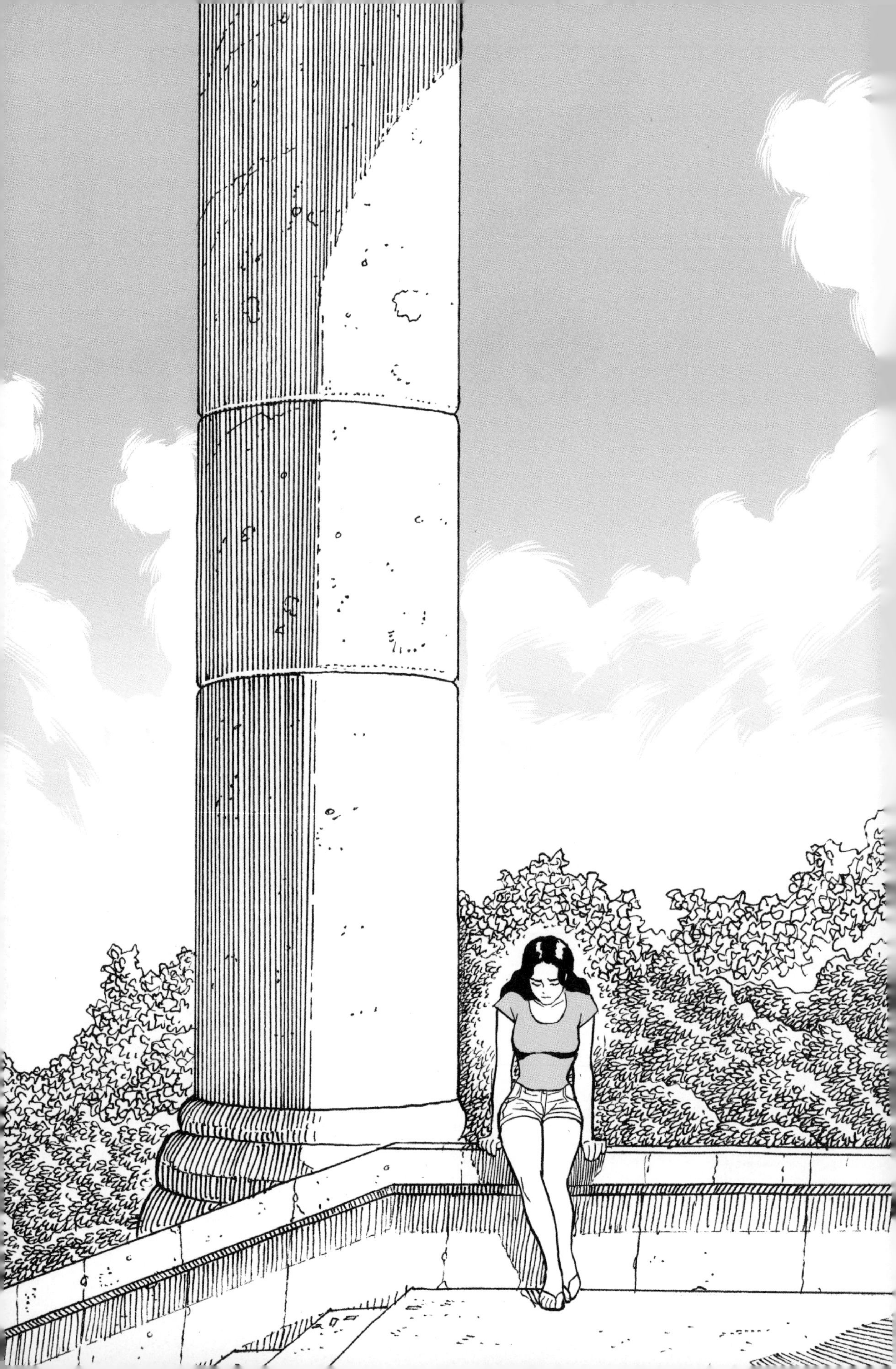

Chapter 7
Thoughts Of You

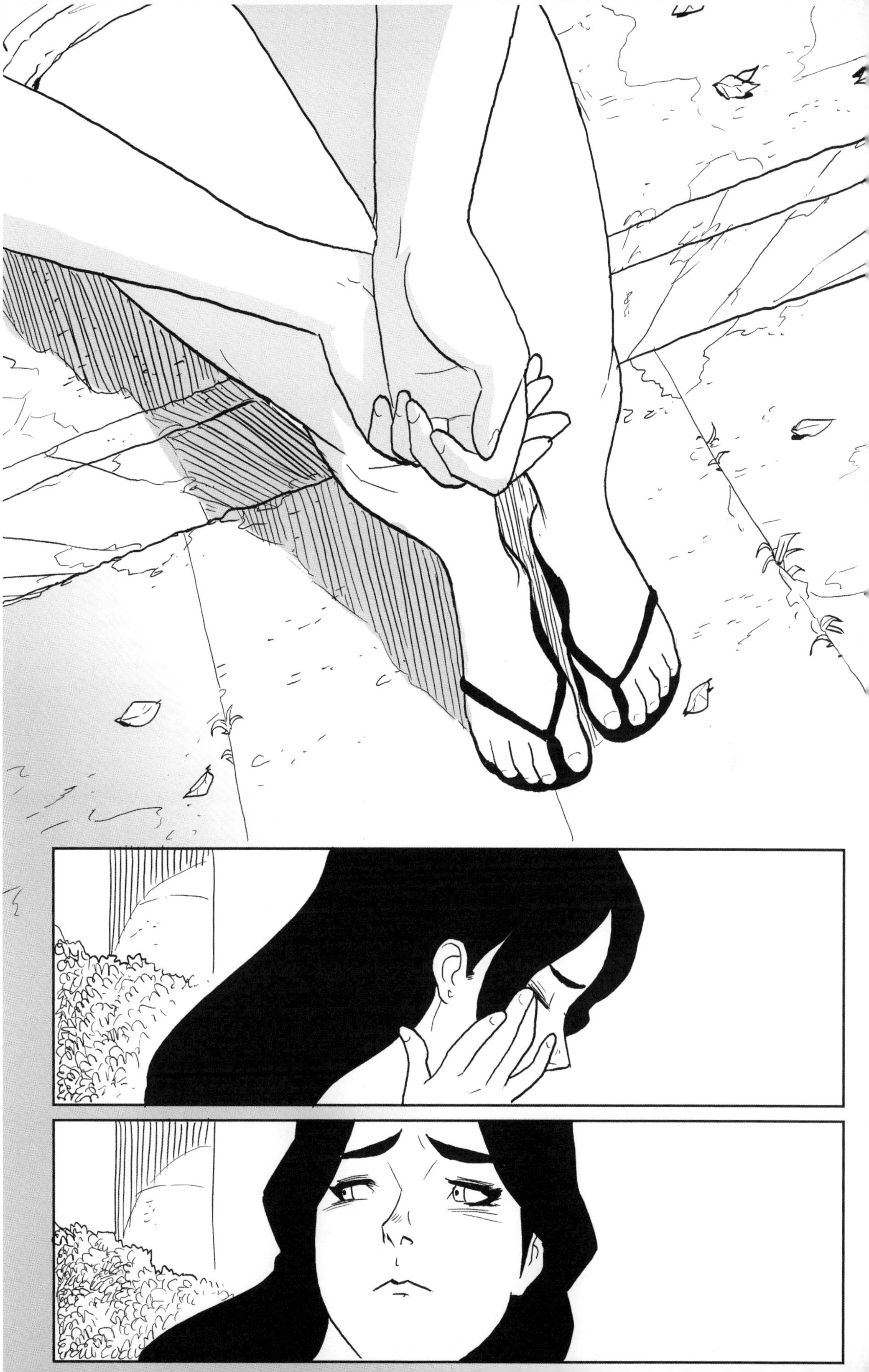

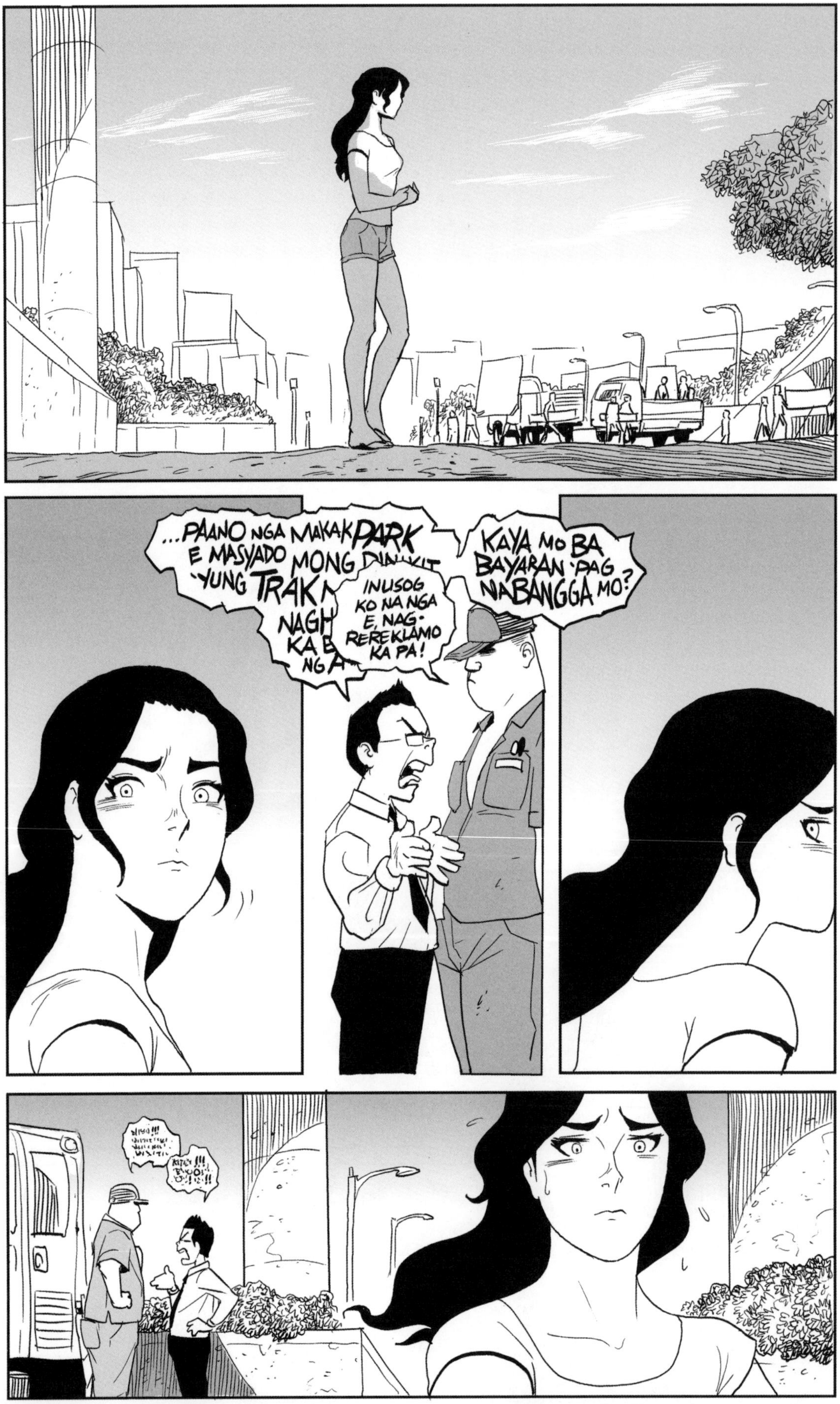
...PAANO NGA MAKAKPARK E MASYADO MONG DINIKIT 'YUNG TRAK
INUSOG KO NA NGA E, NAG-REREKLAMO KA PA!
KAYA MO BA BAYARAN 'PAG NABANGGA MO?

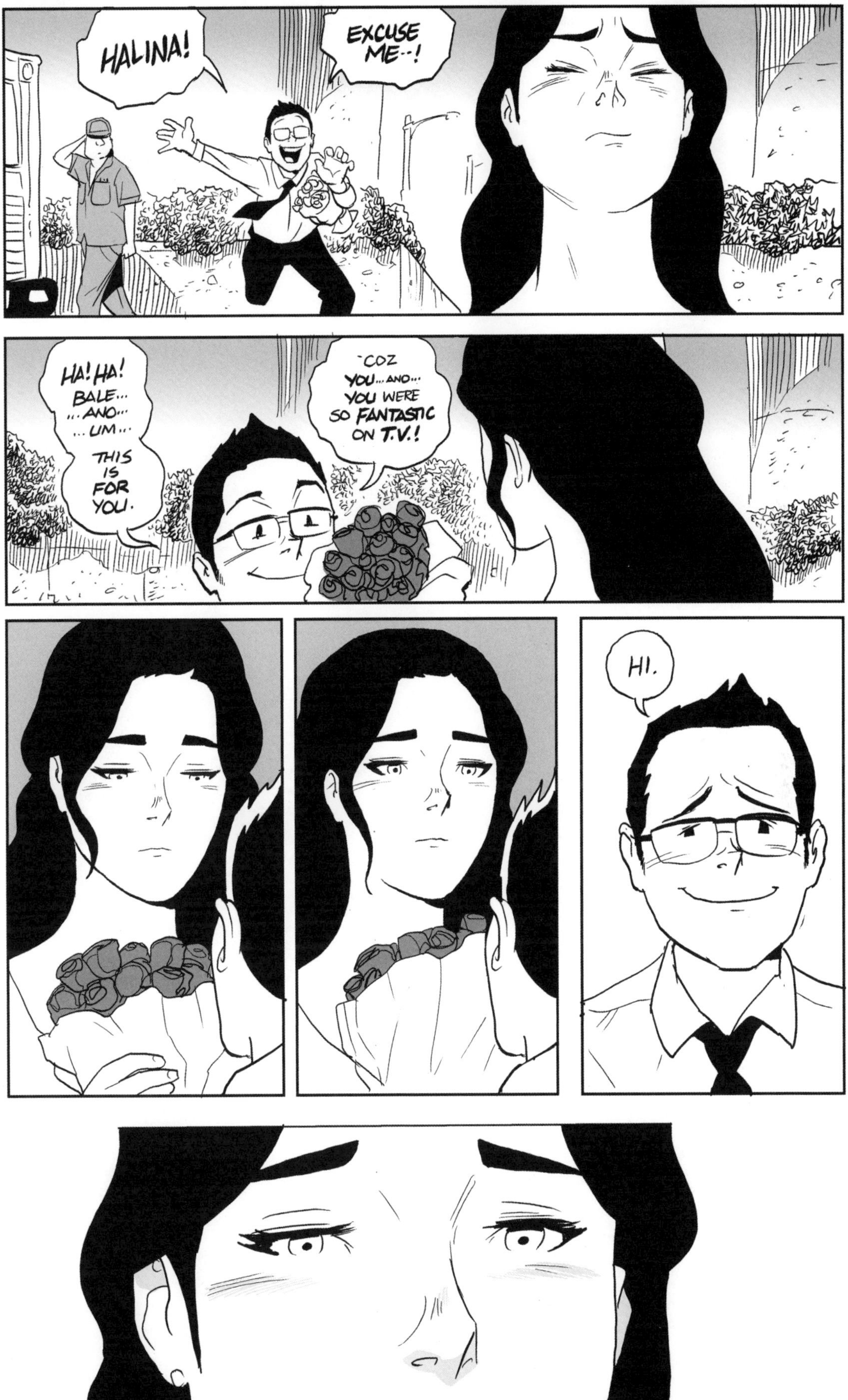
HALINA!
EXCUSE ME--!
HA! HA! BALE... ...ANO... ...UM... THIS IS FOR YOU.
`COZ YOU...AND... YOU WERE SO FANTASTIC ON T.V.!
HI.

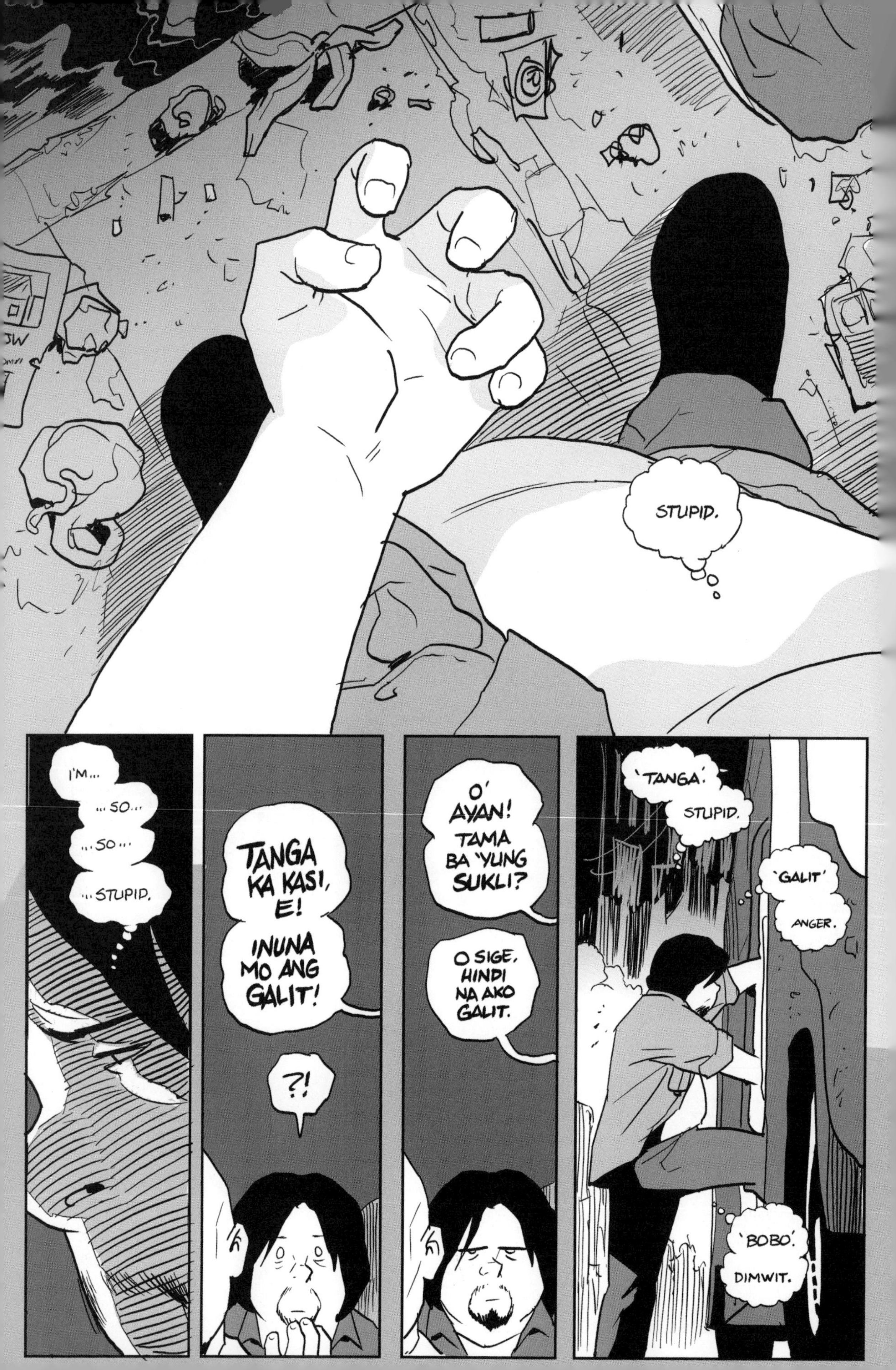
STUPID.
I'M...
...SO...
...SO...
...STUPID.
TANGA KA KASI, E!
INUNA MO ANG GALIT!
?!
O' AYAN! TAMA BA 'YUNG SUKLI?
O SIGE, HINDI NA AKO GALIT.
'TANGA'.
STUPID.
'GALIT'
ANGER.
'BOBO'.
DIMWIT.

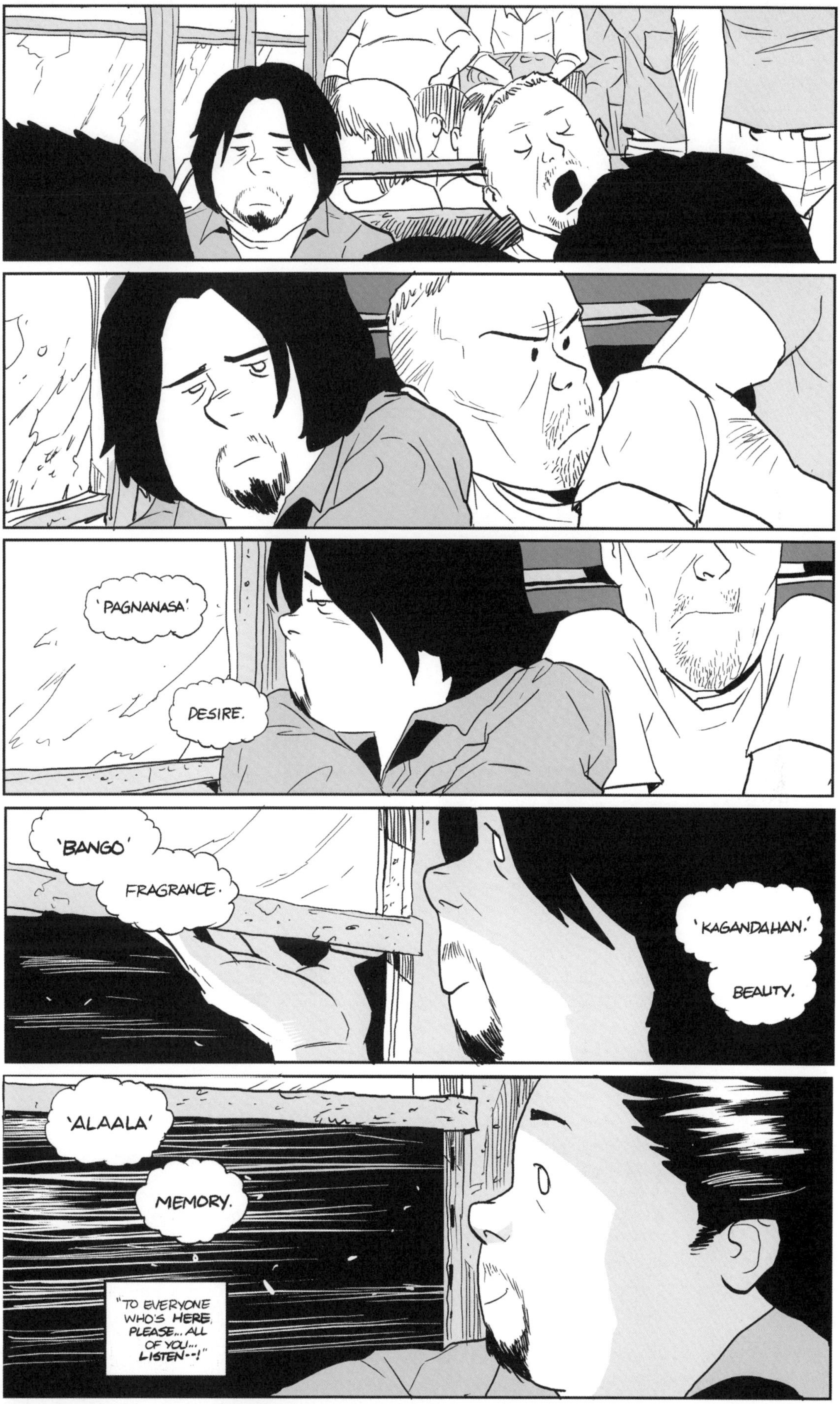
'PAGNANASA'
DESIRE.
'BANGO'
FRAGRANCE.
'KAGANDAHAN.'
BEAUTY.
'ALAALA'
MEMORY.
"TO EVERYONE WHO'S HERE, PLEASE... ALL OF YOU... LISTEN--!"

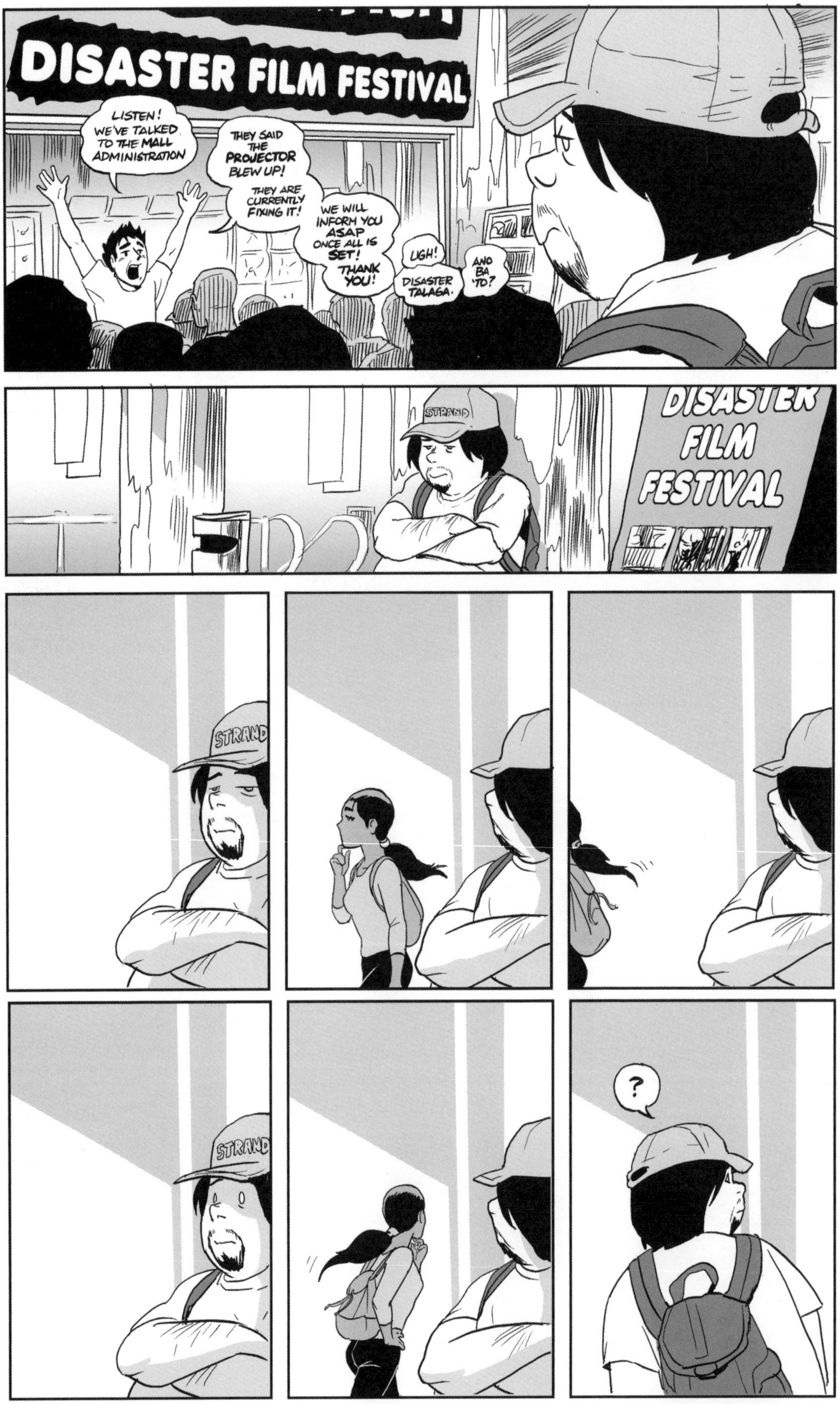
DISASTER FILM FESTIVAL
LISTEN! WE'VE TALKED TO THE MALL ADMINISTRATION
THEY SAID THE PROJECTOR BLEW UP!
THEY ARE CURRENTLY FIXING IT!
WE WILL INFORM YOU ASAP ONCE ALL IS SET! THANK YOU!
UGH!
DISASTER TALAGA.
AND BA 'TO?
STRAND
DISASTER FILM FESTIVAL
STRAND
STRAND
?

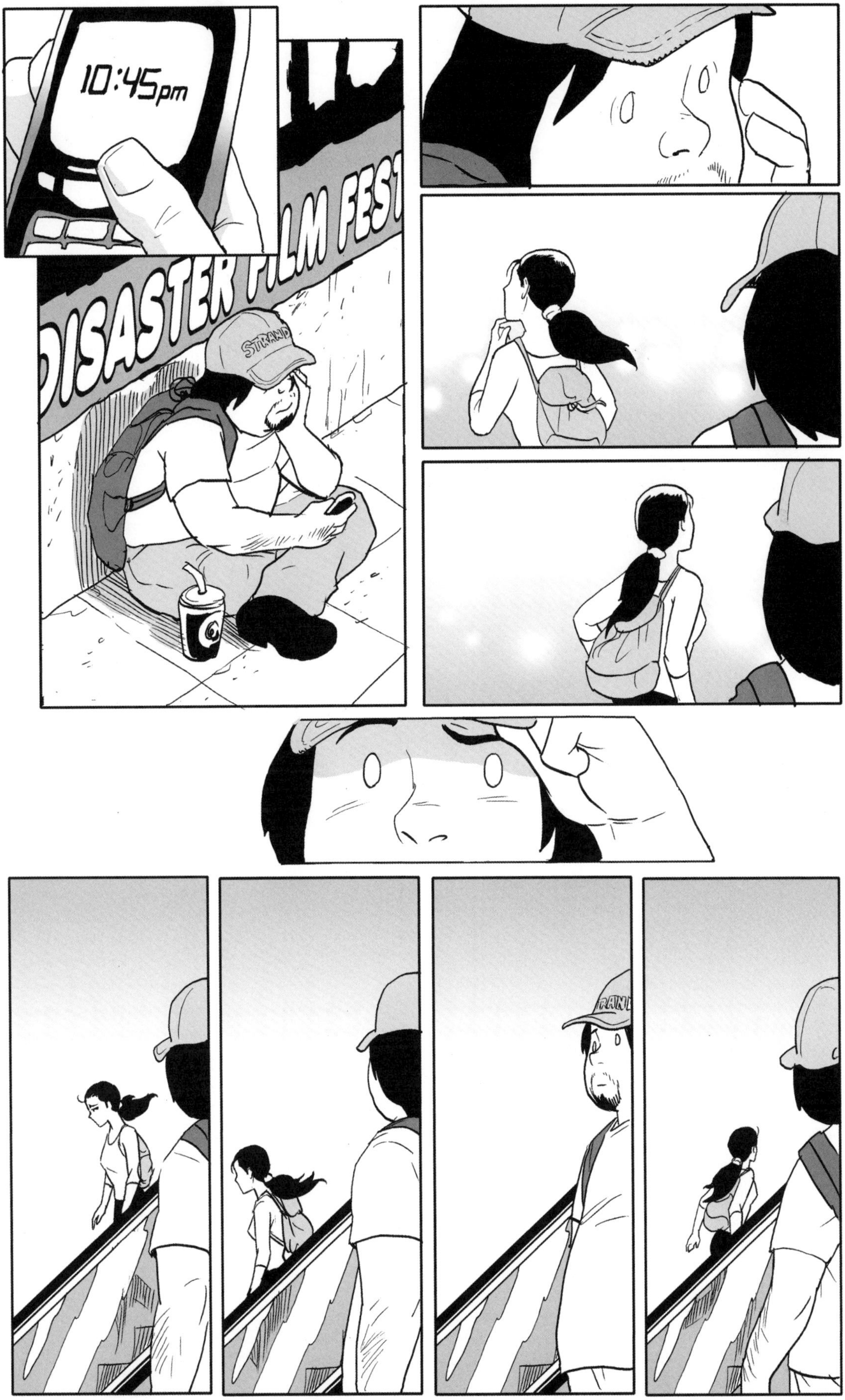
10:45pm
DISASTER FILM FEST
STRAND

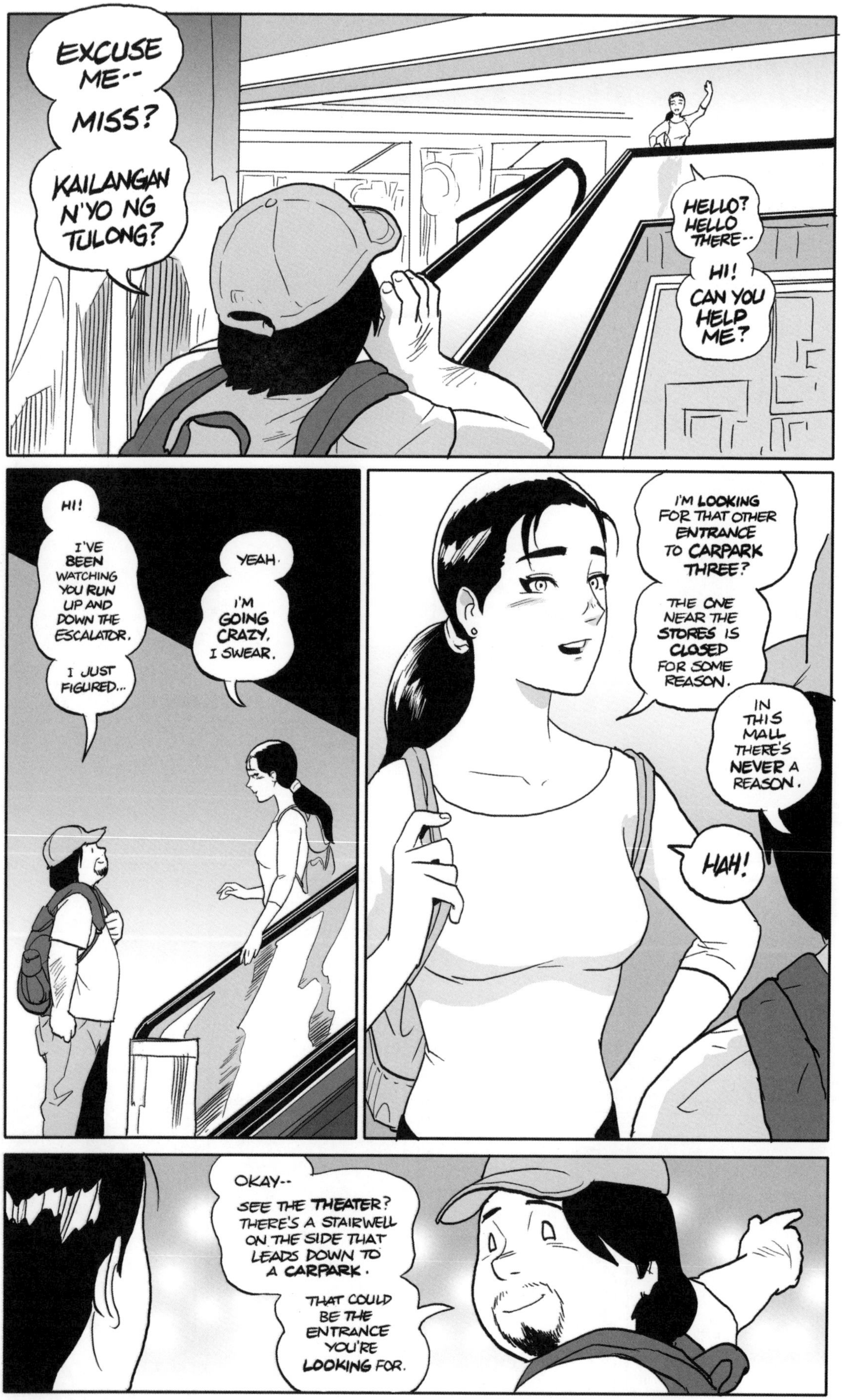
EXCUSE ME--
MISS?
KAILANGAN N'YO NG TULONG?
HELLO? HELLO THERE--
HI! CAN YOU HELP ME?
HI!
I'VE BEEN WATCHING YOU RUN UP AND DOWN THE ESCALATOR.
I JUST FIGURED...
YEAH.
I'M GOING CRAZY, I SWEAR.
I'M LOOKING FOR THAT OTHER ENTRANCE TO CARPARK THREE?
THE ONE NEAR THE STORES IS CLOSED FOR SOME REASON.
IN THIS MALL THERE'S NEVER A REASON.
HAH!
OKAY--
SEE THE THEATER? THERE'S A STAIRWELL ON THE SIDE THAT LEADS DOWN TO A CARPARK.
THAT COULD BE THE ENTRANCE YOU'RE LOOKING FOR.

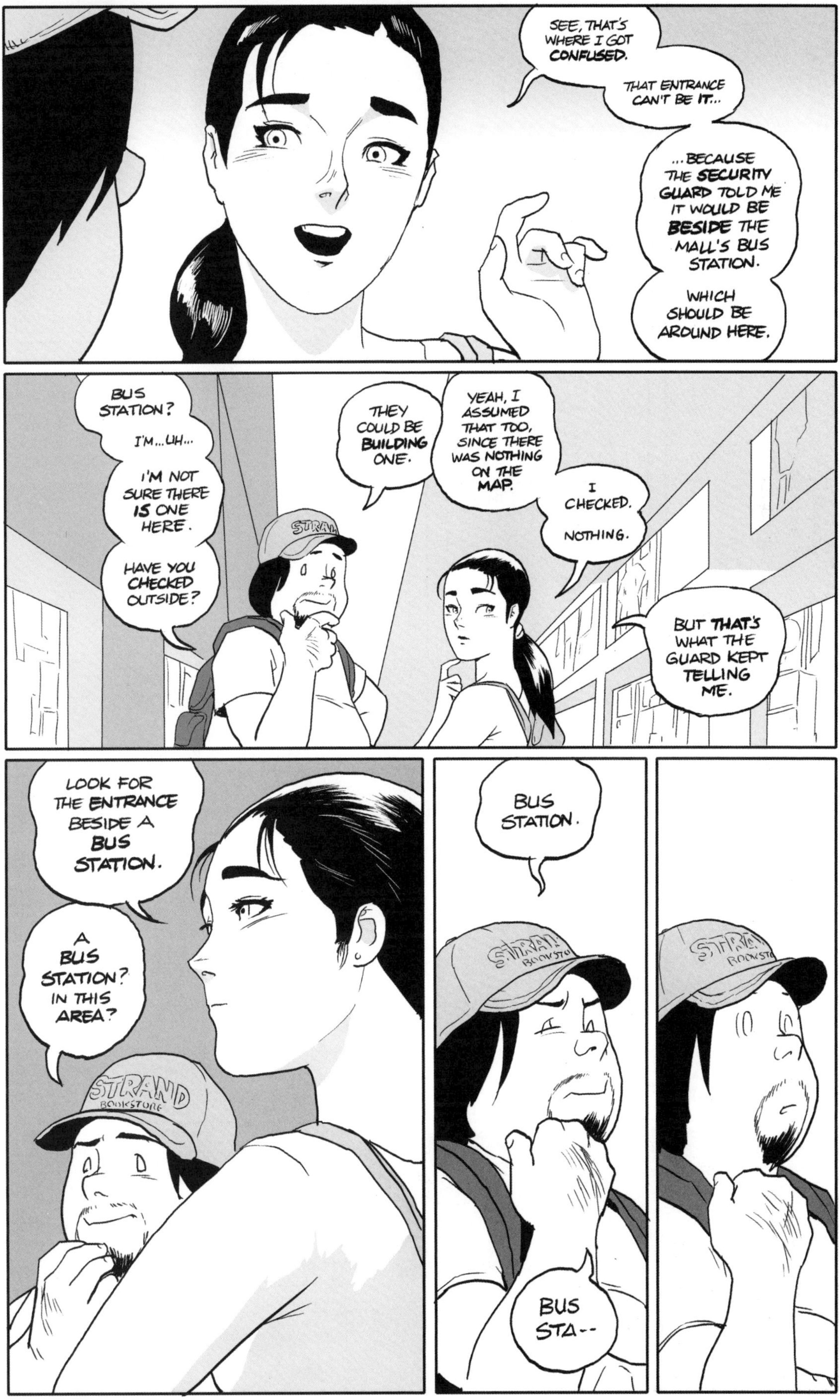

SEE, THAT'S WHERE I GOT CONFUSED.
THAT ENTRANCE CAN'T BE IT...
...BECAUSE THE SECURITY GUARD TOLD ME IT WOULD BE BESIDE THE MALL'S BUS STATION.
WHICH SHOULD BE AROUND HERE.
BUS STATION?
I'M...UH...
I'M NOT SURE THERE IS ONE HERE.
HAVE YOU CHECKED OUTSIDE?
THEY COULD BE BUILDING ONE.
YEAH, I ASSUMED THAT TOO, SINCE THERE WAS NOTHING ON THE MAP.
I CHECKED.
NOTHING.
BUT THAT'S WHAT THE GUARD KEPT TELLING ME.
STRAND
LOOK FOR THE ENTRANCE BESIDE A BUS STATION.
A BUS STATION? IN THIS AREA?
STRAND BOOKSTORE
BUS STATION.
BUS STA--

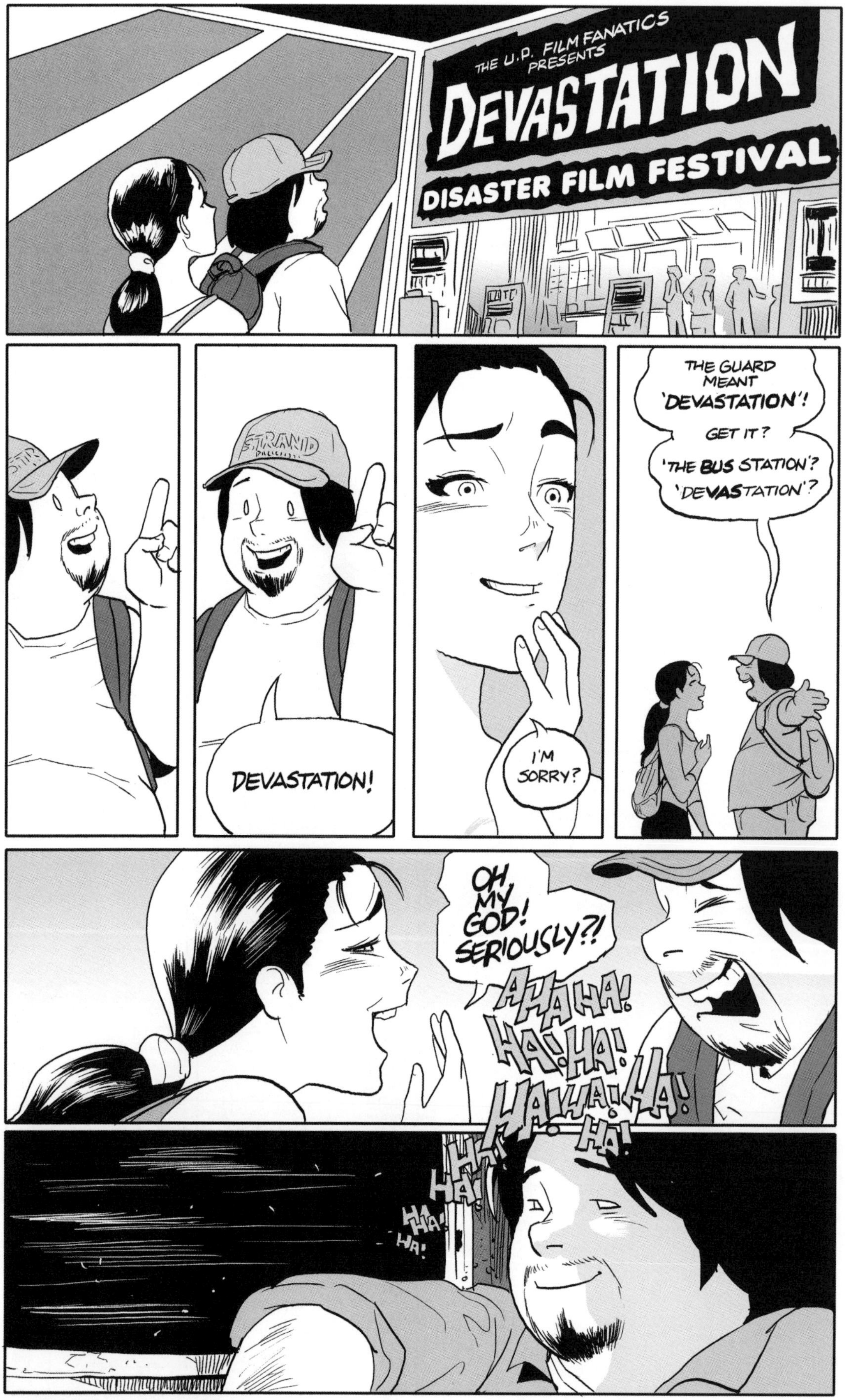
THE U.P. FILM FANATICS PRESENTS
DEVASTATION
DISASTER FILM FESTIVAL
STRAND
DEVASTATION!
I'M SORRY?
THE GUARD MEANT 'DEVASTATION'! GET IT? 'THE BUS STATION'? 'DEVASTATION'?
OH, MY GOD! SERIOUSLY?!
AHAHA! HA! HA! HA! HA! HA! HA!
HA! HA!
HA! HA! HA!

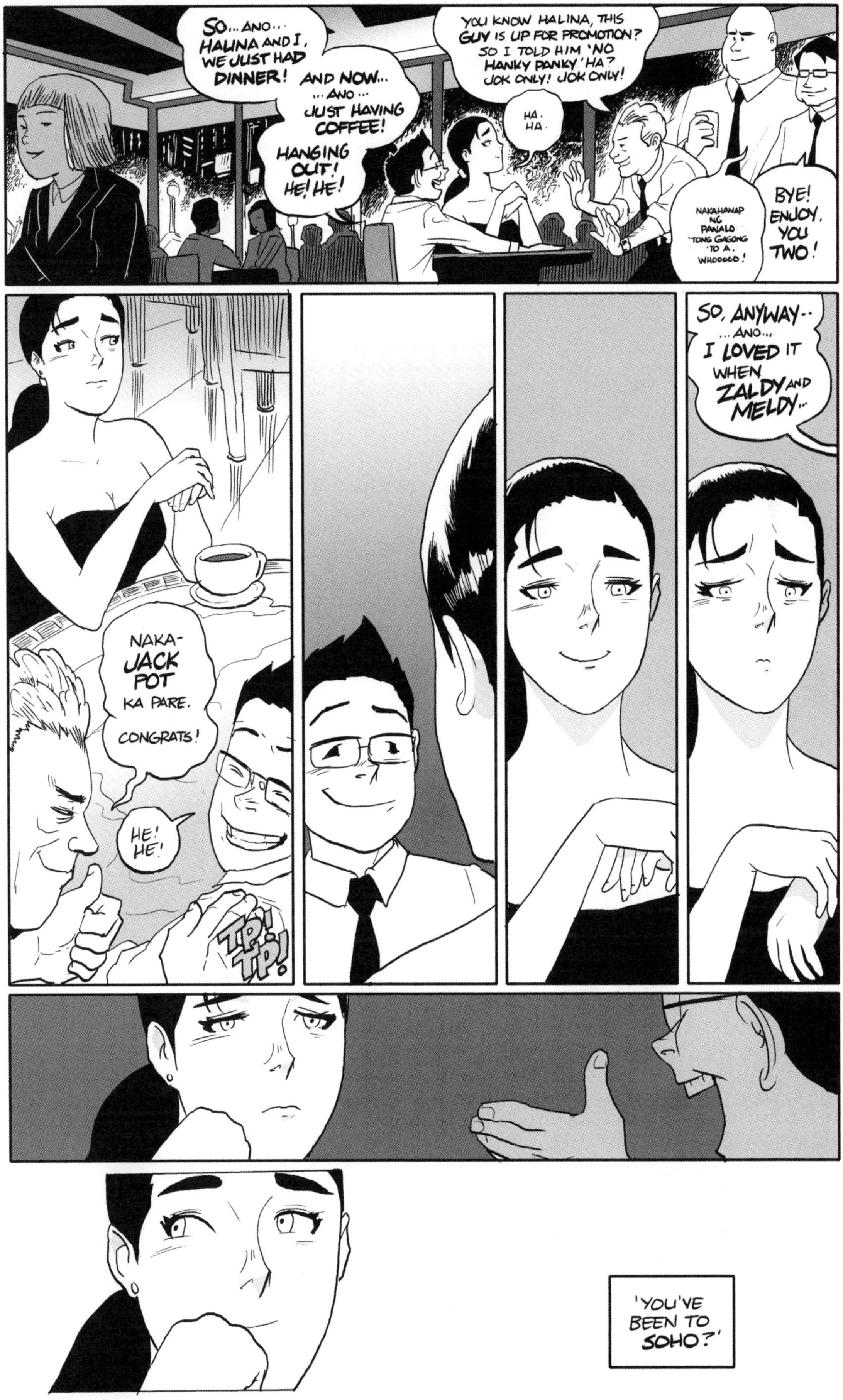

SO... ANO... HALINA AND I, WE JUST HAD DINNER!
AND NOW... ...ANO... JUST HAVING COFFEE!
HANGING OUT! HE! HE!
YOU KNOW HALINA, THIS GUY IS UP FOR PROMOTION? SO I TOLD HIM 'NO HANKY PANKY' HA? JOK ONLY! JOK ONLY!
HA. HA.
NAKAHANAP NG PANALO 'TONG GAGONG 'TO A. WHOOOOO!
BYE! ENJOY, YOU TWO!
NAKA-JACK POT KA PARE.
CONGRATS!
HE! HE!
TP! TP!
SO, ANYWAY.. ...ANO... I LOVED IT WHEN ZALDY AND MELDY...
'YOU'VE BEEN TO SOHO?'

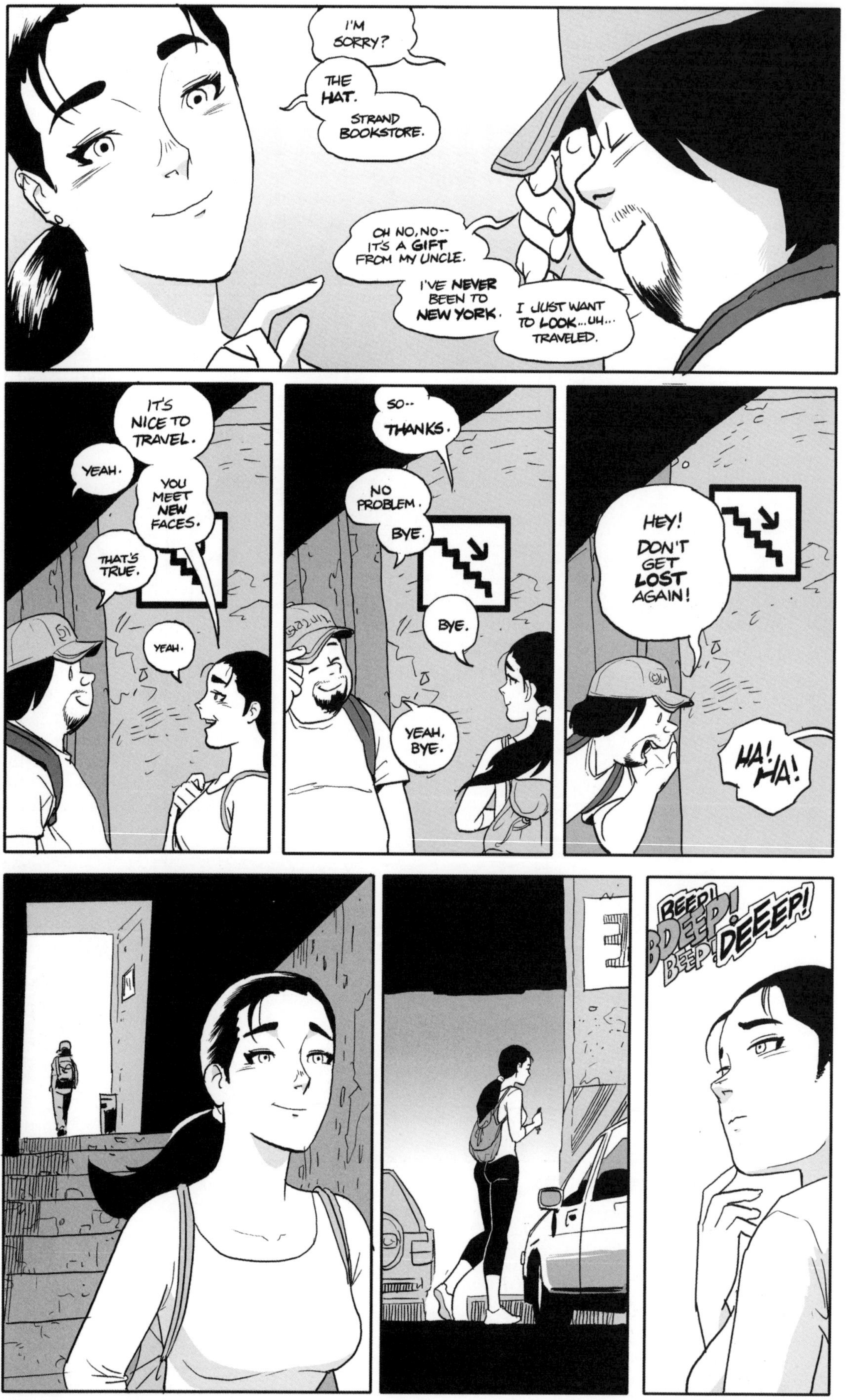
I'M SORRY?
THE HAT.
STRAND BOOKSTORE.
OH NO, NO-- IT'S A GIFT FROM MY UNCLE.
I'VE NEVER BEEN TO NEW YORK.
I JUST WANT TO LOOK... UH... TRAVELED.
IT'S NICE TO TRAVEL.
YEAH.
YOU MEET NEW FACES.
THAT'S TRUE.
YEAH.
SO-- THANKS.
NO PROBLEM.
BYE.
BYE.
YEAH, BYE.
HEY! DON'T GET LOST AGAIN!
HA! HA!
BEEP! BDEEP! BEEP! DEEEP!

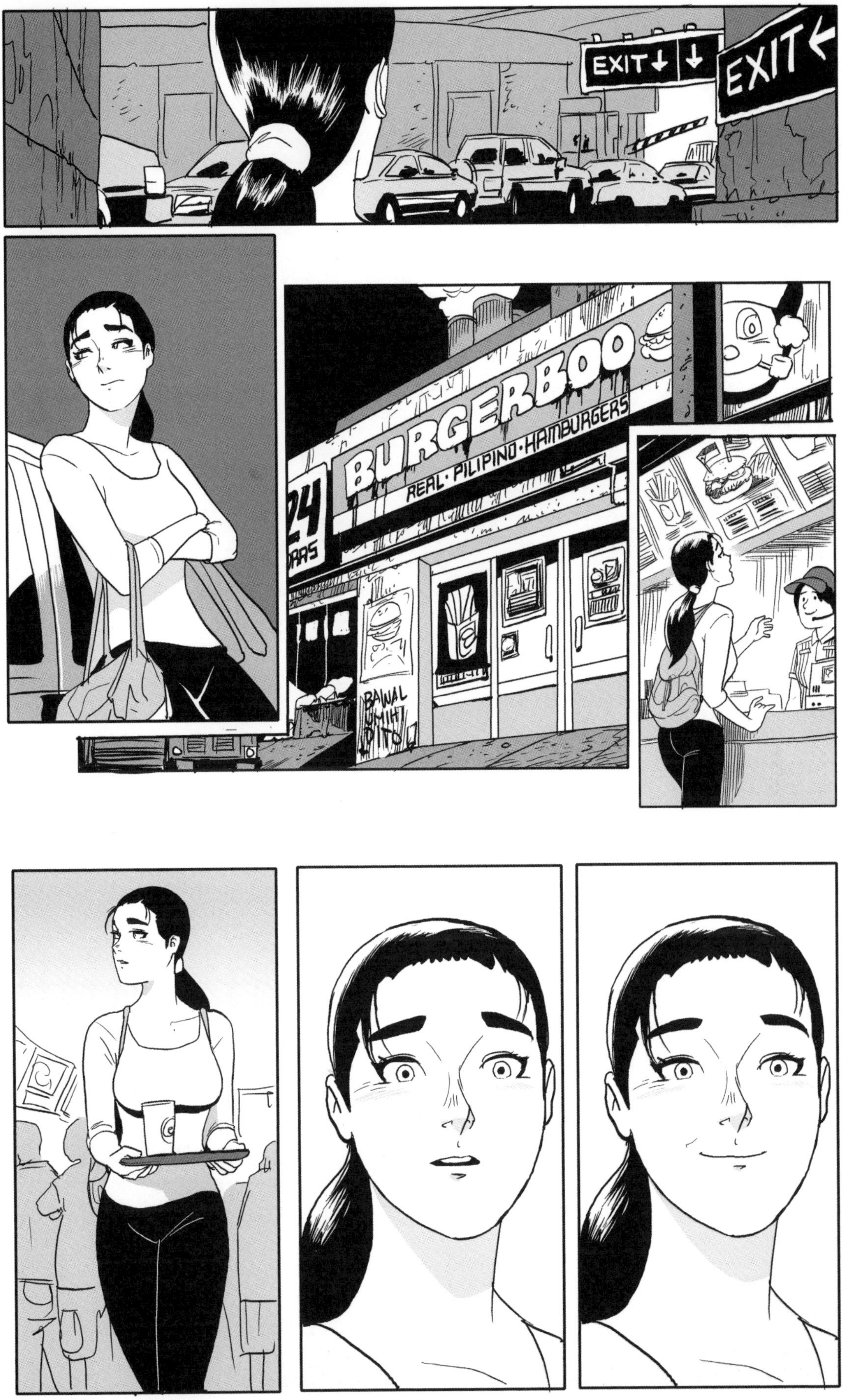

EXIT ↓ ↓
EXIT ←
BURGERBOO
REAL · PILIPINO · HAMBURGERS
24
ORAS
BAWAL
UMIHI
DITO

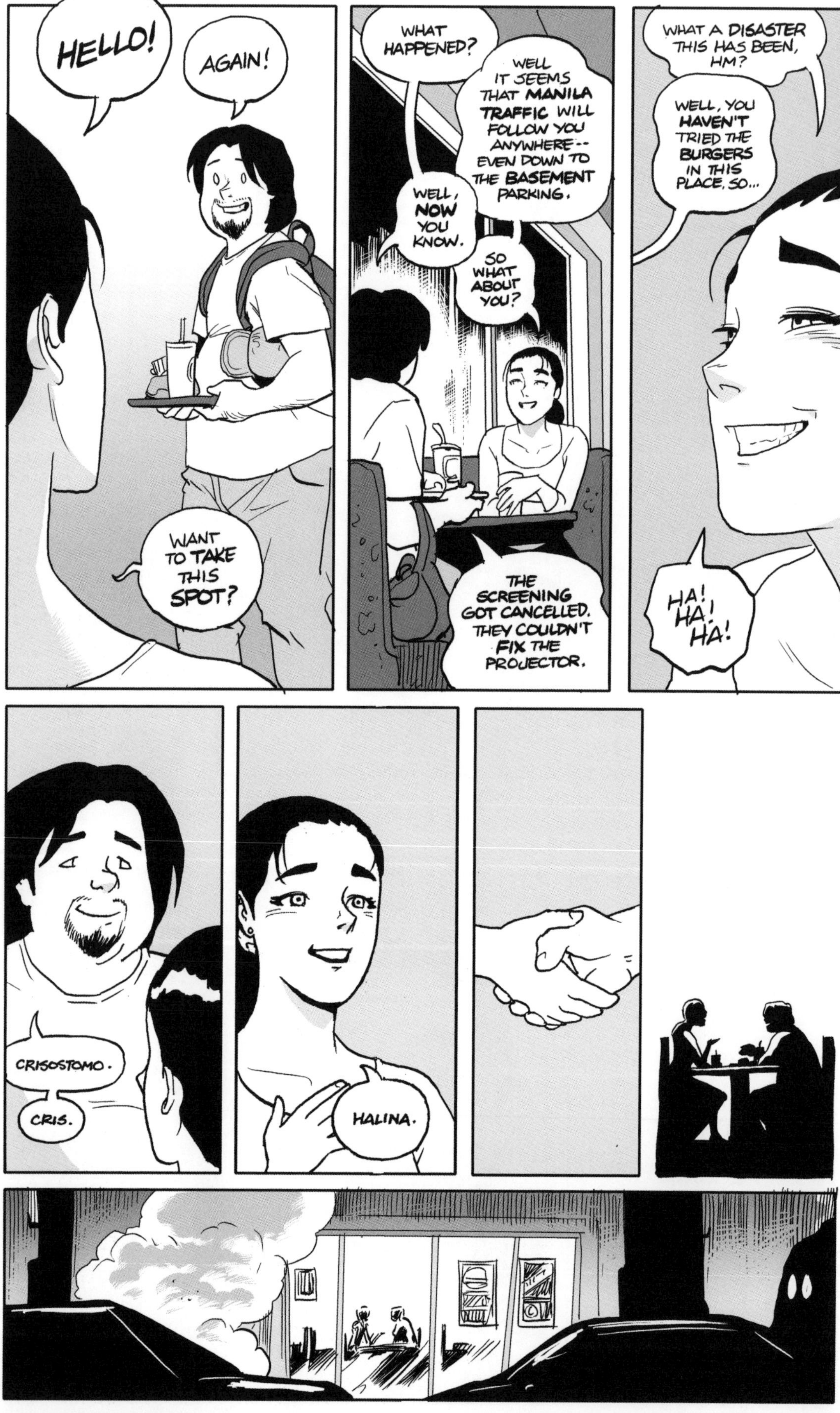
HELLO!
AGAIN!
WANT TO TAKE THIS SPOT?
WHAT HAPPENED?
WELL IT SEEMS THAT MANILA TRAFFIC WILL FOLLOW YOU ANYWHERE-- EVEN DOWN TO THE BASEMENT PARKING.
WELL, NOW YOU KNOW.
SO WHAT ABOUT YOU?
THE SCREENING GOT CANCELLED. THEY COULDN'T FIX THE PROJECTOR.
WHAT A DISASTER THIS HAS BEEN, HM?
WELL, YOU HAVEN'T TRIED THE BURGERS IN THIS PLACE, SO...
HA! HA! HA!
CRISOSTOMO.
CRIS.
HALINA.

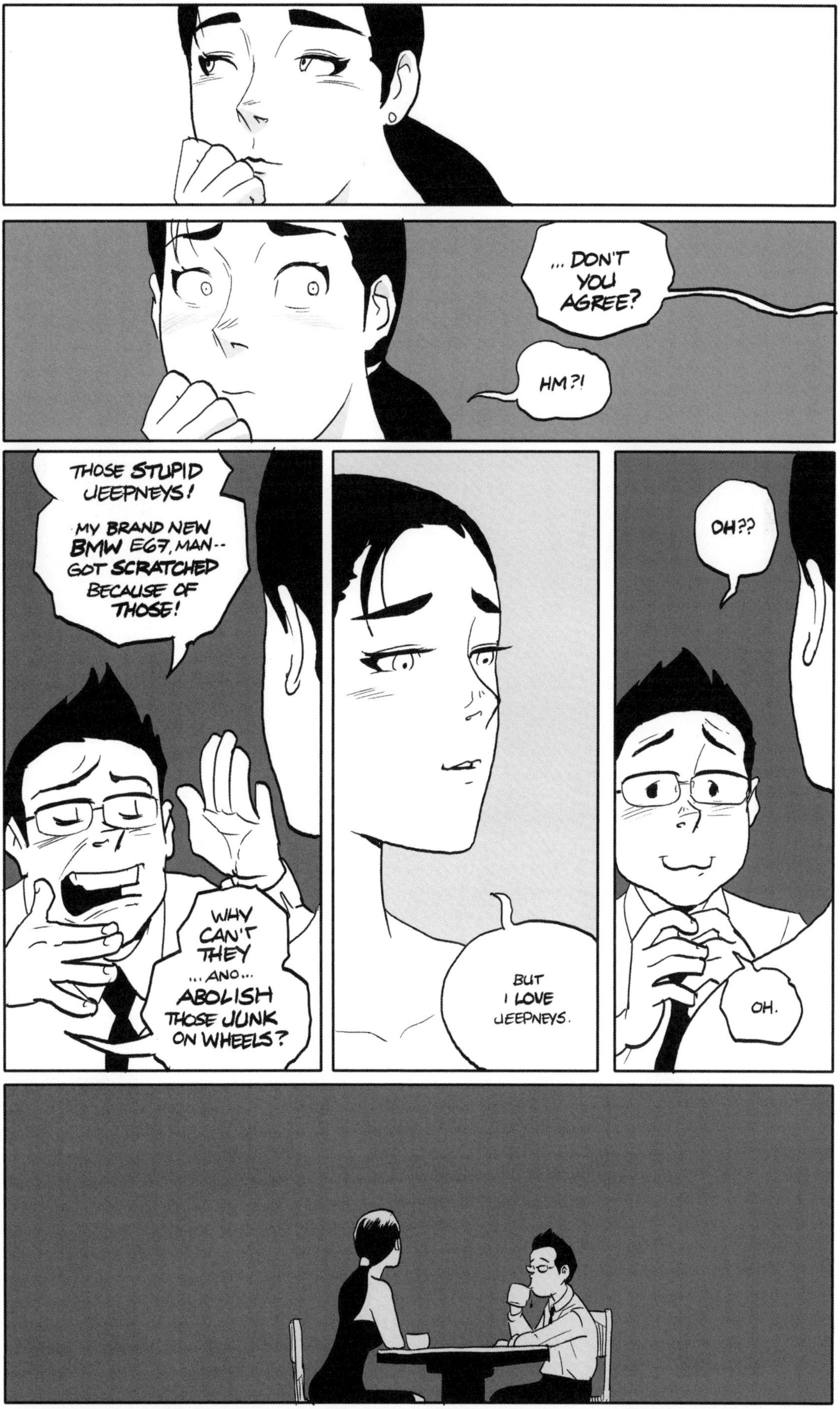
... DON'T YOU AGREE?
HM?!
THOSE STUPID JEEPNEYS!
MY BRAND NEW BMW E67, MAN-- GOT SCRATCHED BECAUSE OF THOSE!
WHY CAN'T THEY ...AND... ABOLISH THOSE JUNK ON WHEELS?
BUT I LOVE JEEPNEYS.
OH??
OH.

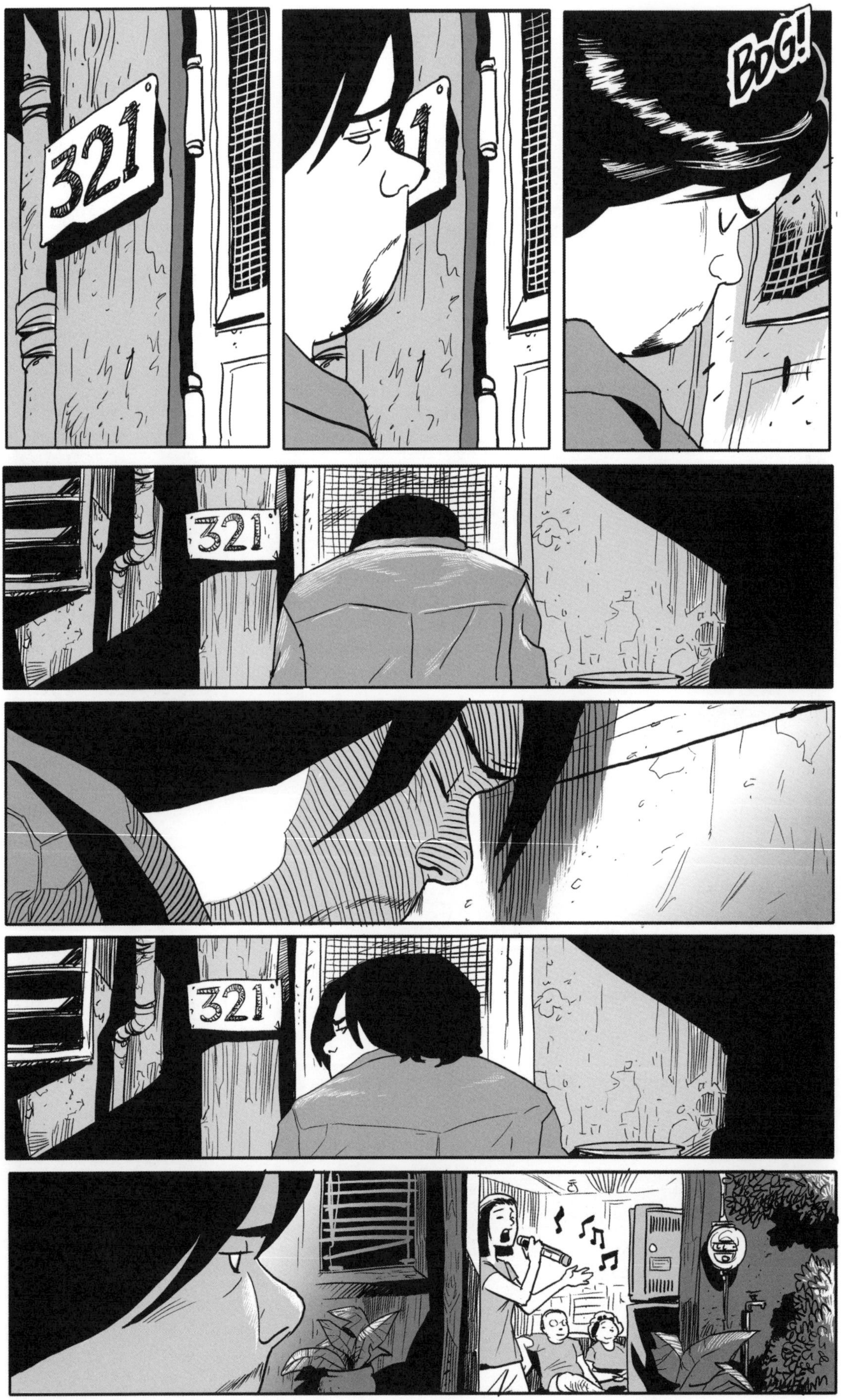
321
BDG!
321
321

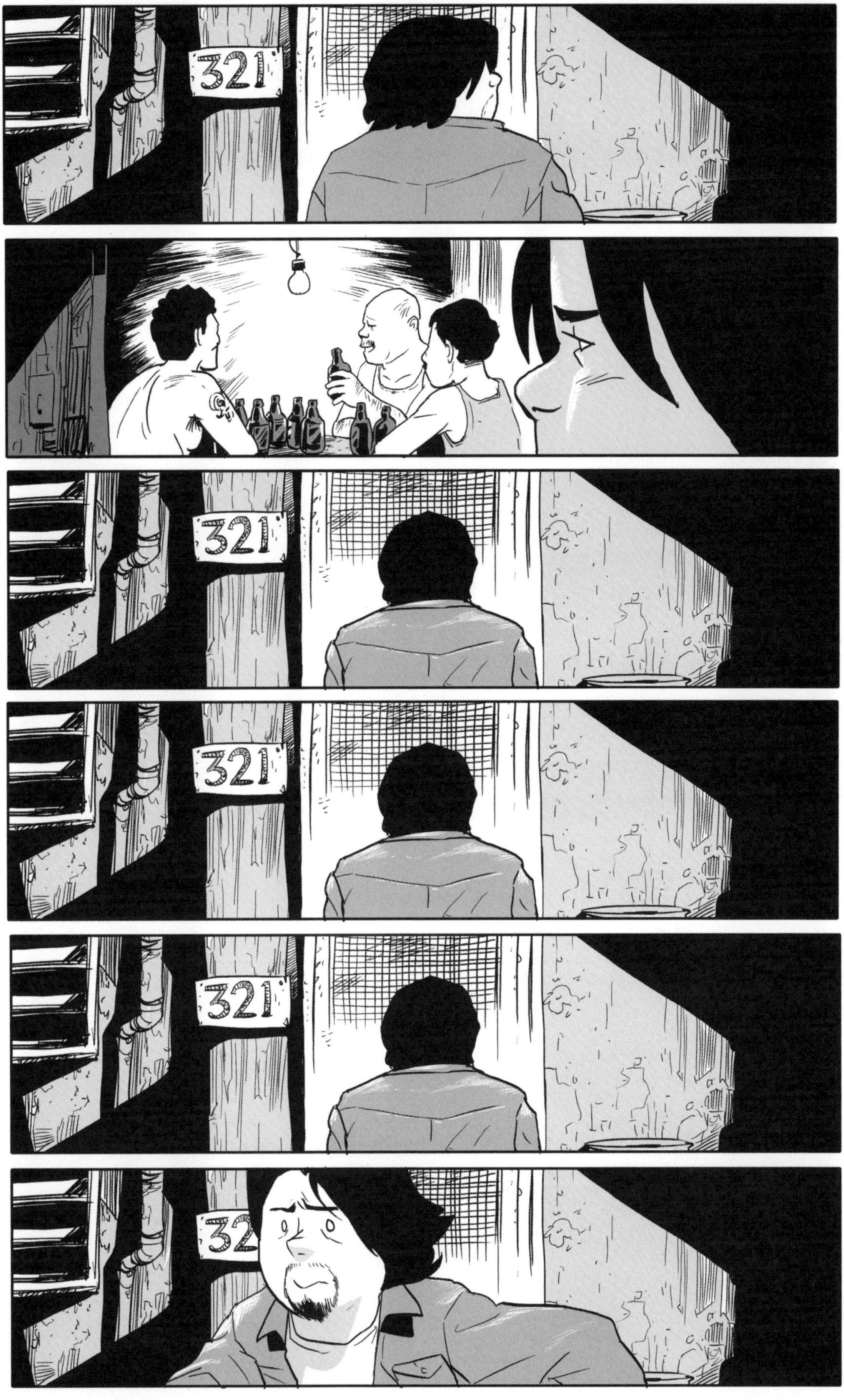
321
321
321
321
32

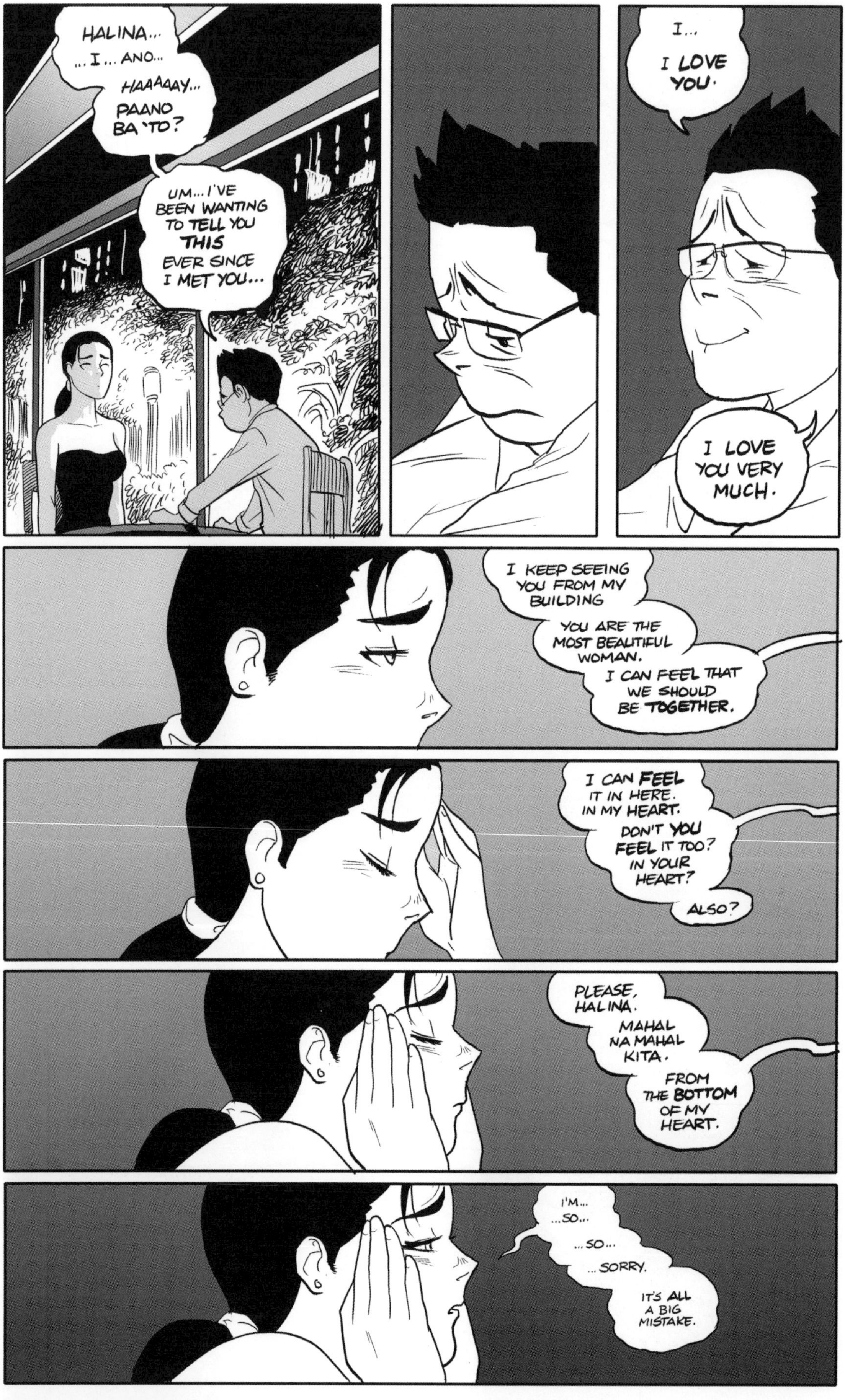
HALINA... ...I... ANO... HAAAAAY... PAANO BA 'TO?
UM... I'VE BEEN WANTING TO TELL YOU THIS EVER SINCE I MET YOU...
I... I LOVE YOU.
I LOVE YOU VERY MUCH.
I KEEP SEEING YOU FROM MY BUILDING
YOU ARE THE MOST BEAUTIFUL WOMAN.
I CAN FEEL THAT WE SHOULD BE TOGETHER.
I CAN FEEL IT IN HERE. IN MY HEART.
DON'T YOU FEEL IT TOO? IN YOUR HEART?
ALSO?
PLEASE, HALINA.
MAHAL NA MAHAL KITA.
FROM THE BOTTOM OF MY HEART.
I'M... ...SO... ...SO... ...SORRY.
IT'S ALL A BIG MISTAKE.

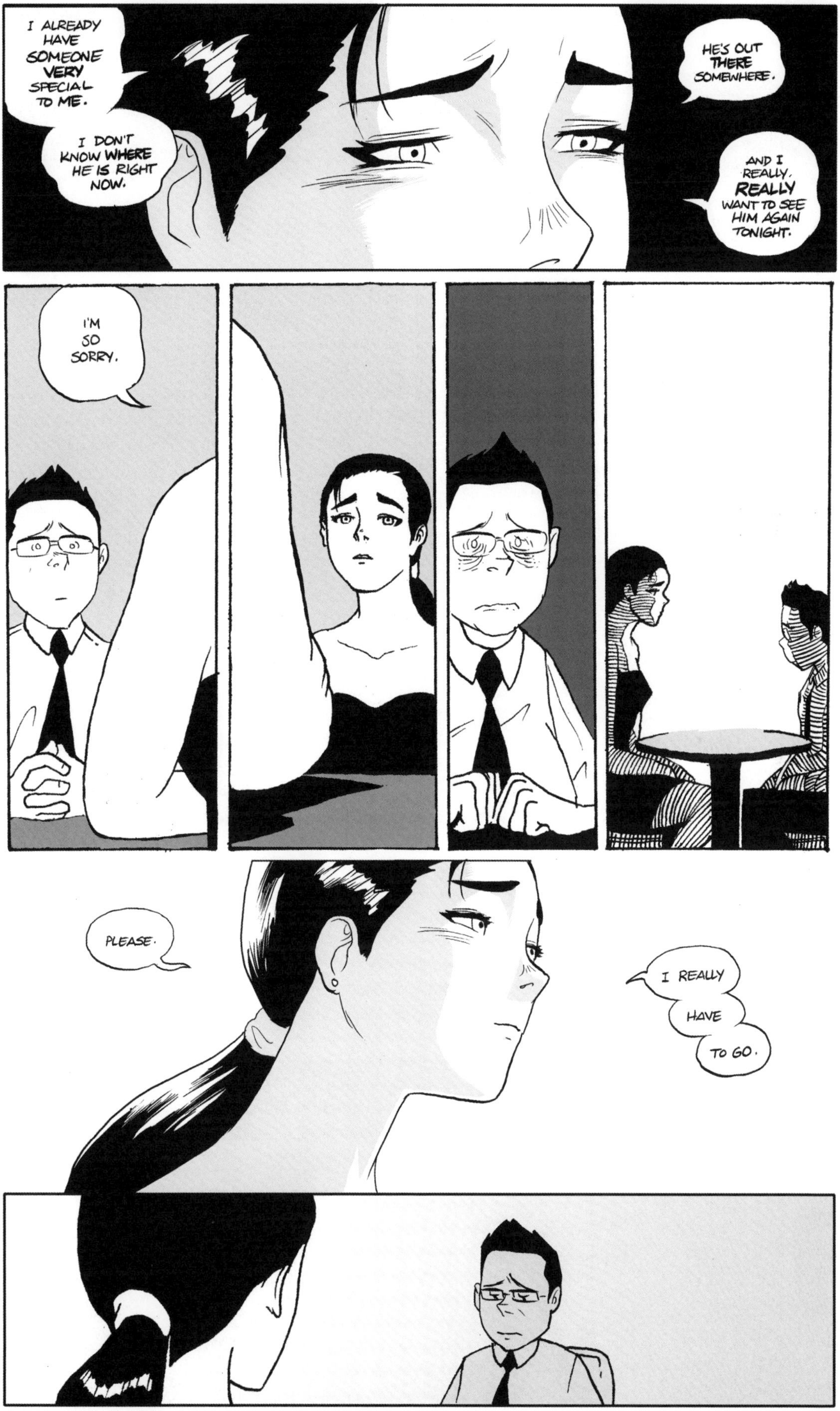
I ALREADY HAVE SOMEONE VERY SPECIAL TO ME.
I DON'T KNOW WHERE HE IS RIGHT NOW.
HE'S OUT THERE SOMEWHERE.
AND I REALLY, REALLY WANT TO SEE HIM AGAIN TONIGHT.
I'M SO SORRY.
PLEASE.
I REALLY
HAVE
TO GO.

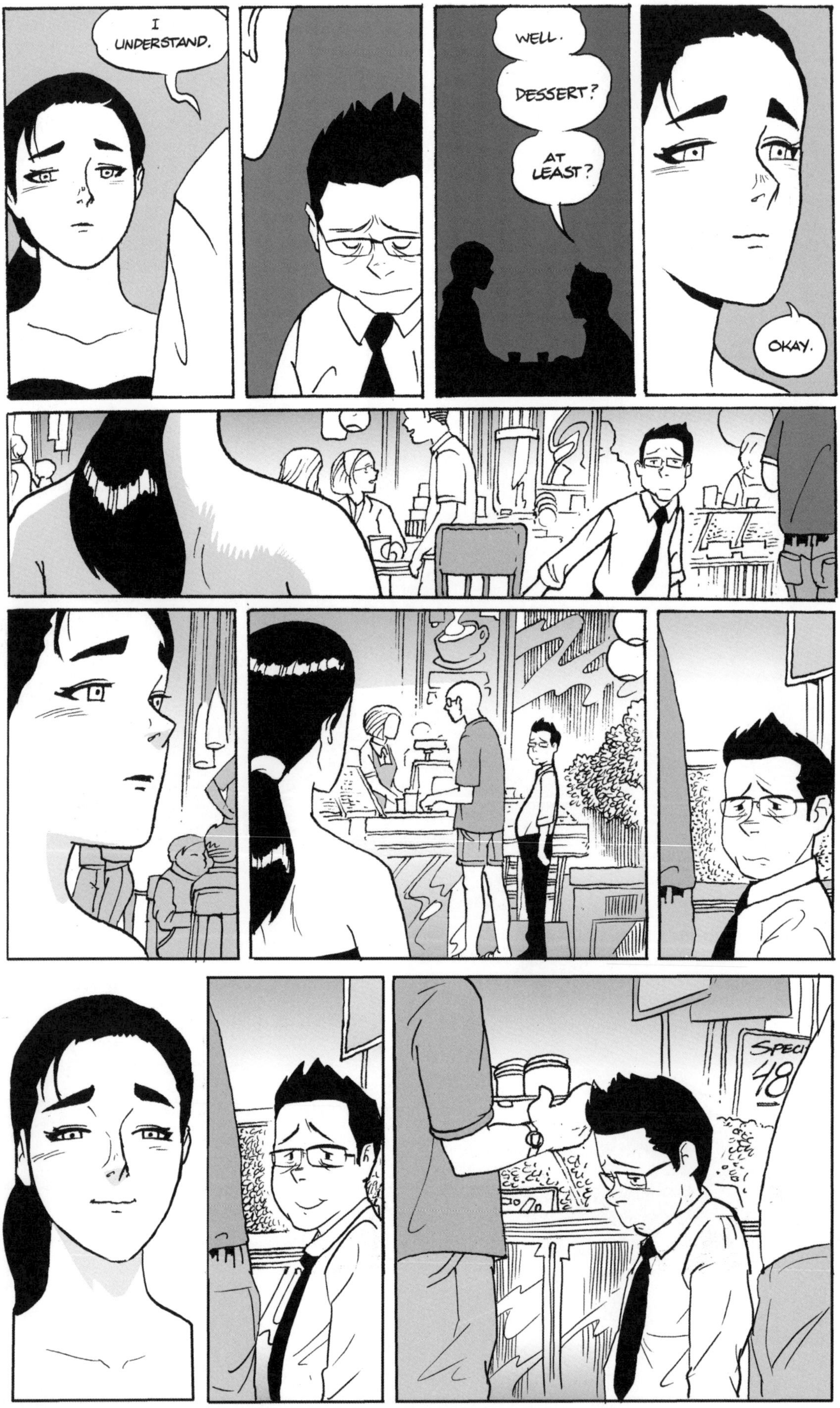
I UNDERSTAND.
WELL.
DESSERT?
AT LEAST?
OKAY.
SPECI
18

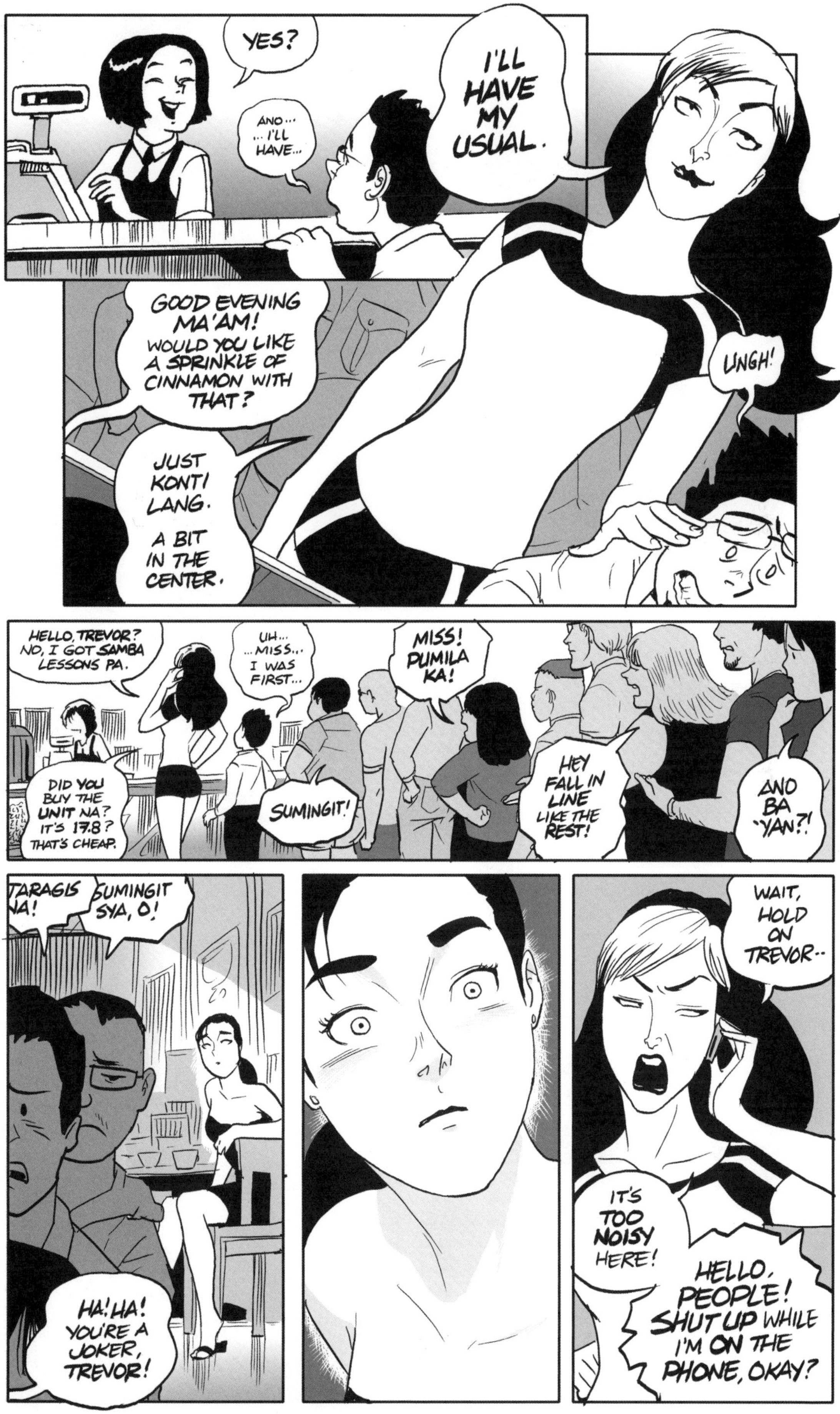
YES?
ANO... ...I'LL HAVE...
I'LL HAVE MY USUAL.
GOOD EVENING MA'AM! WOULD YOU LIKE A SPRINKLE OF CINNAMON WITH THAT?
UNGH!
JUST KONTI LANG.
A BIT IN THE CENTER.
HELLO, TREVOR? NO, I GOT SAMBA LESSONS PA.
UH... ...MISS... I WAS FIRST...
MISS! PUMILA KA!
DID YOU BUY THE UNIT NA? IT'S 17.8? THAT'S CHEAP.
SUMINGIT!
HEY FALL IN LINE LIKE THE REST!
ANO BA 'YAN?!
TARAGIS NA!
SUMINGIT SYA, O!
HA! HA! YOU'RE A JOKER, TREVOR!
WAIT, HOLD ON TREVOR..
IT'S TOO NOISY HERE!
HELLO, PEOPLE! SHUT UP WHILE I'M ON THE PHONE, OKAY?

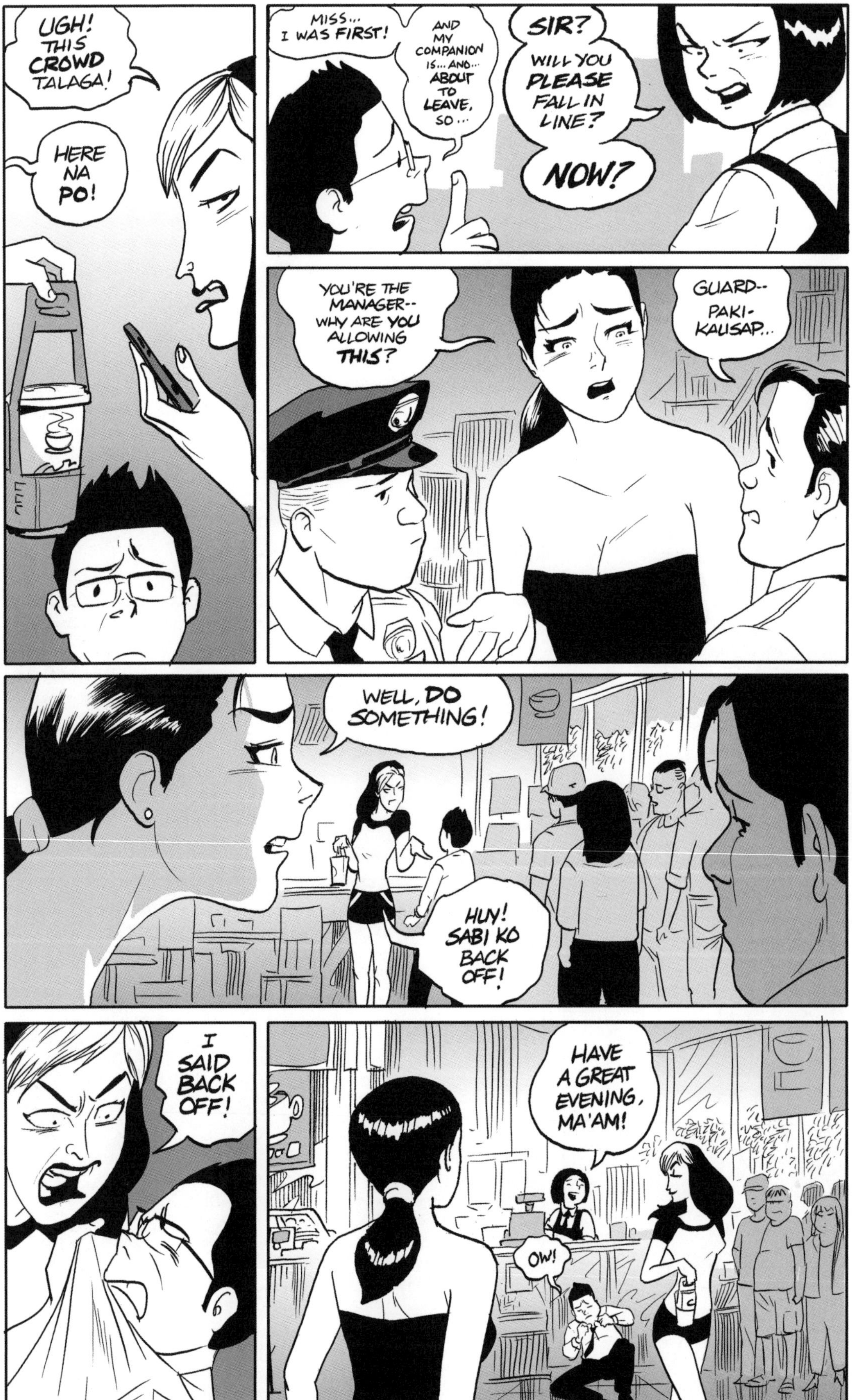
UGH! THIS CROWD TALAGA!
HERE NA PO!
MISS... I WAS FIRST!
AND MY COMPANION IS... AND... ABOUT TO LEAVE, SO...
SIR? WILL YOU PLEASE FALL IN LINE?
NOW?
YOU'RE THE MANAGER-- WHY ARE YOU ALLOWING THIS?
GUARD-- PAKI-KAUSAP...
WELL, DO SOMETHING!
HUY! SABI KO BACK OFF!
I SAID BACK OFF!
HAVE A GREAT EVENING, MA'AM!
OW!

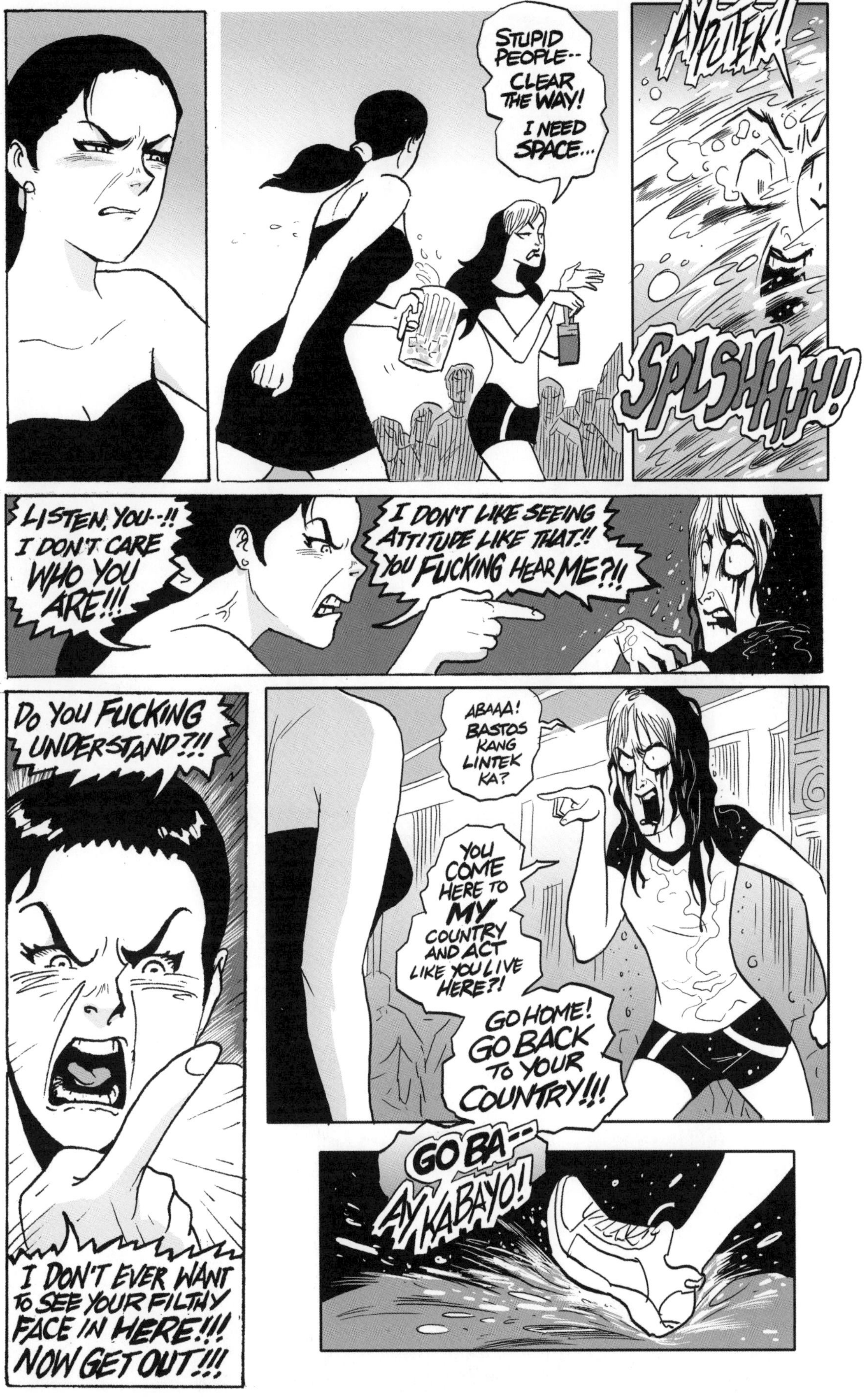
STUPID PEOPLE-- CLEAR THE WAY! I NEED SPACE...
AYPUTEK!
SPLSHHHH!
LISTEN, YOU--!! I DON'T CARE WHO YOU ARE!!!
I DON'T LIKE SEEING ATTITUDE LIKE THAT!! YOU FUCKING HEAR ME?!!
DO YOU FUCKING UNDERSTAND?!!
I DON'T EVER WANT TO SEE YOUR FILTHY FACE IN HERE!!! NOW GET OUT!!!
ABAAA! BASTOS KANG LINTEK KA?
YOU COME HERE TO MY COUNTRY AND ACT LIKE YOU LIVE HERE?!
GO HOME! GO BACK TO YOUR COUNTRY!!!
GO BA--
AY KABAYO!

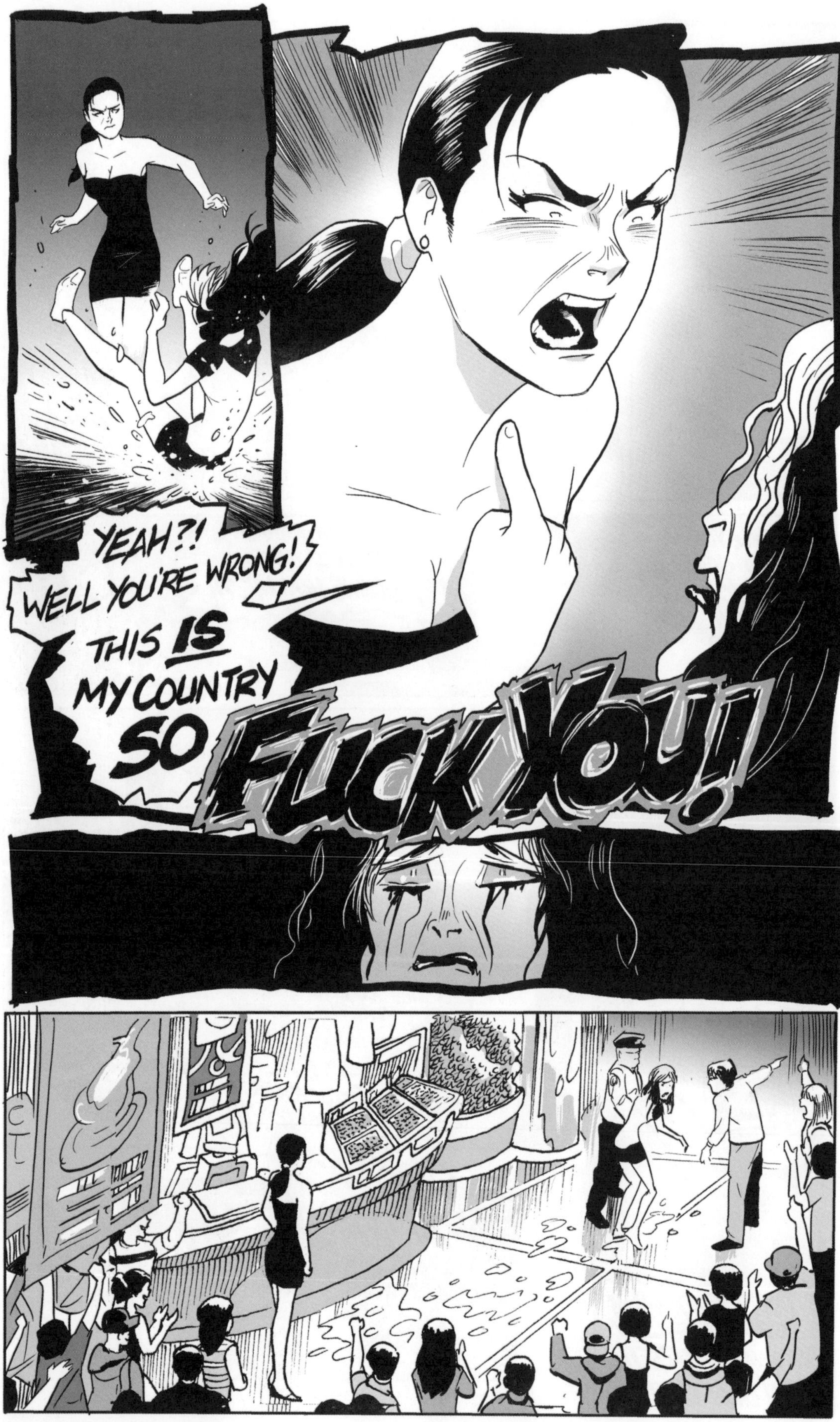
YEAH?! WELL YOU'RE WRONG! THIS IS MY COUNTRY SO
FUCK YOU!

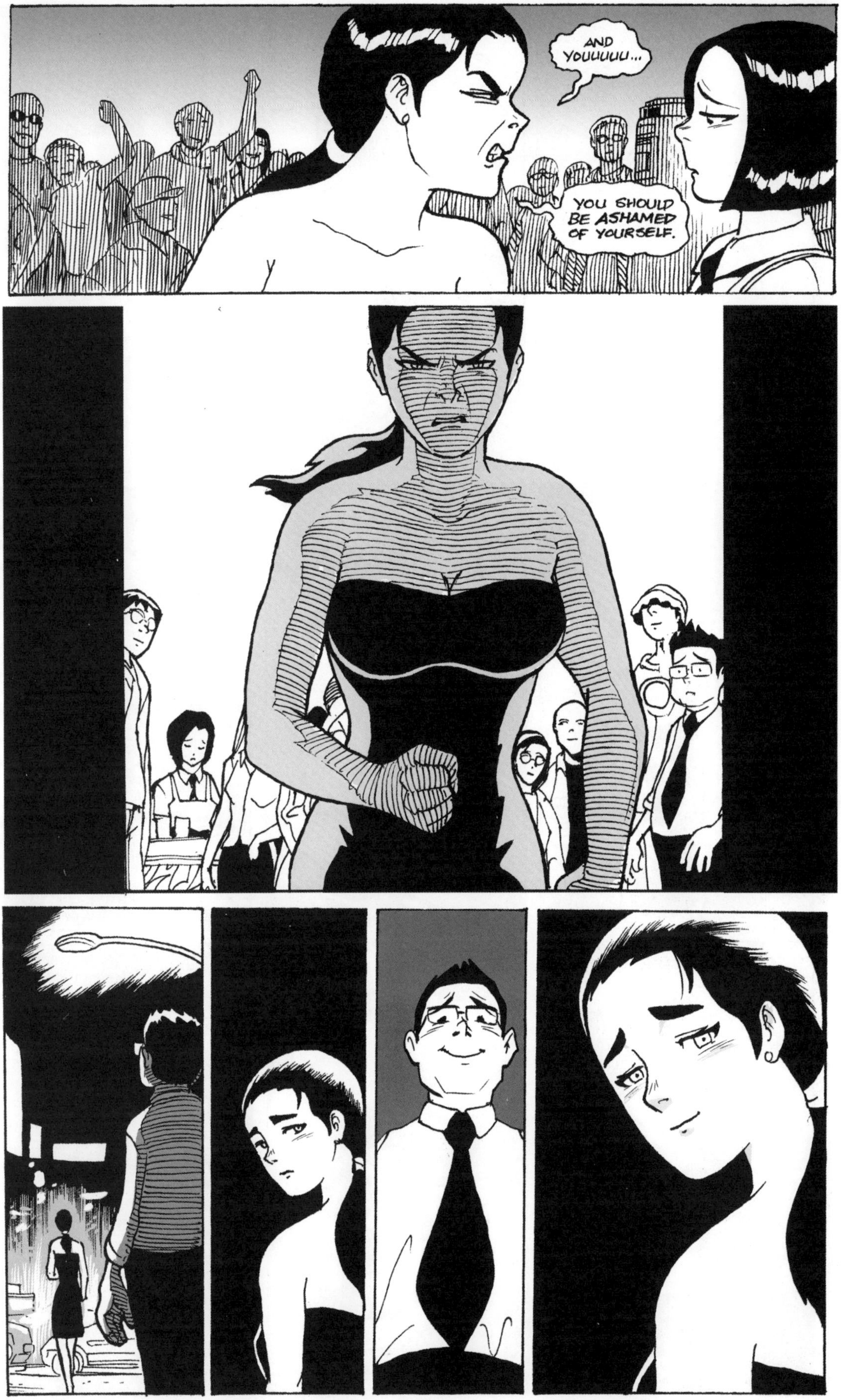
AND YOUUUUU...
YOU SHOULD BE ASHAMED OF YOURSELF.

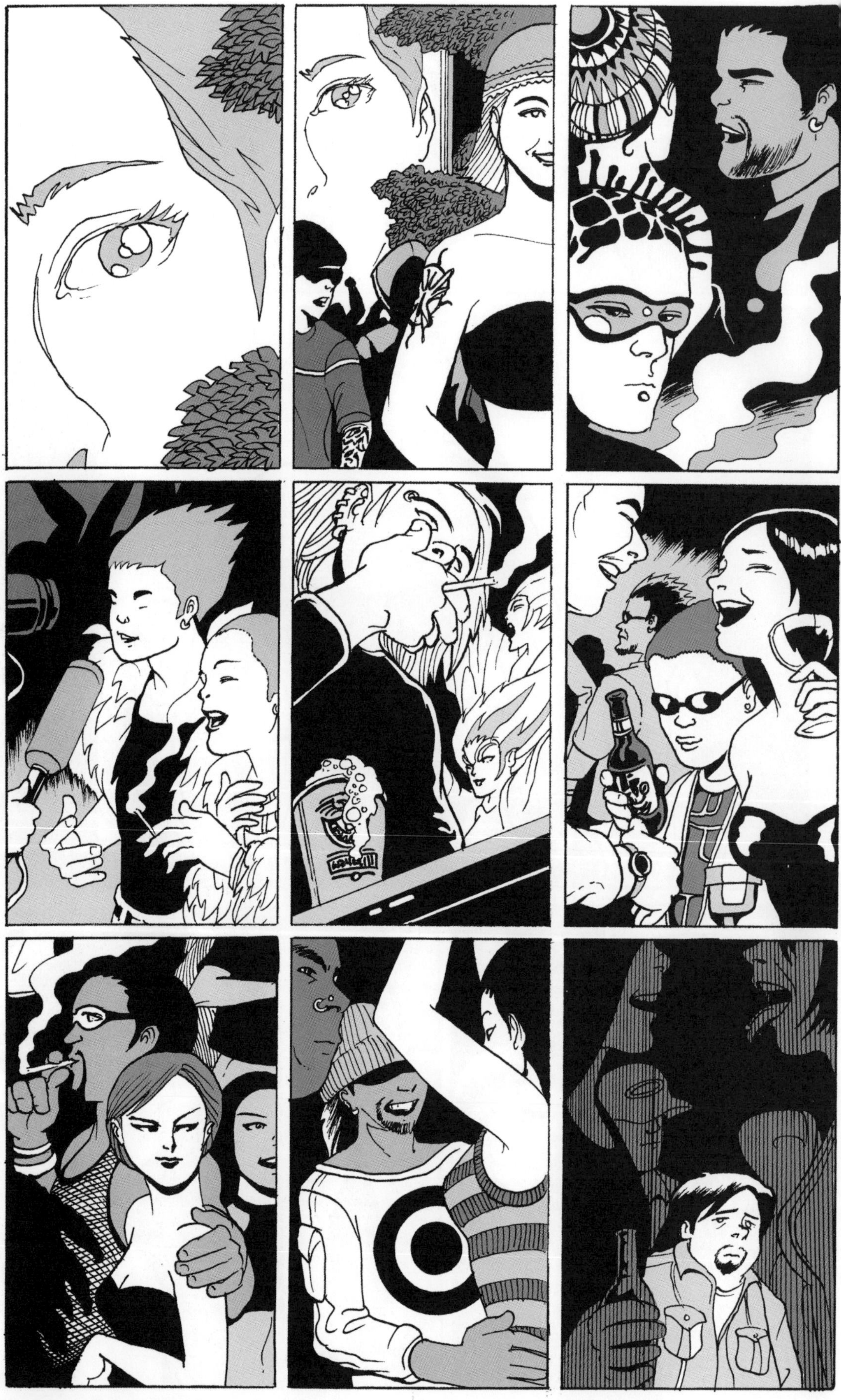

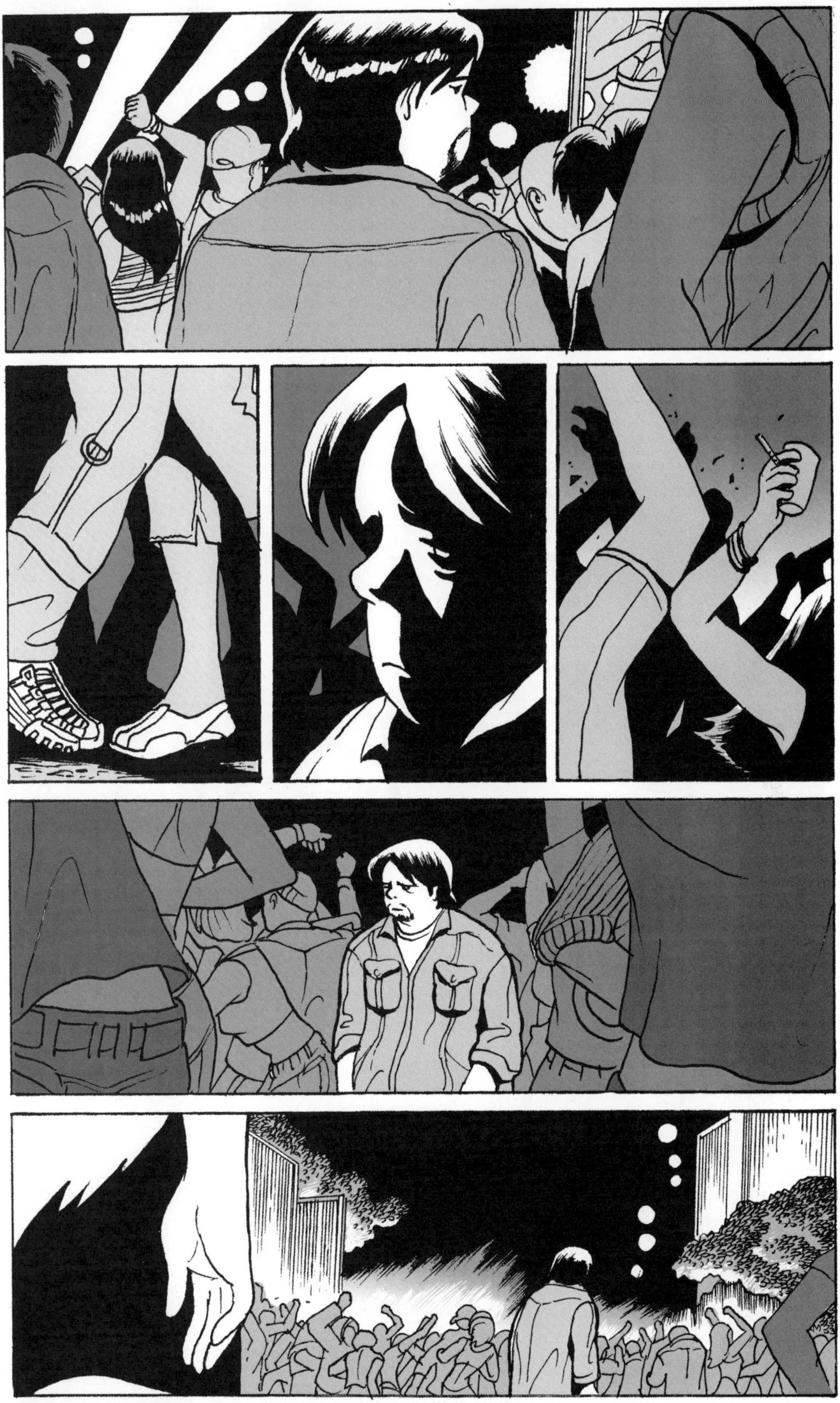

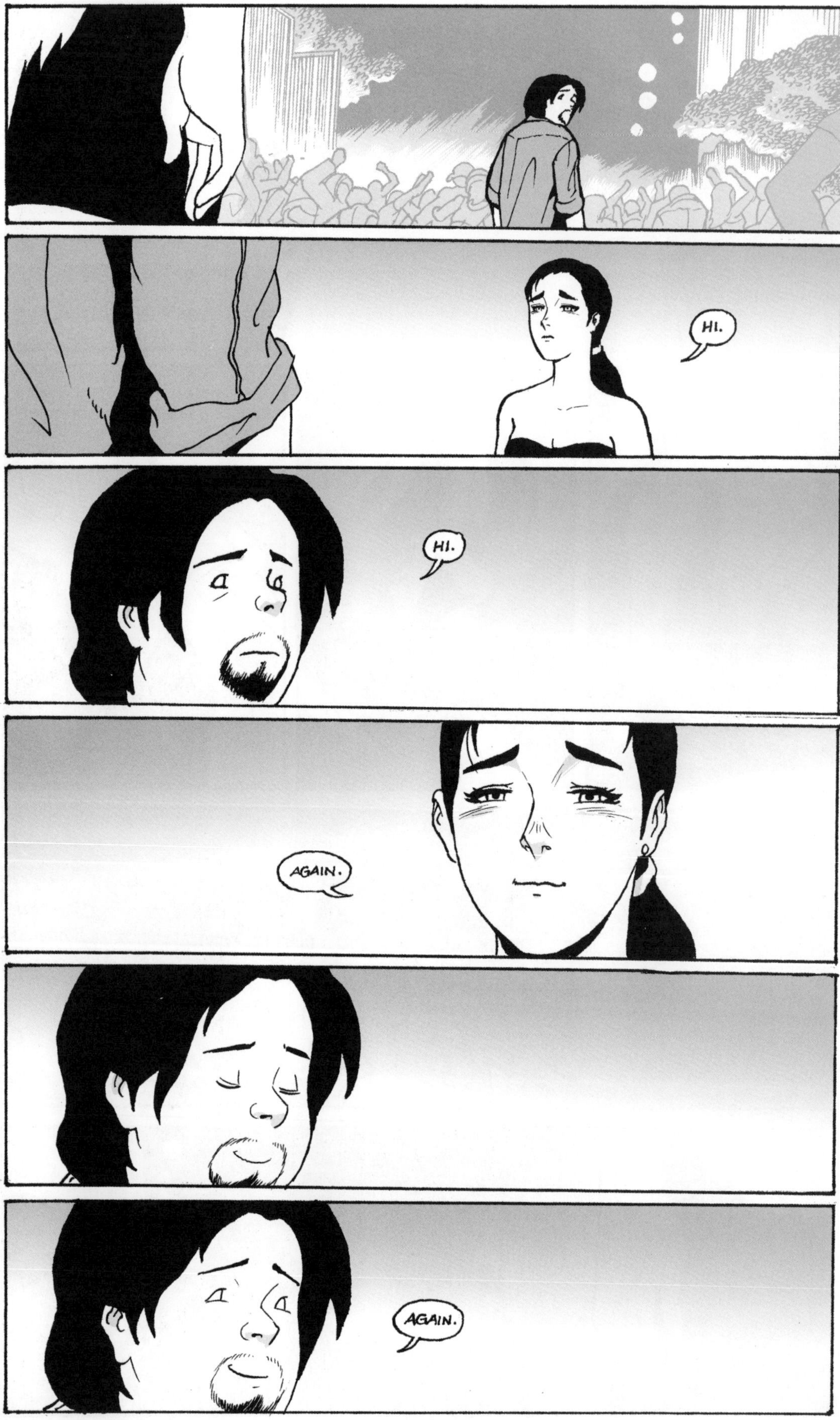
HI.
HI.
AGAIN.
AGAIN.

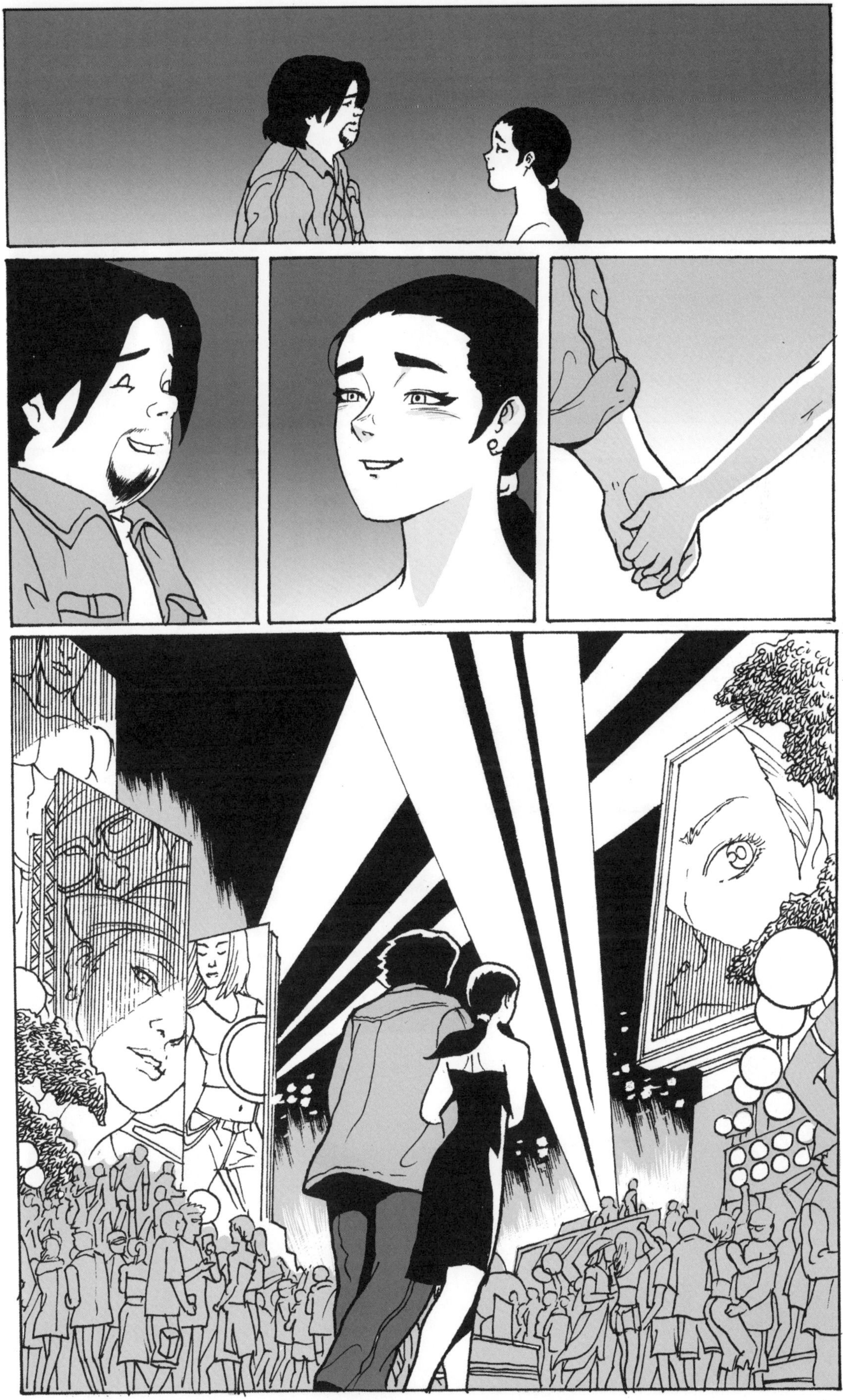

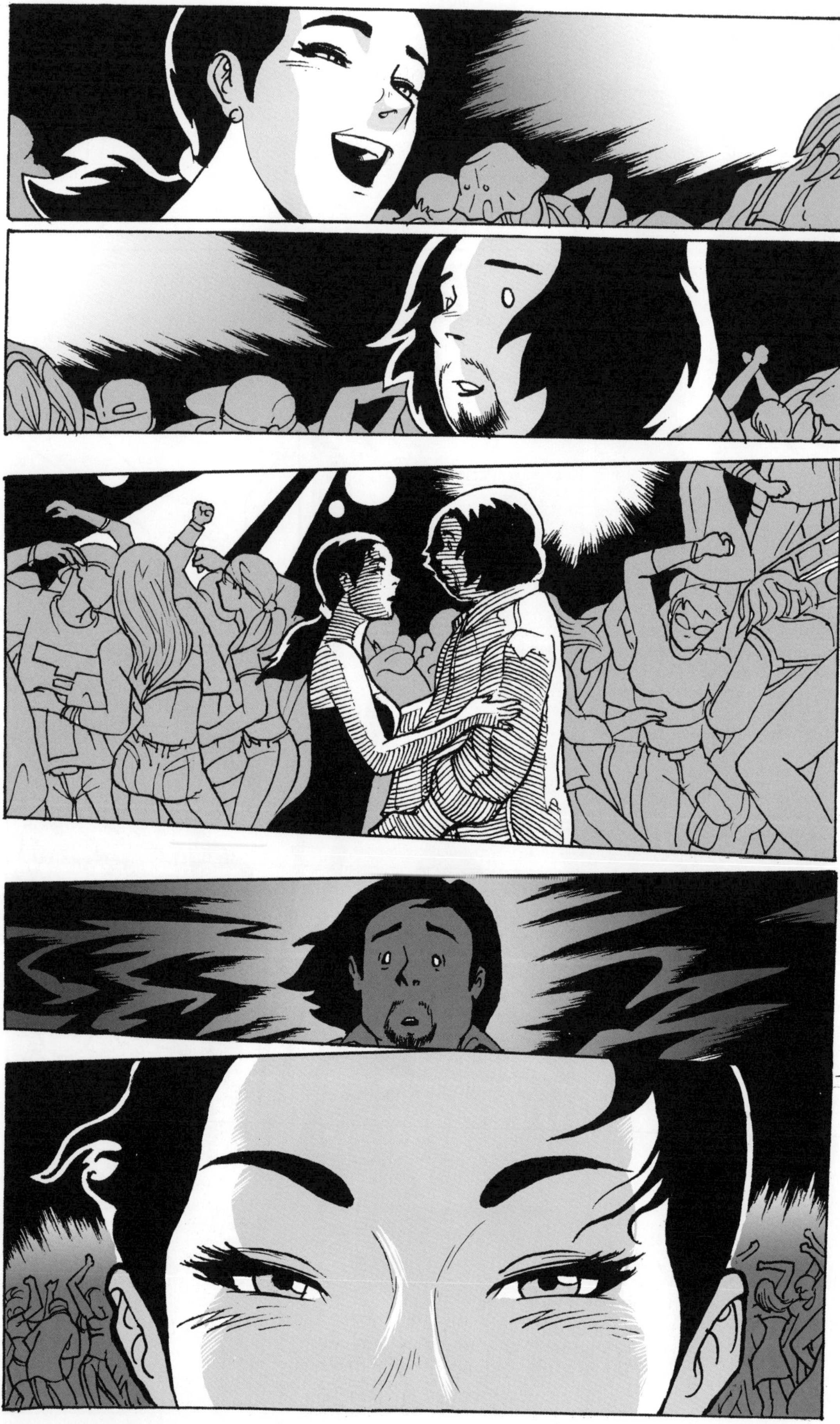

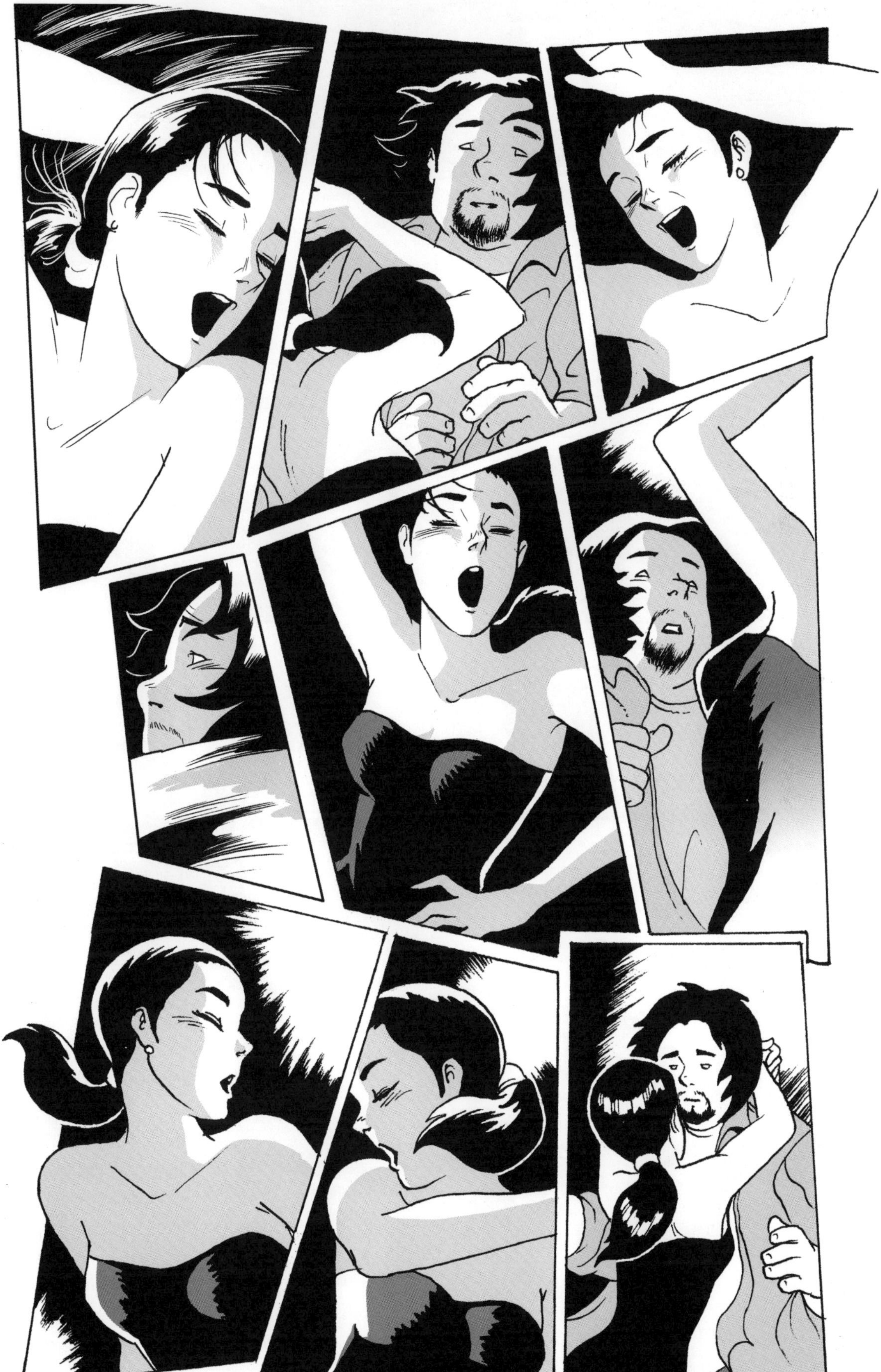

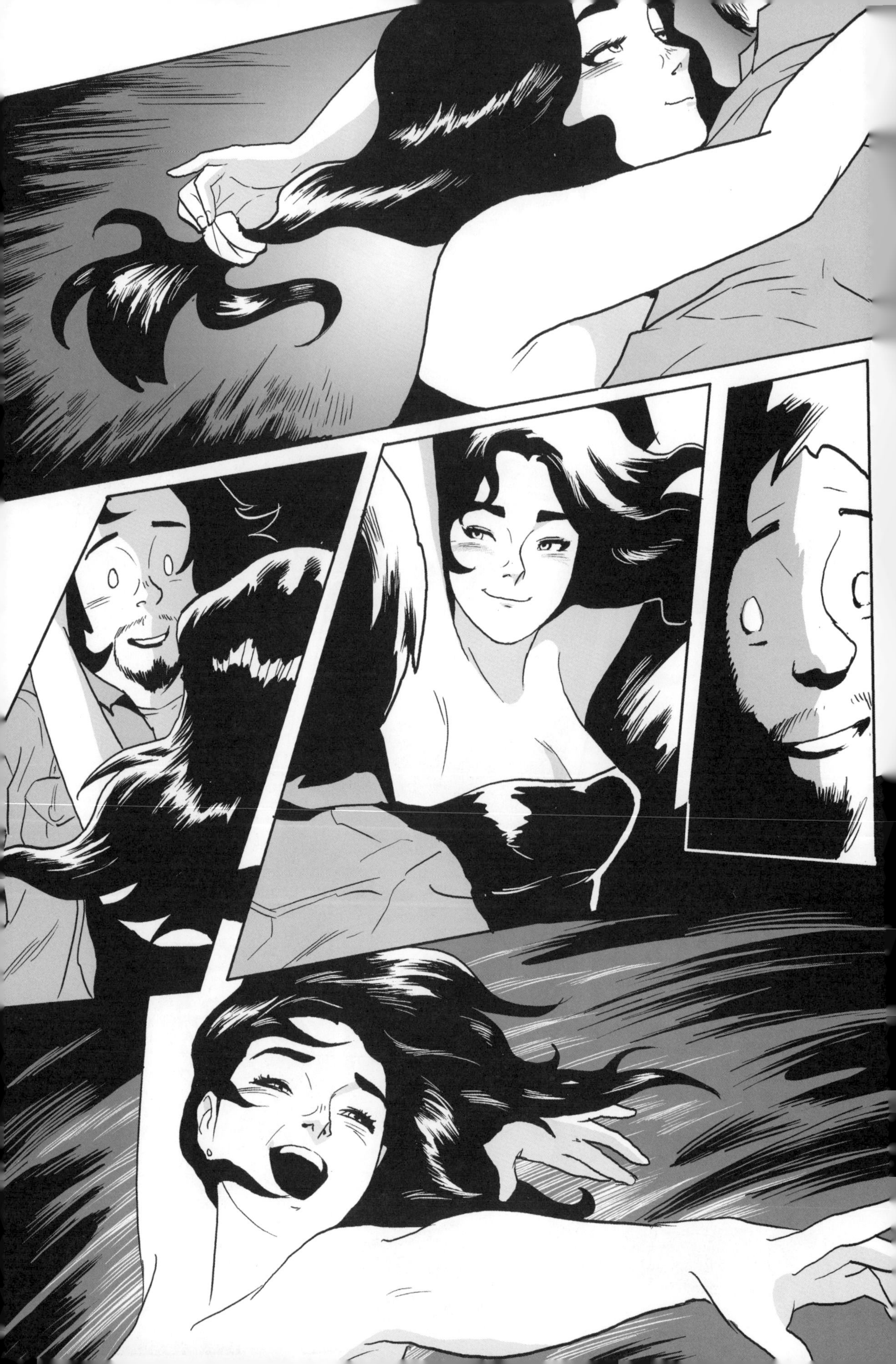

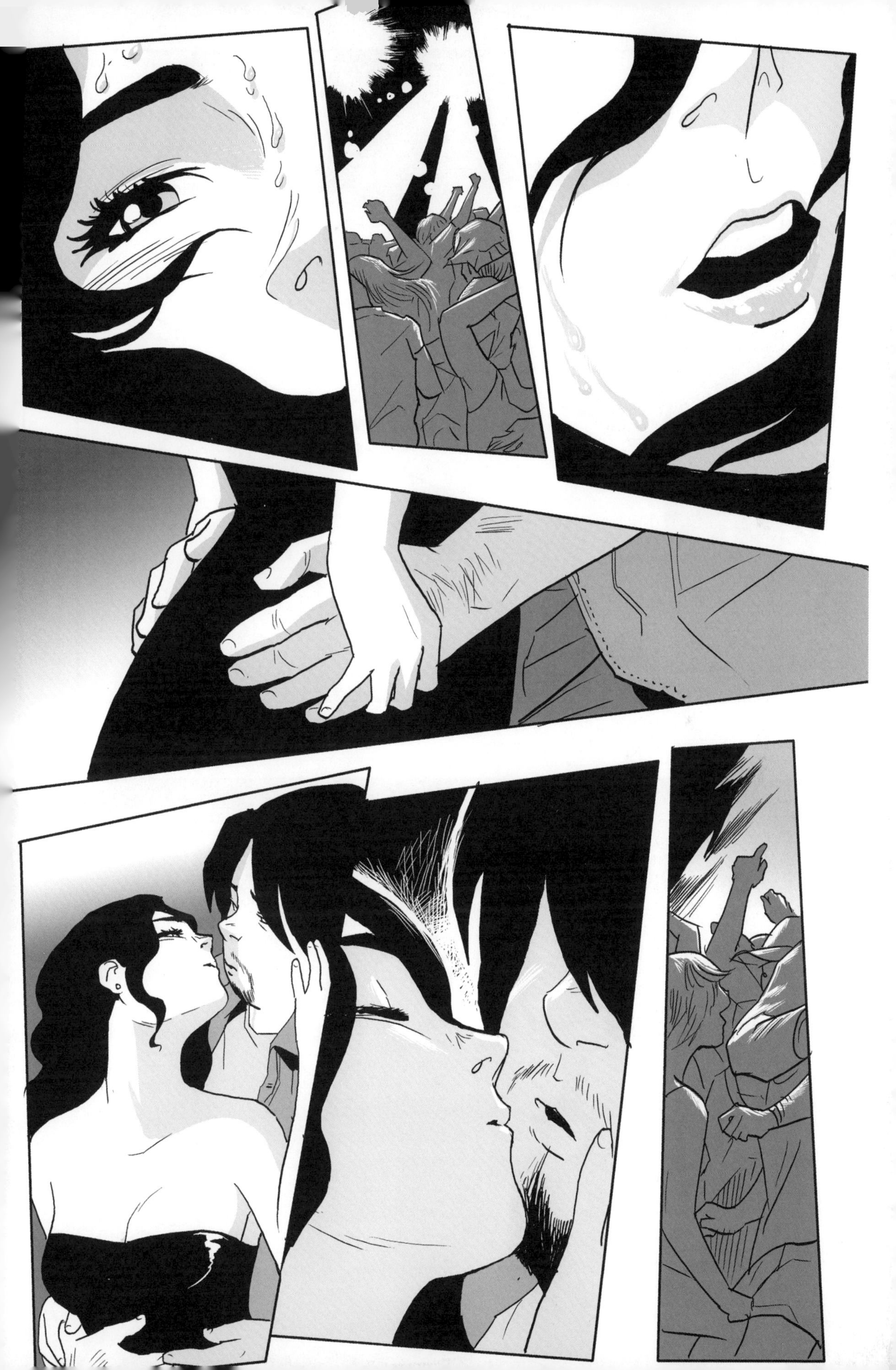

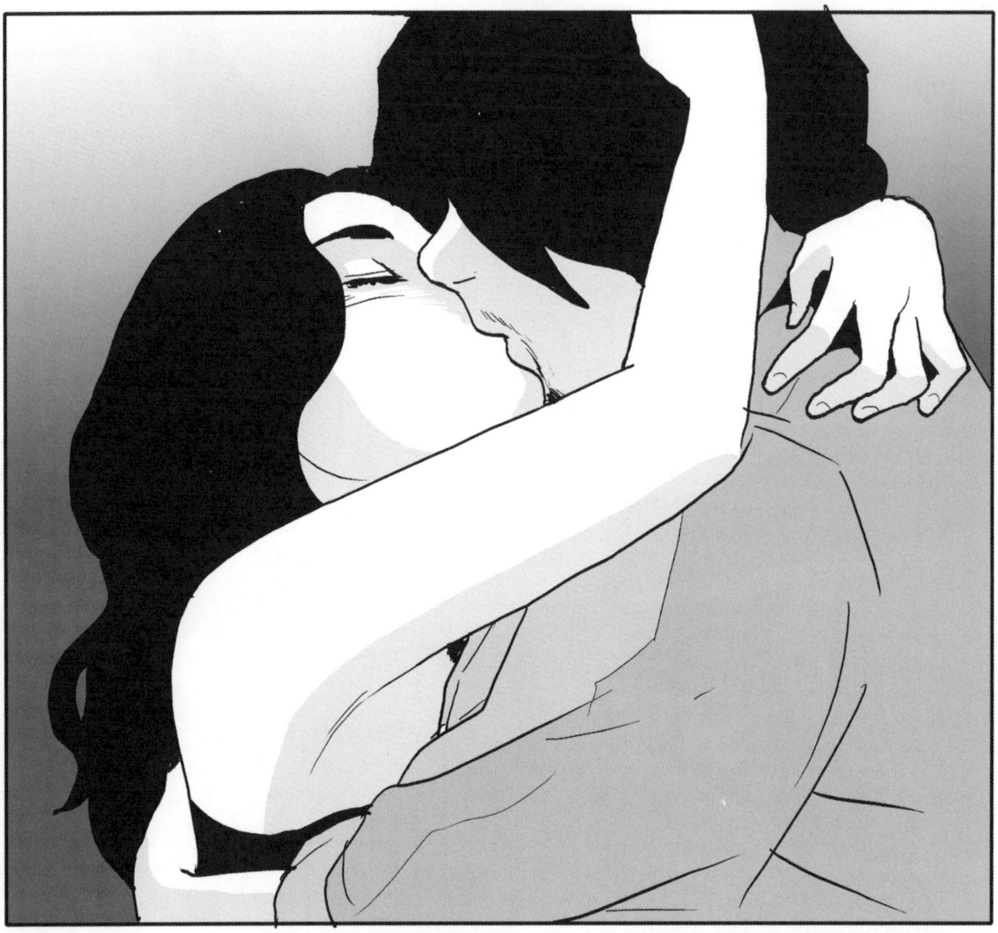
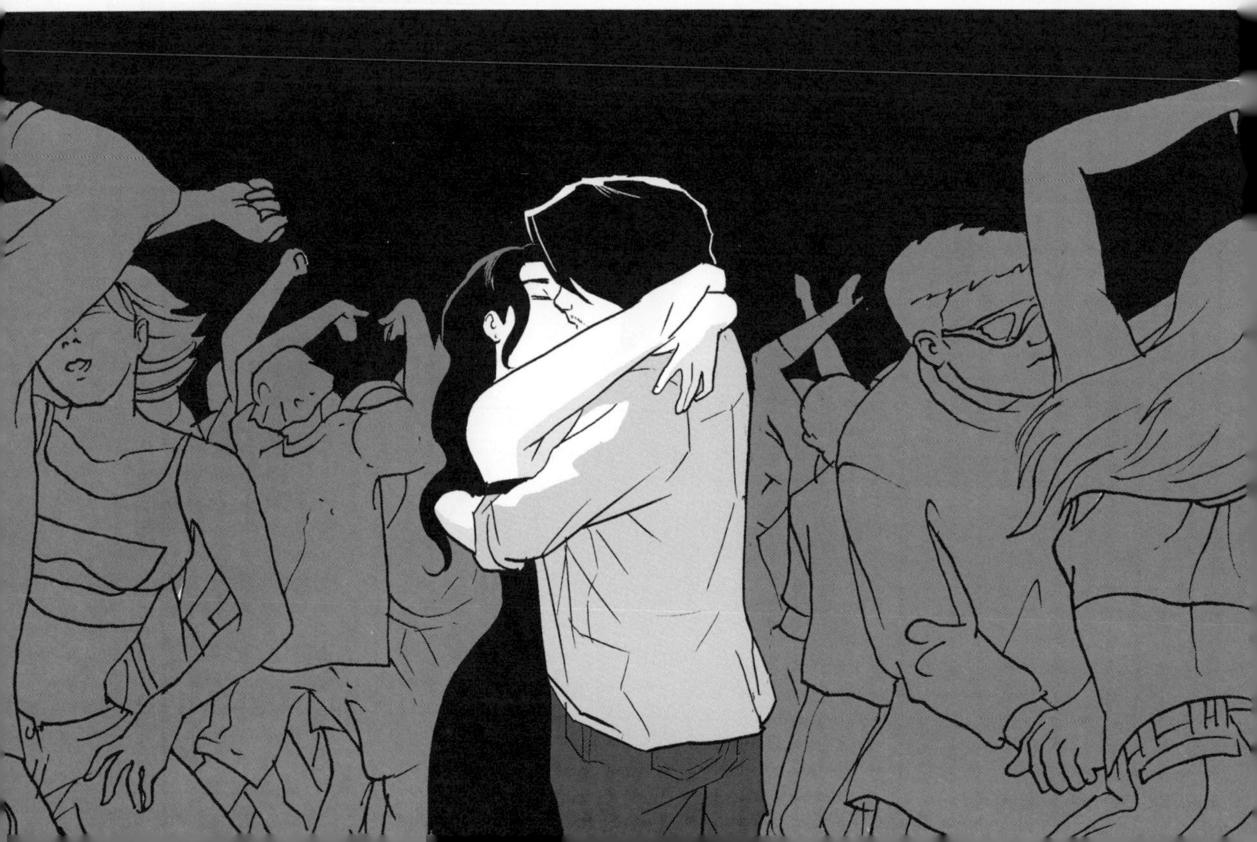

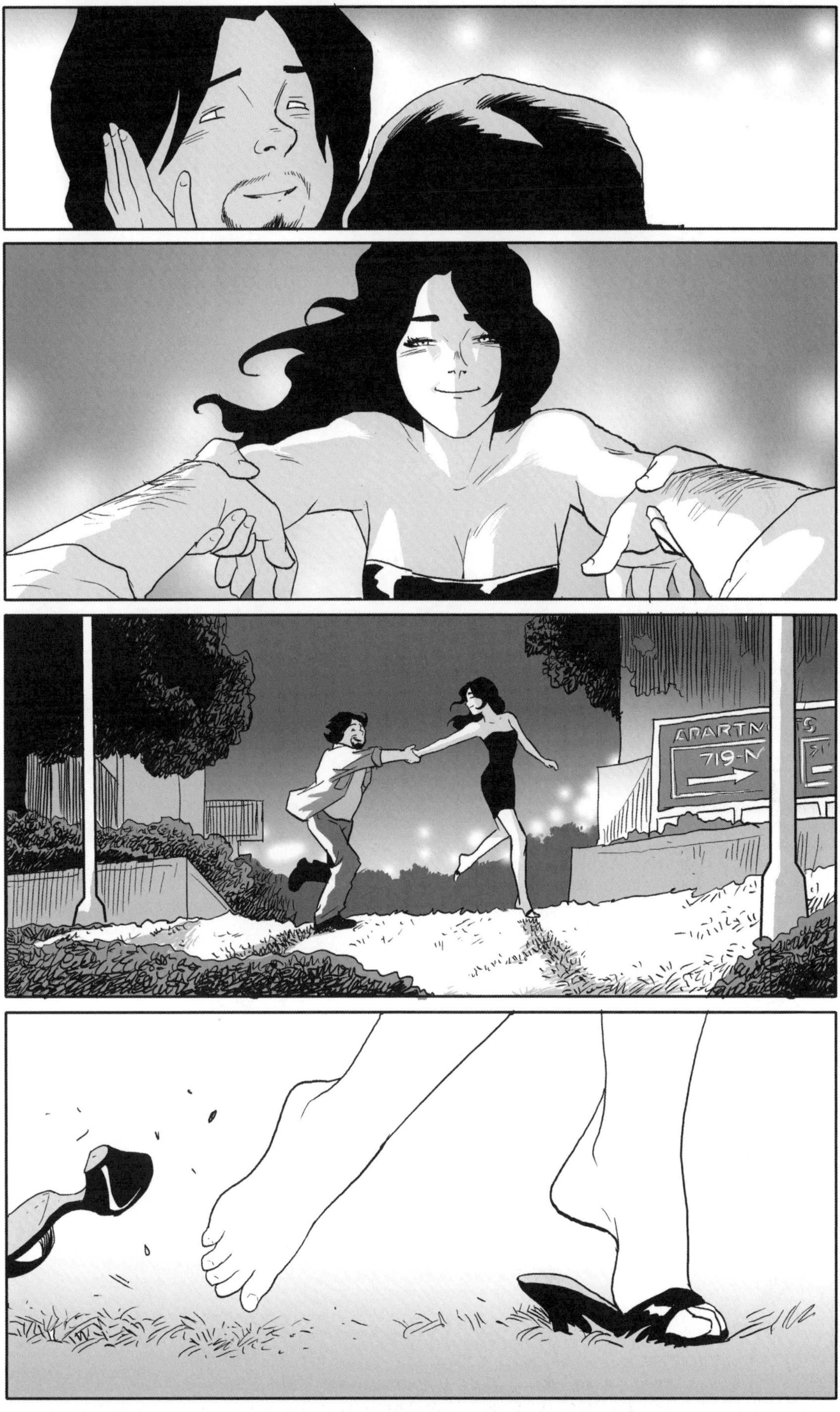

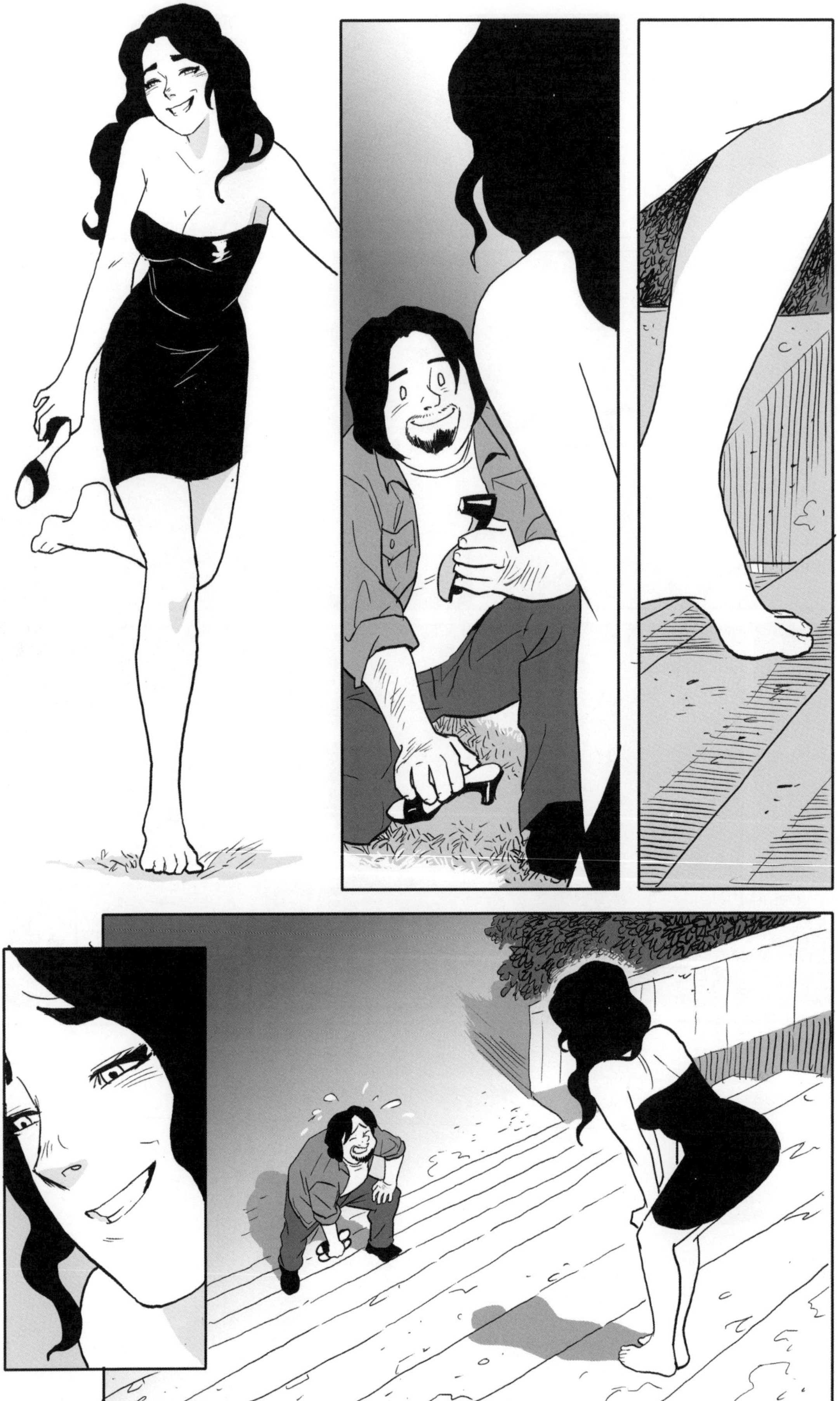

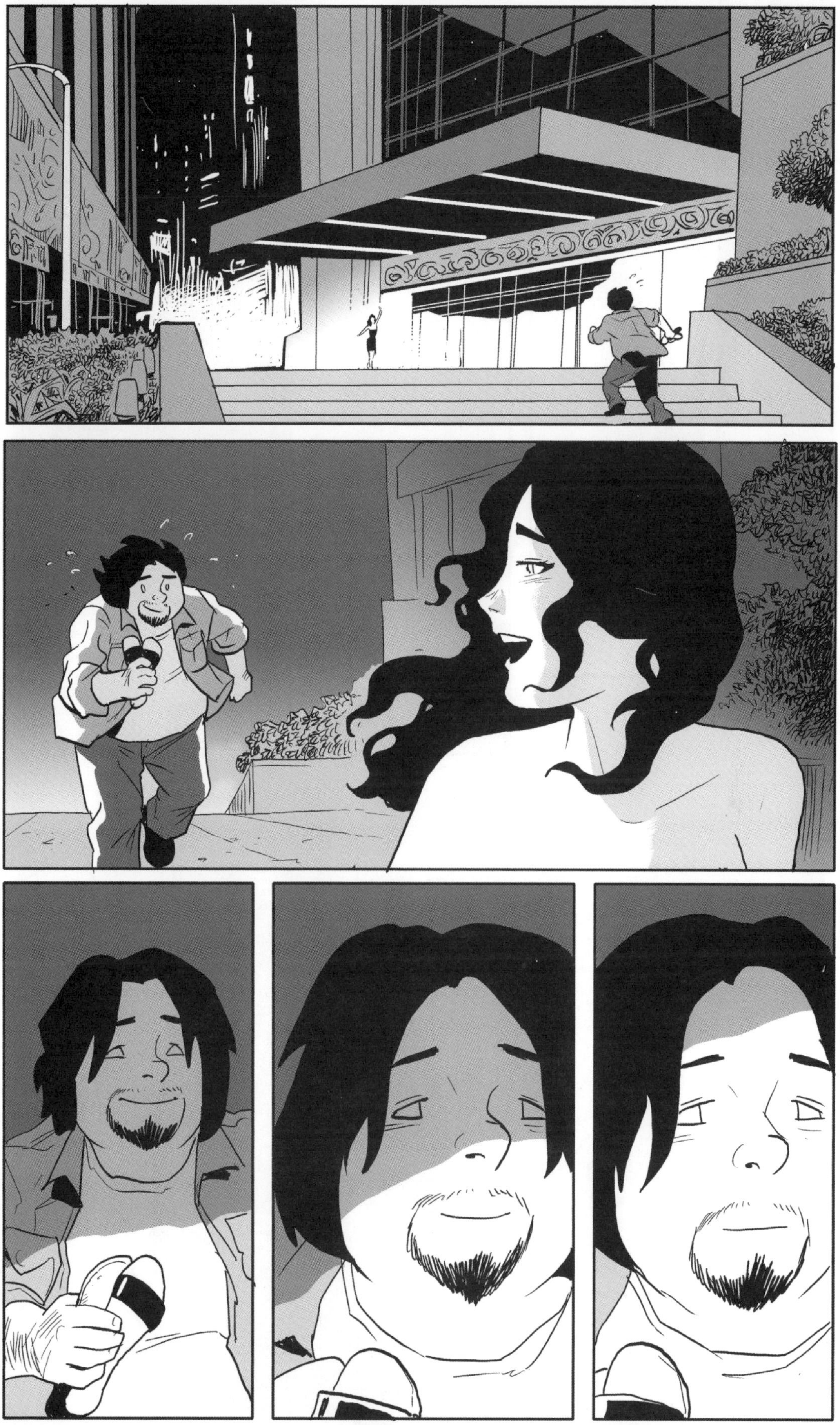

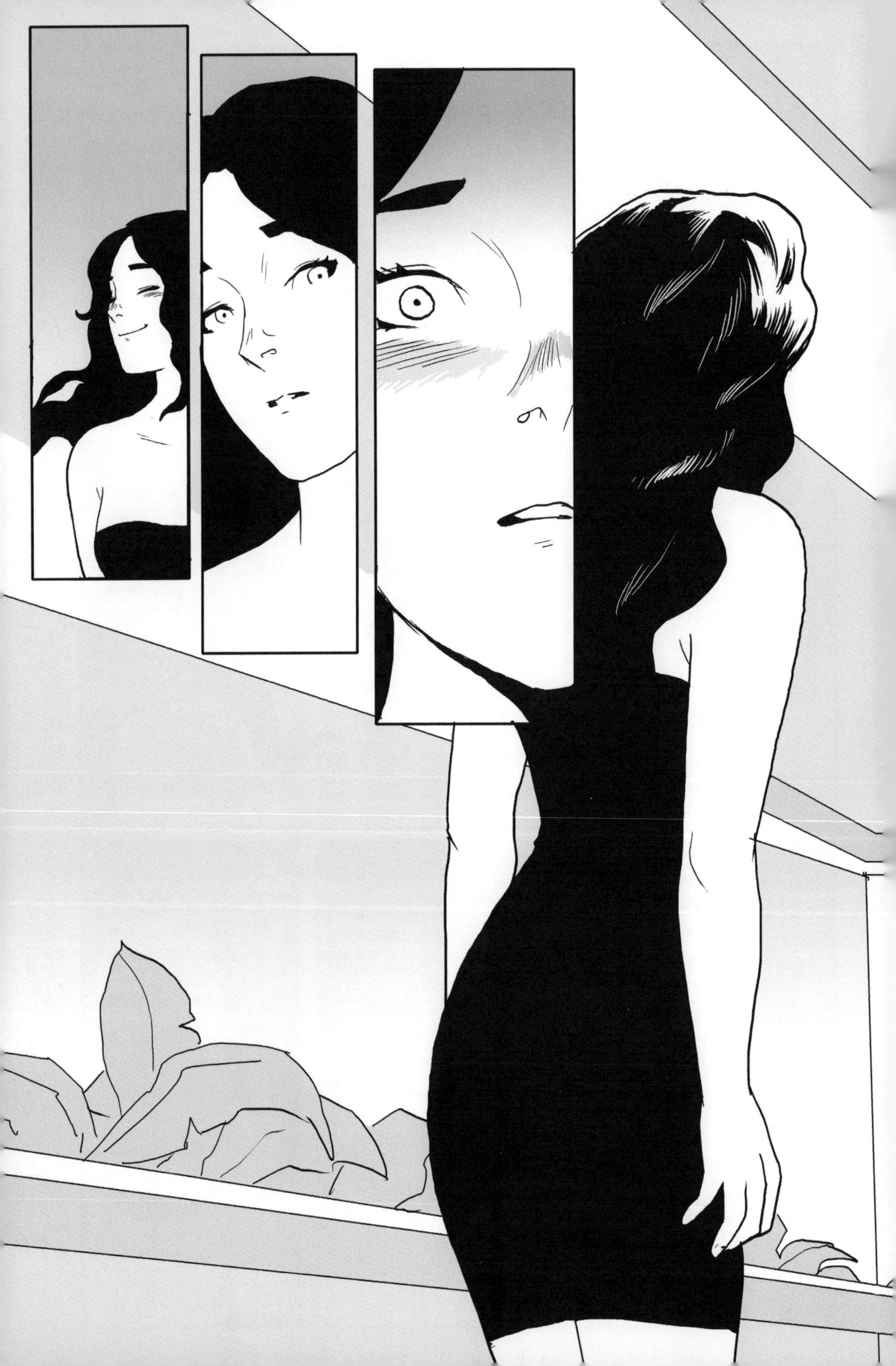

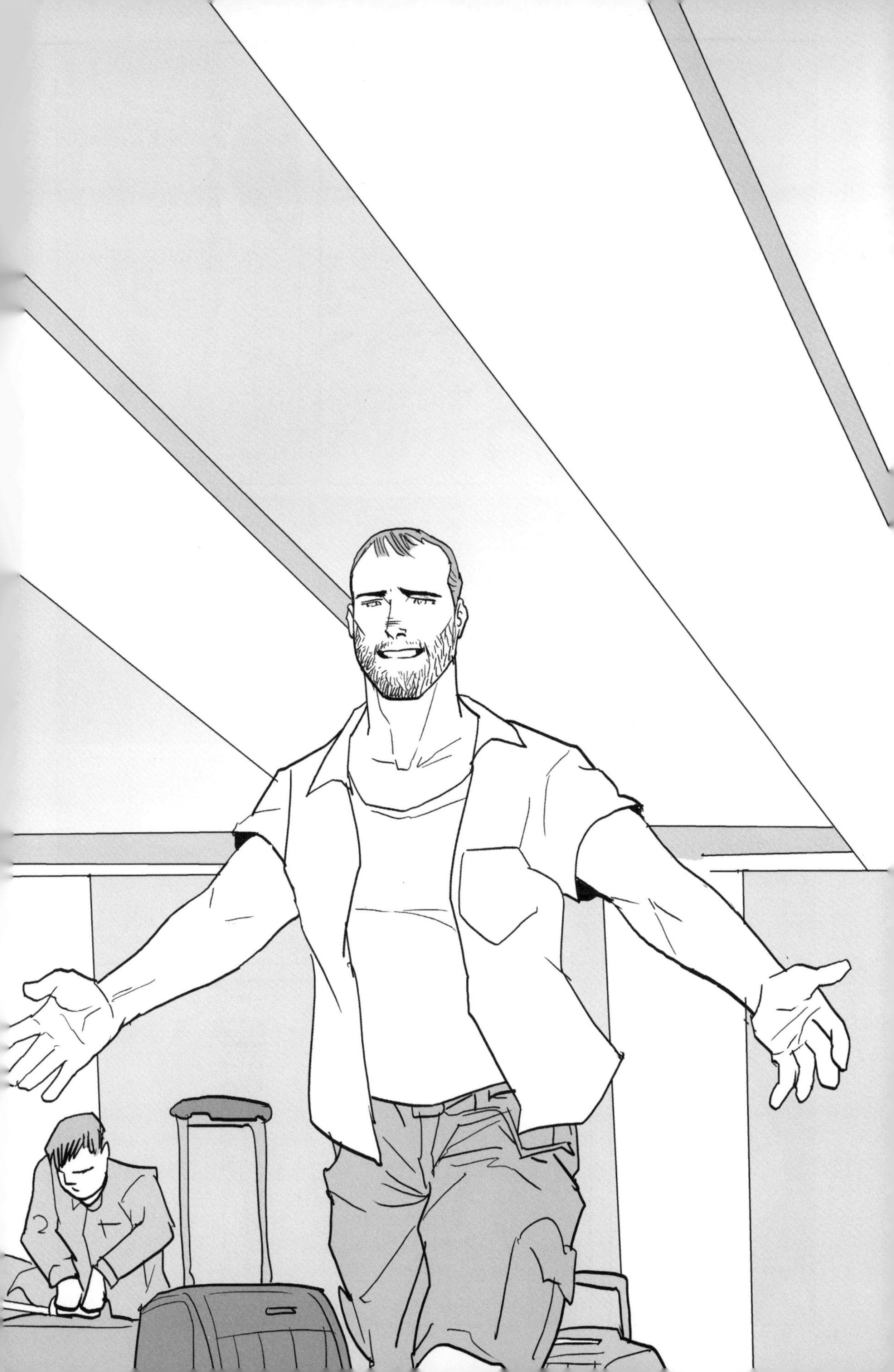

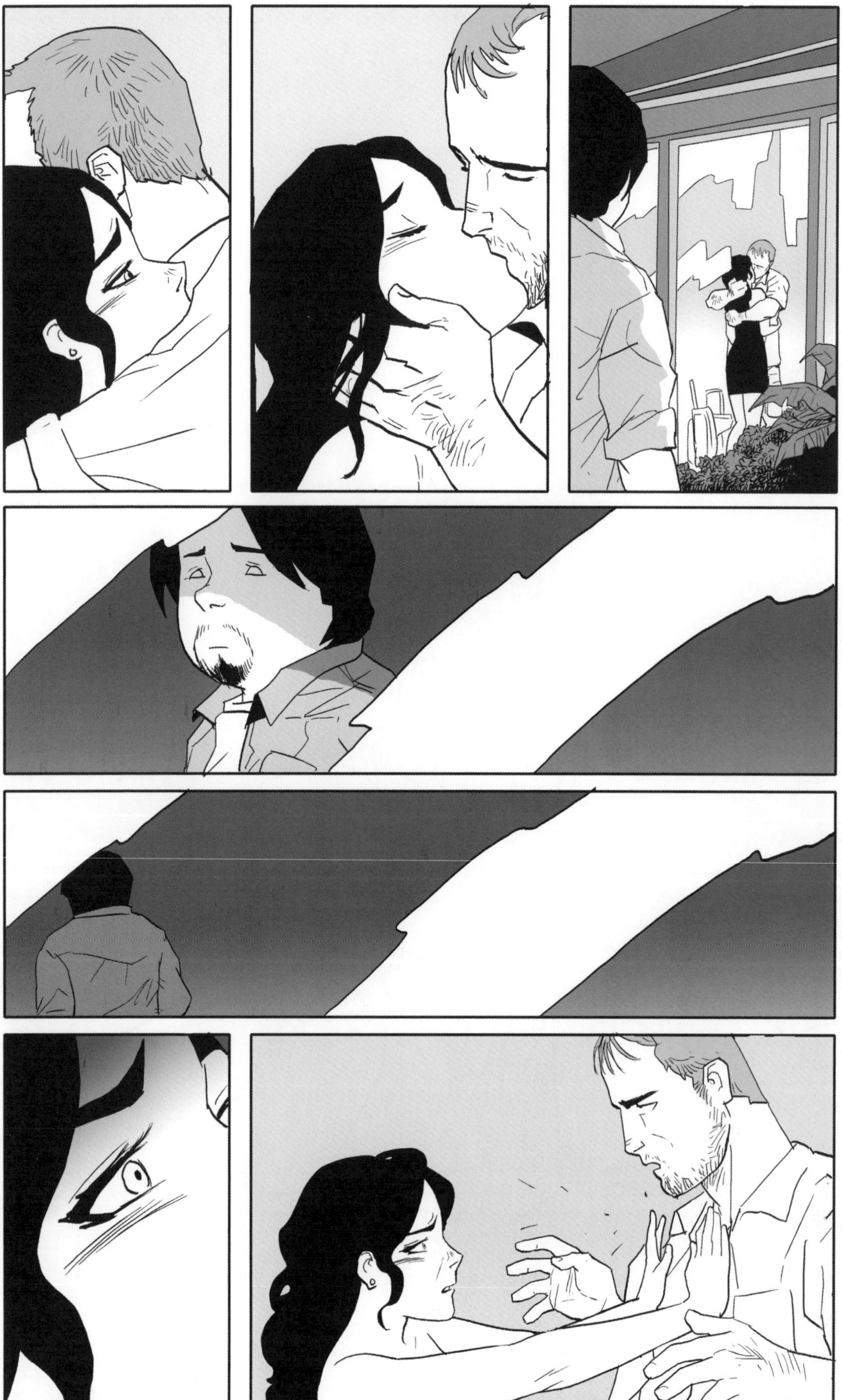

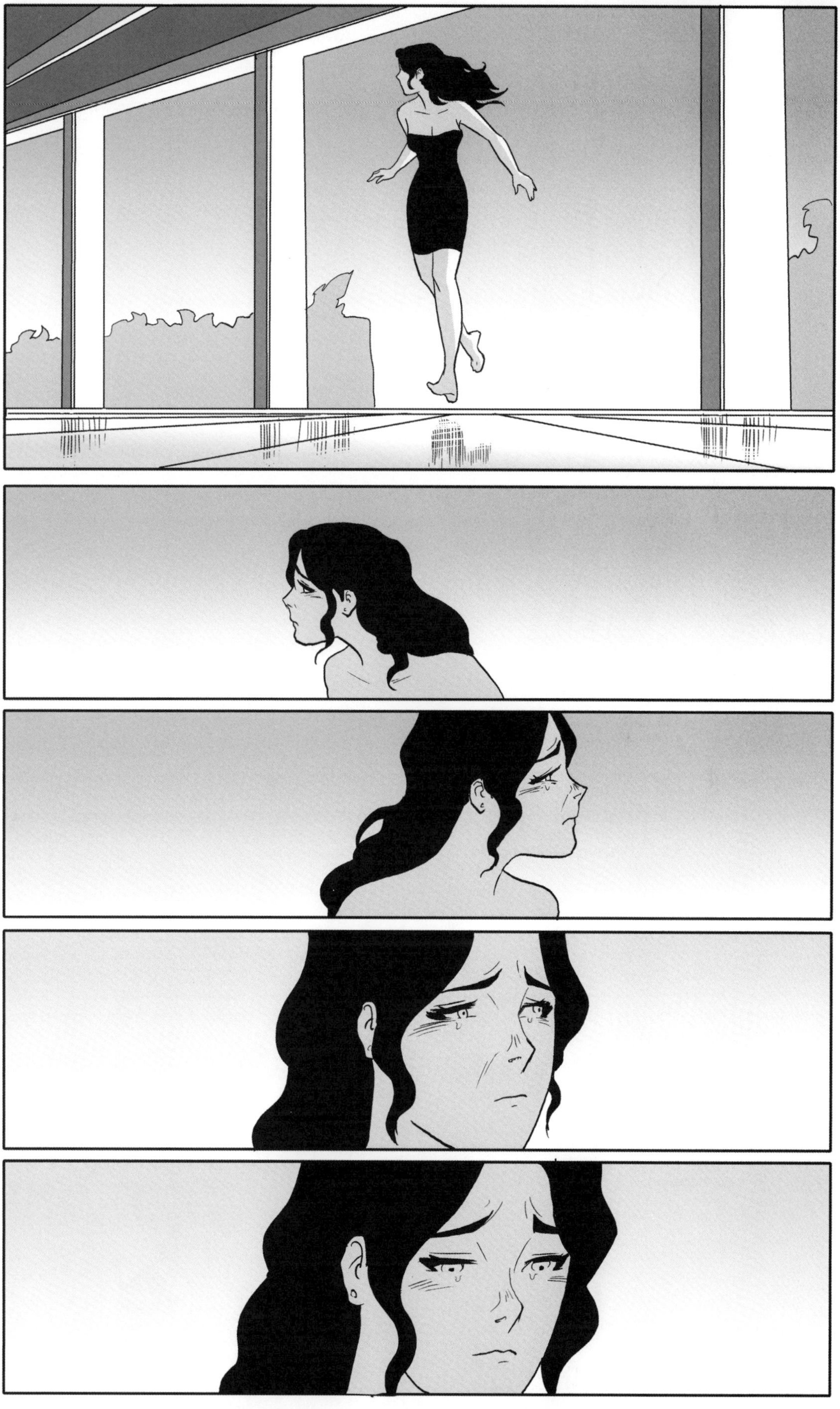

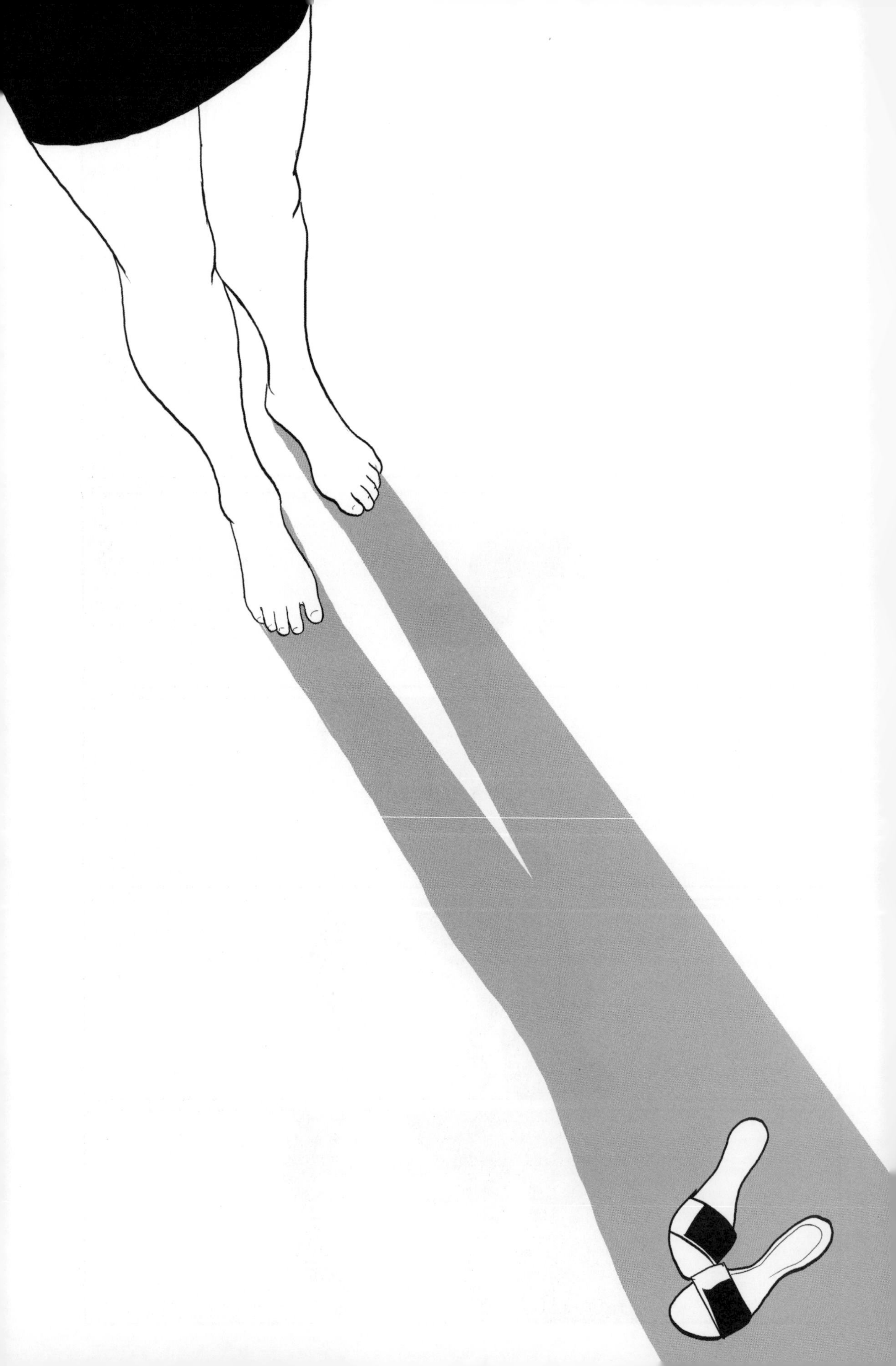

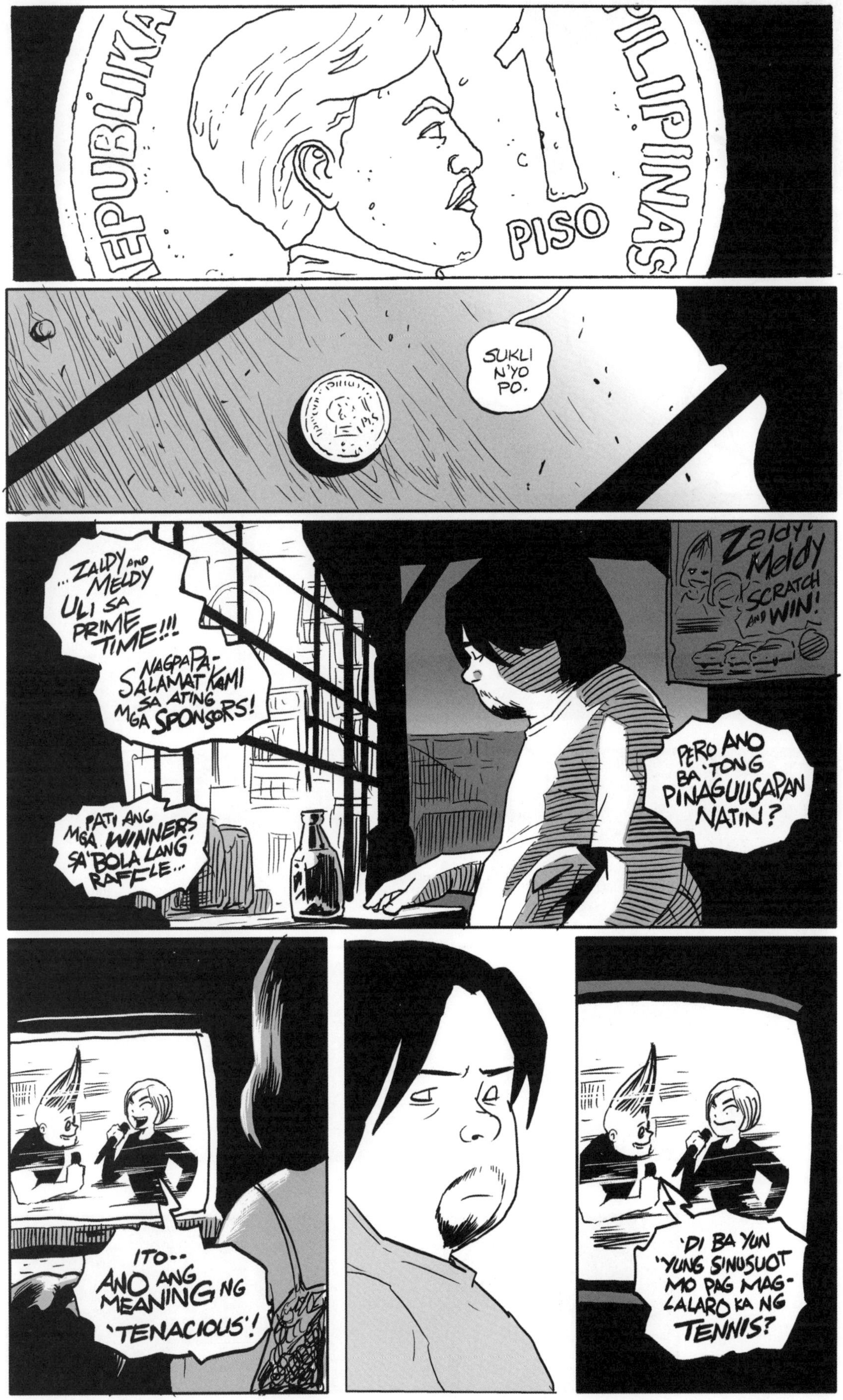
EPUBLIKA
PILIPINAS
1 PISO
SUKLI N'YO PO.
...ZALDY AND MELDY ULI SA PRIME TIME!!!
NAGPAPA-SALAMAT KAMI SA ATING MGA SPONSORS!
Zaldy Meldy SCRATCH AND WIN!
PATI ANG MGA WINNERS SA 'BOLA LANG' RAFFLE...
PERO ANO BA 'TONG PINAGUUSAPAN NATIN?
ITO.. ANO ANG MEANING NG 'TENACIOUS'!
'DI BA YUN 'YUNG SINUSUOT MO PAG MAG-LALARO KA NG TENNIS?

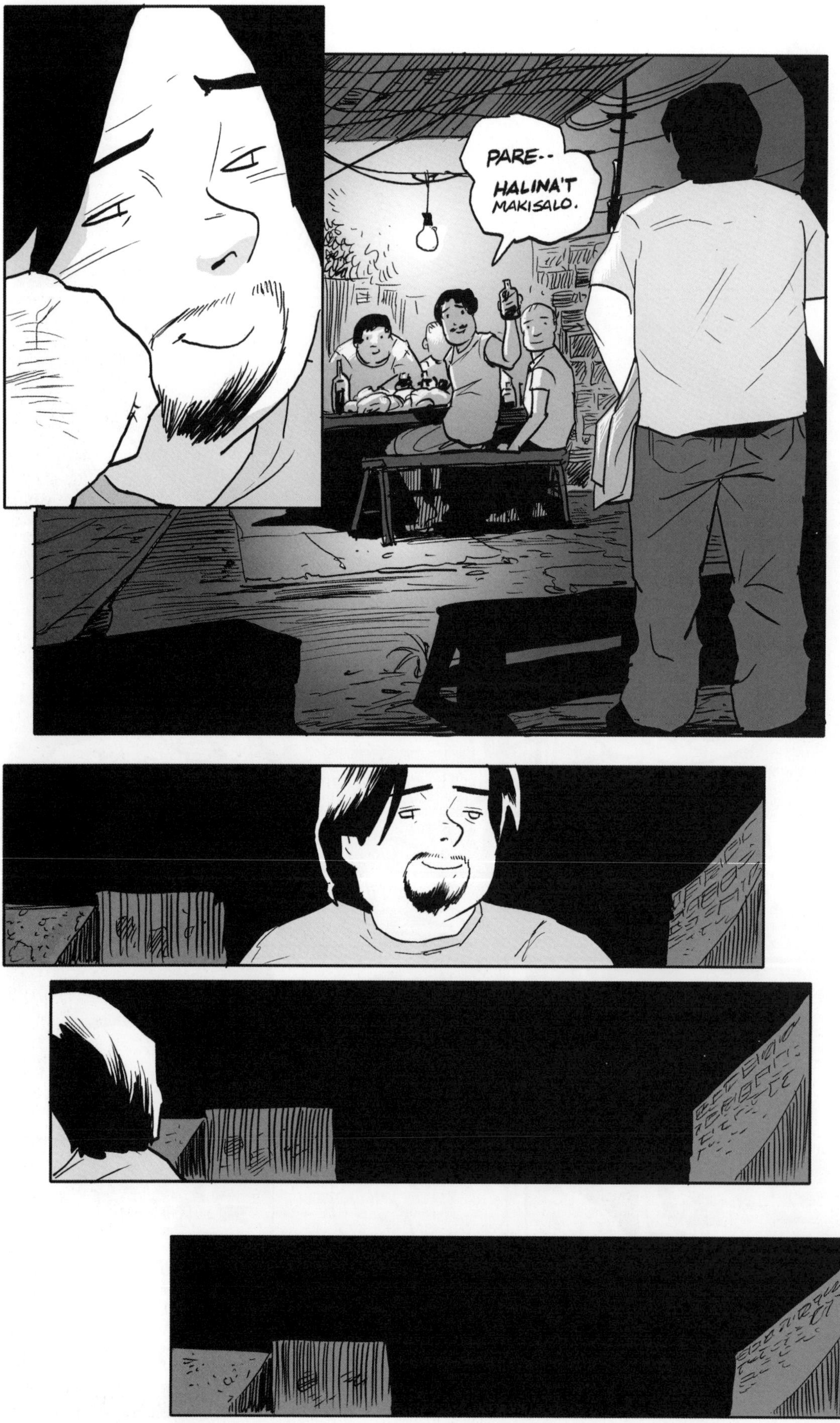
PARE--
HALINA'T MAKISALO.

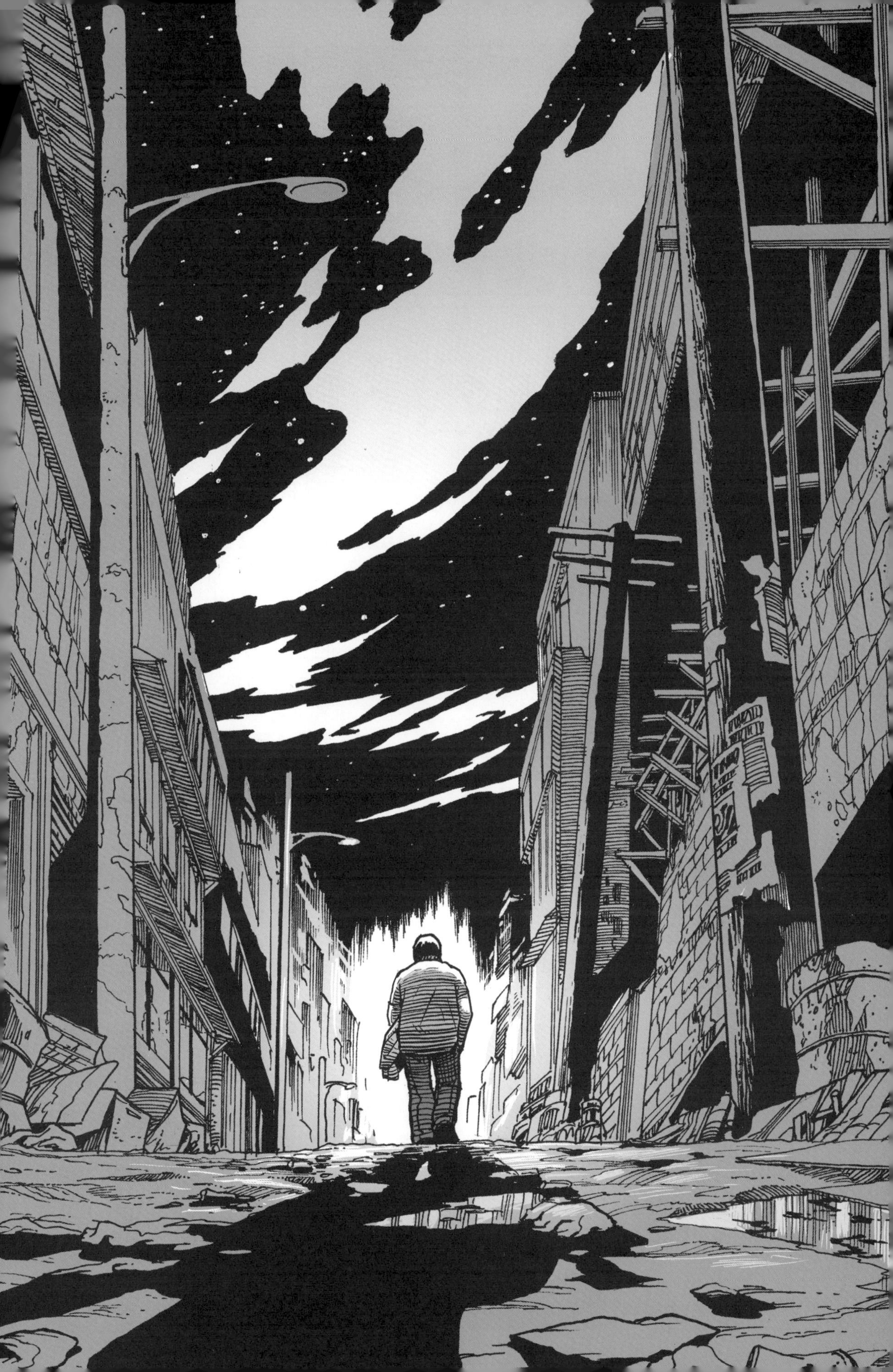

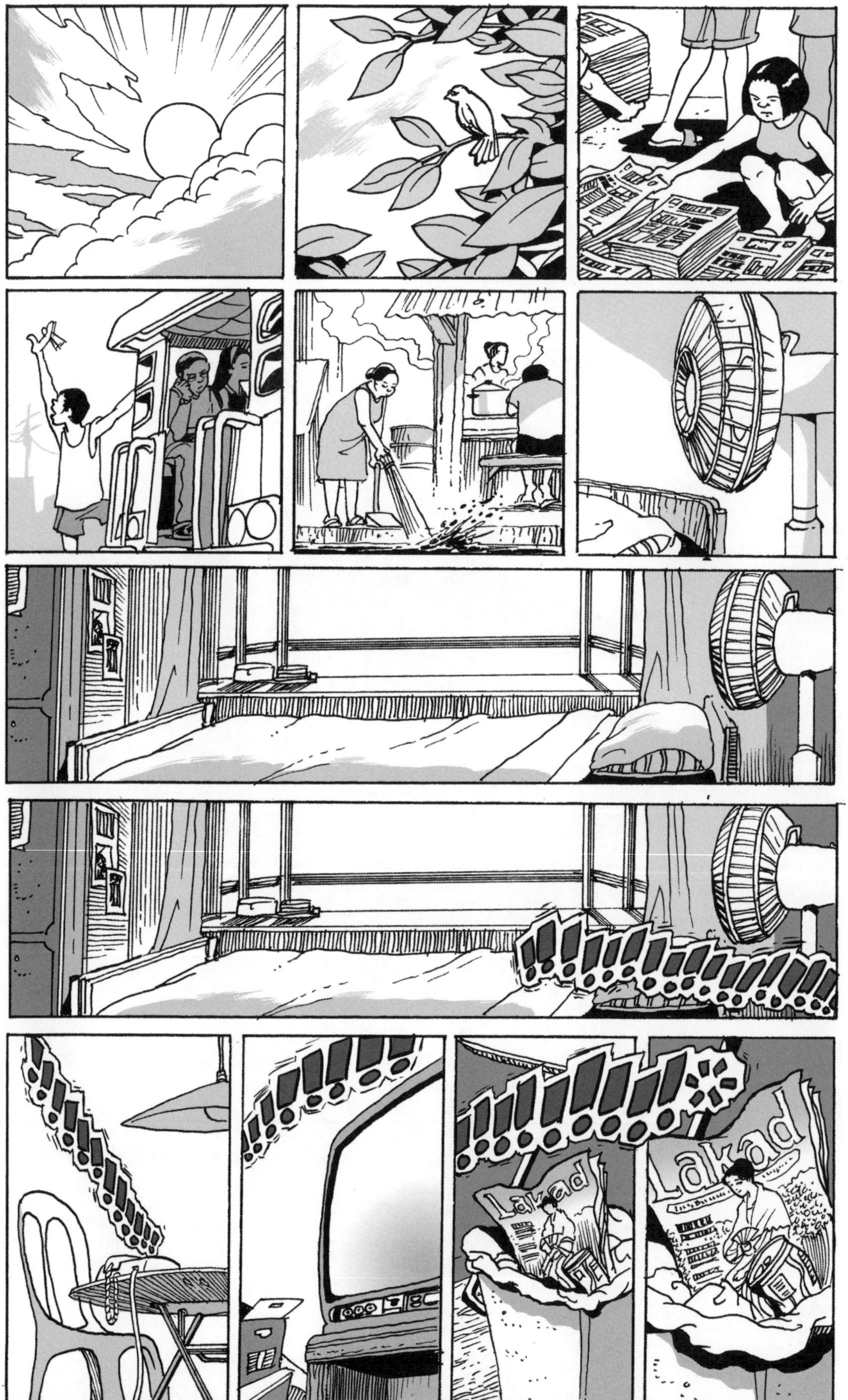
Lakad
Lakad

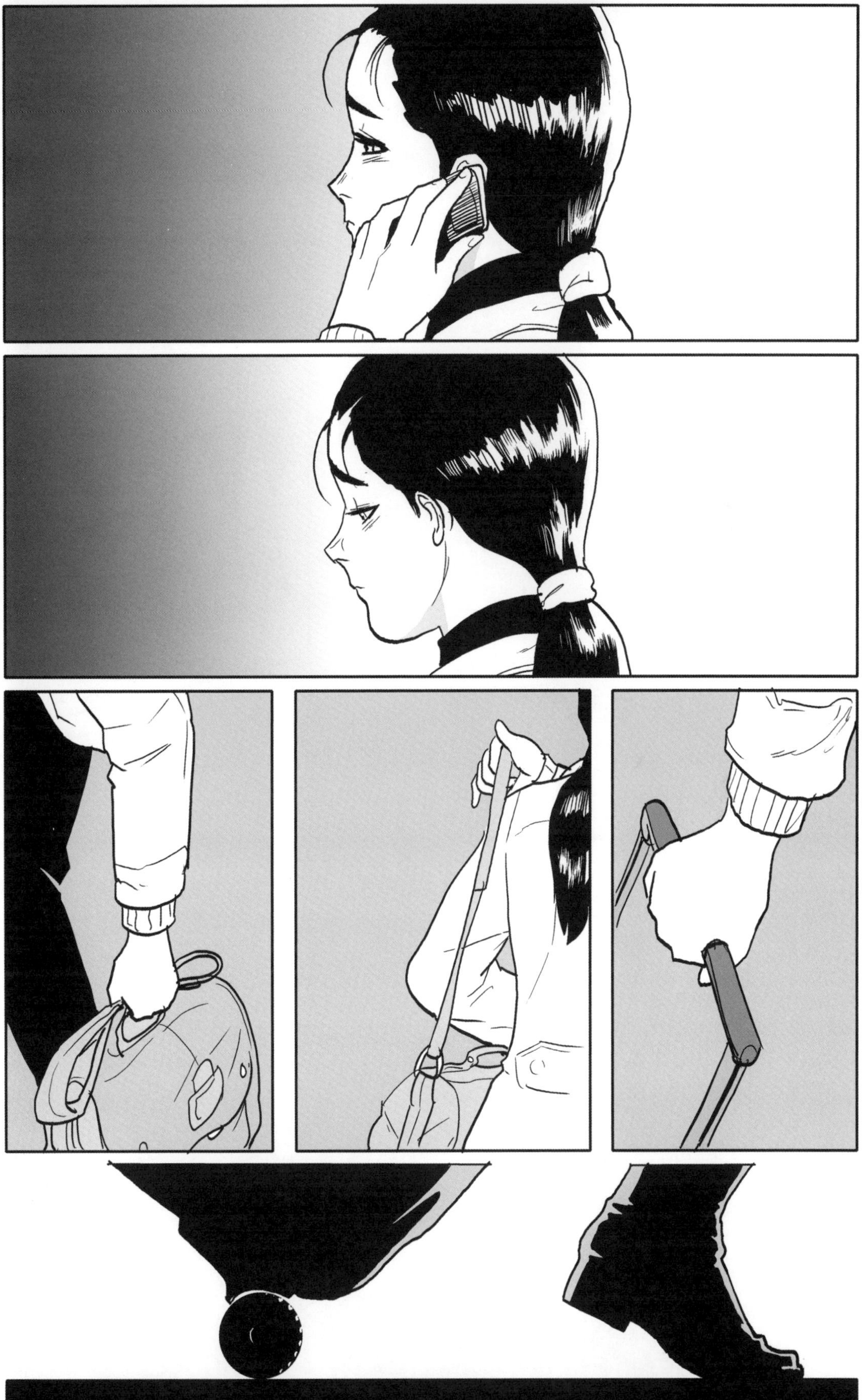

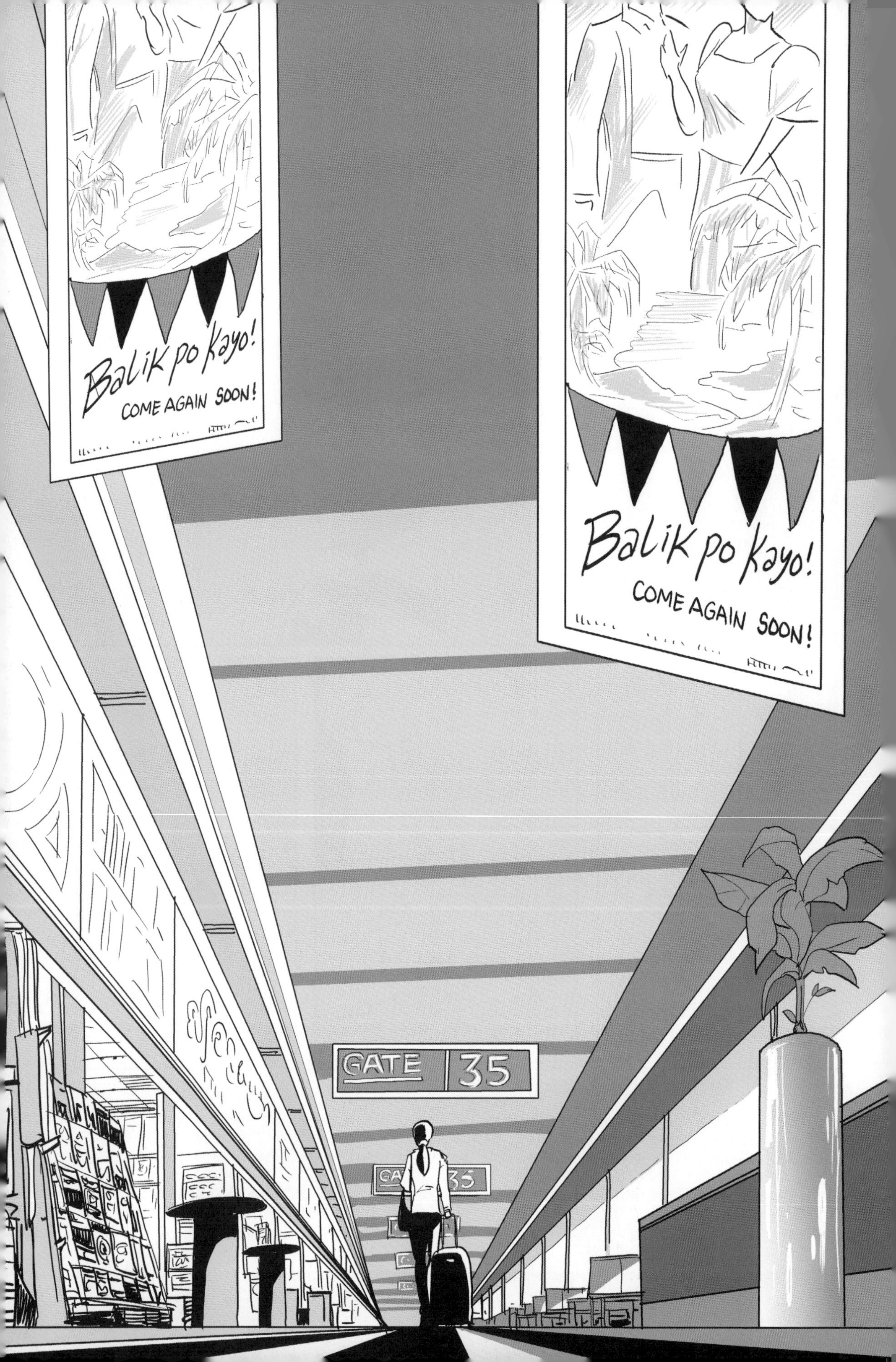
Balik po kayo!
COME AGAIN SOON!
Balik po kayo!
COME AGAIN SOON!
GATE 35

Chapter 8
The Right Words

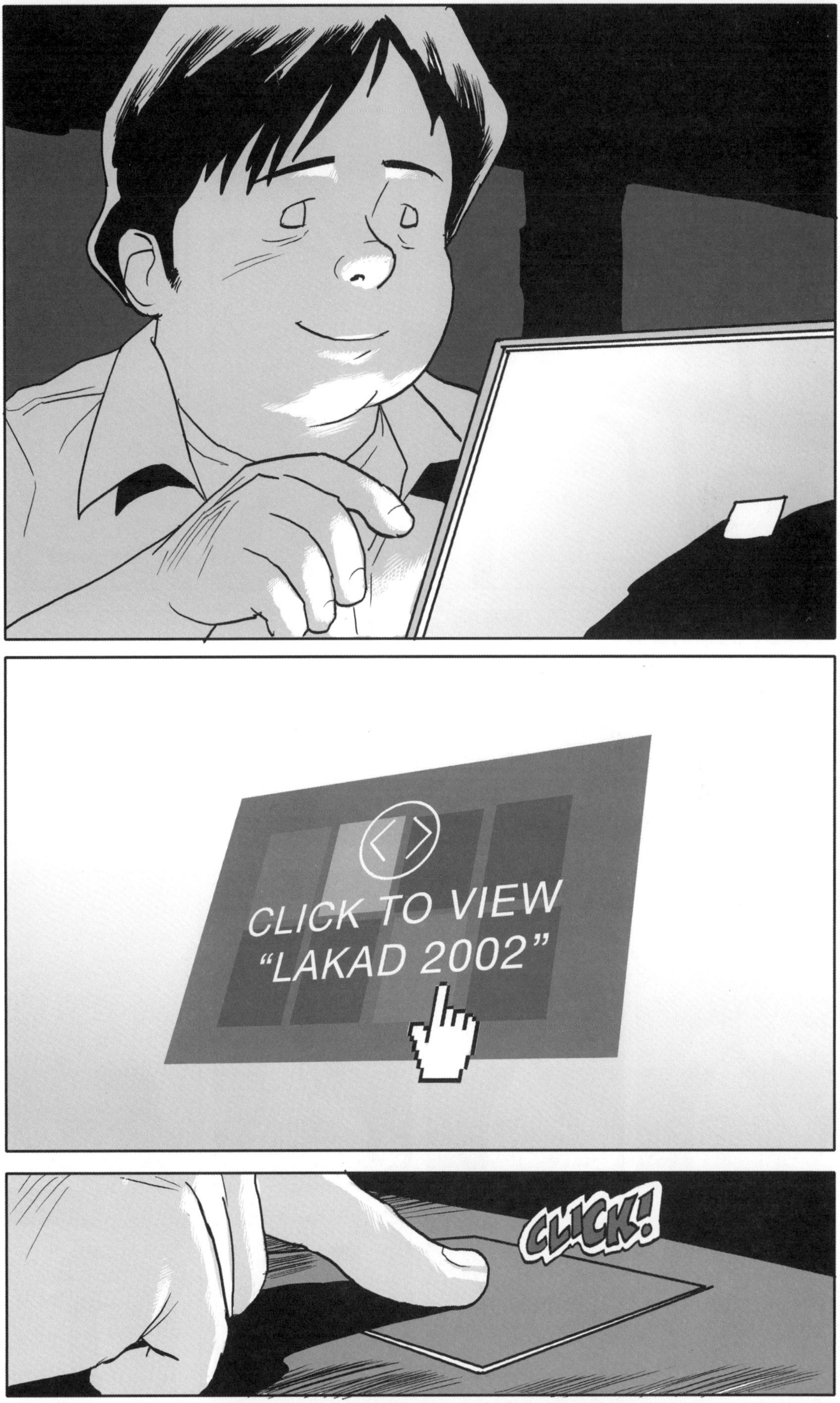
CLICK TO VIEW
"LAKAD 2002"
CLICK!

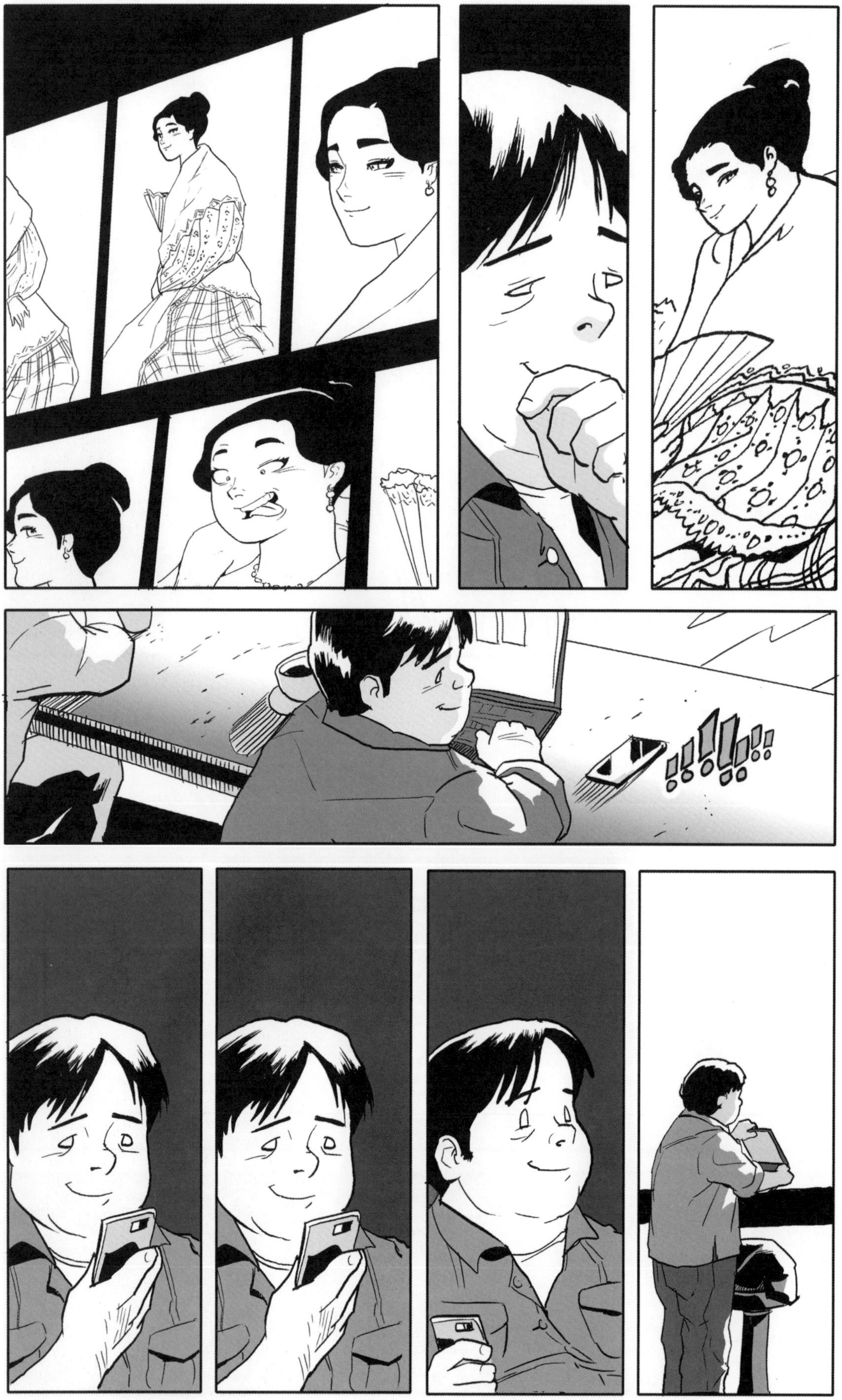

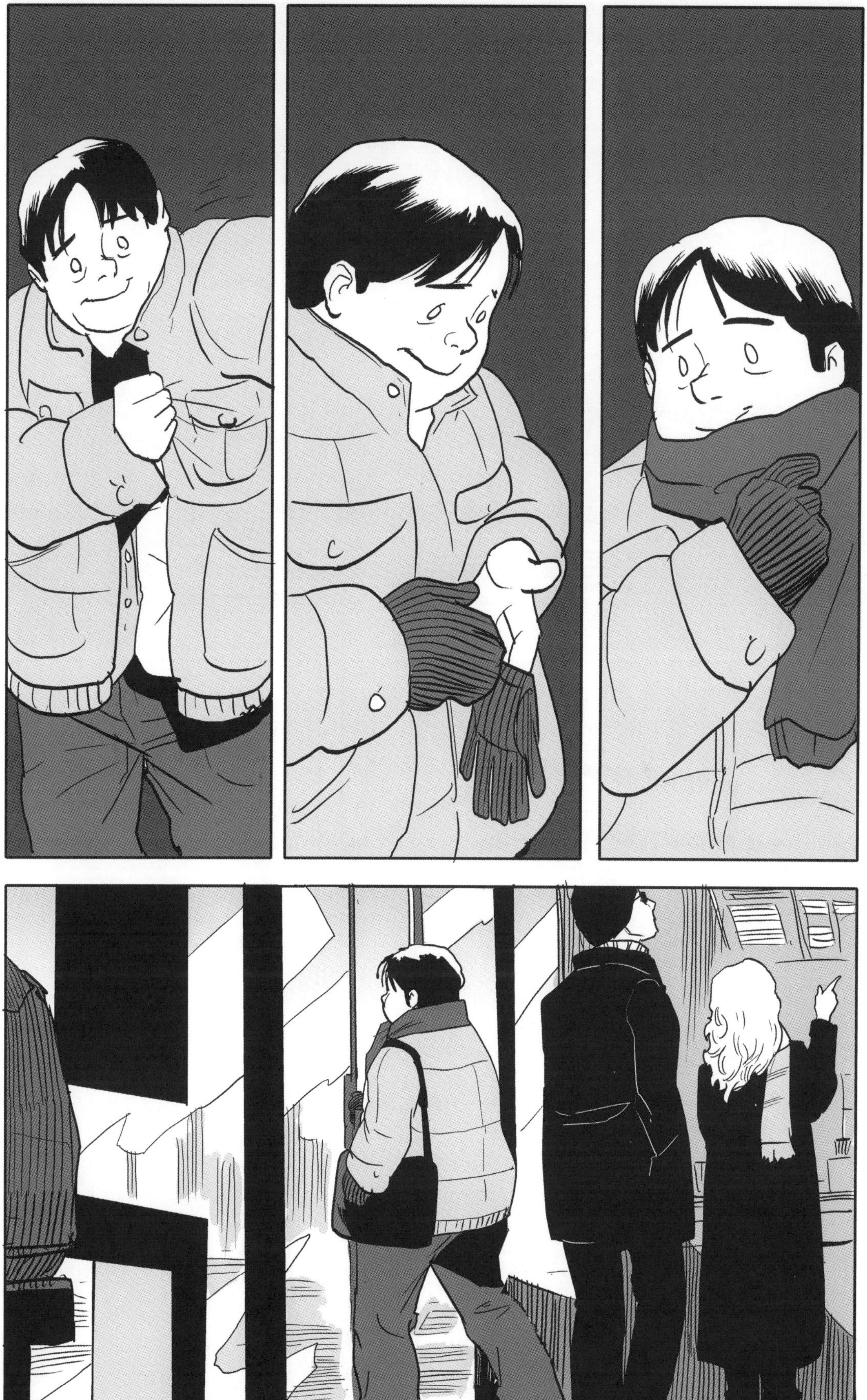

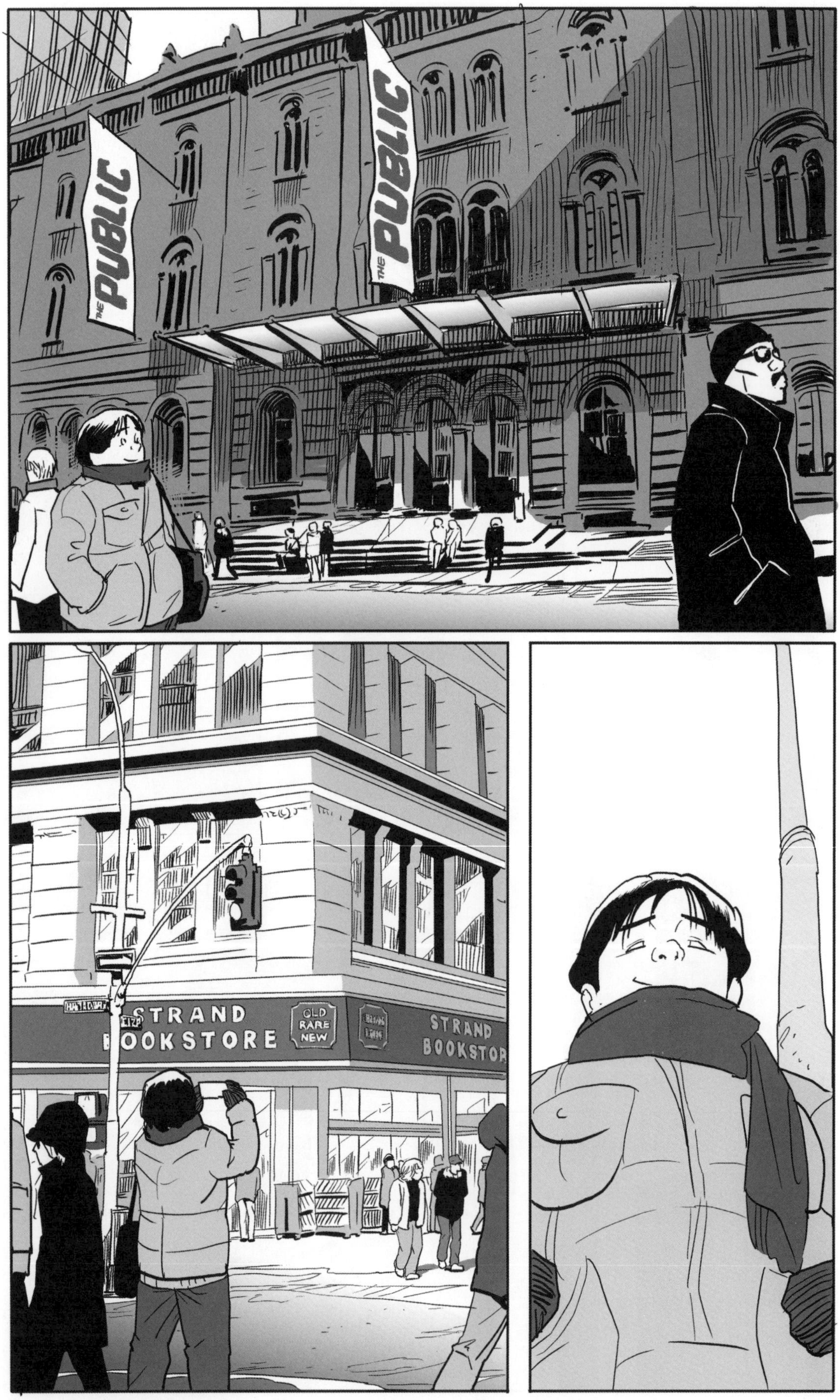
THE PUBLIC
THE PUBLIC
STRAND BOOKSTORE
OLD RARE NEW
STRAND BOOKSTOR

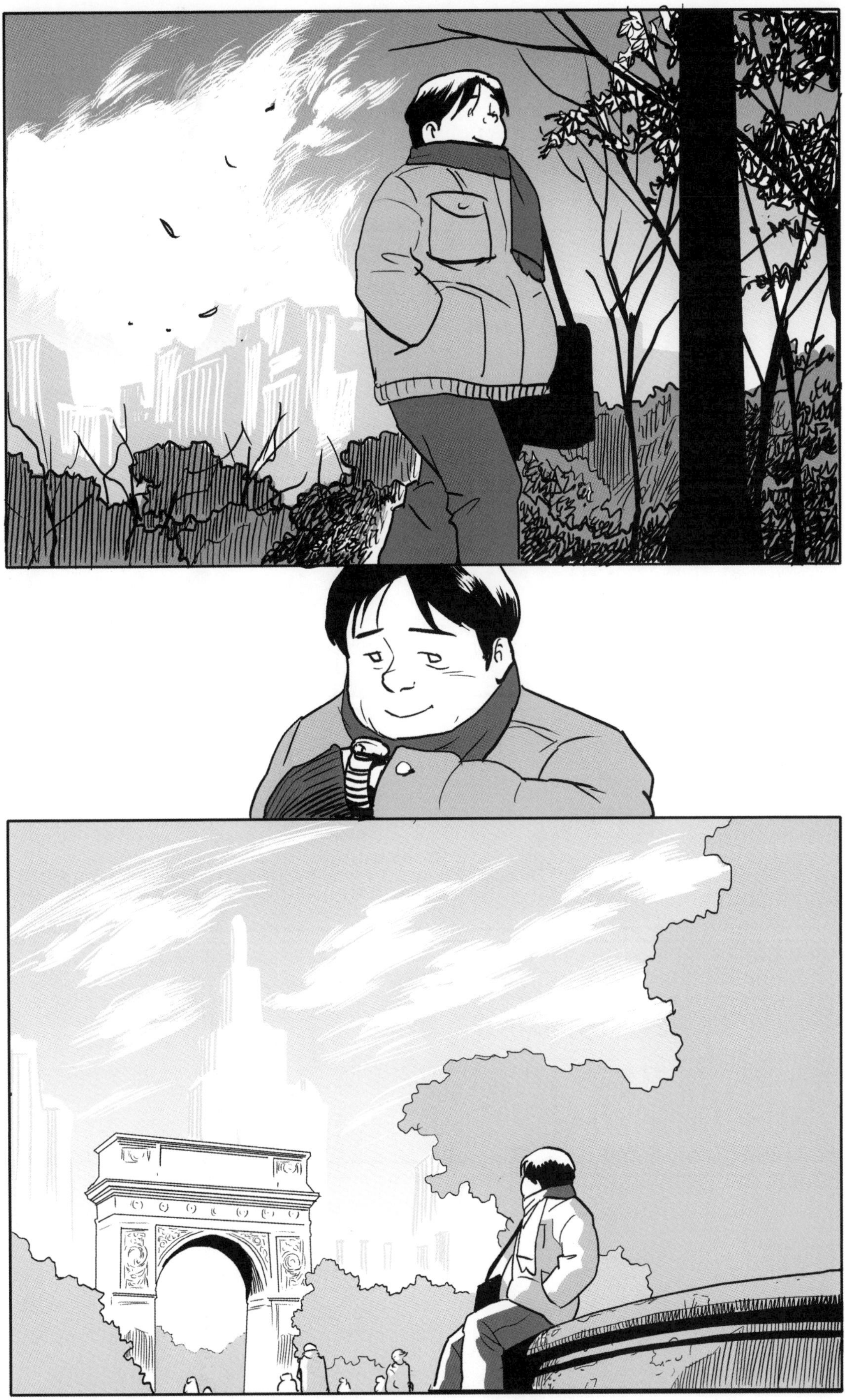

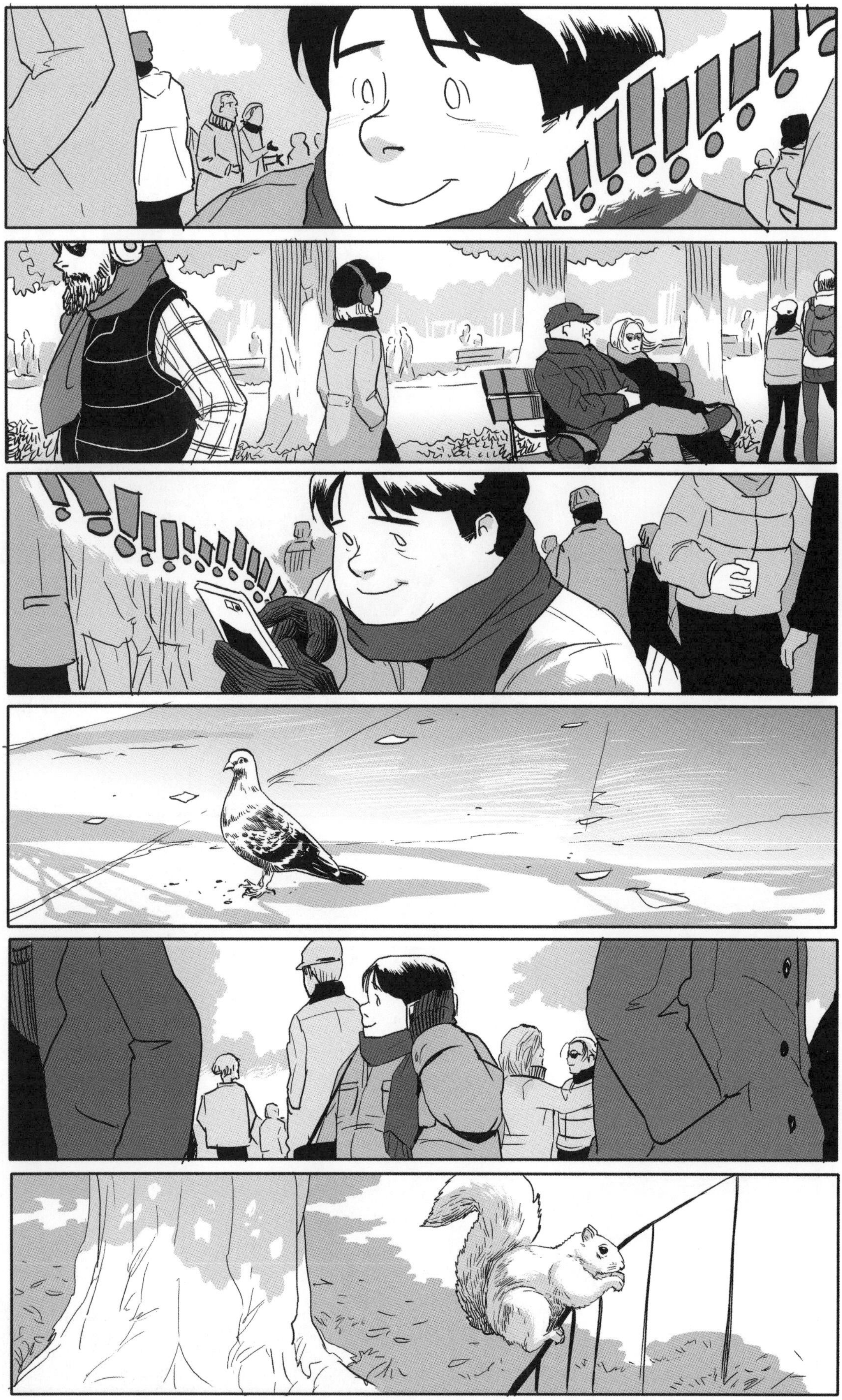

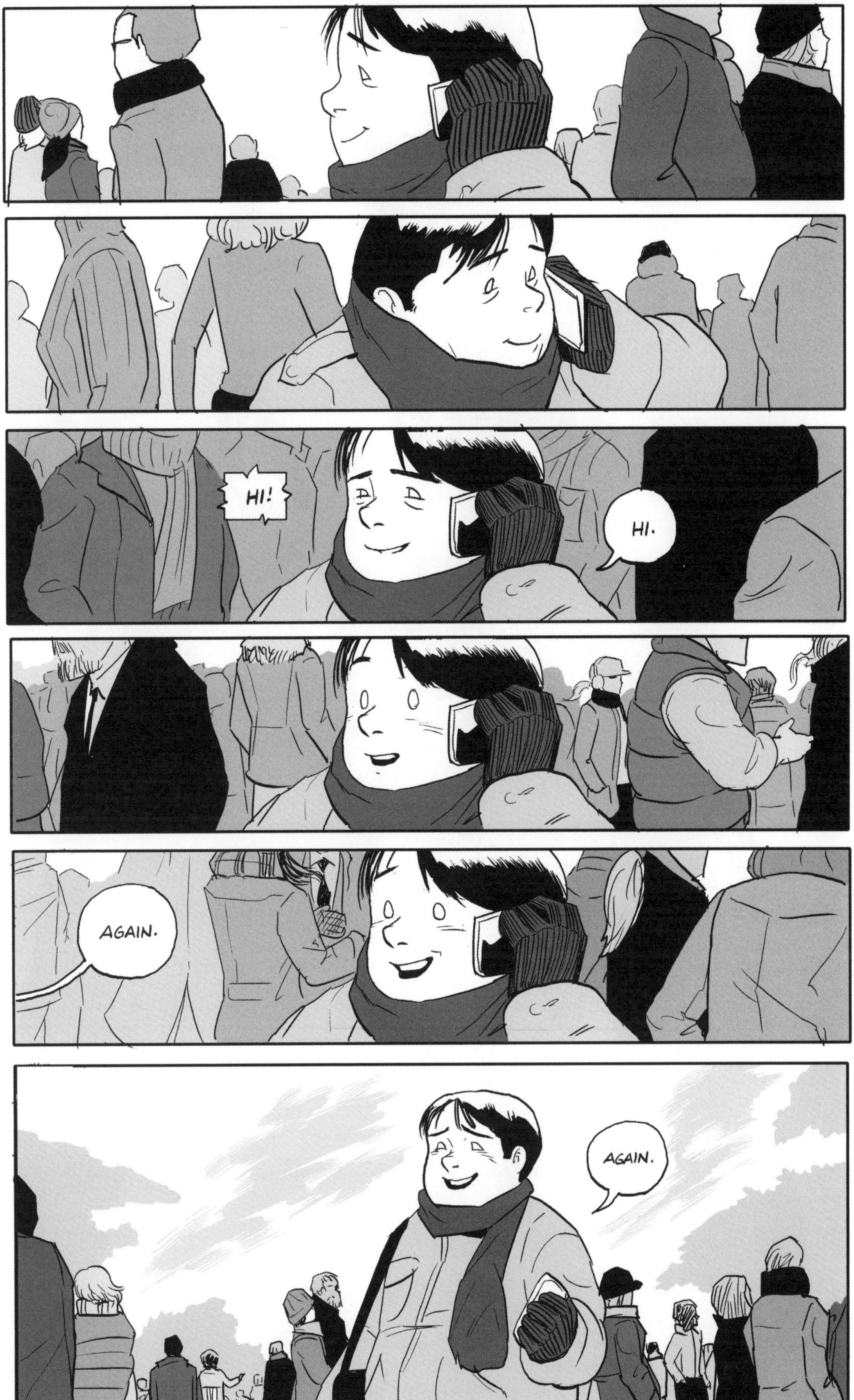
HI!
HI.
AGAIN.
AGAIN.

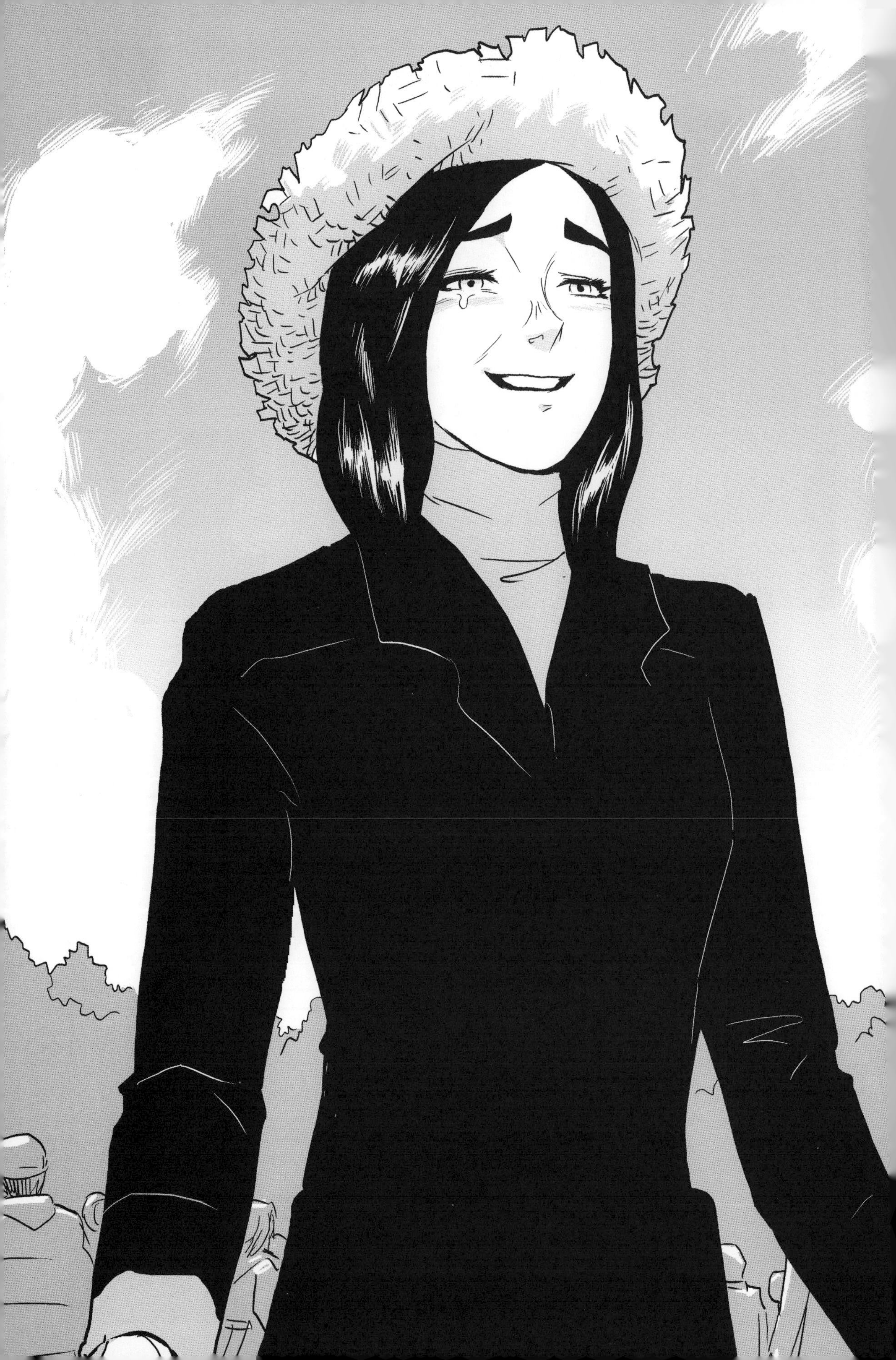

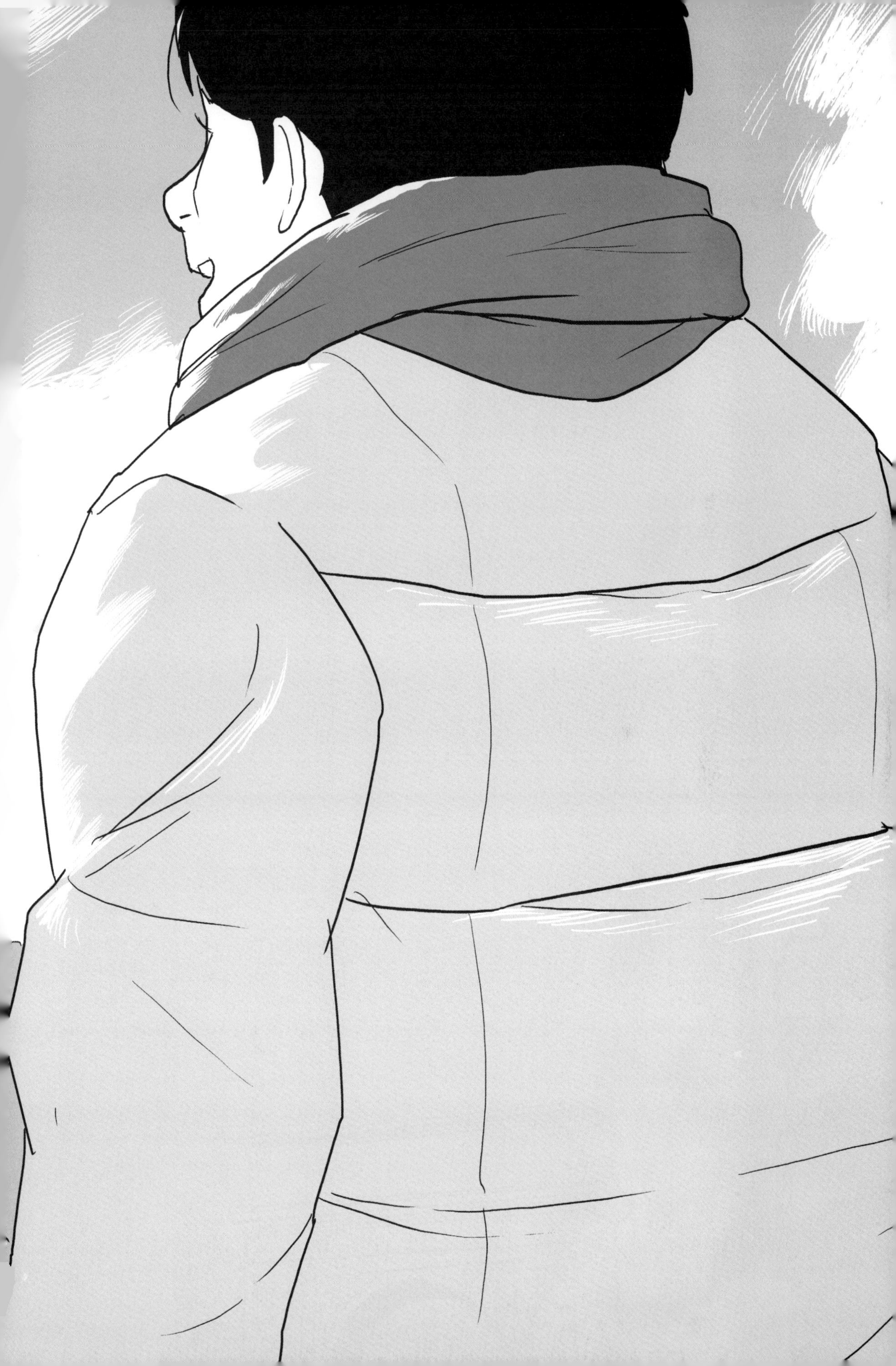

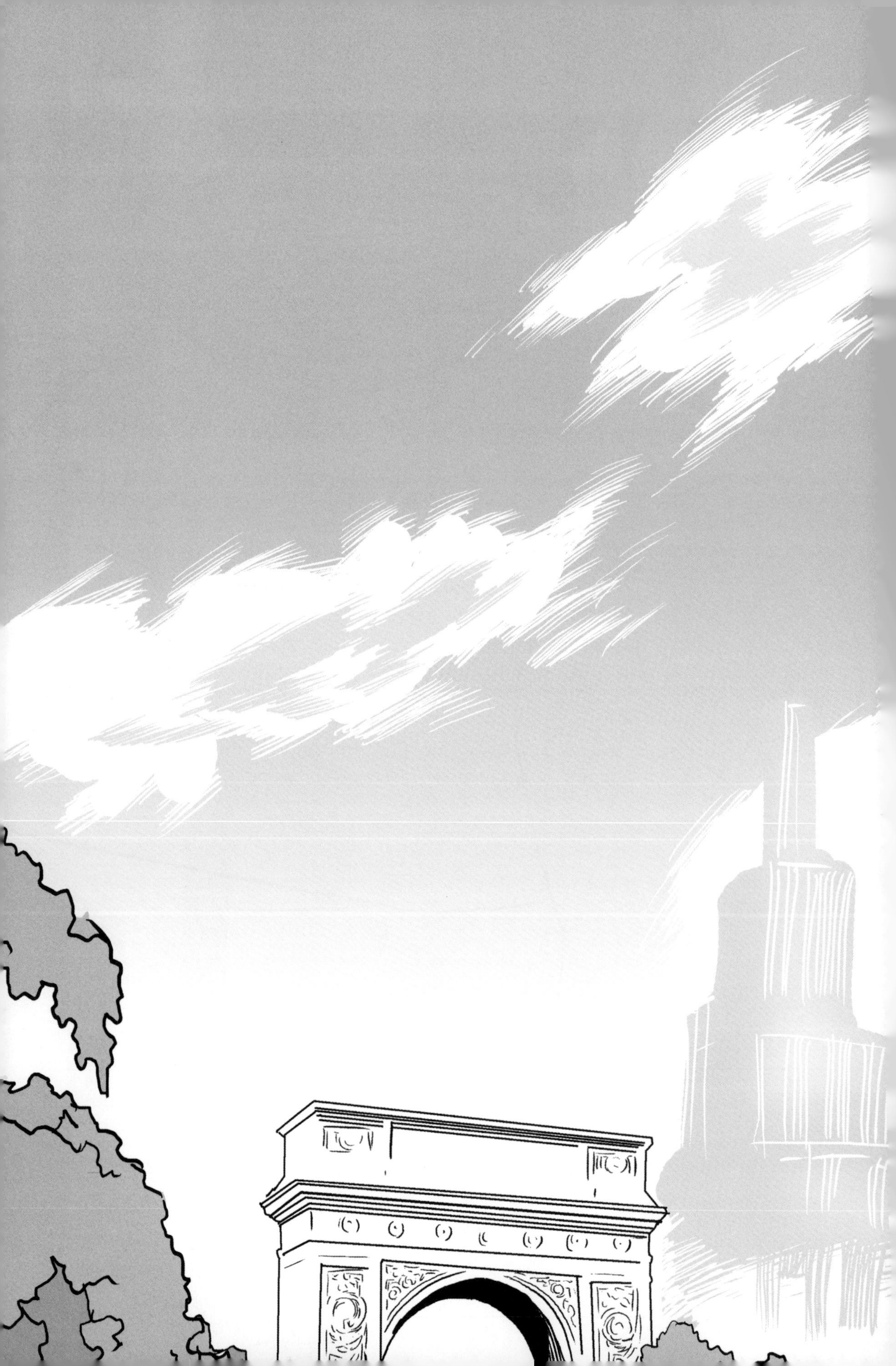

Hello. Again.

Notes on Halina Filipina's 13-year journey

Halina Filipina was written in the hot summer of 2002 and was completed in three months. I disciplined myself into fulfilling a modest page count of one hundred because I have a tendency to go overboard. I wanted it to be a no-frills relationship story, something cozy compared to my other works *The Mythology Class* and *After Eden*. No interweaving subplots here – just two people realizing their differences and falling in love despite them. There's a lot of beauty to be found in stories that are simple – simple but not ordinary. I found working on one to be a delightful experience since I also didn't have to worry about drawing many pages with a big cast of characters.

And so the original *Halina Filipina* graphic novel was completed... but later on shelved. *For 13 years.*

Missed Opportunity

I can only think of two reasons for having kept *Halina Filipina* hidden for so long. To me, releasing yet another romance story following "After Eden" would be too predictable and maybe even a bit self-indulgent. I was also very interested in creating an edgy Filipino super power book at the time. I wanted something different and it manifested in *Andong Agimat*. Andong provided a complete contrast to the clean visage of Jon and Celine and the stuff they had to go through in their seemingly problem-free lives. For that reason, the

Below: Panels from the original "Halina Filipina" graphic novel in 2002. Here, Halina owns a clothing store inside the mall where she first meets Cris. I discarded this idea and opted for her just having a limited stay in the Philippines.

POPCORN
YOU TAKE CHARGE NOW WHILE I PLACE THIS SOMEWHERE.
REMEMBER-- FIFTY PERCENT OFF ON RACK SEVEN.

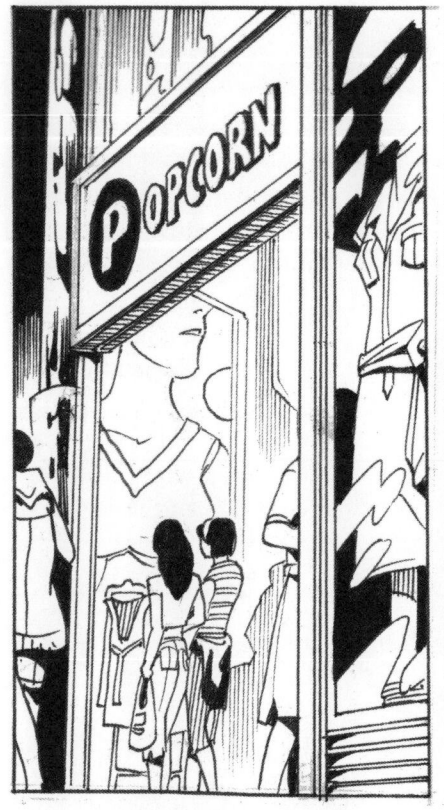

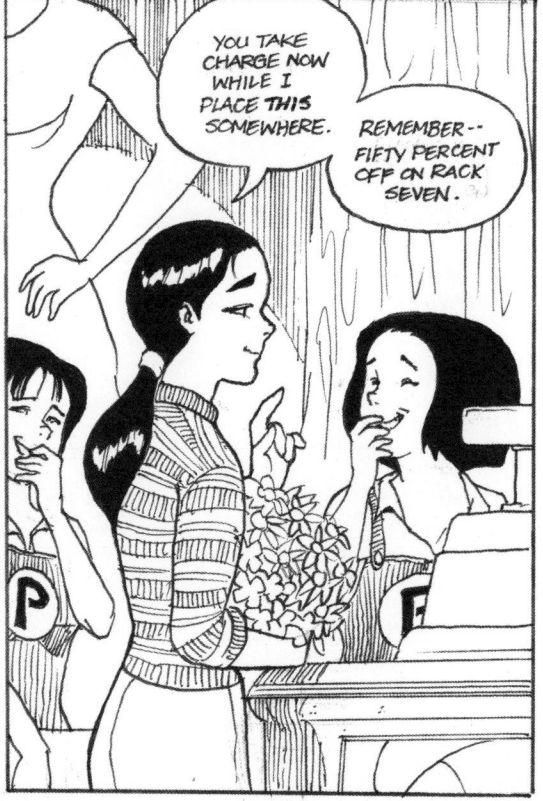

PA-DELIVER--
NUMBER EIGHTEEN!
NUMBER
ANO?!
HOLY--
HEY!!!
IS IT
REALLY
YOU?!

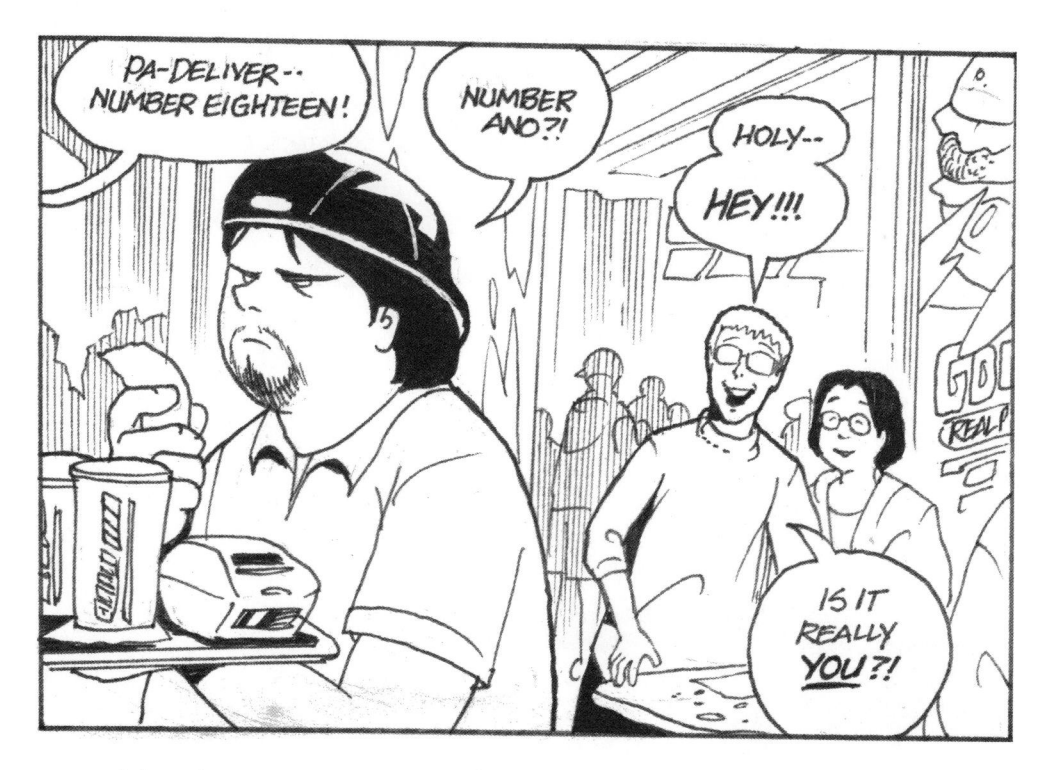

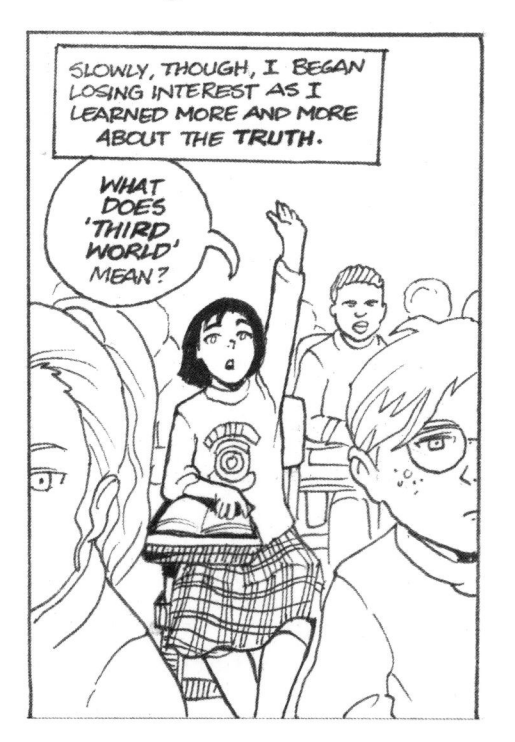

Above: *Originally, I intended for Cris to be working in a fast food joint where, between breaks, he would write his film reviews.*

story of the talisman-wearing Fernando Asedillo, the vigilante who lives in a crime-riddled Manila, became my third novel.

The other reason was *Halina* itself. After rereading the book – the simple relationship story that I thought would be interesting, the novel with the modest page-count – felt completely flat. 2002 was a turning point for me as an artist. There were many issues that I wanted to tackle, from Filipino society to politics to world problems and, later on, my own problems. There were more things I wanted to talk about but I ignored the opportunity. Simplifying something for the sake of it didn't work. Instead of shouting at things that pissed me off, I went for the polite whisper. Without the political and societal issues to set a backdrop for the story, Halina and Cris were just two people eating, talking, maybe arguing a bit. And then one leaves and it all ends. I might have just as well trapped them inside an elevator and the story would've been more interesting. I guess not even having a "cozier" page count could salvage what became an ordinary tale.

SLOWLY, THOUGH, I BEGAN LOSING INTEREST AS I LEARNED MORE AND MORE ABOUT THE TRUTH.
WHAT DOES 'THIRD WORLD' MEAN?

Left: Part of an unused page from the original book showing a flashback of Halina at age 12.

WHAT'S THIS CALLED AGAIN?
HALO HALO.
IT MEANS 'ALL-MIXED -UP.'
ALL MIXED UP.

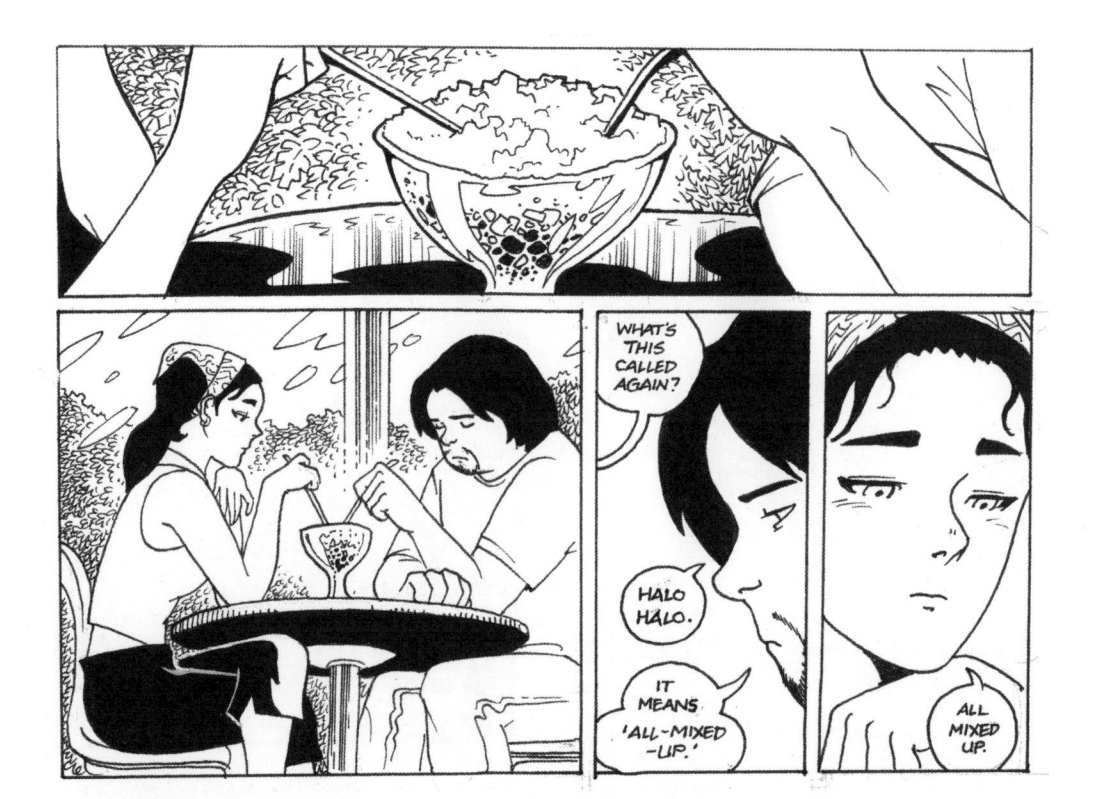

Above: The original scene where Halina first encounters the term "Halo-Halo."

Endings and Beginnings

Some of the initial ideas I had in *Halina* spilled over to *Martial Law Babies*, the novel I would release six years later in 2008. For you who've read it, you probably noticed some similarities, especially with Carol's showbiz baptism of fire which was a fate more cruel than what Halina experienced (lucky her!). Also, Bertrand Faustino Jr., the film critic in that novel is none other than Cris using a pen name – one of my little attempts at a crossover between my books.

The trials of Allan's barkada and all the craziness that ensued – the media bombardment, stories of corruption filling the headlines, and his friends leaving for greener pastures mirrored what I saw happening around me. However, unlike in 2002, this time I had something to say. Overall, I was very satisfied with *Martial Law Babies*. In fact, Allan's barkada mirrored Nicole's in *The Mythology Class*. Only this time instead of them encountering engkantos, the monsters were in the guise of unfulfilled dreams and lost friendships – real problems we face everyday.

But between working on novels and the occasional graphic design projects

Below: Halina was supposed to have spent most of her childhood in California. This panel shows her visiting New York City for the first time.

THEN ONE DAY, AFTER LEARNING ABOUT MY IRRESPONSIBLE PARENTS, THE FASCINATION JUST SIMPLY ENDED.
... SO WHAT DOES HALINA MEAN, UNCLE?
FUNNY, I ALWAYS THOUGHT IT SOUNDED HAWAIIAN, OR NEPALESE, OR SOMETHING.

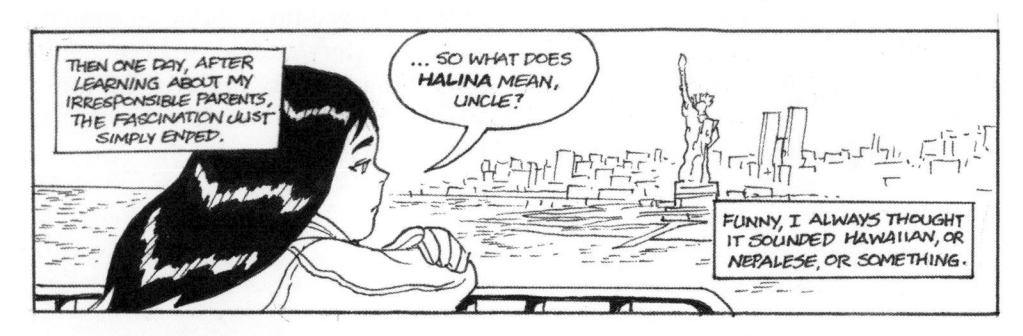

...THIS.
YOU PUT IT HERE...
...HERE...
...AND HERE.
PARA?
MAGANDA?
24

(and soon, animation projects), I would find myself scanning through pages of *Halina Filipina* and noticing how relaxing, almost calming, the book was with its minimal line work and with just the two characters moving the story along. I suddenly remembered how fun it was working on a book about a Fil-Am girl who just wanted to know what being Filipino is all about. Plain and simple.

That excited reaction I had towards the character was also shown by the audience during my Pecha Kucha talk in June of this year where I showed everyone two pages from the unreleased work – the scene were Halina steps out in a saya dress. Seeing their reactions was enough to make me re-evaluate the entire book.

Like Meeting Old Friends

Now the new *Halina Filipina* is complete – reworked, redrawn and streamlined. You are holding a book that went through many changes and, at least to me, looks and reads so unlike

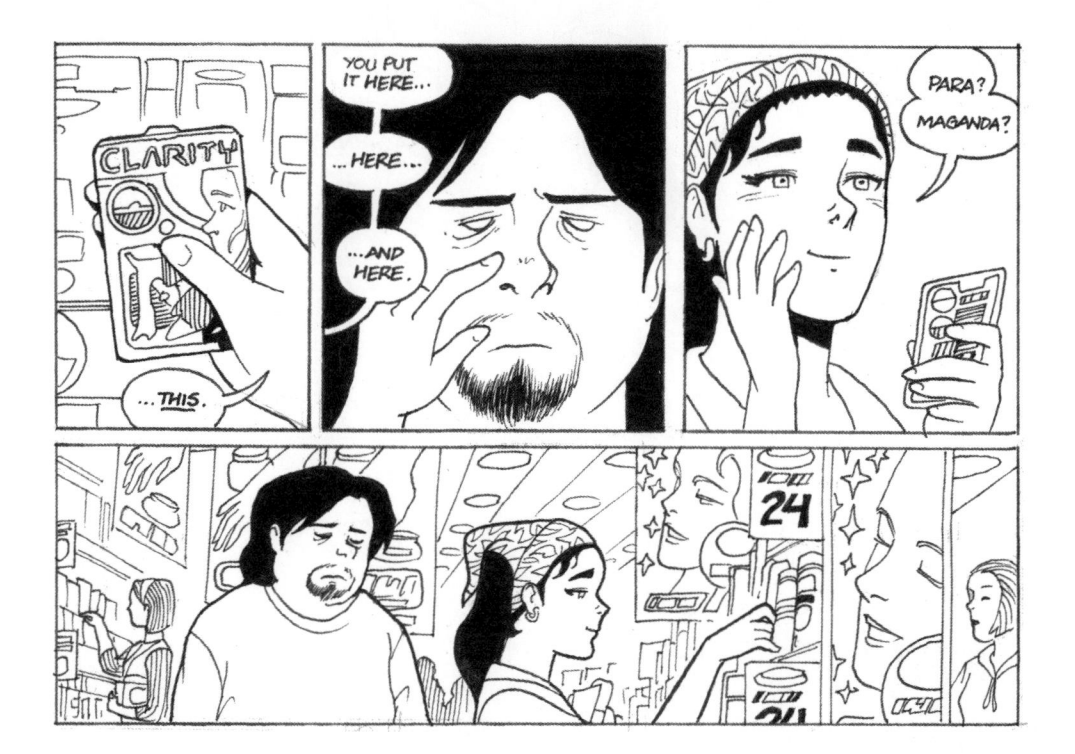

Above: Cris trying to be a gentleman, helping Halina with her shopping.

the previous draft. I would compare this feeling to that of visiting your old town and finding it not looking anything like how you remember it. However, the landmarks are still there. And so are the people. Much like Halina and Cris whose looks have changed since the original draft but are still the same characters I knew so well. Returning to the book and working on it again felt like meeting old friends. Your outlook has changed through the years – you're wiser and more experienced and so are they. Yet somehow they still have the charm and certain qualities that endeared them to you the first time.

And suddenly all those years seem like they never happened. Yes, even when 13 years have passed.

Hello, again

And what of the ending? By following Halina and Cris' story as it unfolded, it was very clear to me – especially near the second act – that their relationship,

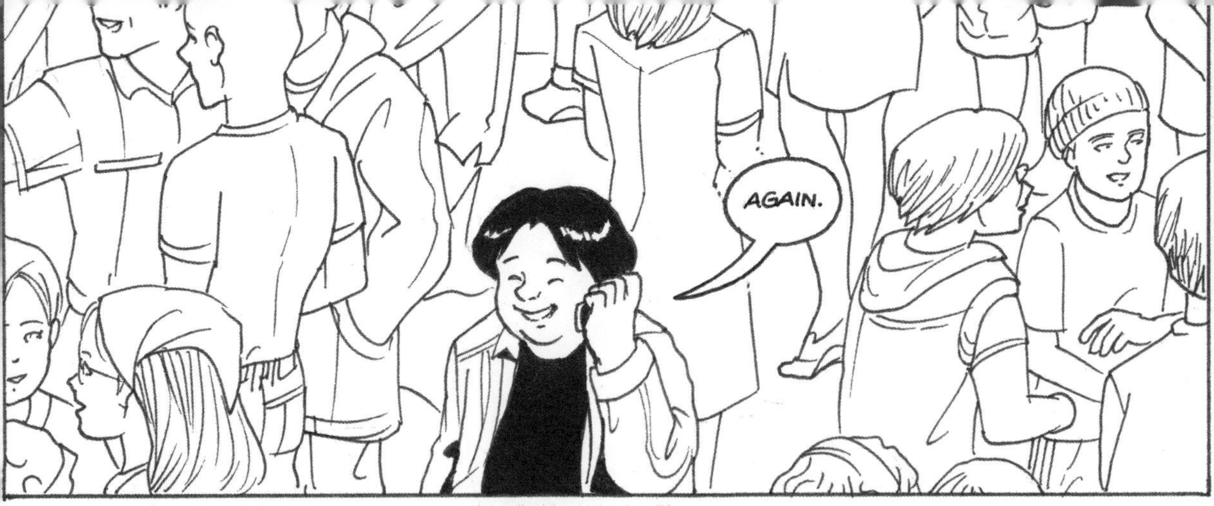
AGAIN.

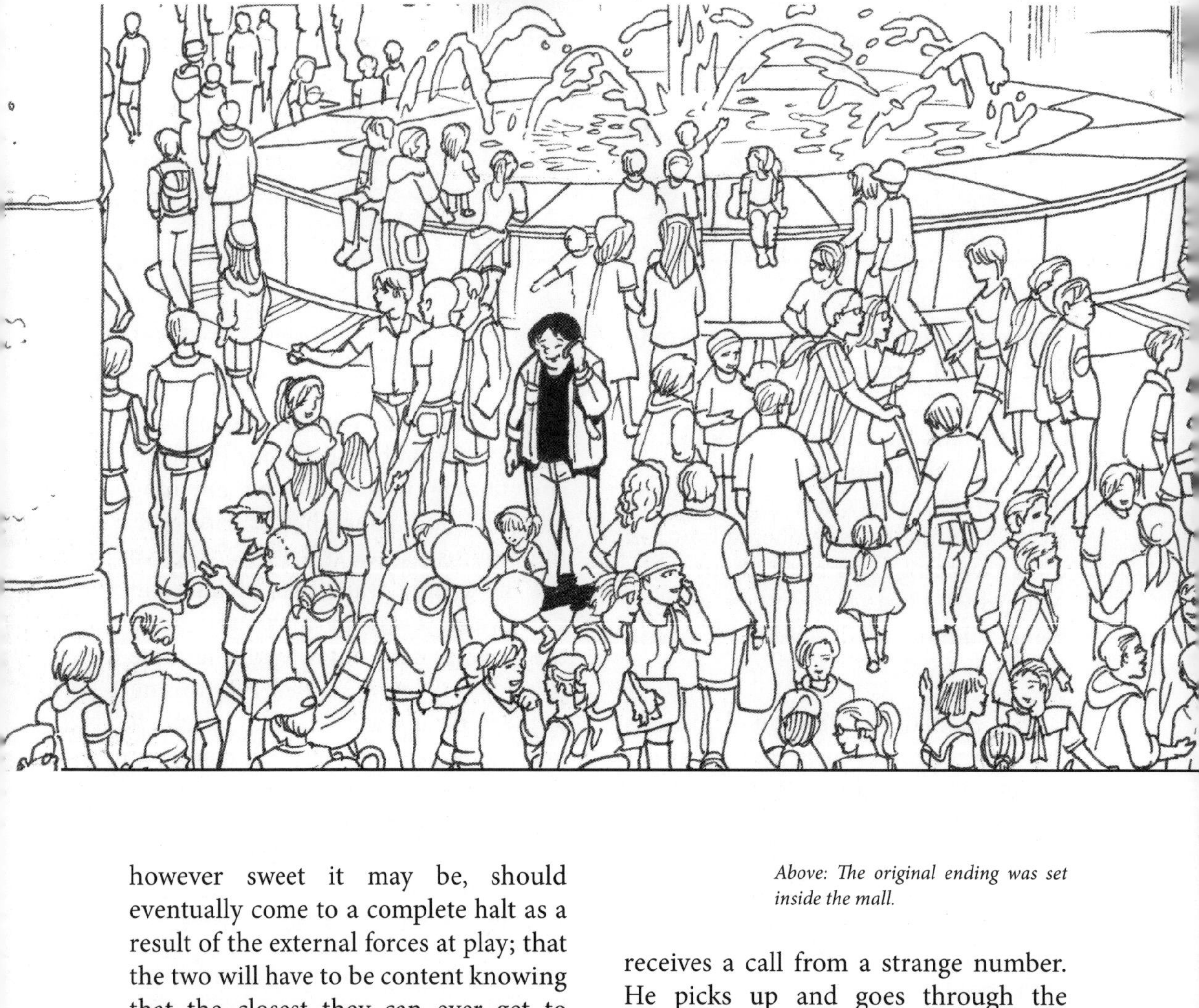

however sweet it may be, should eventually come to a complete halt as a result of the external forces at play; that the two will have to be content knowing that the closest they can ever get to being intimate would have to be calling or texting each other.

The original ending went something like this: after about a year since Halina's departure, we find Cris in the same mall were they meet in Chapter 1. Cris then receives a call from a strange number. He picks up and goes through the "hello, again" bit which hints that it's Halina making the call without the need to show her. The two talk as more and more people enter the scene, leading to a final full page where Cris is surrounded by the crowd but is oblivious of it. The emotion in that scene suited the story.

Above: The original ending was set inside the mall.

That approach was one that I wanted to keep for the new ending, except that instead of setting it in the old mall, I moved Cris to Washington Square. And instead of a strange number calling, it is apparently Halina who set the meeting.

There was temptation to completely change the ending and see where the new direction goes, but I guess keeping it was my way of giving my old 2002 self a break. It still works for me anyway, and ultimately the book's original theme when I first thought of it years ago stays the same. It's about Halina's attempt to find her roots and Cris' willingness to help her – the result being both resignation and hope. I say resignation because Halina decided that the Philippines wasn't really for her and never truly found her Pinoy self. But then there's a sense of hope when we see her wearing the rattan hat that Cris gave her. In fact, everything that Cris and Halina built to strengthen their relationship during that short period of time is represented by that hat – a tiny piece of our culture on top of Halina's head, keeping her warm on a freezing New York afternoon.

I'm glad that this book finally got the chance to be published, read and, hopefully, enjoyed, thanks to Nautilus Comics. It's a very personal story and I'm happy to share it. And this time, unlike with Nicole, Jon, Allan and even Andong, there are no huge barkadas in the picture.

After all *Halina Filipina* is just a cozy story about two friends talking, learning from one another, and sharing the quiet surroundings. Which is fine by me.

Arnold Arre
Quezon City 2015

Acknowledgements

My deepest thanks first and foremost to Cyn who loves everything about my work more than anyone else and for being the most patient person in the universe. To my family–Leonardo & Nancy Arre, Leslie & Aurora Bauzon, Lenn, Ate Ruby, Gian, Jing, Gladys, Calvin, Inches for being my favorite people.

This book wouldn't even have been made if not for Jamie & Iyay Bautista and Nautilus Comics who placed their complete trust in me.
Big big thanks to you both!

I owe a great deal of gratitude to Buddy & Earnest Zabala for always believing in me and for being such trusted friends all these years.

A big thank you to Emil Flores & Robert Magnuson who, since Baguio in 1995, taught me the value of telling fictional stories to bring sense in a mad world.

Special thanks to Gerry & Ilyn Alanguilan for giving me the chance to experience the strange but fun world of "Rodski Patotski," and for keeping the Pinoy comic book reader interested in the classics.

To Karen Kunawicz, Yvette Tan, Dino Ignacio, Marco Dimaano, Leinil Yu, Manix Abrera, Ed Tadeo, and the magnificent Whilce Portacio – thank you for your creativity that keeps inspiring me.

Thank you Jerrold Tarog for your wonderful films and for restoring my faith in Philippine Cinema.

Marie Jamora, Quark Henares, Ramon de Veyra and Neva Talladen. I am indebted to you guys for your friendship, creativity, and support.

To Ely Buendia, what would this generation be – in fact what would this entire nation be without your awe-inspiring music? And along with Buddy Zabala, Marcus Adoro and Raymund Marasigan of the Eraserheads, you have all done us proud with your brilliance.

To RA Rivera, Ramon Bautista, Jun Sabayton, Jr. and Lourd de Veyra for their wit, wisdom and humor that always entertains.

Thank you Mike De Leon, Clodualdo Del Mundo Jr., Cesar Hernando, and Mark Gil whose genius I have, with great sincerity and love, paid tribute to in this book.

And finally, to Luis Katigbak, the first person to have read the original *Halina Filipina* graphic novel in 2002, whose opinion and thoughts I value so much. Thank you for writing stories that inspire.

Credits

Pages 46 to 47: scene loosely based on the film *Batch 81* (1982) Directed by Mike de Leon, screenplay by Clodualdo del Mundo, Jr., art direction by Cesar Hernando, starring Mark Gil. Used with permission.

Pages 83 to 85: from the song Torpedo by the Eraserheads from the album *Cutterpillow* (1995), written by Ely Buendia. Used with permission.

About the Author

Arnold Arre lives in Quezon City with his wife Cynthia and their marmalade cat Abby. He's been drawing & writing comics for more than 20 years and is also currently honing his skills as an animator.

Visit www.arnold-arre.com

Halina Filipina

http://www.facebook.com/HalinaFilipina

Use **#HalinaFilipina** on Facebook, Twitter, and Instagram

Other Graphic Novels by Arnold Available From Nautilus Comics

http://www.nautiluscomics.net

THE MYTHOLOGY CLASS

TRIP TO TAGAYTAY

MARTIAL LAW BABIES

"Books to Span the East and West"

Tuttle Publishing was founded in 1832 in the small New England town of Rutland, Vermont [USA]. Our core values remain as strong today as they were then—to publish best-in-class books which bring people together one page at a time. In 1948, we established a publishing office in Japan—and Tuttle is now a leader in publishing English-language books about the arts, languages and cultures of Asia. The world has become a much smaller place today and Asia's economic and cultural influence has grown. Yet the need for meaningful dialogue and information about this diverse region has never been greater. Over the past seven decades, Tuttle has published thousands of books on subjects ranging from martial arts and paper crafts to language learning and literature—and our talented authors, illustrators, designers and photographers have won many prestigious awards. We welcome you to explore the wealth of information available on Asia at **www.tuttlepublishing.com**.